REPRIEVE FROM ETERNAL LIFE

"We haven't brought you back from the freeze-chamber because we've had any change of heart about the treatment of condemned criminals. You're aboard a starship—a long, long way from Tanagar.

"You've been sleeping for a long time. The only way you can actually find out if someone will last a million years is to try it. You were put away in the earliest years of the penal system—one of the first individuals sentenced to eternal life. We chose you partly for that reason—all the others we've revived come from a more recent period. You've been frozen for eight thousand years, Cheron Felix. *You're the oldest active human being in the universe.*"

The Castaways of Tanagar

Brian Stableford

DAW BOOKS, INC.
DONALD A. WOLLHEIM, PUBLISHER

1633 Broadway, New York, NY 10019

For Sheila

FIRST PRINTING, APRIL 1981

1 2 3 4 5 6 7 8 9

DAW TRADEMARK REGISTERED
U.S. PAT. OFF. MARCA
REGISTRADA. HECHO EN U.S.A.

PRINTED IN U.S.A.

Part One

POISONED DREAMS

1

Burning.

The sensation drowned him. He had no thoughts, only the pain.

I—

It was the only concept that his mind could frame, but it was enough. There is a thought that is "I," therefore "I" exist. Without that desperate clutch at the straw of identity, he would have doubted.

Burning.

From a sea of yellow light swam shadows, slowly taking shape. Rounded, coming closer.

Heads. Bending over. I am flat on my back. And burning. . . .

There was sound, too. White noise that coalesced into slow syllables. He remembered that life was all questions, always questions. He could make no sense of the words, and tried to shake his head. He failed, but his eyes must have signaled. The heads bobbed, exchanging noises.

"Too soon. . . ."

The first words that his mind understood told him nothing, and yet they seemed significant. They echoed in his mind, until their meaning was drowned by the *next* word uttered—a word directed at *him*; a word whose significance could not be doubted; a word trailing streamers of memory extending back into the further reaches of his clouded past.

"*Control.*"

The word echoed, too, reverberating in his mind long after the shadows retreated into the pool of light and the light itself withdrew into tender darkness. It floated in his mind while the burning ebbed away, and like a magic wand it seemed to force the pain down and away, lightening his bur-

den at every ritual repetition. Control of self; control of
body; endorphin control; control of destiny. . . .
   Control.
   Mens sana in corpore sano.
   Mensana.
   Poor sensual.
   Victim of passion.
   *The seven temptations: recklessness, anger, and malice; ec-
stasy, love, and fear; and the seventh is. . . .*

The cloak of darkness swept across his consciousness, and
the train of thought ran into a tunnel from which it never
emerged. He did not follow through to the catalog of the virtues, nor did he complete the list of the temptations.

The name of the seventh temptation, which was pleasure,
retreated into the safekeeping of memory.

2

He opened his eyes, blinking. The light was dull and
orange-colored. There was a shadow to the left, but the
source of the light was above it, and his eyes shied away
from the prospect of looking directly into it. He tried to
move his arms, but they were trapped inside some kind of
mesh. His fists clenched convulsively, but the tension was
draining out of him into a flood of well-being. He felt numb
and weightless.

"Do you know your name?" The voice seemed slow, the
words heavy. His thoughts were sluggish, and for a moment
he did *not* know his name. He had to grope for it. It was as
if the sudden challenge had made him forget how to use his
memory, how to use his mind.

Finally, he managed to say "Cheron." The syllables were
slurred, and it was not enough to satisfy him. After a long
moment of hesitation, he added: "Cheron Felix."

"Good," said the voice. The voice was female. He forced

his eyes to look to the left, despite the hazard of the direct light, and fought to resolve the image.

She had dark hair cut short, and was wearing some kind of uniform. She seemed to be moving slowly upward, but without getting anywhere. Relative to the light, she was motionless, and he decided that it must be an illusion. He had been drugged, obviously.

"Don't try too hard," she said, her voice unnaturally deep because of the sensation of slowed time. "You've had a rough ride. Can you count to ten?"

He counted to ten. Then he recited the alphabet. Then he started on the table of temptations, but she stopped him after six. He felt curiously relieved, as if he might not have been able to go on.

"Never mind that," she said. "Can you remember the last thing that happened to you?"

He tried.

"You've been asleep for a long time," she told him, trying to prompt his reluctant memory. "Asleep without dreaming."

Eternal life.

Guilty of a crime of passion.

Eternal. . . .

He struggled to speak, and managed to say: "Why . . . ?"

She didn't reply. Perhaps she hadn't understood the slurred syllable, or perhaps there was just too much that might be said in response to such a simple question.

He struggled against the effect of whatever drug was confusing his thoughts and perceptions, but the moment his head began to clear, the pain began to rise inside him.

Control.

It was useless. He didn't have control. Between the devil pain and the deep blue sea of synendorphin he was caught tight. The problem was beyond him, and he felt as if a shadow of shame had been cast across him.

Poor sensual. Born Hedonist.

He felt a sudden impulse to laugh.

"What is it?" asked the woman, obviously seeing some expression cross his face.

"Did I . . . serve out . . . my sentence?"

Eternal life!

"Yes," she said, softly, and without humor. "In a manner of speaking, you did. You won remission." She interrupted herself with a sardonic cough, and added: "For good behavior."

He didn't see the joke. The phrase meant nothing to him. He tried to move his head, but couldn't. Only his eyes were free to move.

"I can't move," he said.

She leaned across him, and put something in front of his face. At first, he couldn't make out what it was, and was slightly alarmed by what he saw. Then he realized that it was a mirror. She was holding it so he could see himself, flat on his back, encased in some kind of rubbery web from the neck down. His head was supported by some kind of plastic molding. It had been shaved, and there were silver wires laid across his skull, disappearing into the flesh above and behind his ears.

"Sensory bypass," he said, in a whisper. "You've wired my head. You can't. . . ." The effort required to go on was too great.

She removed the mirror.

"I'm sorry," she said. "Perhaps I shouldn't have shown you. I'd forgotten. In your day. . . ."

She let the statement dangle.

Control.

He fought against the drug, and almost welcomed the tide of pain. He needed something sharp to feed his senses, something that would force his brain to be active.

"Illegal," he muttered, his voice slurring again as he gasped out the word.

"It's not illegal," she said, slowly. "It hasn't been illegal for quite some time. You served quite a stretch of your sentence. You've been asleep a long time. The wires are for piping dreams, not for changing your personality. There won't be any destruction of memories. We only want to add to your repertoire of skills. New languages, new abilities, new responses. You'll still be Cheron Felix. That won't be changed."

He knew she was lying. She was drawing false distinctions. What does it take to change a man's identity? New skills, new responses, new dispositions. He'd still be Cheron Felix, but he wouldn't be the *same* Cheron Felix. *Whatever* they sent along those silver wires, bypassing his senses, would go clean through the censorship devices by which he held something inviolate and constant that he called his mind, his personality, his essential *self*.

"You can't," was all that he could find to say.

She didn't answer. She didn't need to.

Obviously, she could.

"Where am I?" he asked. His voice was twisted with fear now, though he had better control of the slurring effect induced by the drug.

"It's not what you think," she said. "We haven't brought you back from the freeze-chamber because we've had any change of heart about the treatment of condemned criminals. We aren't going to readjust you for life in *our* society. You're aboard a starship—a long, long way from Tanagar."

His immediate response, absurdly, was to think: *That's the uniform. Interstellar exploration.*

"It wasn't easy, bringing you around," she said. "You've been sleeping for a long time. We weren't entirely certain that we could revive you. There's supposed to be no damage, physical or psychic, no matter how long you're frozen, but there's never been any real test of that supposition. The only way you can actually find out if someone will last a million years is to try it. You were put away in the earliest years of the penal system—one of the first individuals sentenced to eternal life. We chose you partly for that reason—all the others we've revived come from a more recent period. You've been frozen for eight thousand years, Cheron Felix. You're the oldest active human being in the universe."

He stared up into her face.

I ought to be stunned with astonishment, he thought, *but I'm not. What's the difference between eight years and eight thousand in the vaults? Or is it the drug, protecting me from panic?*

He decided, after a moment's hesitation, that it wasn't the drug. He really didn't care.

He tried to remember that infinitely dreamless sleep, but couldn't. Naturally not. All he could remember was the burning pain of returning consciousness. There had been no such pain when they put him away. The anesthetic had taken care of everything. There was no gap in his memory between the execution of the sentence and that brief sojourn in hell that was the moment of his reawakening. If they were to be decoupled in his memory, then it would have to be a conscious act of intervention. What could he interpose between them?

Eight thousand years.

Only the words. What else was there?

"Who are you?" he asked.

"My name is Teresa Janeat. I'm an officer in Interstellar Exploration. You're aboard the *Sabreur*, a special-project ship."

"You're the captain?"

"Starships don't have captains. They don't have crews, either. They have passengers, who work on projects."

"You're no Intel."

"There's an Intellectual on board, in charge of the project. His name is Cyriac Salvador. You'll meet him, in time."

His gaze rested on the insignia that dressed the collar and shoulder of her tunic. They were, of course, quite meaningless so far as he was concerned.

"You're just the one who gets things done," he said, feeling more relaxed with every minute that passed. Both the pain and the cushioning effect of the drug had retreated a little now, leaving him a margin of existence that he could occupy in reasonable comfort and with moderately good control of his faculties.

Eight thousand years, he thought, calmly, *is a dozen lifetimes for an Intel, forty for a sensual. Among my kind, my lifetime must be ancient history.*

"You say there are others—from the vaults?"

"That's right," she said.

He realized that she wasn't looking at him. She was studying something beyond his head—presumably the display panel of the medical monitor. He tried to detect some change in her expression that would tell him how he was faring, but her face was quite relaxed and impassive. She had good control, considering that she wasn't an Intel. But then, she wasn't a Hedon either. Striver through and through, he decided. Perfectly stable. Rumor said—*had* said, eight thousand years ago—that the ones who looked most relaxed, most perfectly composed, were the jeckles; but there always had to be exception. Teresa Janeat must be exactly what she seemed. There couldn't be much scope for hydeyhigh on a starship.

"How many?" he asked.

"Twenty," she replied. "You may see one or two of the others in time. Some freedom of movement will be permitted. The wires can be disconnected temporarily. The traction web is for exercising your muscles by induced calisthenics. It shouldn't be necessary after the first few days—there's been very little tissue wastage. Effectively, you're almost as fit right now as you were when you were put away."

"Not only eternal life," he whispered, "but eternal youth."

He wanted to look around, but his head was held fast. All he could see was the ceiling and the light. The walls were quite featureless. All the display panels were above his head, out of view. Life was going to be very boring, if he was intended to spend much time awake. The sensory bypass suggested, though, that there was no such intention. He would be drugged into trance while the wires fed him synthetic experience: powerful dreams that would take their place in the array of his memories, adding to his stock of skills and languages.

"Languages!"

The incongruity of it had only just struck him.

"Yes," she said, quietly. She was looking at him again, staring calmly into his eyes. "That's right."

"I'm on a starship," he said, as though the words had suddenly turned deadly. *"Where am I going?"*

"A new world," she told him. "As I told you, your sentence has been commuted. From eternal life—to exile."

She reached out and touched something beyond the reach of his eyes. Immediately, he began to feel the change. The synendorphin was being fed directly into his bloodstream; now something else was substituting for it. His consciousness was being put out like a light bulb that was no longer necessary. He was being switched off.

He opened his mouth to protest, but no sound came out.

Apparently, she had found out what she needed to know.

He was alive, and his mind was working. She had been talking only to make sure. The information he had gleaned was a kind of bonus.

The impulse to scream some kind of insult died with the retreat of his consciousness. He could not have carried it out.

Teresa Janeat, however, noticed the brief flare in his eyes before they shut.

Stupid sensual, she thought, her reactions dancing on the puppet strings of her educational programming. *Victim of passion, Murderer.*

3

Cyriac Salvador was hunched over his desk like a perching bird, the material of his jacket gathering at the shoulders into the suggestion of folded wings.

Deliberately ill-fitted, thought Teresa Janeat. *A petty symbol of unworldliness. How ironic that Intellectuals should be just as childish, in their way, as Hedonists.*

She was, of course, committed to the view that the middle way was the best way—the only truly adult way. As Cheron Felix had correctly judged, she was Pragmatist through and through. Jeckling was not one of her vices. The only temptation to which she frequently fell prey was malice.

Salvador studied the screen before him for a few more seconds, and then placed his bony finger firmly on the PAUSE button.

"They're all revived," she said. "You have the data on Felix. I've just talked to him. He seems to be as well as can be expected."

"Have you talked to Jerome?"

"Yes. He doesn't like what we're doing to him. The others, beyond token complaints, don't really seem to care. It's not costing them any effort, and it's not particularly unpleasant—in fact, they appreciate the sweetening. It's only to be expected that Jerome would feel different. His only real thought is the attempt to analyze what it's all *for*. I've never understood that. Why just one Pragmatist among nineteen Hedonists?"

"He's supposed to become the leader," said Salvador.

"He won't. He'll abandon the Hedonists and strike out on his own."

"You underestimate his sense of social responsibility," replied the Intellectual, dryly. "Also, his need for civilized companionship. Not to mention the extent of his self-confidence. He won't abandon the Hedonists until he's sure that it's safe to do so—and that will be never, unless he's forcibly separated from the others. Did you tell Felix how long he's been frozen?"

"Yes. It didn't bother him. I cut him off when he began to get too inquisitive about where he's going, but I gave him enough data to give him a reasonable knowledge of his situation. He's alarmed, for the moment, but he'll soon come round to the same point of view as the others. Any kind of life is better than eternal life. Effectively, they've been brought back from the dead. What can they lose, even by dying again?"

"But Jerome isn't prepared to accept that?"

"Jerome's already passed through *that* phase. The Hedonists are prepared to wait and see what happens, but he can't rest without a plan in his head. If he could think of a way to do it, he'd be figuring on taking over the ship and heading back to the system to take over one of the outer satellites as stage one in the new revolution. He probably thinks he's some kind of folk hero as far as the present generation of dissidents is concerned. He's a fool."

Salvador shook his head—another oddly birdlike gesture. She tried to imagine him as a bird of prey, but failed. That wasn't quite right. She couldn't think of the right parallel among the few birds of Tanagar's cities she was familiar with. To find the right analogy she would have had to go back to the Motherworld records, and that would have involved far too much pointless mental effort.

"Jerome isn't a fool," said the Intellectual. "Quite the reverse. If anything, he's a shade too clever. A duller man would have been more pliable, more predictable, but I wanted Jerome. He has the kind of big ideas the experiment requires. He won't settle for finding a way of life—he'll want to change things. And he'll have the opportunity. On Tanagar, he was out of place. I'm taking him where he belongs."

"And the others?" she asked. "Do *they* belong where they're going?"

Salvador shrugged. "A Hedonist belongs nowhere," he replied. "Nowhere except the inside of his own skull. In a way,

they're Jerome's raw material. His instruments. He knows
how to deal with them, how to manipulate them."

"He's a jeckle, of course," she replied, as if that were sufficient explanation of any facet of Jerome's character that
Salvador might care to mention.

Salvador allowed the comment to dismiss the line of argument from their conversation.

"We can start Felix on the program," he said. "He'll be the
last. His mind should be quite receptive. I don't anticipate
any problems, at least until the recapitulative stage. Who's
the man we started first? Talvar, isn't it? We can move on to
phase three there—let him get up and start using his body
again. It's all very well for him to dream his way through rigorous exercises while the machine tones up his muscles—he
needs practice. He can have the run of the connecting corridor that links his cabin to the complementary ones. We can
let him talk to Felix. It will help Felix readjust and will save
you from being plagued with questions about eight thousand
years of history. Talking over their situation will help them
get used to it. And if they feel the need to indulge their new
fighting skills they can try them out on one another. Over the
next twelve days we can release them all, one by one. We'll
be able to check any trouble if it develops. Talvar's already
back on a solid diet, I take it?"

Teresa nodded. "Do you expect them to put the new programs into action?" she asked, warily. "While they're still on
board the *Sabreur*?"

"I don't expect them to start killing one another," replied
Salvador. "We're programming them with the *ability* to fight,
not the lust to kill. It's possible they'll test themselves, though.
Quite carefully, of course. You don't have to worry about
being attacked. Everything that's been put into their skulls
has been put into ours too. It will be necessary for us to
spend at least some time on surface over the next hundred
and fifty years. You don't feel any desperate urge to attack
anyone, do you?"

"I'm not. . . ." She realized the stupidity of what she was
about to say, and stopped.

"You're not a criminal?" said Salvador softly. "There's no
hint of crime of passion in *your* personal history. Of course
not. They're not killers through and through, you know. For
most of them, the crime for which they were condemned was

a momentary lapse. They probably don't approve of their actions in retrospect any more than you do. They're Tanagarians, after all. You mustn't forget that in the long run, we're all fallible. *There, but for the grace of God. . . .*"

He was mocking her. She knew that it was a kind of joke, and that there was no real malice in it. Salvador found her amusing, but not in any scornful way. Nevertheless, she resented his manner. He was idiosyncratic enough to have to admit his own imperfections, to make a joke out of his fallibility, but *her* control was entirely adequate, and she resented any implication that it was not, however good-humored.

She stood up, rather stiffly.

"I'll release Talvar," she said. "No doubt he'll be suitably grateful."

Salvador bowed his head. "And no doubt," he said, "you'll accept his gratitude for what it is worth."

4

Though his eyelids were closed and he was not fully awake, Cheron registered the fact that the light in the ceiling had been switched on. Rather than opening his eyes wide he peeped through the lashes. The secretive impulse was quite ridiculous, but the suggestion that he had at least *some* degree of choice in what was happening to him was valuable.

The face which hovered above him, haloed by the glare, was not that of Teresa Janeat. It was that of a young blond-haired man. His shoulders were wide, and he gave the impression of being powerful. He looked down at Cheron with an expression of faint amusement.

"How are you feeling?" he asked.

"Tired," answered Cheron. "I won't say that I've been exercising—the truth is that I've been exercised."

"I know," said the other. "I've been through it. The whole

course—electronic massage and poisoned dreams. I'm Vito Talvar. They said I could come in to see you—help you through. The woman's not one for telling long stories to help us understand what's going on. Salvador's different, if you get to see him. Has difficulty sticking to the point, and he's an Intel, of course, but he could pass for human in a dim light. Eight thousand years is a hell of a time to be stuck in the refrigerator. I've only been in twenty-five. You look good, considering."

"What are they doing to us?" asked Cheron, his voice hardly more than a whisper.

"Can you recapitulate the first phase of the hypnopaedic instruction?"

"Not really. It's difficult to grasp. It comes back in fits and snatches. The woman said they'd be feeding me new languages and skills . . . but the programming seems to involve weapons. . . ."

Talvar raised a hand as if to touch his forehead and soothe him, but stopped when the flow of words dried up.

"Don't try to come to terms with it now. They'll reinforce it next session, and eventually they'll ask you to recapitulate. You can chat to the computers about anything you like, in half a dozen new languages. They won't give you much information, though—the limitations will drive you into a fury. The physical part is different. It's going to be some time before we can start practicing that. We can shadow-box, and run and jump a little, but the cells are so tiny, and the corridor isn't much better. Anyhow, the ship's spin only gives us an apparent *g* force half Tanagar's. I don't know how things will be where we're going, but the *g* force is bound to be greater there than here."

"Where *are* we going?"

Talvar looked faintly surprised. "She didn't tell you? Bitch. We're going to the Motherworld. Earth."

Cheron shut his eyes momentarily, and cursed himself for not having guessed.

"The Motherworld," he said, as if to fix the idea in his mind. "Home. I suppose there's a sense of poetic justice about that. We were condemned to eternal life—at least, *I* was—for displaying behavioral traits similar to those our remote ancestors are credited with. Now, instead of remaining frozen solid through all eternity, they've decided to send me back to the place those ancestors came from. How appropriate. When did Interstellar rediscover our long-lost home?"

Talvar shrugged. "Who knows? They didn't tell the happy Hedonists for fear of disturbing our carefully guarded tranquility. Maybe a thousand years ago. It takes a long time, of course, for the ships to go back and forth. Several centuries, I believe, though time is said to pass more slowly on the ships themselves—I'm told these things are purely relative. Even the Intel didn't stay active all the way, though. He was on metabolic retardants for the first couple of hundred years. He's pretty old, in fact—can't have more than a hundred and fifty years to go. He'll never see Tanagar again. We're approaching sol-system at the moment. The training program doesn't last long—you'll be just about finished when we reach orbit."

"Centuries?" said Cheron.

"Tanagar isn't as far from home as we once thought," Talvar told him. "Sure, the *Marco Polo* was searching for a new world for several thousand years ship's time—more in the Motherworld's terms, I suppose—but she had to keep accelerating and decelerating to check star systems for hospitability, and her course was distinctly erratic. The impression given in the records that the shipborne generations virtually crossed the universe is misleading. In terms of the size of the galaxy we hardly moved at all—a mere flea jump."

"There are still people on Earth? People like us?"

"Another minor deception incorporated into our legendary history. The myth that the Motherworld was destroyed turns out to have been a matter of premature diagnosis. The self-destruction which was supposed to happen once the seven ships had been launched was apparently less than wholehearted. They had their war, of course. Several, in fact. They devastated much of the surface of the world, and precipitated a geological cataclysm, but after things had calmed down there were still habitable areas here and there, and enough Adams and Eves to repopulate them. In time, new territories became available as life reclaimed the derelict parts and the newly elevated land. Terrible though it is to contemplate, the rebirth of civilization must have been well under way while the *Marco Polo* was still hunting for any kind of world that could support human life. Mind you, it hasn't gotten very far *since* then. Civilization on Earth seems to have been reborn with certain very awkward physical handicaps. No fossil fuels, you see, and precious few readily exploitable mineral resources. Unlike the valiant founding fathers of Tanagar, the new men of Earth found themselves in possession of a second-hand world that had been pretty well used by its former owners. The glorious ascendancy of Tanagar to its peak of technological achievement—things got even better after your day, of course—contrasts rather sharply with the poor showing that Earth's new masters have so far made. They were handicapped by not *knowing* very much, mind. *We* had the science of the twenty-first century secure in the *Marco Polo*'s memory banks, while *they* had to rediscover agriculture. I take it that by now you more or less have the picture?"

Cheron tried to nod his head, forgetting that he couldn't.

"Why are they taking us there?" he asked quietly.

"I presume that we are the ambassadors of Tanagar," said Talvar, with a wry smile. "They haven't exactly said so, but I can't think of any other explanation. It isn't as absurd as it seems at first. We're murderers, for the most part—criminals, anyhow. Therefore we're expendable. The diplomatic mission in which we are to be engaged is one that has a certain amount of risk involved. Intels are very cautious where risk to life and limb are concerned. I don't know how things were in your day but the Intels of today are very jealous indeed of their seven-hundred-year life-spans. They tend to be somewhat reserved; they don't like to get involved, in *anything*. If I had to guess I'd say that Interstellar probably rediscovered Earth a couple of thousand years ago, but that all that's happened in that time is that a small group of Intels have been studying it carefully. By carefully, I mean from a distance. Probably from orbit, using electronic spy-eyes of one kind or another."

"They'd use Strivers," said Cheron.

"Sure they would—if they could persuade a few that there was something to be gained. But what competent Prag is going to risk his or her neck for the sake of doing a few Intels a favor? There's no prestige at stake—not yet. No wealth, either. Earth is more dangerous than a snake pit, as you'll realize when you check the vocabularies they're feeding you. They're giving you the extended course in self-defense because they think you're going to need it. We're the advance party, Cheron. The Prags will move in once we've cleared the way for them."

"That's not quite what I mean," said Cheron. "I can see why a Striver wouldn't want to go to Earth on his own account, but what I don't see is why they picked *me* out of the vaults when they could just as easily have picked a Prag. *You're* a Hedonist, aren't you? I presume the distinctions still apply, even after eight thousand years."

"They apply," said Talvar, a shade sourly. "There's one Prag on our team—a man named Sarid Jerome. He tried to organize some kind of coup a few centuries back—a rising of the Prags against the Intels, I guess. It didn't work. I suppose they didn't put more in because they were worried about Prags getting too involved with affairs on Earth. There must be a lot of opportunities down there for men of ambition. All *I* want to do is win a ticket home to Tanagar, and I hope that's the prize we'll be offered for succeeding in what we're required to do. That's the only way it seems to make sense. Anyhow, there probably aren't all that many Prags in the vaults. Crimes of passion are mainly a failing of our kind. When a Prag commits murder it's usually premeditated, and the courts very rarely demand the full penalty. You were one of the first, of course, so I guess you couldn't judge how things would turn out."

"They obviously didn't turn out the way they were intended to," said Cheron. "The idea was that freezing out the vile creatures who let their emotions conquer their reason would soon extinguish the tendency from human nature. Negative eugenics, of a sort. It doesn't seem to have worked, if they're still having to freeze people eight thousand years later."

Talvar smiled. "No," he said, "it didn't work. You'd better ask Salvador why not. I'm only a poor sensual. I don't understand the differential calculus, let alone the lessons of history. Not that there's *been* much history lately. All the cant about the stable society must have been fresh in your day, I suppose?"

Cheron found that he couldn't laugh properly while his head was secured. "Completely stale," he replied. "As old as forever. A few extra measures were taken to increase security—like the vaults—but there were no disputes regarding principle. It was all a matter of mere tinkering. The groundwork had been laid centuries before. Before the *Marco Polo* even landed. They built Tanagar in their imagination during the long years of the search. They made their minds up so well that three thousand years wasn't enough to shift the pattern of thought more than the tiniest fraction."

"Nor was eleven thousand," said Talvar. "We *possess* more, I suppose, but the things we believe in haven't changed at all. Odd, when you think that so many of us spend so much of our lives telling ourselves in secret that we don't *really* believe in them at all."

"We're only Hedonists," said Cheron. "We don't count. The Intels *have* to believe, because they live their beliefs. They really have the control they try to cultivate in us. They really do stabilize themselves, physically, mentally, and socially. They're the living proof of their own rightness . . . seven hundred years of living proof. That's another thing, I presume, that hasn't changed."

Talvar nodded his grudging assent.

"What's your feeling," asked Cheron awkwardly, "about the Motherworld?"

Talvar had no trouble detecting his meaning. "I'm frightened half to death," he said, abruptly. "But I keep telling myself that even life in that kind of hell is better than eternity in an icicle. No matter what happens to us, it's all profit. Every last second."

Cheron savored that thought long after the blond man had left, until the machines that entombed him sucked him back into their nets of illusion.

5

Cheron had been subjected to hypnopaedic instruction before. It was a recognized way of learning particular physical skills, and his work had involved the cultivation of several such skills. In that distant past which seemed so close and so familiar he had been hospitalized three times in order to be taught the instrumental knowledge of his trade. Each time, though, it had been a matter of a few hours' indoctrination and a few more hours' recapitulation. Even when they had wired him internally for the sensory-bypass capacity when he was still a small boy, it had been a minor operation that had caused him no particular inconvenience.

The session aboard the starship was very different. The machines controlled him absolutely. He felt like a caterpillar tightly wound into a silken cocoon, helpless in the grip of processes that were working a literal metamorphosis. As the new synthetic memories and skills were formulated in his cells, capable of taking hold of his reflexes, amenable to conscious contemplation, he felt that his whole *being* was draining away, to be refilled by alienness.

The man of Tanagar remained in his brain, but was no longer, in some special sense, *him*. His former self was just that—someone he had been, but was no longer. He knew that such a distancing process could happen quite naturally—that he was no longer the person he had been twenty years ago, and no longer the child that had grown to maturity under the tender care of Tanagar. Nevertheless, he had a surprisingly strong sense of the propriety of *that* kind of personal change which he contrasted very sharply with what was happening to him—being *forced upon him*—now.

The kinds of things that he was being trained to do—even the kinds of things that he was made able to *say*—were actions unthinkable in Tanagarian society. In themselves, they were a strange kind of punishment, for in essence what they were doing to him was making him into a killer. The reason that he was here, of course, was that he had been condemned to the vaults *as* a killer, but that was not the kind of killer they were making him. His had been a crime of passion. (Jealousy, of course—there was a saying to the effect that jealousy was the passion of Hedonists, while anger was the passion of Pragmatists. The saying was all the more appropriate for leaving unsaid the fact that Intellectuals, characteristically, had no passion even to beware of.) They were making him now into a creature for whom killing was a *skill*—an instrument of survival. They were giving him reactions that would allow him to commit murder in a quite passionless way, reflexively, without so much as a passing thought, let alone a burst of passionate rage. It seemed a terrible thing that he should be made into that kind of being—a horrible cruelty. After all, the reason a crime of passion warranted the ultimate penalty, by contrast with a premeditated murder, was precisely the fact that it was an arbitrary event quite out of keeping with normal character, and hence both uncontrollable and unpredictable.

He had (as, of course, he was supposed to) despised himself for the action that had resulted in his condemnation. He had felt all the shame and guilt that was reasonable. He had seen the justice in the sentence of eternal life that had been passed at the end of his trial. He had been able to approve of his own removal from society as the best means of preventing him from ever repeating the outburst of violence that had resulted in a woman's death. But now he was being recreated as the kind of man who might kill and kill again as circumstances dictated.

Would they expunge his sense of guilt, his sense of self-loathing? The question seemed desperately important for a while, before he realized that in all probability they would not have to. Such reactions would probably die of their own accord.

And in the meantime. . . . *Control.*

That, in the final analysis, was what was required of him. Control of his glands, control of his nervous system. The machine would help him, for now. Afterward, he would be expected to help himself. He could do it, if he needed to. Everyone knew that. Control was possible—*perfect* control—if only one had the will. Hedonists, for the most part, didn't. Poor sensuals; victims of passion. A mere two hundred years of life—just enough to demonstrate that the triumphs of control *could* be won, and just enough to demonstrate, too, how much better was the control of the ordinary Pragmatist, and how *very* much better was the true *mensana.* (The term, of course, was an insult precisely because it was a corruption, a deliberately slurred phrase: a sound mind devalued in being described by an unsound word.)

He dreamed of murder. He dreamed of conversations, too, in all kinds of barbaric tongues; he even dreamed of all the things that Hedonists habitually dream of, but it was the dreaming of murder which upset and obsessed him. He knew, all along, that he was destroying mere phantoms of the imagination, but he also knew that it did not matter—that the victims might as well be real, and some day probably would be. It was not a prospect that he relished. He quickly came to envy Vito Talvar his obvious complacency in the face of what had been done to him.

I am the plaything of nightmares, he told himself once, in a period of restful wakefulness. *I am becoming a creature of nightmare.*

The phase wherein he conjured up such awkward statements of his predicament soon passed, but he never quite escaped from the notions themselves.

6

Sarid Jerome accepted the seat that was offered to him, noting without surprise that Salvador had chosen to keep the bulk of the desk between them. The Intellectual's face had a curious pink glow that was reflected from the mutely glowing screen in front of him. The room's main lighting was partially dimmed.

"I suppose you realize," said Jerome, "that I now know a dozen ways of killing a man quickly and efficiently, without the aid of weapons. Don't you think you're taking something of a risk?"

"You couldn't do it," Salvador assured him. "I won't explain why—just take my word for it."

Typical mensana, thought Sarid. *Always the clever bluff. Always make use of uncertainty.*

Salvador pressed three of the buttons on the desk and pointed to the blank wall to his left. Sarid turned in his chair to watch a panel slide back and the screen behind come to life. It displayed a map. Salvador dimmed the lights a little further.

"Do you recognize it?" he asked.

"Hardly," said Sarid. "The geography of the Motherworld

isn't one of the things I've taken pains to study. The instruction tapes don't seem to have included much in that line."

"The outlines of the continents aren't quite the same as those indicated on the memory-bank maps in any case," said Salvador. "The upheaval which followed the tectonic disturbances initiated by the atom wars raised some new land and sank some. There was a warm-up, when the north polar ice cap melted and returned a great deal of water to the oceans, inundating some low-lying areas. That was suddenly reversed, though, when the ash and dust added to the atmosphere during the period of accelerated vulcanism screened out enough solar heat to precipitate a quick cooling. The ice age wasn't very violent and didn't last long, but it affected most of the northern hemisphere. As far as we can ascertain, the new period of migration, when people expanded out of Africa into southern Europe—including the newly elevated lands in the north and central Mediterranean—began about seven thousand years ago. It took another thousand years or so for the climate to settle down properly, but it's been reasonably stable since then. Writing was rediscovered about four thousand years ago. There's no need to bore you with the history of the new civilization, except to mention that archaeology became the queen of the sciences in the more advanced parts of the globe sixteen or seventeen hundred years ago. It wasn't easy finding the right places to dig, and the business of reconstructing the knowledge of the ancient world has been fraught with all the difficulties imaginable, but they're making progress. It has been a long, slow renaissance, but it's bearing fruit."

Sarid turned away from the map to study Salvador's face.

"Why tell me all this—here? Why not force feed my mind the way you did with all the other information?"

"It's not just information," said the Intellectual. "I'd like to hear your reactions."

"What's there to react to?"

"We rediscovered Earth nearly a thousand years ago, in their terms. Their year is longer than ours by some fifteen percent, if you want to convert back into Tanagarian terms. At that time, their renaissance had hardly begun. What would you have done, in our place?"

"In the place of your immediate predecessors, you mean?" Salvador shrugged off the trivial correction.

Sarid kept his eyes on the Intellectual's face while he paused to think. Finally, he said: "I don't want to play guessing games. Obviously, Interstellar decided not to interfere, and the Senate backed the decision. They declined the opportunity to become midwives supervising the rebirth of the Motherworld, if you'll pardon the mixing of the metaphor. Why should I bother to figure out the reasons? Intels can always think of excuses for not doing anything. The status quo is sacred, remember."

"That's not what I asked," Salvador pointed out. "I asked what *you* would have done."

"How do I know? I'd have looked around, and made a decision on the basis of what I saw. You want me to say that I'd have interfered—played God in order to help the miserable remnants of the ancient world back on to the high road to civilization. Well, maybe I would. I don't know. What's the point? The situation I'm in *now* is entirely different. You're going to throw me into the test tube and watch my every reaction. I'm an experiment—a fascinating one from the point of view of the Intels watching from a distance. I can smell the curiosity from here. The hell with it—why should I cooperate? You want to know what I'll do, you wait and see. I suppose you've planted some kind of electronic leech in my head that will see what I see and hear what I hear, and relay it all back to the data banks in your listening posts. I can't do anything about that, but I can refrain from voicing my thoughts. They're private."

"You're not very cooperative," observed Salvador, not sounding too concerned.

"What did you expect?"

"I expected a little more enthusiasm—not for the project itself, but for the business of learning as much as possible about its nature, and the intentions of those running it. I *can't* detect curiosity radiating from you, and I find that strange."

Sarid shrugged. "All right," he said. "Tell me what the plan is. Then I'll know what I'm supposed to do when I get down to the surface. It won't make any difference, of course, in what I actually decide to do."

Salvador smiled. "I'm not going to give you any orders," he said evenly. "What would be the point? I'm not even going to make suggestions. What you do is up to you. You're per-

fectly entitled to keep your plans and your innermost
thoughts entirely to yourself."

He stopped and paused, obviously waiting for Sarid to take
the initiative. Sarid was in no hurry to do so. He looked back
at the map, then at the Intellectual. Finally, he said: "Fair
enough. I'm curious. What exactly are you trying to do?
What are you hoping to achieve? Do you expect twenty Tanagarians—nineteen of them Hedonists—to be able to take
control of the history of an entire world? Do you expect us to
become the mentors you're reluctant to become yourselves?
Why go to the vaults to find your ambassadors?"

"That's better," said Salvador.

"Now you've made me ask the questions," said Sarid sarcastically. "I suppose you'll refuse to answer."

"The situation on the Motherworld is an interesting one,"
said the Intellectual slowly. "There's a sense in which their
renaissance has almost run to completion. They've recovered
much of the knowledge of the ancient world. The scholars of
Macaria have managed to recover and preserve a great deal
of pre-catastrophe writing, including scientific textbooks of
various kinds. They know enough to begin an industrial revolution that would remake the world in half a dozen generations. The knowledge, however, is not enough. You see, they
lack the resources to get any kind of industrial revolution
started. They have no coal, no oil, no uranium. There's iron
in plenty in their world, but far too much of it is in the form
of oxides. They have both steam engines and internal-com-
bustion engines, but the former use wood or charcoal as fuel,
and the latter use alcohol distilled from wood or sugar. The
Macarians know about electricity, but the materials they have
for *using* what they know are highly limiting. It's a curious
historical predicament—one without parallel in *our* history.
The people on Earth who are most advanced are facing the
prospect of having to develop an alternative technology, and
at present it seems as if that technology will be far more limited than that of their distant ancestors. If we were to put *our*
technology at their disposal, things would be very different—
they'd then have access to the resources of the solar system.
They'll never gain that access on their own. In effect, we
could absorb them into our way of life—move them into
Tanagar's cultural orbit. It would take a long time, but we
could do it. The alternative, obviously, is to leave them be,

and see what kind of history they make for themselves, with the means at their disposal. That might be interesting. There isn't much scope in a stable and uniform society for the study of social science—experiments in history. It would be interesting to see what other forms of social organization are possible, and to be able to observe the dynamics of social change. We might learn something."

"However," said Sarid Jerome, cutting across Salvador's rather lazy discourse, "you appear to be doing neither of those things."

"True," said Salvador. "What we're doing instead is to introduce into the situation a kind of catalyst—something that will help change to happen."

"That's what I'm supposed to be—a catalyst?"

Salvador didn't bother to affirm the fact. Sarid stared at him for a few seconds, then said: "I suppose it's typical of Intel thinking. Stand back, don't get involved, but shake things up a little. Disinterested observers, who couldn't possibly compromise their objectivity by taking an active part in the situation, trying to stimulate a little action. The fascination of the scientist. You don't even know what you want me to do. You don't have a plan for me to cooperate with. You just want to see what will happen. The Motherworld is your plaything, like everything else in the universe except Tanagar, and you're beginning a game. You'll play the game with nations, and peoples, and socio-political systems, and the patterns of history, but it might just as well be wooden pieces on a checkerboard or microscopic organisms on a slide. The attitude is the same.

"Of course, the attitude to Tanagar itself is precisely the reverse. There, stability must be preserved at all costs. Stability itself is the cardinal virtue. All change is threatening, and hence must be suppressed. You take the catalysts *out* of Tanagarian society, instead of throwing them in. The social world of Tanagar is the secure base from which you can look out upon the wonderful universe—the one unquestioned thing that makes you free to ask all the other questions. That's right, isn't it?"

Salvador again ignored the rhetorical question. Instead, he rose to his feet and went over to the wall-screen. He placed a thin finger on the map.

"This is Macaria," he said, "the most advanced nation on

Earth. It exercises some degree of political control over all of what used to be southern Europe and most of what used to be North Africa, including the new land bridge. It's not exactly an empire—some of the other nations are supposedly independent allies, others are subject states incorporated by conquest. The significant fact is that Macaria has economic control everywhere, and is still expanding. The equatorial belt is very sparsely inhabited, and is covered by very dense forest. Similarly, northern Europe is mostly forested with no substantial concentrations of population. At present, expansion is mostly eastward, but the Macarian elite already have plans for crossing the Atlantic and establishing themselves in America.

"You speak Macarian, as do all your companions. You speak it like a barbarian. In fact, you don't speak any language like a native. Wherever you find yourselves, you'll be strangers. You'll have to establish identities for yourselves. The Macarian ruling elite is notionally highly exclusive, but that's a sham. The political expansion of its realm of influence has been so rapid that it's recruiting both from the lower ranks of Macarian society and from the ruling elites of other nations. There are opportunities to rise to the top, and I'm sure that you'll find them if you need them.

"We won't be dropping you in Macaria itself, but in Dahra, which is a long way to the south. Strangers attract far less attention there—no one's expected to be carrying papers, and it will be easy enough to establish identities for yourselves if you're careful. The hazards, of course, are appropriately greater. We'll provide you with money—counterfeit, of course, but in terms of the value of the metals less corrupt than the actual currencies used in exchange. We'll give you some basic medical supplies, too, though we'll disguise them a little. We don't want you to be carrying anything that will unequivocally testify to your extraterrestrial origin."

"Why not?" Sarid interrupted.

Salvador smiled. "We have a base on the surface. Occasionally our observers move about there. We'd rather our presence wasn't known. We don't want to deflect the attention of the Macarian scholars into . . . unproductive channels. We've taken elementary precautions to assure that it will be difficult for you to be entirely honest without being considered insane. We'd rather your influence was subtle. Do you see the point?"

"I see," said Sarid sourly. "It wouldn't do for the pieces in the game to be too aware of the players. They won't necessarily be stupid, you know. If they've recovered so much material from the ancient world they'll know about starships. They may even know about the *Marco Polo* and her six sisters. Perhaps the truth wouldn't sound so implausible, if it were told to the right people."

Salvador nodded in agreement but made no further comment.

"Even if I *can't* persuade anyone else that I'm telling the truth," said Sarid, softly, "*I'll* know. Don't ever forget that."

"I would never underestimate you," said Salvador quietly. "You can depend on that."

7

Cheron lay back on the bed, dabbing sweat from his face with a disposable towel. He was breathing heavily, and there was a warm ache in his arms and legs. After his long sojourn in the tight-fitting plastic web it was an immense relief to have freedom of movement—even to turn his head was a luxury. For the first time since the moment of his revival he felt *human* again. From now on he was no longer an experimental animal, controlled to the least twitch of his nervous system and the chemical cycles of his metabolism.

He was free.

He almost laughed at the absurdity of *that* thought as he looked round at the narrow walls of the tiny cabin but there was enough truth in it to make the irony redundant.

He reached behind his head to touch the small patches covering the wounds in his skull. The skin would soon heal, and the hair was already beginning to grow back on his head. Talvar was far enough ahead of him to have found it necessary to cut his own hair, cursing the fact that he could not style it properly.

There was a knock on the door, and Talvar entered without waiting for him to call out an invitation.

"How do you feel?" asked the blond man.

"Good," replied Cheron.

"Back on solid food?"

"Nearly. The soup was perceptibly thicker. It's pretty foul, though."

"I think they may be preparing our digestive systems for the unpleasant experiences the Motherworld has in store. It's difficult to be sure. I haven't seen Salvador or Teresa Janeat for some time—not that they're ever eager to explain themselves. The idea is to force us to converse with the computers in order to make sure we know our languages properly. Stupid."

"Common sense," Cheron contradicted him. "Everything they've put into our heads they've put in with a purpose. I want to make sure I have command of every last vestige of it. It's the price of survival. Now that I've got a second life, I don't want to lose it through carelessness."

Talvar shrugged. "It's all profit," he said. "I resent having to participate in this ridiculous persecution. I hate being treated like a laboratory animal. And I hate not being able to do something *about* it."

"Control," said Cheron, with heavy irony. "It's all a matter of control."

"Sure," said the other. "Are you going to take up meditation? If you could make yourself into an Intel you could maybe live forever. Learn to determine your metabolism and evert your entire gut at either end. A Hedonist with a masochistic interest in asceticism—a jeckle in reverse."

"I don't want to be an Intel," said Cheron. "Not even a Prag. I just want to be a live Hedonist instead of a dead one, I'm willing to work at *that*."

Talvar shrugged. "Once we're on the ground, I'll make sure I stick close to you. That way I'll be safe without having to punish myself in the meantime."

Cheron turned on his side, and then sat upright, rejoicing in the freedom of movement. Talvar sat down, bracing himself against the cabin wall.

"You're getting fat," observed Cheron.

"I *am* fat," Talvar replied. "This is the real me reasserting itself after being pounded out of shape by that wretched elas-

THE CASTAWAYS OF TANAGAR

tic machine. All Hedonists tend to be endomorphic. It's glandular. We're born as well as made, you know. Maybe you don't, coming from so far back in time. The separation of types has a natural basis—it's not a matter of arbitrary imposition. In the final analysis, our values are written in our metabolic sub-routines."

"How does that account for changelings? Or jeckles?"

"I didn't say that it was *absolute*. Anyhow, metabolic patterns change sometimes. An underactive thyroid gets triggered by some happenstance of nature, and a cheerful, easygoing person like me is transformed overnight into a ravening Prag, driven to obsession by some kind of chemical command system. Being a Prag is unhealthy anyhow—nobody can be obsessive all the time. Mind you, the jeckles are even obsessive about their shameful bouts of pleasure-seeking. Do you ever see a *real* Hedonist behaving like a Prag on hydeyhigh? Hedonists have a sense of proportion that the other types lack."

"Is all that supposed to make sense?"

"How would I know? I'm not an Intel."

"I'd have thought eight thousand years would have permitted further advances in understanding than *that*. As far as I can see, the system has actually failed. In my day, the justification for putting people like me into the refrigerator was that it would remove the disturbing elements from the system and allow it to perfect itself. From your accounts, it seems that things in your day were—are—actually worse. Jeckling was supposed to be a flaw that would work itself out. Changelings were supposed to be a temporary phenomenon too."

"Oh, we've advanced," Talvar assured him. "We now know that our remote ancestors—or, to be strictly accurate, the not-so-remote ancestors of the present generation of Intels—were a little naïve. Utopian optimism, I believe it's called. As far as I can make out they thought that the separation of the three types would not only stabilize the system but bring it some kind of *ultimate* stability, in which Intellectuals, Pragmatists, and Hedonists would become distinct castes following distinct ways of life, whose collaboration would contribute to the social body all the forces needed to maintain it.

"The Intellectuals of that generation thought that they could—or perhaps already *had*—purge themselves of all

34 *Brian Stableford*

shameful emotion and become creatures of pure reason. The passions would be left to the other castes, in moderation of course. Pragmatists were allowed to be hungry for success, Hedonists for pleasure, but the Intellectuals' hunger for enlightenment was purer and didn't count. Nowadays, the Intels tend to chuckle a bit at such crude thinking. The cant has changed its character. Now it's obvious—or so they tell us— that to separate reason and emotion as though they were opposites is silly. The keynote now is inner harmony, depending upon idiosyncratic circumstances. Jeckling is a sad necessity for those thus metabolically inclined, and such are the frailties of human flesh that there will always be changelings. Nobody ever changes into an Intel, though. I've often wondered about that. You can be thrown out of the Intel class by a metabolic quirk, but not into it. I think it's because being an Intel is a form of hereditary insanity."

"Did you learn all that at school?" asked Cheron.

"Of course not. I learned *much* more than that, and it all made sense—at the time. Mercifully, I managed to forget most of it almost immediately."

Cheron threw the towel into a disposal slot. He was quite cool now.

"What did you actually *do* to wind up in the vaults?" he asked, conscious of the indelicacy of the question. Talvar, however, accepted it in the same spirit as he would any other inquiry.

"Killed a man, of course."

"Why?"

"I'm not exactly sure. I was at the time, but after the Intels had worked on me to try and figure it out to *their* satisfaction I lost confidence and began to wonder. Crime of passion was the verdict, of course—my plea of premeditation never had a chance. I could never think of a convincing motive. I had so much difficulty that I began to find my *real* motive unconvincing. It was a simple matter of vicious opportunism. He was an Intel, of course. If he'd been a Prag they might not have frozen me, but if he'd been a Prag I probably wouldn't have hated him enough to kill him. There's something about Intels which always makes me want to vomit. Even the ones I don't have anything specific against make my flesh creep."

"What did he actually *do* to you?"

"I was relocated. Half across the planet. Retraining, the

works. It wasn't that, of course—happens all the time. But he
kept *explaining* it to me. Necessity, opportunity, making use
of resources, make me even happier. I kicked for the sake
of kicking, but he was so *patient* and so patronizing. He was
too fine and sensitive a soul to belong to *this* world. Do you
think I'm crazy?"

"Probably," said Cheron.

"What did *you* do?"

"Persistent failure of self-control. Sexual jealousy. Violence. I don't know for certain that I did kill anyone. That
wasn't the issue at the trial. Self-indulgence, deliberate failure to contain aggressive impulses. Well, they've paid me
back in kind, now. They won't ever take us back to Tanagar.
You do realize that, don't you? They're going to land us on
the Motherworld and leave us there to rot."

"The thought had occurred to me," said the blond man, in
a more sober tone.

"But what the hell," said Cheron. "It's all profit."

8

Cyriac Salvador stared at the schematic diagram displayed
on the screen above his desk. He beckoned to Teresa Janeat
and pointed out the red spot in the lower left-hand corner
that was winking steadily on and off.

"What is it?" she demanded.

"Ironically enough," he said, "it's the self-repair facility. A
case of physician, heal thyself, in mechanical terms."

"There's no actual loss of function?"

"No. Not yet. It's a warning of vulnerability. The ship had
to be modified quite considerably to accommodate this project—structurally, of course, but more importantly in terms
of circuitry and programming. Something was bound to go
wrong eventually. The problem is that now that it *has*, it

means that we're that much less able to cope with any further malfunction."

"Can you do anything?"

"I've already done it. It didn't work. The system needs a closedown overhaul, but we can't close down for several days yet—not until we dock at the satellite after dropping Jerome and his companions."

"Nothing much can go wrong in that time," said Teresa, with more hope than conviction.

"The ship is now providing life-support for twenty-two people—and not at minimum subsistence level, either. It's not exactly a strain, but it's a lot of activity. Jerome and the others have limited access to the control network, too. Everything's under safeguard, but it's one more factor that we can't entirely account for. With the self-repair function deteriorating, other things are bound to deteriorate too. The probability of something serious going wrong is very small, of course, but it pays to be aware of small probabilities."

Intel caution, she thought. *Cowardice.*

Aloud, she said, "Even if we lost half our systems, they'll be able to pick us off from satellite."

"Satellite would get a little crowded with twenty extra men on the station."

"In that case," she told him, "we'd better make certain that whatever else happens, the drop goes ahead. Does it really matter if we lose a few of the sensuals?"

He looked at her sharply. "That's a little callous," he observed.

She shrugged.

"I worry when things begin to go wrong," said Salvador calmly. "I've invested the greater part of my lifetime in the Motherworld, and in this particular project. It took a great deal of effort to get authorization. I don't want *anything* to go wrong—not the tiniest detail. I don't want to lose any of the resurrectees, at any stage. We can't expect them all to live to be two hundred down on the surface, but I don't want them wasted. We've brought them a long way."

"You're in charge," she said, in an offhand tone. "I only get things done."

He made no reply, but waited, impassively, until she left the room. Her dislike was, of course, of no consequence. It had not yet created any real difficulty, and there was no reason why it should. It was a fact of life, no more. It might have been easier had she been able to like him, but an Intellectual never expected to be popular. Neither Pragmatists nor Hedonists envied his class in the sense that they could appreciate the rewards of knowledge and asceticism, but they nevertheless resented Intellectuals for the superiority that was made evident by their longer life-span. It was a burden that all his kind had to learn to bear, along with all the other burdens.

It was, of course, a burden which Cyriac Salvador was glad to shoulder, though he would have denied that he got pleasure from it.

Or, indeed, from anything else.

9

Cheron strapped the leather belt around his waist, adjusting some of the pouches that were fastened to it.

"The jacket goes over the top?" he asked.

"So it seems," replied Sarid Jerome. "The belt contains everything we expect to help keep us alive—especially money. We don't want to leave it exposed."

"This clothing is *appalling*," complained Talvar. He was already fully dressed, and had come with Sarid Jerome to Cheron's room. The three of them were to be the first party through the airlock when the ship made its pass through the atmosphere. None of them had ever seen any of their future companions. The corridor where they were lodged had no access to the others.

"I look absurd," observed Cheron, echoing Talvar's sentiment in a token fashion.

"Get the jacket on," said Sarid. "We have to move out. Time's catching up."

"Suppose we refuse to move?" said Talvar. "What then? What are they actually going to *do*?"

"Gas us and throw us out, probably," Sarid replied. "This isn't the time for a rebellion. I'm sure they have ways to take care of noncooperation. They've had no difficulty so far in treating us exactly as they wish. Let's go."

He led the way through the narrow doorway of Cheron's cabin, and they followed him along the corridor, Talvar bringing up the rear. For the first time, they were allowed through the bulkhead into the main corridor of the ship's central section. Sarid led them unerringly to the airlock. There was no sign of Cyriac Salvador or Teresa Janeat. No one was going to wish them farewell.

"We're getting lighter," observed Cheron.

"They're stopping the section from spinning," said Sarid. "We're braking as well. We'll probably be hitting the atmosphere in a matter of minutes. They'll start the countdown once we're in the lock. The parachutes are in a locker along here."

Once they were in the airlock there was a long pause while the pressure was equalized to that of the appropriate stratum of the atmosphere. Cheron felt his ears popping, and he was conscious of having to breathe more deeply. His throat was dry.

The countdown was screened for them. Instructions appeared on the screen at intervals regarding their parachutes. Most of the instructions were redundant. They already knew what they were doing.

Cheron felt sick as the temporary weightlessness began to give way to a gravitational pull that was not in the direction he had previously thought of as "down." He didn't speak but studied the faces of his companions carefully.

Control, he told himself.

Sarid Jerome was quite impassive, and apparently calm. Vito Talvar, too, was showing less sign of strain than Cheron had anticipated. He felt ashamed of his own apprehension, which—he felt sure—must be manifest in his features. Neither of the other two were showing him any particular attention, and he was sure that the reason for this was to save him embarrassment.

The screen flashed the word: READY.

The countdown had reached twenty. The computer clearly had a poor opinion of the reaction time of human beings.

Talvar touched him on the shoulder, but whether to reassure him or to seek reassurance there was no way to tell.

The READY signal blinked off, and the countdown number disappeared too. The screen, in fact, went completely blank. Then the light went off, leaving them in total darkness for three seconds. For one terrible moment Cheron thought that this was the end, and that he was returning to the oblivion which was tantalizingly out of reach of his memory.

Then the airlock opened, and they lurched out, pulled sideways by the gravitational well. Cheron saw the great silver bubble of the starship overhead as he spun, and then he found himself hurtling toward a silver-tinged horizon lipped with ridges of dark cloud. For a second, nothing made sense, and he was startled by the coldness of the air that stung his face, and by the fact that it wrenched the breath from his lungs so furiously that he was sure there had been a miscalculation of conditions.

When the parachute opened and he was able to discover once again which way was down, he was appalled to find that he was headed into Stygian darkness—the distant rim of dawn was receding as fast as he fell. There were a few distant flares of yellow light, but directly below him there was nothing but an abyss.

He seemed to fall for a long, long time. The darkness closed in on him, and was lightened only by a single bright flash of white that he saw from the corner of his eye in the final minute of his descent. He was unprepared to meet the ground, which seemed to smash into him with far more force than it should have. He might have broken both his legs, but he was saved by an unexpected reflex which he had not known that he possessed. It folded his legs and allowed him to roll over. The soil was hard, and his hip and arm were battered by the collision, but he sustained no serious injury.

His body knew what his mind did not, and before he could collect himself sufficiently to take purposive action, he had already slipped from the harness of the parachute, and was struggling to rise to his feet. The struggle was a painful one—he weighed half as much again as he had on the starship, though he was lighter than he had been on his homeworld, eight thousand years before.

He cursed himself as he came to his feet—for his clumsiness, for the pain that he was feeling, for his lack of self-control, and most of all for the alien programs in his brain which seemed to know what was happening and what was necessary so much better than did his conscious mind.

He was on the Motherworld, hundreds of light-years from Tanagar, eight thousand years from his own time, but in a strangely disturbing fashion he *belonged* to this place already.

He had been here before, in his dreams.

Part Two

THE PRICE
OF SURVIVAL

1

It was midday when they found the road winding through the valleys and gullies of the semi-desert. When new, its surface must have been almost jet black, but dust and sand had drifted across it, lodging in tiny cracks opened up by the fierce heat of the sun, so that now it had a curious mottled appearance. Occasionally, as they approached, vitreous scars gleamed with reflected sunlight. There was no sign of any kind of vehicle.

When they reached the side of the road, they sank down with a weariness that suggested they could have gone no farther for the moment. To Cheron, at least, it came as a great relief to have found something so obviously man-made—something shaped for human use by human effort.

"I'm so *heavy*," moaned Talvar. "It's stupid. They were supposed to be preparing us for *survival* here."

"We weigh less here than we would on Tanagar," Sarid reminded him. "Our muscles haven't wasted. Once we've acclimatized ourselves, we'll be unnaturally strong and powerful. It will only be a matter of days."

Cheron struggled out of his jacket and laid it down on the parched ground. "These clothes seem remarkably ill-adapted to the circumstances," he said. "Last night it was too cold; now it's far too hot."

Sarid Jerome made no reply. He was staring into the blue infinity of the sky, with an expression of intense concentration on his face. Cheron watched him for a few minutes and then said, "What are you thinking about?"

"The parachutes," replied Sarid.

The parachutes had been constructed from some kind of synthetic protein. Soon after they had landed the polymer had begun to break down. By morning there had been noth-

ing left but shriveled streamers of organic waste which might
have been almost anything.

"Why?" asked Cheron.

"There's nothing to show that we're from another world.
Nothing except the ideas in our heads. Everything has been
set up so that the only realistic course for us to adopt is to
pretend that we're men of this world. In effect, Salvador
wants us to *become* men of this world. We're like some kind
of drug, injected into its bloodstream."

"So?" This time the question came from Talvar.

"It would be interesting to know what Salvador intends us
to do—what he believes that we will do. Not knowing, *whatever* we do we'll never be able to be sure that we're not acting exactly as he intended that we should."

"Does it matter?" asked Cheron.

"Maybe not," said Sarid. "To *you*."

"The immediate problem," said Talvar, "is finding the others. The road seems to run more or less north to south. Or
the other way round. Either way, it's not the line the ship was
following."

Sarid sat up and looked along the road to the north, scanning the horizon. There was nothing but bare hills. While no
one was speaking there was utter silence, broken occasionally by the plaintive calling of some invisible bird.

"We're in Dahra," said Sarid. "About twenty-six-hundred
kilometers north of the equator. The mountains in the east
are in a region which the Macarians call the Kezula. It's territory they don't occupy and don't control. Inhabited by nomadic herdsmen and scattered villages. No towns. The
nearest Dahran city is Sau, where the road presumably goes
if we head northward. It could be fifty kilometers, or two
hundred. Probably nearer two hundred—this is wilderness.
The others will be strung out in a long line extending across
the northwest section of the Kezula, back into Dahra and
then into the southern borderlands of Merkad. Some of them
might be nearer to the Merkadian city called Zedad than to
Sau, but they'll head for Sau anyhow, because they know
that's where *we'll* be heading for. We'll be doing the sensible
thing if we follow the road. Or do you want to head south?"

"Why should we?" asked Cheron.

Sarid shrugged. "Maybe we'd be better as three instead of

twenty." After a pause, he added, "Maybe I'd be better still on my own."

No one replied to that comment, and Sarid refrained from venturing further along that particular line of thought.

Cheron closed his eyes and tried to conjure up some kind of mental picture of Dahra—some kind of understanding of what the city of Sau might be like. He failed. It was not that he lacked information, merely that he did not have the imaginative power to gather it and organize it into any kind of coherent assembly. His body ached, and the ache demanded the full attention of his consciousness. He envied Sarid the ability to think—the *determination* that forced him to think.

I am no longer a Hedonist, he told himself. *I am no longer a Tanagarian. I have undergone a crucial metamorphosis, and I am now just a man. I must learn the values of a Pragmatist, perhaps those of an Intellectual too. I am no longer living in a protected environment whose stability and security are guaranteed. I cannot afford the luxury of limitations.*

He paused, trying to force that message to become a part of him—more than meaningless chatter. He doubted that he was capable of living up to its demands.

He wondered whether butterflies already knew how to be butterflies while they were still caterpillars. It seemed unlikely.

"Salvador is tormenting us," said Talvar bitterly. "All this is really a punishment. It wasn't enough to sentence us to eternal life. They decided that we must spend eternity in hell as the price of our sins. None of this is real, of course. It's just one more poisoned dream. We're still frozen, or at least in metabolic retardation. They're feeding us vicious dreams. Even if it *is* an experiment, that's all that's happening. It's simulated. That's why it makes no sense. We've never left Tanagar. The Intels have made the vaults into their own private inferno, and we're the damned souls they want to torment. It's a game, you see—a game of judgment and damnation."

"Shut up," said Sarid baldly. "Fantasizing isn't going to get us anywhere. Get up on your feet and walk."

The blond man sat up, and for a moment he seemed about to react violently, but the moment passed. He shook his head, and said, "Poor Pragmatist. It's not the pain, it's the anticipation. How *do* you live so long under all that stress?"

"Control," said Sarid steadily. He rose to his own feet, standing upright, without the least sign of strain in his features. "You're not exhausted," he told the blond man. "You're not heavy. That's only self-indulgence—masochistic surrender. Stand up and get your head straight. We're going to walk to Sau, whether it's fifty kilometers or two hundred, two days or ten. Concentrate on hardening your feet. You don't want to blister like a five-year-old child, do you?"

Vito Talvar rose to his feet, and struck the same kind of pose as Sarid. Cheron, after watching their faces for a moment, stood up too.

"We can't afford this," he said. "We have to cooperate, and we can't do that unless we can stop despising one another for what we are."

Sarid glanced at him, and acknowledged the truth of what he had said with a nod. Talvar relaxed, but said nothing.

"Now that I'm here," said Cheron, stooping to pick up his jacket and slinging it over his shoulder, "and dressed like this, I realize how little there is inside my head that makes me a Tanagarian. How much of Tanagar's knowledge do *I* have— or even *you*, Sarid? On Tanagar, we had other people to do *our* knowing for us. What are the things I can *do*, outside the things that were drilled into my mind by the dream-machine on the ship? Is any one of them of any use here on the Motherworld? The one thing that equips us to survive here is the one thing that was quite inconsequential on Tanagar—our simple physical size and the strength that goes with it. That's not exactly the legacy of Tanagarian culture and civilization, is it? Have you stopped to think how little of that legacy is actually invested in *us*?"

"Yes," said Sarid. "I have."

"That's why he thinks he might be better off without us," said Talvar. "At least his way of thinking fits. You have to be a Prag in a god-forsaken place like this, just to be able to exist."

"We'd better start learning, then," said Cheron. "Hadn't we?"

"Let's walk," said Sarid. "It's a long way to Sau."

2

Some ten or eleven kilometers to the north they rounded a shallow bend and were presented, quite unexpectedly, with the sight of a village. The change in the character of the land was both sudden and spectacular. They could look back and see nothing but a patchwork of gray and yellow, with patches of mean grass and dull thorn scrub, where only ragged cracks in the stony ground provided any kind of roothold. They looked forward now, though, to slopes which were green with vegetable plots and small stands of fruit trees, where brown soil was protected from the hot wind by walls of chipped stone and thick hedges of tangled thorn bushes. There were small, square houses made of clay and friable brick, clustered in half a dozen groups, with pens for chickens and connecting pathways. A few tethered she goats were cropping weeds from the open spaces between the houses.

Some distance from the village itself, set back a little way from the road, there was a larger building made of some kind of stone-and-plaster conglomerate. Farther away still was another building, this time set at the roadside—a long, low edifice with several doors and numerous windows, much more angular in construction and dark gray in color. This was clearly the product of a different way of thinking, and of a different culture. They would have recognized it as an alien presence and attributed it to Macaria even if its nature had not been manifest in the fact that soldiers in uniform were sunning themselves on benches on the south side of it. There were lines where undershirts and uniform tunics hung drying in the sun, and from somewhere in the rear came the sound of metal horseshoes clicking and rasping on stone floors. Behind the barracks was a series of crude wooden shacks— some no more than shelters roofed with tarpaulin. Wisps of smoke drifted from a chimney at one end of the building.

"Civilization," said Sarid, letting the irony show in his voice.

"No roadside inn," commented Cheron. "Not many travelers pause here."

"Except for those that are welcomed by the army," Sarid pointed out.

They had already been seen by the village children, and the men and women who were in the fields or sat outside the houses obviously knew they were there also. It was the children, though, that reacted to their presence. Half a dozen came running to meet them, carrying baskets and panniers of fruit. The race was won by a child of twelve or thirteen, dark-skinned and ill-clad. He offered grapes and some larger orange fruits they could not put a name to.

Sarid reached into his shirt and struggled with the flap of one of his belt-pouches, finally pulling out a couple of small coins—thin silver sequins no bigger than the nail of his smallest finger. The child accepted them both and surrendered half the contents of his basket. Then he began to herd the other children back, protecting his customers from undue pestering. Cheron found two similar coins and bought the whole contents of a lesser container from a smaller child—an act that caused some dissension among the children.

"We were probably cheated," observed Sarid, as the mob finally withdrew. Talvar, however, had already fallen upon Cheron's purchase with indecent haste. Cheron, too, made no attempt to mask the relish with which he bit into a fruit. They took their prizes to the roadside and methodically worked their way through the meal. Some of the children stayed close by, watching them curiously. Then two troopers carrying rifles came slowly down the road toward them. Cheron watched them come, uneasily.

"Behave as if we have a perfect right to be here," advised Sarid. "If we want to use the road, we're going to have to meet a lot of soldiers. The Macarians didn't build it for the convenience of the natives."

The uniform which the soldiers wore consisted of loose white trousers and a pale blue jacket worn over a white shirt. There were silver epaulettes on the jackets, and metal insignia on the breasts. Both men wore flat caps with large peaks and flaps protecting the back of the neck from the sun. The rifles which they carried had forty-centimeter bayonets attached to them. They carried the weapons in a relaxed manner. The soldiers were obviously foreigners, somewhat lighter in skin than the villagers; clean-shaven and generally taller. They remained, however, some fifteen centimeters shorter than Cheron, who was the shortest of the three Tanagarians.

The soldiers looked them up and down for half a minute, while no one spoke. Finally, one said, in Macarian: "Foreigners."

"That's right," replied Sarid, in the same language.

The soldier who had spoken frowned, plainly surprised either by the language or the pronunciation.

"Where from?" he asked.

"Camelon," replied Sarid, naming a province of Macaria in western Europe."

"You're not men of Camelon," said the second soldier. "You're barbarians from the far north. No one but a barbarian talks the way you do."

Sarid shrugged. "What does it matter where I was born? I'm from Camelon now. A seaman. We lost our ship off the coast of Zarh. We've been moving east for weeks."

"You've crossed Zarh! And Ksah too?" The soldier plainly did not believe the story.

Sarid shrugged again. "It wasn't easy," he said.

"You have papers?"

"No," said Sarid. "No papers, no possessions. We lost our ship."

"You gave money to the children."

"So?" Sarid put on a show of being annoyed. "Everyone has to eat."

"Come with us," commanded the soldier.

Sarid glanced at his companions, nodding imperceptibly. It was hardly necessary. Cheron and Talvar were quite content to follow his lead.

As they walked along the road to the barracks, Cheron wondered why Sarid had told such an implausible story. Why pretend to be seamen in the middle of a desert? Cheron had no idea how far this place might be from the nearest seaport, but he knew that it was a very long way.

They were taken into the long building and hustled along a narrow corridor to a small office, where a man who was plainly an officer was laid right back in a chair, his feet on a stout table, letting the current of cool air from a large fan play on his face. The fan appeared to be powered by electricity, and Cheron noted that there was an electric light bulb set in the ceiling. The place obviously had some kind of generator. This was more than he had expected—even the glass in the windows seemed to him to signify a higher level of technological achievement than he had imagined.

The officer showed no more than token annoyance at being interrupted. He listened while the soldier repeated the story Sarid had told him.

"Barbarians from the northern forest," said the officer, when the report was complete. "The last thing I expect to come limping along my road. They say there are giants in the north, but I never believed it until now."

"We grow large because of the cold," said Sarid. "We need our bulk."

"It isn't cold *now*," observed the officer. "But you look fit and well. Do ships from Camelon really trade with Zarh?"

"Certainly," Sarid told him. Cheron was already beginning to feel that they were completely out of their depth, but Sarid maintained his mask of serene self-confidence.

"And how have you lived while crossing Zarh and Ksah?" inquired the officer.

"As we could," replied Sarid, with another one of his masterful shrugs.

"By banditry, no doubt," said the officer smoothly. "It's our task to protect the people of these friendly states from banditry. It's the service we perform in bringing law to lawless lands . . . the gifts of civilization. You wouldn't understand the gifts of civilization, being forest demons from the north. Demons, of course, love the snows—you must be *very* unhappy in these parts. Or do your brother demons of the desert succor you?"

"We are men," said Sarid evenly. "We are not bandits."

"That is good," said the officer. "You could not be soldiers of Macaria if you were demons. And if you were bandits, we would be required to hang you. You are not only men, but henceforth you are civilized men. You must learn to speak like civilized men, and not like barbarians whose tongues are too large. But then, everything about you is too large. The quartermaster at Talos will not find uniforms to fit you. Don't despair, though. We will *make* uniforms, so that you may have the privilege of serving Macaria and God. You have heard of God, I hope?"

Cheron swallowed hard, and even Sarid seemed shaken.

"All we want is to return to Camelon," he said. "We intend to go to Sau, and then into Merkad. It will take many months, but in the end we will find the Calm Sea again, and a ship that will take us to our own place."

"I could not be so cruel," said the officer pleasantly. "You have no idea how things are in Dahra. Since we brought the rewards of civilization to this poor land, so long wrecked by disastrous war with Merkad, we have increased the hopes of every raider and pirate in the Kezula. We have built a road, so that trade caravans may safely pass from one place to another—and by doing so we have told the raiders exactly where they may be sure of finding caravans. Even worse, we have shown them the power of our arms, and they will not rest until they have captured weapons that will let them fight us on equal terms. There are ambushes everywhere.

No one can pass along the road without an escort without facing terrible danger. The people of Zarh and Ksah are so gentle, and so untroubled—you would not believe how terrible the men of Kezula are, and how they act when they sweep west into our protectorates. Only with the army to protect you can you hope to live long in Dahra. Besides, it is the law. Macaria needs men to help her cause in these lands, which are so far from the homeland. We cannot take the young men from Dahra's villages, for it is they we are here to protect—unless, of course, they beg to join us. Foreigners are another matter. If you belong to Camelon, as you claim, you belong to Macaria. You are in the army. It is as simple as that. If you wish to argue, I should remind you that you are now subject to army discipline, and the punishment for insubordination is cruel. We must use rigorous methods while we are so far from home—you agree?"

It was not altogether clear what Sarid was being asked to agree to. What was clear, however, was that his agreement would make very little difference. Cheron glanced behind him, at the troopers with their bayoneted rifles. Sarid would not meet his eye. Talvar seemed to have become unnaturally pale even for one as light-skinned as he.

"Very well," said the officer, taking his feet off the table and turning to a chest of drawers that stood by the wall. "We

shall remedy your unfortunate lack of papers. You will carry
the papers of soldiers of Macaria. It is a great honor. You
will be expected to fight like forest demons whether you are
forest demons or not, if there is fighting to do. Indeed, it may
be that we have forests where there is need of you. If not,
then there are roads that will be built all the more quickly
with the help of your well-fed bodies."

From the top drawer he began to draw out sheets of paper,
one at a time. There seemed to be three different sets of
three.

"What are your names?" asked the officer.

Sarid, accepting the inevitable, told him.

"These are *names*?" said the officer, showing a trace of ex-
asperation for the first time. "I think you are making them
up. I do not care, however. I am a generous man, and would
as soon call a man a man as a dog."

The papers were quickly completed. None of the three
was invited to add any mark or signature.

"Put them away," said the officer to the two soldiers.
"Lock the door, in case the convoy is late and they want to
leave us under cover of darkness. If they *do* try to leave,
shoot them."

They were taken back down the corridor and guided into a
bare stone-walled cell. The door was bolted from the outside.
The soldiers, presumably made cautious by the size of the
new recruits, handled them gently and politely.

"All right," said Talvar bitterly—in his own language—
"what's the *next* stage in the master plan?"

"We wait," said Sarid. "What alternative do we have? The
others are likely to run into similar situations. With luck, the
Macarians will gather us all together and save us the trouble
of finding one another. What's more, there's probably a good
deal in what the little man said. Before, we were on our own.
Now we have an army to protect us. Also, we have papers.
Already, we are accepted into a way of life."

"In fact," added Cheron, "if we hadn't been inducted, we
would have volunteered."

"I *told* you this was hell," said Talvar. "You wouldn't believe me, but it's true. Eternal torment begins right here."

"Why did you tell him that stupid story?" Cheron asked
Sarid Jerome.

Sarid sighed. "If I'd told him anything less bizarre, he'd

have *known* we were lying. This way, there's just the faintest possibility that we were telling the truth."

"That's devious enough to be Intel thinking," said Talvar.

"I hope it is," replied Sarid quietly. "As Cheron said, it's time we began learning to be whole men. From now on, we have to do our own Intel work. That's the price of survival."

3

As he dangled from the parachute caught in the branches of the tree, struggling to release himself, Cyriac Salvador reminded Teresa ever more strongly of a great black bird netted by a hunter: confused, desperate, completely out of his element. His coat was flapping about his shoulders and his left arm was trapped at an awkward angle, projecting from his shoulder like a damaged wing.

Teresa looked up at him from the ground. He must have been there for nearly thirty minutes. The cords that bound him would go into their decay cycle soon, but for once he did not seem to appreciate that patience was all that was required.

Once he realized that she was there, though, he stopped, conscious of his lack of dignity.

She clambered up the trunk of the tree, finding footholds with no difficulty, until she was in a position to begin snapping the cords, one at a time. She let him down gently to the ground. Once he was free, he quickly reverted to his customary manner. He was dressed in his normal clothes, except for the coat and the belt that had been looped hastily round his waist. Teresa herself had three of the belts—two of them looped over her shoulders like bandoliers. It was she who had known what to do when the systems started to fail. She had made contingency plans. He had not.

Salvador watched her climb back down to the ground, kneading his numb left arm with the fingers of his right hand.

His face showed no sign of strain. He did not feel pain if he did not choose to.

"Thank you," he said. It was a phrase that covered a great deal of necessary thanks. But for her, he would have died in the ship, along with the seventeen other men who had been brought back from eternal rest only to die a long way from home.

"We seem to have come down to the surface a little sooner than you intended," she said evenly. "It's perhaps as well that we're as well-equipped as Jerome and the others."

"We're not," answered Salvador. "We may have added the languages to our repertoire of skills, and we have a good deal of knowledge that they actually lack, but there's one vital difference. They have implants to transmit information back to the satellite. We don't. Satellite won't know we're alive. In fact, they'll presume that we're dead. They know what happened to the ship. I didn't have time to signal our intentions."

"I couldn't give you the time," she replied. "We had to get out."

"You were ready to act," he said. "You knew exactly what to do. Do you always make plans for million-to-one chances?"

"If the million-to-one chance is that I'll get killed, why not? It didn't cost much, in terms of mental effort, and it's not as if I was overburdened with other things to think about."

She turned her back on him and scanned the hillside that extended away below them. Bare black stone showed through in thin streaks. The grass was coarse and yellowed, though it grew greener in the shade of the gnarled trees that stood in ragged clumps here and there.

"It's the same on the other side," she said, pointing with her thumb at the ridge over which she had come. "Not very exciting."

"We're in the borderlands of the Kezula," said Salvador. "It's poor land, but there should be herds of grazing animals nearby—villages of tents, too. They have oxcarts, so there should be navigable trails of some kind. Our one problem will be persuading the natives not to kill us. The tribesmen may be a little insular, and they probably resent intruders."

"We have to reach the surface base," said Teresa. "That's

not going to be easy. The northern reaches of Macaria are a long way from here."

"Merkad isn't far away," said Salvador. "It's more or less civilized. We'll be able to buy horses there. We have enough money to buy our way to the base in reasonable comfort. A matter of weeks, if we stay alive. We're likely to be in the base for a long time, though. The shuttle doesn't operate on a once-monthly basis."

"We have no alternative," she said. "Unless you want to become part of your own experiment. Not that there'd be much point in that, as our experiences aren't being recorded. Still, think of the extra insight you'll obtain through having experienced the rigors of surface experience at first hand."

Salvador came to stand beside her, looking away down the slope.

"You know," he said, "I'm almost surprised that you bothered to get me out."

"I may need you," she said calmly. "You know more than I do. You see more than I do. And two people are a more effective fighting force than one."

"That's good," said the Intellectual, without any particular sarcastic stress. "I was afraid your motives might have been altruistic."

She looked at him sharply, not knowing how to interpret the comment. It took her some time to decide—correctly—that he was mocking her. An Intel joke, too subtle for normal people to appreciate.

"How's your shoulder?" she asked.

"Under control," he assured her. He added, "I think Merkad must be *that* way."

They began to move off down the slope, heading north.

He isn't afraid, thought Teresa. *It's not simply a matter of not showing it. All this, to him, is something he can take in his stride. He's an observer, detached from everything, including his own potential feelings. But without me, he's lost. He's never in his life been called upon to do things. There've always been machines, and Prags, and sensuals.*

"We need weapons," she said. "And less-conspicuous clothing, too. Our best hope of proceeding safely is to be ordinary."

"We're too tall," replied Salvador. "And there are no people with skins as light as ours this side of the Macarian border—except perhaps for a handful of soldiers. Pretending to be ordinary isn't going to be easy."

They crossed the floor of the valley and began to move uphill again. Salvador's pace was measured and quite steady.

"Sarid Jerome probably doesn't know that the ship crashed," said Teresa eventually. "But he'll come north any-how, looking for the other murderers. Suppose he finds us? He won't want us to reach the base—not without taking him and I wouldn't like to guarantee that he won't have more imaginative plans for us than using us as hostages."

"If we keep moving north," said Salvador, without the slightest trace of anxiety, "he'll never catch up with us, will he?"

Another million-to-one chance that he isn't going to worry about, thought Teresa. *So much for Intel caution.*

Then, inevitably she began to wonder if she might be making a fool of herself. Maybe he *had* thought it all out. Maybe he hadn't needed pulling out, on board the ship. Maybe he had foreseen every last detail of what had happened. Maybe he was letting her think the way she was thinking.

That was the trouble with Intels. You could never be sure just how much cleverer than you they were. Even when they acted stupidly, you could never be certain that they weren't being more subtly clever than a mere Prag could ever appreciate.

Quietly, she cursed him, and tried to fall into step beside him.

4

The vehicle into which Sarid, Cheron, and Talvar were bundled in the early hours of the next morning was an elongated truck. It was loaded with sacks and bales now, but there was evidence that it had been used in the not-too-distant past for transporting cattle. It was part of a convoy of

five vehicles, each loaded with goods but not fully laden, so
that each had space near the tailboard for half a dozen men,
recruits for Macaria's army. Each group was attended by a
uniformed man carrying a light machine gun. There were
other armed men in the cab of each truck.

The convoy was headed south—an unwelcome revelation
as far as the Tanagarians were concerned.

"What kind of fuel do these things use?" asked Cheron,
marveling at the presence of such vehicles in a supposedly
primitive world.

"Alcohol, probably," was Sarid's terse reply. "Maybe some
kind of gas. Can you see any of our men on the other
trucks?"

Cheron craned his neck to inspect the groups of men in the
truck ahead, until he was forced to get up into his own truck.

"I can't see much," he replied. "There may be others, but I
couldn't tell."

It was obvious that none of the men waiting in the vehicle
to which they had been consigned was a Tanagarian. Only
one was as tall as Cheron, and he was massive compared to
his companions. There were five in all. The tall man turned
out to be Merkadian, as was one of the others—a much
smaller, thinner individual. Two were Dahran volunteers,
considerably younger than the conscripts. The fifth was a
black-skinned man who claimed to come from Khepra, a nation far to the east and somewhat to the south, beyond the
boundaries of the Macarian sphere of influence. His presence
in Dahra would have been no less surprising than the presence
of the northerners Sarid and his companions pretended to be.

The large Merkadian gave his name as Mondo, and proved
extremely taciturn. His companion, Midas, explained that
they had been conscripted from the prison in Sau, along with
every other non-Dahran prisoner. The black man gave his
name as Baya-undi, and explained in Macarian that was far
more perfect than their own that he had been conscripted illegally, and that the Macarians were virtually committing an
act of war against Khepra (the only genuinely civilized nation on Earth, in his version) by violating his person. The
two Dahrans clearly felt very much out of place in this company, and knew too little Macarian to follow conversation in
that language. When Cheron asked them in their own tongue,
though, they gave their names as Qapel and Malaq. There

was a further string of syllables which was identical in each name, and they explained that they were brothers and that only the personal names need be remembered.

Midas proved the most communicative and most informative of their new companions, especially when he discovered that Sarid and his fellows spoke Merkadian. The advantage of this was that it allowed them to talk without being understood by their guardian, a Macarian named Spektros. (Not that he had anything against Spektros, Midas explained, but one never knew what Macarian troopers might report back to their superiors.)

The Merkadian explained that he and many others had been literally bought from the authorities in Sau, and complained bitterly of the injustice of the fact that while he had been sentenced to two years' imprisonment and Mondo to ten, both had been taken into the army to serve an indefinite term. Macaria, he said, had always held a special grudge against Merkad, and no Macarian would ever pass up an opportunity to humiliate one of his own kind. Merkadians had risen in valiant revolution against their northern masters several times, but had always been ruthlessly suppressed, quite often with the help of the vile Dahrans. Now the Macarians had such weapons and such means of transportation that they would be unconquerable for the time being, but Merkad's day would undoubtedly come. He, Midas, hoped that his sons might live to fight in that greatest of battles. In the meantime, he hated all Macarians and would do his level best to sabotage their war effort. He evinced great interest in the supposed origin of Sarid's group, saying that he trusted them implicitly because they spoke Macarian so badly, and because everyone knew that the demons of the northern forests were the only people—if they *were* people—that the Macarians really feared.

"Where do you suppose they're taking us?" Cheron asked of Midas.

"For now," replied the Merkadian, "we will go to Talos. There they will school us to be soldiers. It will not be bad— men like you and me already know well enough how to be soldiers. They will see what we are good for, and they will find that we are good for almost anything, which is more than can be said for these peasants who cannot understand the pure tongue of Merkad. They will be sent to dig sewers and build barracks and cut trees. Eventually they might aspire to drive such disgusting machines as this one. They will make *us* into fighting men, which is a much better life just so long as we do not actually have to fight. They will move us here and there and give us guns and tell us whom to shoot. If we are lucky, we stay here in Dahra. If we are less lucky, we may go to the Kezula, or to the far east. The only disaster that may strike us would be to go south, across the sea of Hamad to the great forest, where it is too hot and the demons of the forest have more powerful magic than Macarian guns. But perhaps you will not mind that, if you too are forest men?"

Cheron did not have time to formulate his next question. Baya-undi interrupted to say: "I understand the impure tongue of Merkad well enough, though it is not fit for civilized men. I am not a peasant but an educated man, and I can fight. Nevertheless, I shall *not* fight where the Macarians can see me. While I am in Dahra, whether it is to build factories or to dig ditches, I am safe from harm; and if I had a vehicle such as this I might find a way to return to my own country. Once into the mountains of the Kezula the Macarians could never catch me."

"You could not escape," said Midas scornfully. "Everyone knows that the Macarians will not let deserters free. And not a man but a dog would prefer digging to shooting. There are ways to live and ways to live but that would not be any of them."

An argument was building up, but it was interrupted when the convoy pulled in to the side of the road and came to a halt.

"Time to eat!" said Midas. "The Macarians are such clock-worshippers that no sane man can tolerate them. We start early with empty bellies and must suffer until the clock says that it is time to eat—astonishing."

The tailboard of the truck was let down, and the recruits jumped to the ground one by one. Now, at last, they were able to look at the men riding in the other trucks, and Cheron scanned them all eagerly, hoping to find kindred among them. There was, however, no one who could possibly be taken for a man of Tanagar.

"So it seems we are to be three and not twenty, after all," said Vito Talvar.

"It means nothing," said Sarid. "The others will have been

scattered over a wide area, farther from the road than we were. Most of them will not have headed for the road, and even those who chose the right direction may have been picked up too late to join this convoy. If any of the others share our fate we will meet them at Talos during the next few days."

The food that they were given was hot, having been kept in sealed pressure cookers insulated with straw. It was a thick soup containing lumps of well-stewed meat and chopped vegetables. They were also given dry bread and a little cheap wine, heavily watered and spiced with some kind of herb whose function (Midas informed Cheron) was medicinal.

"We get to eat twice a day," Midas told him. "The hours are fixed and immutable, as if their lordly God had passed a commandment. It is not always the same. Sometimes the meat is from a goat, sometimes from an ox, sometimes a dead horse. Sometimes the bread is the greasy stuff they make from rye, sometimes it is hard and gritty because of the seed husks of bitter corn. Sometimes the quartermaster has bartered away the wine and we get filthy black coffee. There are two things to be said for it: they do not often substitute offal for real meat, because they believe that soldiers should be strong, and it is much better than the filth they feed you in Dahran prisons. I am no more than skin and bone because of that prison. Mondo has managed to stay fat, but *I* don't know how. He says that a whore used to bring him food, but that is incredible, if you care to look at his teeth, being careful not to breathe in while you do it. If he were not a countryman of mine I would think that he ate his cellmates, but only a dog-worshipper would do that, and I'm told the meat tastes terrible anyhow. Perhaps he was lucky enough to have a rat-infested cell and a fire to cook the ones he caught. The rats moved out of *my* cell because they would have starved to death had they stayed. Things were bad, I can tell you. I think the black man has money—he has a bag full of possessions—perhaps we could persuade him to buy fruit if we stop in a village. I would steal it, of course, except that we are in the army now, and men have so few real possessions that they are sacred, and so thieves are apt to have their noses slit or their tendons cut. You can cripple your fellow troopers, but don't steal from them. What have you got in those pouches in the belt you wear inside your shirt?"

Cheron smiled rather ruefully. "A little money," he confessed. "Some stone bottles containing medicines."

The little man made a gesture of scornful disgust. To him, medicines were magic, and were for the most part either useless or poisonous. It was obvious that he considered the carrying of medicines to be the practice of a fool.

When the meal was over they scoured their bowls with dry sand, and returned them to the cook—a man whose career was written in the rolls of fat which spilled from his body at every convenient point. The tin cups and spoons were simply thrown back into the stock.

Once they were under way again, Cheron found himself engaged in conversation with the two Dahran volunteers, who asked him much the same questions as he had asked Midas. He passed on Midas's comments and advice. They seemed relieved by the fact that someone could give them explanations of what was going on in their own language, and insisted on telling him the story of their lives. It was not a long story, and proved to be far from exciting—a point they themselves made frequently. They chattered about the magnificence of Macaria's army, and the pride they felt as Dahrans because their nation was an ally of Macaria and not a conquered nation like Merkad. They waxed eloquent on the subject of the futility of life on the land, growing crops for the landowners and hardly having enough left over to live on, even without the problem of blight and the frequent raids by bandits. They were convinced that they would become fighting men, and had no doubts about their ability to show remarkable prowess when tested. They had never handled guns, and they believed with all their hearts that a man with a gun was a virtual demigod.

As the day got hotter the back of the truck became increasingly uncomfortable. The road was good, but the truck's suspension was not, and they were jolted and jarred continually. They had some sacking and their jackets to protect them from the harder edges that surrounded them, but the cushioning effect of these makeshift shock absorbers was very limited. Because they were in the rearmost truck they were traveling in a perpetual cloud of dust raised by the wheels of the other vehicles, and this got into their eyes and throats.

They passed close to half a dozen small villages, and once the truck slowed down so that they could reach down to snatch baskets of fruit from the children who bounded alongside hopefully. Cheron threw a few small coins from the truck in payment. The juice of the fruit soothed their throats, and even the trooper, Spektros—who had hitherto held himself aloof from their conversation—became infected by fellow-feeling and repeated in Macarian much of the information they had already obtained in Merkadian and passed on to Qapel and Malaq in Dahran.

"We need many more soldiers," explained Spektros. "Not because we are planning a war or because we need to defend ourselves, but because we need to occupy and make safe some of the land to the south of Hamad. This does not mean, of course, that you are all bound for the Bela settlements. It is more probable that you will stay here and allow more seasoned fighting men to go south. For centuries—some say thousands of years—men have stayed away from the great forest because it is so unpleasant. In the interior it is pitch dark, and the forest savages—subhuman creatures with four arms and no legs—work powerful magic that makes men sicken and die. But the tropical forest grows quickly, and it makes good sense to build great factories where there is most wood, to make charcoal and alcohol which can feed the factories of Asdar. In Macaria, you see, we have our own forests to the north, and great rivers that flow south to the Calm Sea and the Bitter Sea, but they can only supply Macaria's needs—if the *world* is to be civilized then we must conquer the forests of the south. Macaria has claimed the great forest, and now must make the forest its own. We might also have to conquer Kyad, of course, but it is such godforsaken country. Dahra is so much better, and the Dahrans are wise enough to ally themselves with Macaria. Dahra will one day be a great nation, second only to Macaria."

No one dissented from this view of things—at least, not in any explicit way. Midas maintained a tactful silence, while Baya-undi muttered something in a language which not even the Tanagarians could understand.

Later, Baya-undi took the opportunity to correct a few misleading impressions by lecturing to Midas, Cheron, and Vito Talvar in Merkadian. "Macaria," he said, "is not truly civilized. Macarians do not know the meaning of the word. They worship machines and material possessions. They do not understand that moving a metal box along a strip of black-tarred imitation sand has nothing to do with civilized *values* and a civilized *way of life*. The Macarians are both vulgar and brutal, as evidenced by their treatment of a genuinely civilized man. My country was old before the name Macaria had ever been spoken. It will still be the only civilized nation on Earth when the name Macaria has been forgotten."

Midas offered the opinion that all this was mere noise. Cheron and Talvar refrained from agreeing with him overtly, but failed to persuade Baya-undi to give a more elaborate account of Khepra's qualifications as a civilized nation. He seemed so vague about it, in fact, that Midas voiced the suspicion that he had never been near Khepra and that his blackness was the result of a freak birth. The resentment caused by this remark led to Baya-undi's withdrawal from the conversation.

When Cheron asked Sarid Jerome, in their own language, what he thought of this small cross section of Macaria's army, Sarid predicted that even Vito Talvar would be a general before his eightieth birthday.

5

They found the bodies late in the evening, sprawled by the side of the rough mountain path which they had been following. There were three—all men. All were dressed in loose robes that had been a uniform pale gray in color before being stained with blood. There was a great deal of blood. Whoever had stabbed the poor unfortunates to death had not been adept in the art of *coup de grace*.

Teresa had mixed feelings as she looked down at the bodies. She was not quite sure what significance they had for her. They were a reminder of the fact that danger lurked between these mean and shabby hills which only *seemed* bleak and empty. They were reassuring proof that this world w indeed, inhabited. (She was surprised, of course, by the relief which betrayed that she had been in need of such proof in some irrational, emotional, *uncontrolled* way.) They also served to symbolize the commonness of death, and to tell her that if she were dead (as she soon might be) she would look just as absurd as *these* creatures did.

Why were they killed? she wondered. They couldn't have had anything to steal—not dressed as they were.

Salvador knelt down to examine them more closely.

"Their sandals are virtually worn through," he said. "They seem to have been walking for several days. They're itinerant priests—probably Merkadian. They may have come here to preach to the tribesmen, or they may have been driven out of Merkad by the Macarians. Notionally, they worship the same single god, but they have rather different views of him. To the Macarians, he's a king, to the Merkadians he's a sponsor of holy men who help the oppressed and lead them in unsuccessful revolutions. The theological disputes tend to be rather more vicious and bloody than brawls in the docklands of Ophidion."

He began to detach the bloodstained robe from one of the bodies.

"What are you doing?" demanded Teresa.

"Stealing it," he replied equably.

"You're crazy! That kind of disguise is the last thing we need. It was enough to get *them* killed. How is it going to protect us?"

"It won't," he answered. "Not here. But once we're over the border into Merkad. . . ."

Teresa thought about it for a moment, then said, "Oh."

"It will allow us to get away with seeming strange," added Salvador. "People expect priests to be odd—they're not common men, by definition. We're not likely to be able to pass for peasant farmers or merchants, but we might just get by as holy men. Inconspicuously conspicuous, if you see what I mean."

"I suppose the Merkadians have female priests?" she said.

"You're taller than the vast majority of local men, you don't have large breasts and your hair is cut short. What makes you think you look female to the natives?"

She pursed her lips, but noted that one of the men Salvador was busy stripping wore no beard, though he clearly hadn't shaved for at least three days. She resented the usurpation of her planning role, but the merits of his argument were unassailable. She took the two robes that he passed to her, and rolled them up into a bundle, which she tied with the cords that had gathered the garments about the waists of their wearers.

"We'll wash them in a stream when we find one," she said. "The bloodstains won't come out, but we might be able to get rid of the worst of the parasites."

Salvador left the corpses their tattered undershirts. When he stood up his face seemed grim, and she was pleased to note that he had not been completely unaffected by the sight and touch of the lacerated flesh. No doubt his stomach was under strict control, but he did have feelings of *some* kind.

"What happened to them can happen to us," she said.

"Except that we both know twenty ways to defend ourselves against men with knives," he replied.

"Cheron Felix claimed that he'd been changed by those hypnopaedic treatments," she said. "He said that having that kind of knowledge made him a different kind of man—no longer a sensual, no longer a Tanagarian. The same things that did that to him are in your mind and mine. They don't change me—they're just something to be used. But I wonder what difference skills like that might make to an Intel."

"What you have to remember," he said, wiping his hands on a lichen-covered stone and then on his jacket hem, "is that it doesn't matter what kind of knowledge you have in your head. The thing that matters is keeping it under control. Nothing changes an Intellectual. Nothing there is to know can change a man who can cope with knowledge. Only sensuals can't—and, in a rather different way, Pragmatists."

"With a voice like yours," she said, "you could tell the most blatant lies and still be convincing. Maybe even to yourself."

"I don't need to lie," he said. "Not to you. I trust you, just as you trust me."

She threw the bundle of bloodied cloth to him, and he caught it reflexively.

"You can carry them until we need them," she said. "After all, it's your plan."

He made a small mock bow, and said, "As you wish."

6

The convoy reached Talos about an hour before nightfall.
The recruits acquired uniforms and were given pallets of hide
and straw to sleep on. The pessimism of the recruiting officer
about the possibility of finding uniforms to fit the Tanagarians proved unfounded—all three of them, and Mondo too,
were unhesitatingly issued garments which were no more ill-
fitting than anyone else's. The makeshift mattresses, however,
made no allowance for the possibility that men might have
such generous proportions. Despite the discomfort, Cheron
slept deeply and peacefully. A few minutes' concentration
was sufficient to soothe the aching of his bruised limbs, and
the unfamiliar heaviness of his body, once he allowed himself
to notice it again, dragged him quickly into unconsciousness.

The forty men who shared the dormitory were roused
again shortly after dawn, and conducted to a communal
shower-bath where they were required to stand beneath
streams of lukewarm water for ten minutes. Several of the recruits kept their undershirts on without drawing any protest
from the corporal in charge of the operation. Sarid, Cheron,
and Talvar removed their belts and placed them on top of
their bundles of clothing, and kept an eye on them throughout, but no one attempted to touch them.

There followed a long session of queueing while each recruit was given a cursory inspection by a medical orderly.
Medication, where it was deemed necessary, was administered
via hypodermic syringes of awesome size. Cheron was glad to
note that there seemed to be adequate facilities for steriliza-
tion of these instruments, but he and his companions were
passed as healthy. Not until the whole batch of recruits had
been attended to were any of them allowed to proceed to the
halls where the first meal was served. Here there were perhaps a thousand men forming long queues and filling rank

upon rank of places set at narrow tables. Though the officers—with the exception of some below the rank of sergeant—were all Macarians, fewer than one in thirty of the troopers had the features of northerners. Most were Dahrans and Merkadians, though there were several other men with skins as dark as Baya-undi's. Baya-undi made no effort to seek out their company, and seemed to regard them as disdainfully as he regarded everyone else.

Rifles were issued in midmorning, and the recruits were then separated out into squads for drilling and training. No bullets were issued on the first day—or for several days thereafter—and the early training was in the use of the bayonet.

Much of the routine which Cheron and his companions found themselves required to learn was obviously quite pointless, save that it occupied time. Cheron found that he could perform most of the tasks he was commanded to do with consummate ease, but he also found that there was no reward for efficiency. To do a job quickly did not liberate time for idling, thinking, or talking. To have nothing to do was a cardinal sin, and he quickly learned by his own experience and that of others that the gift of being occupied with a slow but not too onerous task was a privilege not to be despised. He found no difficulty in understanding that tasks were performed for their own sake, and for the sake of making sure that the time and lives of the troopers were completely under control of their officers, and he anticipated no difficulties in adapting himself to such a regime.

Sarid, by contrast, found that everything he was required to do grated on his nerves. Once he had demonstrated that he already knew well enough how to handle a bayoneted rifle, he considered the matter ended, and resented having to go through the same rituals of practice as men like Qapel and Malaq, who had never handled such weapons and had not had the benefit of hypnopaedic instruction to compensate. Sarid was a man who habitually acted purposively, who did not like to do *anything* save as the means to some end. Above all else he valued achievement and production, the reaching of targets and the fulfillment of goals. By the evening meal of the first day he knew that adapting himself to army life was going to pose a terrible problem in self-control and discipline. He set *that* as his target, and launched himself

forth on an inner struggle that would exempt his attention
from the actions themselves. It was far from being an ideal
solution, and he was very soon working on a variety of
schemes to alter his situation. He considered desertion, and
he considered becoming an officer. Both ideas seemed realiz-
able, but only in the long term. He set them aside for constant
revision and refinement, knowing that there was nothing he
could do immediately. He observed the fact that Cheron and
Talvar fitted in much more easily and naturally, and was not
surprised. He did not communicate to them the fact that he
was making contingency plans.

Not until the evening of the third day were the recruits
given a first taste of the freedom that they were allowed under the benevolent rule of Macaria's army. After dark on that
day they were allowed to go into the town (with the exception of those delegated to guard the camp and those who had
already invited punishment upon themselves). Cheron, Sarid,
and Talvar set off with Midas and Baya-undi. Mondo was
one of the unlucky few who had occasioned the wrath of an
officer, and hence was absent from the group. Several other
Merkadians had tried to attach themselves to the Tanagarians, but Midas had prevented them from doing so by one
means or another; he preferred to be the only penniless man
to keep company with four men who all had money.

The Macarian base contrasted sharply with the old town of
Talos. Macarian architecture—in its military manifestations,
at least—was square and angular. Its building materials were
dull in color and utilitarian. The windows were invariably
square, and where they were glazed the glass was divided into
rectangular panes. Doors were also rectangular, and made of
heavy wood, precisely shaped, usually equipped with heavy
metal locks. Dahran architecture, on the other hand, was
much more devoted to curves. The houses and public buildings frequently had domed roofs—even the meaner dwellings.
Rounded turrets jutted up everywhere into the skyline. Windows were usually slits, and where they were wider than a
few centimeters they were arched at the top. Most were
screened by braided curtains or ornamental wooden shutters,
but where they were glazed there tended to be complex mo-
saics of colored glass. There were hardly any metal locks to
be seen, and the wooden bolts that secured the doors were
usually discreetly placed. The poorer buildings were made of

yellow brick and clay, but many of the public buildings, no matter how crudely constructed, were made spectacular by being painted in pastel shades of blue, orange, and brown. Most of the woodwork was tinted with gloss and varnish.

The streets of Talos were narrow, obviously constructed to allow the passage of men, donkeys, and small handcarts. Only the main thoroughfares were wide enough to take Macarian trucks, and these were so full of people, animals, and various kinds of stalls that taking a truck along one would have been a slow and frustrating process. All the streets stank of animal droppings, and the principal sanitary measure adopted by the authorities seemed to be strewing dry gray sand liberally upon the fouled streets and sweeping up the resulting conglomerate to load it on to dung carts which patrolled each street about once in every ten days.

Once, Talos had been a market town, operating as a point of exchange for goods of all kinds, mediating between several coastal towns, the fertile belt and the towns of the far north. The Macarian road had enhanced this role, and the establishment of the military base had resulted in great changes in the economic profile of the back streets, where cafes, wine shops, and brothels blossomed as never before.

Midas had never visited Talos, but he had no difficulty in finding his way about. He found Cheron and the others dull company, however, by his own exacting standards. They were relatively uninterested in wine, and completely uninterested in women. After several unsuccessful attempts to urge them to great efforts, he decided to settle for the quieter tempo that they obviously preferred. After all, as Vito Talvar might have reminded him, from his point of view it was all profit.

Cheron found a certain fascination in observing the night life of Dahra. All of the men and women he saw idling, drinking, fighting, and gambling were obviously committed Hedonists, even if they were only jeckles on hydeyhigh. They were living for their moments, trying to squeeze the excitement of pleasure from lives that were all too obviously reluctant to yield it. He found little difficulty in empathizing with them. And yet there was something that marked them off as being very different from the Hedonists of Tanagar. At first he could not quite identify it, but eventually he realized that there was a furious *intensity* in their behavior that was unfamiliar even in connection with the wildest jeckling. They did not take their pleasures cheerfully, but seemed possessed with a bitterness and ferocity that exaggerated their gestures and responses. The males used every action and every activity to display a show of strength, an aura of power. They yielded quickly to any emotional impulse, and seemed desperately keen to yield, as if their impulses were their true selves, and when they were not in the grip of some motivating force they somehow had only a phantom existence.

There's no control, he thought. *But it's more than simply a lack of it. There's an active denial of it, a rejection of it. Where there is no natural fervor, they manufacture or fake it. They are not irrational, but they put no value on the force of reason. Calm of mind is the last thing they desire, and they do not number it among the pleasures. Their virtues are our temptations, and our temptations are their virtues.*

The only exception to this judgment that he felt compelled to make was in favor of the Macarians, but not all of them. The Macarians of the lowest class—the troopers and some of the camp-workers—were little different from the men of Merkad. It was the officers, and one or two well-dressed men he took for merchants, who were partially exempt from the pattern which made the Motherworld seem an inversion of Tanagar's Hedonic culture. He wondered, absently, whether the Macarians had any kind of Intel culture—for they clearly had their Pragmatists—and whether the same kind of inversion might pertain to that. It did not seem to him to be a particularly fascinating question.

They returned to the camp at the designated time, still quite sober. In both instances they were exceptional. Most of the recruits, as expected, abused the privilege they had been given, and suffered in consequence. Cheron and Talvar noted this without any particular interest, but Sarid found it almost infuriating; it led him to despise his fellow soldiers even more fiercely than before. Outwardly, though, he was always calm, and only those closest to him—Midas and perhaps Bayaundi—were able to suspect his hidden rage. Both reacted, perhaps subconsciously, by allying themselves more with Cheron and Talvar than with Sarid, who was much more isolated in spirit than either of his companions.

In the days which followed hundreds of recruits were assigned new roles in Macaria's military organization and were shipped out north, south, or west. Hundreds of new recruits were brought in to take their place—volunteers, conscripts, the scourings of Dahra's prisons. There was not the slightest sign, however, of any man of Tanagar.

"Something's gone wrong," said Sarid, after they had watched the third new detachment unload from trucks from the north. "*Some* of them would have been picked up. It would have been inevitable."

"Before I touched ground," Cheron told him, "I saw a kind of flash. I didn't think anything of it at the time. Do you think it's possible it might have been the ship—that something happened to it?"

"I saw the flash too," said Vito Talvar.

"It could have been anything," said Sarid. "But it's possible. Perhaps there're just the three of us in all the world. Maybe whatever happens to Earth as a consequence of our being here is entirely up to us. More important, perhaps whatever happens to *us* is entirely up to us." As he said it, he realized for the first time that he had been *waiting*, not bothering to think about long-term plans until he knew more about his resources. It was now time to stop waiting, and to start planning. The resources he had were all that were going to be available, and he had to start working on that basis.

If only, he thought, *I had two good Prags. They'd be worth more than a dozen lousy sensuals.*

"I don't want to stay in the army all my life," said Vito Talvar. "I don't want to stay in Dahra, either."

"I have no intention of doing either," replied Sarid, his voice heavy with conviction.

"We can't do anything until we're reassigned," Cheron pointed out. "Everything depends on that. It won't be long—they're processing recruits as fast as they possibly can."

"That's true," said Sarid, his mind no longer on what he was saying. He was wondering how difficult a task it might be for one man, with the right knowledge and the appropriate determination, to rise to absolute power within an empire like Macaria's.

7

On the fifth day they spent at Talos they were given bullets
for the first time, and were taken out to the rifle range to display such prowess as they might possess. Two corporals—one
of them the recently promoted Spektros—walked back and
forth along the line giving the benefit of their advice. They
were given three hours to improve their performance. After
that, they were told to put their weapons away.

Later, they were offered an opportunity to display what
they had learned concerning the use of the bayonet. They
were given special bayonets constructed of soft and flimsy
wood, and matched one against another under the eyes of an
officer named Donsella ti Ria and a very small sergeant
named Yaxilis.

In the initial contests Cheron found himself matched
against Sarid, but neither showed any real enthusiasm for
putting on a pointless exhibition. They were cursed for lack
of effort. Vito Talvar, by contrast, found himself facing one
of the less competent Dahran volunteers, and made a fool of
him without having to draw on any significant skill or
strength. The officer apparently decided that stronger measures would have to be employed to put some of the men to a
reasonable test, and brought in two long-serving Merkadian
recruits who acted as instructors. Cheron needed only half a
minute to disarm one of them, and his companions would undoubtedly have done likewise had it not been for the fact that
before their turn came Mondo had knocked the man unconscious and put a twenty-centimeter splinter of wood clean
through the muscles surrounding his armpit. After this, the
other Merkadian was only allowed to test Baya-undi and two
other less fearsome opponents. For the remainder, Yaxilis
himself stepped in.

Yaxilis was nearly three-quarters of a meter shorter than

Mondo, but had such speed that the big man had no chance. He stabbed and jabbed with ritual precision for two minutes, and then repaid the giant Merkadian for his earlier incautiousness which caused injury to an instructor by splintering the stock of the rifle while using it as a club to lay him out.

Yaxilis approached Cheron with greater caution but no less confidence, relying on fast footwork to keep out of range of the bigger man's lunges. Cheron, however, proved a little too fast to permit the sergeant to get in any ponderable blows of his own. After two minutes' wary thrusting and blocking the contest was declared a draw. The result did not please Yaxilis, but he made up for it by humiliating poor Midas, with whom he was much better matched. He laid Midas out alongside Mondo, a little more brutally than was necessary—though whether this was because he was annoyed at his failure to beat Cheron or because he thought Midas was Mondo's friend no one could guess.

He did not try to fight Sarid or Vito Talvar. When he and the officer walked away, deep in conversation, it was left to them to revive the two Merkadians, with the assistance of Baya-undi.

"You did well," said Sarid to Cheron. "I'm not sure I could have kept him out in a mock fight like that. I could have killed him, of course, but we were not taught to pretend. He would have beaten Vito."

"He would not," said Talvar.

"You're too heavy," Sarid told him. "And I don't just mean the gravity."

"It's my glands," said Talvar.

"The cause hardly matters. What does matter is that we must remember not to rely too much on the programs that were pumped into our heads aboard the *Sabreur*. We may be more powerful than these Motherworlders, but at their best, they're faster. Our reflexes may not be enough to keep us safe."

Midas moaned. "When I heard you babbling away in your barbarian tongue," he complained, "I thought for sure that I was in the wrong heaven. Am I in hell or back in Talos? Never mind—what difference could it possibly make?" He looked sideways, to watch Vito Talvar still trying unsuccessfully to revive Mondo. "Drag him to his bed," he advised.

"He'll sleep until midnight. His brain is no bigger than a pea, but when it gets jolted it's bruised all over."

In the end, they had to follow this advice.

"Presumably," said Cheron to Midas, once they had got Mondo back to his bed, "this afternoon's little farce is all the base can manage as a selection procedure. What happens to those of us who pass?"

"How should I know?" replied the little man, clutching his head in his hands. "Ask Spektros, if he'll still talk to you. Rumor says that the army hasn't the time or the will to train us properly here. The Bela settlements are in trouble—unusually heavy casualties. The forest demons get the blame but disease and fever are just as likely causes. Either way, we may be taken to Asdar to wait for a ship, and given such instruction as is convenient there. I hope not. I wanted to go back north."

"You could have missed the target when they gave you bullets to shoot," Vito Talvar pointed out.

"That's an insult," said Midas tiredly. "Besides, I'm too good to miss. And I had to fight that little sergeant in self-defense. *I* didn't know he was going to win anyway. We'll all be burned as black as Baya-undi, you realize. Still, he probably has protective magic. Have you?"

"Not exactly," said Cheron dryly.

Midas lay flat on the mattress. "We've had it easy up to now, you know," he said. "We've been well treated here. Once we're shipped across Hamad we'll be completely in the grip of some evil-livered sergeant with a dog's balls and teeth like poor Mondo. They persecute Merkadians, of course. That's why Yaxilis smashed me over the head with his rifle butt. If I'd done that to *him* I'd have been hanged by my thumbs for four hours."

Cheron met Sarid's eye and said, "The equatorial forest isn't the healthiest place to be."

Talvar turned to the waiting Baya-undi, and said, "*Have* you got protective magic?"

Baya-undi didn't take it as a joke. "I have protection enough against evil spells," he said. "But it is not evil spells that I am afraid of. Ships from Kyad sometimes dock at Asdar, though, and not every man who goes to Asdar reaches the Bela settlements. The best magic is the magic that would take us all to Kyad, and then to Khepra. There are no Macarians in Khepra, and we do not treat civilized men as Macaria has treated us."

Cheron, Sarid, and Vito Talvar stared at the black man for half a minute, until he turned and calmly walked away.

"Don't listen to him," said Midas softly. "He's a fool. It is better if the Macarians ignore a man, but if they will not ignore him it is better for him to be with them than to have them pursue him."

"He's right," said Cheron. Sarid Jerome, however, said nothing at all.

"It's simple," said Midas. "There's a saying we have—if you must live in hell, be friends with the devil. For now, the Macarians are the devil. I hate them all, but I am not about to run away from them if they will chase me, because I know only too well how *they* hate *me*."

"Let's wait and see," said Sarid softly. "Perhaps we will not be sent to Asdar."

The next morning, though, they were put on a truck heading south.

8

Teresa handed one of the fruits to Cyriac Salvador and watched him turn it over and around in his long fingers. He looked up when she bit into hers, and stared at her as if he expected her to be struck down by some quick-acting poison.

"If you don't want it," she said, "give it back."

Her hunger had been painful for a long time now, but he seemed to be made of different flesh. He was far more cautious than she, always willing to wait just a little longer. The way he looked at her always made her feel as if her hunger were little more than simple greed. She had decided that it was not just that he had far better conscious control of his nervous system, but that his asceticism had in it a masochistic element which transformed any kind of discomfort into an uplifting trial by ordeal.

"It's good," she said, finishing the fruit. "It's also safe. I'm going back for more."

He looked up into the thick foliage of the tree behind her. Most of the fruit had already been devoured by the birds that still scuttled along its branches. The tree was not tall, but its thin branches were inadequate to support the weight of a human being. She would have to stay close to the trunk and reach out to shake the branches so that the fruit would fall.

The harvest that she brought down this way was a poor one. He left it to her to pick up the fruit when she came back down, and she selected out the best for herself with a clear conscience. He noted that her feet were bleeding. The shoes that she had been wearing aboard the ship were not designed for walking, and certainly not for the rough terrain over which they had been forced to travel.

When they emerged from the small wood that grew in the shelter of the rocky cleft, she pointed across the fell to another stand of trees.

"With luck," she said, "there will be another tree of the same kind."

"Undoubtedly," murmured Salvador. "The birds are there."

She half-expected him to protest about further delay and began clambering down the slanting rock face without pausing to discuss the matter. He followed, picking his way more delicately. There was no blood on the soles of his own feet, though he had discarded his shoes some time before she had finally abandoned hers. He was able to protect himself against such injuries.

They had been several days in this hilly wilderness, and had as yet seen no sign of the plains of Merkad. Whenever they came to the crest of a hill they saw nothing before them but more hills. Since they left the track in order to pursue a course leading more or less directly northward they had found the going very difficult—fit territory for goats but not for men. The directness of their present route, however, was only part of the reason they had chosen it. Twice they had left the track in order to hide from groups of horsemen armed with long knives and muskets. Had they seen herdsmen or a village they might have risked being hospitably received, but the horsemen were too obviously hunting parties that would almost certainly not be too particular about what they caught. Some such group might well have been responsible for the murder of the three priests.

Teresa had already located a tree carrying purple drupes when he caught up with her. She was trying to find a way up the trunk that would not necessitate putting too much weight on one or the other of her feet. In the end, he lifted her so that she could take hold of the lower branches and pull herself up.

He wandered around the bole of the tree and found two fallen fruits which were the object of a major operation by a band of black insects. Where the raw flesh was drying in the heat the insects were cutting away small sections and bearing them off through the weeds to a crack in the rocks some fifteen meters away.

He watched them patiently, wondering whether the species had existed before the great upheaval that had changed the face of the world. Probably, they were ordinary, humble ants which had continued to exist more or less undisturbed through all the troubles that men had brought upon the Earth. On the other hand, there was a slight chance that they were some new species, aided in the attainment of social habits by the mutagenic storm which had been whipped up by the atom wars. Millions of new proto-species must have been created in a matter of fifteen or twenty years, of which only a handful could have survived. Fifteen or twenty years was fifteen or twenty generations for creatures such as these. Insects were quite prolific enough for a handful of mutants to produce billions of descendants on that kind of time scale. Men had changed very little, but at this biotic level the Earth's ecosystem might have undergone a considerable metamorphosis. If so, the result of it all had been the recapitulation of the same patterns, the same strategies of life. There was no way he could know whether the creatures he was looking at had maintained their present way of life for millions of years, or only a few thousand.

He placed his foot across the path that led from the project to the nest. Some went around it, some climbed straight over it. None seemed confused, and the creatures did not bite.

Then, with a howl of fury and a clatter of snapping branches, Teresa Janeat tumbled out of the crown of the tree, landing heavily on her left leg. Tumbling down with her came a pale green snake, lashing furiously and displaying tiny needle-sharp fangs.

Salvador was only three meters from the place where they fell. He reached them with a single skipping stride, and he snatched at the snake's tail, lifting it as it coiled in readiness to strike for a second time at the woman. He gave the creature a vicious jerk, as though he were cracking a whip, but its spine was too supple to be broken that way. Without pausing to give it time to curl, he smashed its head sideways against the trunk of the tree. This time, the action was lethal.

Teresa had rolled over onto her back. Her face was quite white.

"Were you bitten in the tree?" he demanded.

She nodded, and held up her right hand. There were two faint scratch marks on the back, already swelling with the histamine reaction. He tore at the skin with a ragged fingernail until it bled, and then sucked at the wound, spitting out the blood. He enlarged the cut with his teeth, and managed to make the blood flow more freely.

"Don't stop it," he told her. "Make it flow. A little more. Now . . . arrest the flow. Make it clot. *Concentrate*. What poison is. left won't kill you. Shut your eyes and lie back. Relax."

She did as she was told. She had already put herself into a light trance state in order to control the pain. He began to feel her ankle then. It was already swelling. To make things worse, there appeared to be a fracture low down on the fibula. It was clean enough to mend well, but she would not be able to walk for quite some time.

When she eventually opened her eyes, her voice was thick and slow. She was high on her own internal pain-killers.

"It's broken," she said, looking up at him from beneath half-closed eyelids. "My leg is broken."

"Yes it is," he told her.

"What are you going to do?"

"What would *you* do, if you were me?"

She managed a half-smile. "I'd abandon me," she said. "No way to survive here for a month without so much as a knife. Can't live on fruit. Nights are too cold. Did you ever figure out what season it is?"

"It's not the rainy season," he told her. "I'm sure of that."

9

When the trucks stopped at dusk, they had reached the end of the road. They were still a long way short of Asdar, but for the rest of the journey they would have to make do with a rough track chipped by horseshoes and rutted by countless cartwheels. They spent the night on the fringes of a moving township of tents and vehicles, whose inhabitants seemed to be suffering desperately from the dust and the heat. The gangs of men—most of them soldiers, some Dahran civilian laborers—looked haggard and exhausted as they queued for their food. Some were ill, coughing and red-eyed. Many had shirts stained black with the smoke from charcoal braziers and the tar that they mixed with cement to form the matrix of the surface layer.

All day, Cheron had been debating with himself whether it might not have been better to avoid being attached to a combat unit, but now that he saw the conditions under which these men lived and worked he realized that Midas had been right. It was better to be a fighting man—at least until the time came when they might have to fight.

Of the group which had first come together in the truck which brought them to Talos, only Malaq was missing from the troop that had been sent south. The two brothers had been separated, though whether it was because Qapel had shown substantially more talent in the use of his weapons or it was simply some administrative whim no one could tell. Following Midas's advice, Cheron and Sarid tried to find out from Spektros where the troop was going, and what kind of program had been mapped out for them. Spektros, however, turned out to know little more than Midas had already picked up on the rumor network.

"We will be in Asdar for a few days," he said. "We have too few steamships on the Sea of Hamad to serve our needs

properly, and sailing ships are so unreliable. Something has
gone wrong in the Bela settlements, and we are sending as
many men as we can raise. The success of the settlements depends on Dahran emigrants, but the Dahrans are reluctant to
go there. They are afraid to cross the sea, and afraid of the
forest people, about whom they tell all kinds of ridiculous
stories. They are so *stupid*, these people. We are bringing
them into the modern world, but we have to drag them by
their heels."

"Why do you need Dahran emigrants?" asked Cheron.
"Why not your own people?"

"Macaria is an advanced nation," replied Spektros. "There
is work for our people to do at home. We transport many of
our criminals, but men who simply have no place of their
own are taken into the army or the navy. When the Bela colonies are settled and established, our people will come out to
run things, but as far as labor goes, the Dahran peasants and
herdsmen are much more useful. They are being made redundant on the land, where they lived a miserable and precarious
existence anyhow, but they will not see the necessity of
changing their attitudes and their ways. They would cling to
their traditions forever if they could, no matter that it is
their traditions that keep them poor and desperate. We offer
them knowledge, but nine in ten of them would rather *not
know*. They have no *idea* of change—despite what they say
that life *is*, that it is what it is, and that the world cannot
help but remain what it is until the end of time. They accept
famine, plague, even war, as part of a recurring pattern
which must repeat itself forever no matter what. They are so
fatalistic, progress means nothing to them. They have a dozen
false gods, and see demons everywhere, and they have no understanding of the fact that the Will of God is that man
should advance himself, should make himself free and powerful, better to appreciate the generosity of Creation. If we
could turn them from the worship of these petty misfortune
mongers to the true faith, we might help them do more for
themselves, but they are our allies, not our subjects, and their
rulers are jealous of their tawdry religion. Not that you
northerners are any better."

"Camelon shares the faith of Macaria," said Sarid, who did
not want a religious dispute.

"The Camelonians are heretics," opined Spektros. "So are the men of Vondrel. Is it Vondrel that you're from?"

"Farther north," Sarid told him, deciding not to press his claim to belong to Camelon.

"Giants from the ice mountains," said Spektros. "Do *you* believe in progress?"

"I'm not altogether sure," said Sarid ironically. "But I believe in change. Anyhow, the mountains aren't the end of the world, you know. There are more plains to the north of them. They were populated once, and they will be again. It's good land, and the winters aren't as cold as they once were. Today's barbarians are tomorrow's civilized men—is that what counts as progress?"

"When we need your land," said Spektros, "we'll take it. For the time being, we need land on the south shore of Hamad. It will be a good place to live. There is no one there to stop us except the forest savages who live in the treetops. Once we have shown that we can defend the lands we take, there will be no stopping us. In the end, we must win."

The trouble with Spektros, decided Cheron, was that he was basically incapable of intelligent discussion. He could mouth a few cant phrases about progress, and his vocabulary seemed considerable, but most of the words he knew were just words. He had no real appreciation of the concepts behind them. He was a semi-educated man, able to read and write, but he still thought in slogans. Even so, there was more to him than there was to anyone else they knew, except possibly Midas, whose eccentric ramblings sometimes suggested an unusual, if erratic, perceptiveness.

Cheron confided this opinion to Sarid, who laughed in an oddly bitter fashion. Cheron realized, after some thought, that the Pragmatist held much the same opinion of *him* as he held of Spektros. This was doubly wounding, on the one hand because it was unfair, and on the other hand because Cheron could see no justifiable way that Sarid could claim to be any wiser than he. In the end, he decided that Sarid was stupidly considering that simply because he was from a time eight thousand years in Sarid's past he therefore must be almost as primitive as the men of Earth.

It was peculiar, he thought, how much difficulty people had in overcoming the most absurd preconceptions.

After they left Spektros and returned to their tent, Cheron asked Baya-undi what *he* thought of progress.

"Progress," said the black man, "is an illusion. The Macarians make machines to do what men can already do. It saves time—but what do they do with the time they save? They make more machines. In Khepra, we do not need machines. We do not need to break our backs making roads like this, because we do not have this restless urge to travel. When we do travel, we do not do so with the intention of going as fast as we can. If a journey is worth making, it is worth making slowly. Progress is a word invented by inferior people who know nothing of spiritual enlightenment, so that they may consider spiritual enlightenment to be unimportant and therefore pretend that their inferiority is somehow a kind of superiority."

"But if Macaria were to invade Khepra tomorrow," Cheron observed, "they would defeat you by means of their superior weapons."

"Only a fool or a madman would consider such a stupid thing to be proof of superiority," said Baya-undi, with all the confidence in the world.

"Surely greater knowledge is a kind of advancement," said Cheron. "And the Macarians seem to have recovered far more of the knowledge of the first civilizations of Earth than any other people."

Baya-undi gave him a pitying look. "This story of ancient civilizations is a myth," he explained. "It is all a pretense. Have you ever seen these ruined cities the Macarians claim to have found? Have you seen the messages which they claim to have received and deciphered from these ruins? I know of no one who claims to have seen any of this except Macarians and Merkadians, all of whom are notorious liars. It is a fiction, a legend, and contrary to the revelations of the true enlightenment. Even the Merkadians know that the ruins are not what they seem, that they belonged to people no different from them in terms of their attainments. The Macarians read too much by far into the strange things they think they have found. It is all invention."

"That's not so," said Cheron. "There *was* a civilization on Earth a long, long time ago. It was real. It possessed machines far greater and more powerful than the Macarians have. It sent ships into space—to other worlds of other stars."

Baya-undi dismissed these claims with a rude noise. They were, in his view, fantasies fit only for children to believe.

10

The trucks had been uncomfortable even while they moved on the relatively smooth surface of the Macarian road. Once beyond that surface, the jolting became much worse. Shortly after the morning meal one of the vehicles broke down, and after much discussion it was deemed irreparable. Its complement of passengers was redistributed, and it was abandoned. Spektros observed, philosophically, that it had broken down in just the right place, as the road-builders would catch up with it before it had deteriorated past reclamation. The overcrowding made the journey even worse.

At one point, Cheron found himself clinging for support to the tailboard alongside the Dahran Qapel, who was staring back along the trail, watching the dust clouds thrown up by the wheels dissipate slowly in the sluggish breeze. He explained that the landscape through which they were now moving was as alien to him as it must be to Cheron. This was grassland, where small herds of grazing antelope were attended by flocks of birds, and widely spaced bushes and squat trees, in a permanent state of desiccation, were the only things which violated its infinite flatness. It was a world he had never seen before; effectively it lay as far beyond the horizons of his own valley as the ice-capped poles—or had, until the Macarians had come.

Vito Talvar had taken to giving Qapel the occasional language lesson, and his understanding of Macarian was growing slowly, but he still found it difficult to conduct any reasonable exchange of information except in his own language. Cheron answered a few questions which served to tell the

Dahran what everyone else already knew concerning their destination and likely prospects.

"Will you stay in the Bela settlements when your term in the army is up?" Cheron asked him.

"Perhaps," said Qapel. "But I may have to return home first, in order to find a wife. If the Bela country is worth living in, I may go back there. I must live somewhere. If it is possible for me to have my own land, instead of raising crops for men who live in cities, I would go."

"Your countrymen seem reluctant," said Cheron.

"They cannot think that things might be other than they are," said Qapel. "When their hands are before their faces, they see only their fingers. They have not learned that if they look at what they can see through the cracks, the fingers fade into mist."

"And yet," said Cheron pensively, "the life of the army seems hard compared to the way life seems to be in the villages we pass on the road. The Bela settlements are in a strange and hostile land. You cannot blame people for preferring what they know, as long as they have food enough to live. They know who they are, these people. They are secure in their way of life."

"It is true," said Qapel. "A man is safe in prison, too. The big man with the bad teeth would have stayed in prison if he could, rather than be here. He would like the village life, too. He would bully weaker men, make them work for him as well as for the landowners and themselves. He would make wine and take women, and grow fatter by the year until the flesh rotted from his living body, and be happy . . . all the while be happy. I am a fighter. In my village, men were afraid of me. But I could not go that way. I would not *be* happy. I do not know why."

"I can understand," said Cheron.

"I cannot," said Qapel. "I take pleasure in wine, in women, in the light of the sun, in good meat, in festival days. I can *be* happy. But it does not last. It is something in me. Something wrong. I had to go away. I could not bind myself to the land with chains as my father is bound and his ancestors bound themselves before him. I do not know what else there is, nor whether there is anything else at all, but if there is, then it is for a man with a gun to find and take. It is for men who are more than men. I want to be free."

"*This* is not freedom," Cheron assured him.

"What kind of freedom have *you* known?" the Dahran challenged him.

It occurred to Cheron that it would not be easy to give an account of nouminous Tangarian existence without there being too many parallels with the way Qapel had described the life of his village. Not, at any rate, from the viewpoint of a Hedonist.

Instead, he said: "The freedom which is important is knowledge. You must be able to know all the ways that you can act, and you must be able to foresee at least some of the consequences that will come from your actions. In my land, it was much easier to be certain of the range of choices a man might make, and we knew when we made our choices what the consequences would be. A gun is only one way to widen the number of choices you have. It is not the best way."

I chose pleasure, he thought. *Fully aware of what I was doing. I selected the kind of reward that I wanted from life. Tanagar, in its benevolence, provided that kind of gratification, in full enough measure to satisfy anyone. I was happy.*

In thinking it, though, he was no longer fully convinced. Now, it seemed, he could stand outside himself and look back at the life on Tanagar which had run its course and come to its end. In some crucial sense, it was no longer *his* life but that of another. It no longer seemed so obvious that everything had been right except the unconquerable jealousy that had led him to violence.

"In my land," he added, feeling the need to go on, "we who worked for others in menial ways were well-rewarded. We lived more comfortably by far than those who ruled us."

"I do not believe it," the Dahran said.

"The men who owned by land had no use for wealth or pleasure. They took pride in rejecting them."

"It cannot be so," said Qapel. Despite what he had said about the shortsightedness of his countrymen, he had his own clear ideas about the limits of the possible. His knowledge of human nature was complete and unassailable.

"Could you imagine a world in which no one is poor?" asked Cheron. "Where no one is hungry, and everyone lives in comfort, and no one *needs* to work, though almost all have some kind of task which they like to call their own?"

"Certainly," answered Qapel. "Everyone can. Some men say it lies just beyond the grave, others say that it is beyond the ocean. I have seen dead men, but not the ocean. It makes no difference. Any man can think of such a world, but no man could live in it."

"Once," said Cheron, "there was such a world here on Earth. Almost. It could have been, but it destroyed itself. It *could* have been. Perhaps, this time, the Macarians will succeed in making it . . . though they might need help."

Qapel had lost the thread of the conversation. Plainly, he thought Cheron was rambling, as Cheron had heard Midas rambling, semi-coherently and drunk with dreams and random thoughts. The Dahran seemed to accept the fact with equanimity. He, too, was familiar with streams of meaningless thought that led nowhere.

"I miss my brother," he said, returning the conversation to Earth. "They should not have split us up."

As he spoke, the truck lurched to a halt.

Cheron hauled his backside up on to the tailboard, and peered round the side of the truck, to see what had gone wrong. Riders had accosted the leading vehicle, and were holding excited conversation with the driver. An officer—the same Donsella ti Ria who had attended their absurd trials of strength—emerged from the back of the truck to join in.

Moments later, the column was under way again, but one by one the trucks left the track and headed up a slight slope toward the southwest, where a group of rounded hills loomed up from the savannah like an archipelago in a straw-colored sea.

"Where are we going?" demanded Midas, as Cheron eased himself back inside.

"I don't know," said Cheron. "We're following some riders mounted on white horses."

"Perhaps we are not going to Asdar after all!" said the little Merkadian, obviously enthusiastic at the thought.

"Don't be too hopeful," said Spektros. "The road will still be here when we turn around—or, rather, it will not be here, because I am talking about a cattle track and not a road. In any case, if we have left it it can mean only one thing. We are going to see some action. *Now* we will find out who can shoot and who can fight, and who is only a scavenger dog who barks while standing on his hind legs."

Qapel was now craning his neck to see what lay ahead. Cheron grabbed his belt to save him from falling over the tailboard in his eagerness.

"Don't worry," grunted Mondo, fixing Midas with a mock-benevolent gaze. "If *we* aren't running away, then the others will run when they see us. No one fights unless he is sure to win."

"Merkadian," said the corporal, "for one so old you have a very great deal to learn."

11

Cyriac Salvador moved slowly along the pathway, hardly aware that he was at last within sight of the village. His tread was still measured and precise, but his stride had lost most of its distance, and he moved like an automaton, with mechanical gracelessness. Teresa, whom he carried in his arms, was unconscious, her head lolled back from his right shoulder.

The Intellectual was still barefoot, and wore now the bloodstained robe that he had taken from the body of a dead Merkadian priest in the Kezula. He had dressed Teresa in the second garment. Both the robes were ill-fitting in the extreme, leaving most of their arms and lower legs naked. The three pouched belts were hidden inside their underclothes.

The village children and a number of the women came to watch the strange pair approach, and stood silently by as Salvador walked the length of the main street and laid his burden down beside the stone parapet of the village well. When he put her down her eyes fluttered open, and she looked up into his drawn face, studying the dark, sunken eyes.

"You look terrible," she murmured. "A disgrace to your tribe."

He turned away to face a crowd of staring people and asked for a cup. A child came forward and brought him a wooden bowl. The boy hesitated but did not turn away. In-

stead, he began winding the bucket down into the pit and
fetched the water up so that Salvador could fill the bowl and
force Teresa to drink.

Afterward, he slaked his own thirst, without allowing his
desperation to show in his expression, though he was ready
enough to admit that it might show in his flesh, and ashamed
of it.

When he had handed the bowl back to the boy, he asked if
anyone would offer his companion a place to rest, because his
leg was broken and he had been through a bout of fever
brought on by snakebite.

For a few seconds no one spoke, then a woman said, "Are
you a healer?"

"Yes," said Salvador. "A healer and a holy man."

The woman explained that her daughter was sick, and
might die, and that a healer was welcome in her house. Salvador picked up Teresa's limp form, which seemed far
heavier than it should have been though it was now ten or
eleven days since they had quit the lighter gravity of the ship,
and followed the woman.

"Healer and holy man?" murmured Teresa, in Tanagarian.

As if he were murmuring a prayer, Salvador said, "I'm as
holy as any man, by the standards *they* know. And I *am* a
healer."

The house was set some way back from the street, and was
reached by way of a mud-stained path. It was one of a row
of brick houses, better than some of the ramshackle wooden
dwellings but less impressive than the tall houses with slanting
roofs that could be seen at the other end of the village. The
woman waited while Salvador laid Teresa down on a low
couch in front of the fireplace before leading him through a
doorway protected by a tattered cloth curtain. There was a
small back room, nearly filled by a large bed designed for
sleeping four or five people. There was only one person in it
now—a feverish girl child with dark, staring eyes, whose
breathing was terribly ragged.

Salvador reached out to touch the girl's shoulder, trying to
attract her attention. Her eyes seemed uninterested as she
turned to look in his direction. She coughed, and Salvador
saw that the expectorant was heavy and flecked with blood.

"Get me some water," he said to the woman. "Put a kettle
by the fire and put water in it to boil."

The girl shivered.

"When you've brought the water," said Salvador, "leave me alone."

The woman fetched a bowl of water, then went back to watch the kettle while it boiled. Salvador forced the girl to drink just as he had forced Teresa to drink. Then he began to investigate the contents of his belt.

When he came out of the room again, some thirty minutes later, he found Teresa awake. He knelt and began to check the bandage that secured her ankle.

"I may be able to get some clay," he said. "With luck, I can set the bone and help it to heal cleanly. Otherwise, you'd limp for months, and there'd have to be a corrective operation once you get back to the base."

"What's the matter with the child?" asked Teresa.

"Viral infection. Not dangerous in itself. The fever left her dehydrated, I've fed her fluid and something to reduce the pain. It's best if the fever's allowed to run its course. When her temperature begins to come down, I'll give her antibiotics to take care of any secondary infection. She'll recover in two or three days, though she may have passed the infection on. It'll probably go through the village, if it hasn't already. It won't bother the adults much, unless they already have respiratory difficulties, but the children will need careful handling."

"You'll be able to pay for our keep, then."

"That's right."

"How long will we be here?"

"Long enough. There's no hurry." He got to his feet and checked the kettle that sat on a metal grid beside the fire. There wasn't much water left. The supply of firewood was running low. The woman had gone out in search of food.

Salvador took half a dozen coins from his belt, and went out looking for her.

Teresa watched a harvest-spider amble across the wooden floorboards, and then closed her eyes, listening to the distant sound of voices and the ringing of a mallet on metal.

She hoped fervently that the village had a cobbler—preferably one whose gratitude could be bought with a little elementary medical treatment. After all, they had to conserve what money they had. Once they got through Merkad they had Macaria to cope with.

12

After disembarking from the trucks, Cheron's company was split into three sections. Two were sent out to the right and left, each guided by one of the men who had stopped the convoy. Cheron's section waited for a little while before moving slowly forward, with Donsella himself in command.

"What's happening?" asked Cheron of Spektros, when the corporal returned from a conference with his superiors.

"This range of hills is a long spur extending into the grasslands from the Kezula. It is by no means mountainous, but sometimes the mountain men will come this far south. In the past, the mountain men believed that they had the right to exact tribute from the hill farmers, as rent or taxes. They remember that right whenever they think that Dahra cannot protect this land—which is, alas, very often. They have come now, it seems, because they think that Macaria does not care, or because they have heard that Macaria is sending a great many of its troops across Hamad. At present, they think they are safe, because they think that news will have to reach Talos before help can possibly come. They will be anxious about the prospect of being cut off by troops marching from the northwest. They will not expect an attack from the southwest. Also, they have forgotten or do not realize that the trucks can bring us across the grassland to the very edge of the hills. We will reach them by the evening, and will fall upon them as if from out of nowhere. We will kill them all, and teach them a lesson. All Dahra will know how Macaria guards her friends."

The march seemed long, but the pace was not a punishing one. Cheron's section was making straight for the village where the raiders were lodged, and did not have as far to go as the sections which were moving around to the rear.

They reached the fertile land surrounding the village, as

Spektros had predicted, by late afternoon, when the sun was almost standing on the rim of the western horizon. Here, the section was split again, Donsella taking command of one party, a sergeant the second, and Spektros the third. There was no time to waste if they were to keep the advantage of the light, and all three parties immediately began to make their way across the fields, crouching low in the channels between the cornstalks and sheltering beside walls whenever they could. Spektros's party consisted of Cheron, Vito Talvar, Midas, Qapel, and two other Dahrans. Sarid and Mondo had been detached with the sergeant's group.

It seemed that the raiders had posted no sentries—or if they had the sentries had been watching the wrong avenues of approach and had been dealt with by the section which had been sent to occupy the head of the valley some two kilometers ahead. The first the marauders knew of the attack was when their horses—which had been lodged in a corral for want of an adequate stable—suddenly ran free after being stampeded by the sound of gunfire. From the shelter of a wall, still well out of rifle range, Cheron was able to watch half a dozen men come running out of the larger buildings in the central cluster to see what was going on. Two were cut down by rifle fire from the eastern side of the village before the others reached cover again.

Spektros pointed to three of the small outlying houses that lay between the position of his party and the main part of the village.

"We will check each one in turn," he said. "They may be empty, but if they are not there will be at least one raider there no matter how many others. The raiders would not leave villagers alone in their houses, though they might wish to be entertained there. Cheron Felix—you and I will attend to the door in each case. Midas and Talvar will cover the windows. There will be no back doors. The others will replace any man who falls and will take up our position at the door if and when Felix and I go inside. Shoot at anything that shoots at you. Do *not* fire at anything which moves. It would be an embarrassment if we were to kill villagers even the raiders would have left alive. If possible, do not shoot at all—use the bayonet. If you have no time to think, then duck. Never shoot until you are certain what you are firing at. Now *move!*"

He went forward in a crouching run, leaving no time for argument. Cheron, after a moment's surprised hesitation, went after him, his heart hammering. The others followed.

When they came to the first of the cottages Spektros spared a moment to look around, making sure that Vito Talvar and Midas were going to the windows. Then, as Cheron caught up with him, he kicked out at the door, smashing the flimsy latch. It flew inward. He crouched, swinging the muzzle of his gun as he looked around the two squalid rooms within. One section at the rear was curtained off, but he did not bother to check behind it.

"Next!" he said, tersely. "If they're there, they've seen us by now. Be wary."

They approached the house from the side, tempting fire from the windows but leaving themselves the opportunity to get quickly out of view. Nothing happened as they approached, but this time when Cheron kicked the door in response to the corporal's signal it gave only a couple of centimeters. It was wedged or barricaded.

"Again!" commanded Spektros.

Cheron placed himself better for his second attempt, and lashed out with his foot so that the heel crashed against a spot some thirty centimeters below the latch. There was a burst of sound as whatever had been blocking the door overturned, and this time the gap which opened up was enough to allow a man through. A curved blade nearly a meter long licked out of the shadow like a long silver tongue, aiming to take Cheron's leg off. Cheron caught the blade with the barrel of his rifle and turned it aside. Spektros lunged past him, bayonet extended.

Gunfire exploded from the window where Vito Talvar was taking up his station, and the blond man jerked back, flattening himself against the wall.

Spektros charged through the door, hacking from side to side with the bayonet, bringing forth a scream of anguish from one man who was hit. Cheron tried to follow, but was nearly bowled over when a man came out, thrusting with a short, straight blade. He turned aside to let the blade pass, and when the body of his assailant collided with his Tanagarian bulk it was the other who came off considerably worse.

As the raider reeled, Cheron found—to his astonish-

ment—that he had all the time in the world to adjust the attitude of his weapon and drive the bayonet up into the other
man's abdomen, right through the diaphragm and into the
pleural cavity.

It's so easy! he thought. It did not seem like killing at all.
There was no passion in the act whatsoever. Unthinkingly, he
had even suppressed his fear, to keep his adenalin under
careful control. This Tangarian reflex had combined perfectly
well with the hypnopaedically superimposed neural command
which had told him precisely how to dispense with his enemy.
He was no more emotionally involved in the act than if he
were flicking a spider from his sleeve. It would have seemed
far more significant had he been watching someone else perform the act.

There was the sound of another shot from within the
house, and Cheron followed Spektros through the door, ready
to fire at the rifleman who had already come so close to hitting Talvar. The shot had been Spektros's, however, and that
man was dead. Only one of the four raiders still stood, and
he was at the other window, trying to wrench free the rifle
that Midas had incautiously intruded through it. The raider
himself was armed only with a straight blade. Cheron, without pausing to give Spektros the opportunity to take the initiative, took one gigantic stride forward and drove his
bayonet into the raider's spine. The blade was deflected from
the bone, but the man went rigid with pain and fell backwards. As he lay on the floor, his contorted face upturned,
Cheron finished the job by driving the bayonet down through
his throat.

It was all over.

When Cheron realized that, he relaxed, and *then* there was
a rush of emotion that he could not suppress. There was horror, but also elation, and again the words that came into his
head were: *It's so easy.* He realized quickly enough, though,
how very easy it had been. Only one of the four raiders had
had a rifle. Two had been armed with knives that were really
no better than meat carvers. They had stood no chance
against the soldiers—none whatsoever.

"Move it!" shouted Spektros in his ear. "There's one more
yet."

Cheron's eyes were caught by the sight of a small girl peering from the curtained section of the house. She was no more

than twelve years old, and was naked. There was blood on her legs. She was terrified—no less frightened now than thirty minutes before. What was happening was all beyond her comprehension.

There was someone else in the curtained covert, too. Cheron could hear the sound of weeping—empty, hopeless sobbing.

It was this sight and this sound that really freed the feelings within him. Now, for the first time, he felt fear and anger. He was barely conscious of the fact that Spektros was pushing him, but he did not resist. He allowed the corporal to push him through the doorway. Then he hurled himself flat, as a bullet split the wood of the lintel a handsbreadth from his left ear.

There had been two raiders in the third house, but rather than stay within they had come out to fight. Both had rifles, and they had reached the cover of a low stone wall without being seen. Three shots scattered the attackers, who took cover wherever they could find it.

Cheron crawled back through the doorway, to join Spektros inside. When the burst of firing ceased, the only sound he could hear was the uncontrollable weeping. For some reason, that seemed to be far worse than anything else that had happened or was likely to happen. It was the only thing that lent any kind of human dimension to what was going on. Without that, he might have been back in his conscienceless dreams—poisoned dreams, perhaps, but dreams nonetheless. Everything, he knew, was easier in dreams.

Spektros peered around the door and took careful stock of the situation.

"You!" he said to Cheron. "You speak Dahran. The mountain men probably speak some dialect of their own—more likely to be Merkadian than Dahran. We can't get out. Tell your friend Qapel to get the others around to one side, to flush them out. Keep it quiet, just in case they *do* understand."

Cheron withdrew and went to the window nearest to the wooden chicken-run behind which Qapel and one of the other Dahrans had taken cover. Cheron explained to them that they had to circle around from the back of the house, to force the mountain men from the position they held.

"Did he understand?" asked Spektros, when Cheron returned.

Cheron nodded.

Spektros sighted along his weapon and sent a bullet whining off the crown of the wall where the raiders were hiding.

"Bastards!" he muttered. "Don't fire. Waste of ammunition. Wait."

Cheron looked back over his shoulder at the curtains. Only the girl's face was visible now. She was watching him like a mouse mesmerized by a snake, as if there were no way that she could withdraw her gaze. He wanted to tell her that everything was all right, and that nothing more was going to hurt her, but the words would not come. When he tried to form them in his head, all his languages seemed to clot together in a viscous tangle.

"What's the matter, sea-pig?" snarled Spektros. "We're fighting a battle, here. Watch the wall!"

Cheron accepted the rebuke, ready enough to return his attention to the wall, and to concentrate thereon with fierce singlemindedness.

Control, he demanded of himself.

He continued to repeat the word silently, in a kind of inward chant.

Control . . . control . . . control. . . .

There are seven virtues, he informed himself, in a suitably hectoring tone. *Reason, authority, and gentleness; charity, optimism, and calm. And the seventh is control.*

Qapel and the Dahran who had been sheltering with him suddenly opened fire from some coign of vantage away to the left. The raiders, apparently too stupid to have anticipated the move, half rose as they sprinted in panic for a new position. Cheron put a bullet into the leading man's head. The other lasted long enough to leap over the body of his companion, but in the hail of bullets that came at him from two sides he had no real chance of survival. He was cut down, and was too badly hurt to loose any kind of Parthian shot when Spektros went out to finish him off.

By the time the twilight died, the battle was over. The troop had lost just one man. Twenty-seven raiders had been killed. The spoils amounted to a dozen rifles, thirty blades of various dimensions and various articles of jewelry. Such coin as the raiders had carried was left to the villagers, who were given the job of burying the marauders.

The soldiers stayed the night in the village, accepting the generosity of the grateful people they had delivered from evil. Cheron pointed out at one time to Spektros that they were probably consuming as much as the raiders would have stolen, there being twice as many troopers as there had been raiders, but Spektros cursed him for a fool. Cheron, however, held himself back from full participation in the festivities, uncertain of himself or the situation. He watched the others eat and drink, and he watched the signs of fear and anguish that were submerged just beneath the surface of the villagers' gaiety and gratitude.

He never saw the woman whose sobbing had imprinted itself so firmly in his memory, unless perhaps her face passed unrecognized before him during the night. He saw the twelve-year-old girl, though. No longer naked, no longer bloodstained, she was on her knees between Midas's legs, while he explained to her in imaginative detail precisely what he had saved her from.

13

It was midday when the convoy finally reached Asdar, having set out at dawn. Asdar was a city of some considerable size, with a population of several hundred thousand scattered through a number of districts arrayed about three natural harbors. It was the principal port of the great inland Sea of Hamad, created during the Upheaval by a massive landslip. The rivers that rose in the Kezula fed into it, and so did several Kyadian rivers, as well as the Bela which flowed into it from the south. On the map, the Sea of Hamad had the shape of a snub-nosed pistol with its butt to the south and its barrel pointing west, with a great bite taken out of the chamber by the peninsula of Omman some three hundred kilom-.

eters east of Asdar. Omman was claimed both by Dahra and by Kyad, but was effectively independent, and provided bases for the pirate fleets that harried the merchant ships traveling between Kyad's ports and those of Dahra and Ksah.

Asdar had been an important city long before the Macarians had begun to take such an intense interest in its affairs, but now it was undergoing a period of expansion as Macarian entrepreneurs were buying up surrounding land in order to launch countless different ventures. The land was cheap, and Asdar offered ready access to many different kinds of raw materials as well as providing the main supply point for the Bela settlements. Trade was booming in the city, and factories were growing up around it. Macarian knowledge, Dahran labor, and the resources of Kyad and the Bela territories added up to a powerful combination. The smelting of steel was beginning, using charcoal shipped from the Bela or brought west from Ksah, which claimed dominion over a part of the equatorial forest. The steel supplied shipyards to the east, building steamships to secure regular and certain communication between the north and south, and gunboats to assure protection against the pirates of Omman.

The population of Asdar seemed far more mixed than that of Talos. There were far more pale-skinned northerners from Macaria and her subject states, but there were also black-skinned Kyadians—perhaps even some Kheprans among them. Merkadians, Ksahmen, and the native Dahrans supplied various shades of brown to fill in the color spectrum.

Donsella's company was given lodgings in barracks that lay on the fringes of the eastern docks, a long way from the city's prosperous center. The first thing Cheron noticed was the stench of fish drifting on a slow, warm wind from the wharves where the Dahran fleets landed their catches. The party were welcomed by troops already stationed there with some curiosity; rumors had already preceded them concerning the reasons for their failure to arrive when expected. Mondo and Midas produced the most extravagant and exciting accounts of the battle that had delayed them. The Tanagarians were plagued by demands that they should buy wine in order that the whole company might celebrate, but the unreasonableness of the demands made it easy for them to refuse.

"Apparently," said Sarid, as he, Cheron, and Talvar sat to

one side during the evening meal, "we shall be here for
several days."

"It's not a prospect I relish," said Vito Talvar. "This diet is
becoming tiresome. No doubt they will help us to fill in the
time by marching us up and down and conditioning our reflexes so that we can perform all kinds of meaningless rituals
on the appropriate screech of command. I think we should
find a way to advance ourselves. Let's invent the flame-
thrower or design a better machine gun—or at the very least
become medical orderlies."

"For one thing," said Sarid, "I am not sure that I could
design a better machine gun. Perhaps I could tell them something about lasers, or particle beams, but I couldn't put one
together from materials that come ready to hand. In any
case, I suspect they will already know. It is the means they
lack, not the ideas. If we were to begin to display our odds
and ends of technological knowledge they would simply con-
clude that we had somehow gained access to information that
should have been withheld from us. We would call attention
to ourselves without ingratiating ourselves, and without even
putting ourselves into a genuine bargaining position. The only
way that we could begin to make use of our knowledge is
first to attain a position where we could seem to have a legitimate claim to it. That is not going to be easy, starting from
our present situation. As for finding some safer role within
the army, I fear that we run into the problem of what the
army thinks it needs. It wants fighting men far more than it
wants medical orderlies. We are too big, too bold, and too
good with weapons to be transferred."

"I do not like the way the sky glows," said Talvar glumly,
peering out of the window at the dark twilight clouds which
reflected the red glow of blast furnaces. "I do not like the
smell. I am beginning to tire of the ceaseless mental strife
which is the cost of keeping my feet free of sores and blisters.
This world drags on me so terribly that I cannot imagine how
I ever managed to walk on Tanagar—where, you assure me,
the gravity was greater. I no longer think that this is all a
dream. Plainly, it is Tanagar that is imaginary. We really are
giants from the frozen forests of the far north who served as
seamen on Camelonian trading ships. The long journey across
Zarh and Ksah, which we thought Sarid had invented, was
real enough, though our kindly subconscious censor has

blotted it from our minds. The hot sun addled our brains and made us call up this fake past from the wellspring of fantasy, in order to make our tribulations slightly less terrible. We are not in hell, as I thought—things are far worse than that. We are simply mad."

"You should compete with Midas," said Cheron. "In a story-telling contest you should run him close."

"I could defeat him with ease," said Talvar. "I would only have to tell the truth. I'm sure that being frozen was extremely peaceful. Eternal life has much to recommend it, in philosophical terms—not least the possibility that Tanagar might, in a million years or so, have become sufficiently enlightened to temper its vicious mercy with a little generosity and welcome its stored-up population back to the land of the living. When that day comes they will weep for us, the wasted few who were squandered in some mad experiment by a rogue *mensana*. Thanks to Cyriac Salvador we will miss our Millennium. We will die here, surrounded by subhumans and haunted by the stink of rotten fish. I was wrong ever to think that this second life was profit—it is a terrible loss, compared to the second life we might have had and should have had. Whichever way we turn for spiritual comfort we find ourselves damned."

"You take far too much pleasure in self-pity," said Sarid Jerome with a scowl. "If you spent less energy in savoring the exquisite horror of the moment and more in considering the long-range objectives open to us, we'd be much better off. As a miserable sensual your plans would undoubtedly be useless, but we'd be saved the trouble of listening to your whining."

Cheron feared that Talvar might take offense, but in fact the blond man only smiled in a pitying fashion that was laboriously overdone. "Alas," he replied, "the future is to me far less than an open book. I live in the moment because I am its prisoner. I can never, in my heart of hearts, *believe* in tomorrow. Every time I go to sleep I do so without the conviction that I will wake again. I am the worst Pragmatist that ever was. It's glandular, of course—a trick of the metabolism. I am condemned to live within the margins of pleasure and pain. I see everything in terms of heaven and hell, paradise and punishment, because it is the only way I can see significance in anything at all. It is a terrible thing, I know, that the race of Tanagar can contain a creature such as I. How sad that it should generate us by the billion, more perfectly with every generation that passes. Cheron will help you, if you feel inadequate. He comes from a braver age, when even Hedonists had a touch of the Intel about them. Look at his sober face—it is as grave as your own. But at least he understands what I'm saying, don't you Cheron?"

"I understand," said Cheron. "But I also understand what Sarid says. We're a long way from Tanagar, and we'll never go back. This is the Motherworld, and we must try to come to terms with what it demands of us . . . or die."

"It's a difficult choice to make," said Vito Talvar. "Isn't it?"

"Not for me," replied Sarid Jerome.

14

Teresa emerged from the doorway of the house to look at the assembled crowd. They made no move toward her; it was Salvador, and Salvador only, who had captured their hopes. He was the healer, she merely a companion. She counted three twisted limbs, two blind children, half a dozen men and women so ill that the effort of walking from their own villages must have brought them near to death. Less than half of them had obvious ills. The rest, presumably, simply did not feel well. For those who only imagined themselves ill cures would come easy. About one third of the others could actually be brought back to full bloom of health—temporarily, at least. Some improvement might be made in the condition of the others, but it would require not the talents of a healer—merely some advice on elementary hygiene.

They were patient. Some had been there for two days and more. They had received words of comfort, or even medicines, but they stayed, presumably to absorb something of the holy aura that surrounded the healer. Their attitude, for the most part, was paradoxical. Sickness was something they lived with as a matter of course. They expected it, as part of life's routine. Occasionally, they sought special explanations for their afflictions, hunting sorcerers or rooting out traitors who had somehow offended one of God's many minions. Usually, though, they regarded illness and infirmity as things which needed no explanation—things which simply *were*. They did not apply the logic of cause and effect except to rare and special cases, and even then the specialness was socially defined rather than being determined by the character of the sickness. For these reasons, the role of healer, as they saw it, was a curious one. A healer was a miracle worker, who cut through the normal pattern of earthly affairs. His work was not returning people to a state of normalcy, but rather lifting them out of that state into a condition of blessed superhumanity. Freedom from fever or pain, or the healing of suppurating sores, was not the essence of this condition but merely its sign. The real gift conferred on them by the healer was a supernal sense of special well-being that was incalculably more valuable than the rewards of analgesics and antibiotics.

Within a matter of six days, while she lay on her couch and the small child had recovered completely from her virus infection, Cyriac Salvador had undergone a metamorphosis. He was now more than human in the eyes of these villagers, and his reputation was spreading. As long as people were prepared to believe what others said—and they were so desperately anxious to believe it that they snatched at the idea like drowning men clutching at straws—there was no way that he could be rendered back into an ordinary mortal. Not, at any rate, in Merkad.

This turn of events worried her for two reasons. Firstly, the fact that they would not have to try hard to find friends in Merkad was offset by the anxiety that they might call attention to themselves in an unfortunate way: from skeptical authorities or even from the Macarians. Secondly, the twist of fate made her far more dependent on Salvador than the broken leg. The leg would heal, but the gap in their ascribed status would not. From now on, it was Salvador that would get things done no matter who the Pragmatist was.

Teresa adjusted her hood, and went back into the house, closing the door.

"We're trapped," she said. "They'll let us go north, if we can feed them sufficiently pious reasons, but we'll never get away from them. They'll go with us. An army of cripples for a retinue—so much for being conspicuous in an inconspicuous way."

She limped back to the couch, and Salvador moved aside to let her be seated.

"We're eating well," he pointed out. "It isn't just them who need restoring—it's us. Our good fortune comes cheap—let's not decry it."

"We'll run out of medicine very soon," she observed. "I suppose you're not thinking of setting up a factory to make analgesic and extract penicillin from mold?"

"It would make no difference now if the only thing I did was to lay my hands on their louse-ridden heads and recite the table of the temptations," observed Salvador. "As it happens, though, one or two of their own pharmaceutical methods are far from ineffective. The basis of good treatment is intelligence—simply stopping people from being stupid achieves far greater gains than elaborate medical technology. I *am* a healer—and that won't stop when my little phials are empty."

"What happens when the officers of the church begin to wonder who we are? What happens when we find ourselves faced with Macarians who have a religion all of their own, and medical science too?"

"We avoid cities," said Salvador. "Merkad is a rural nation. We could cross it a dozen times without getting out of this kind of back country. We need never set foot where we aren't likely to be appreciated. In any case, the church isn't likely to interfere; we're doing it far more good than harm."

"I know that charity is a virtue," she said, "but I fear that we may overdo it. Recklessness isn't the worst of the temptations, but it's often the most dangerous."

"I don't need lectures on proverbial morality," said Salvador with deadly amiability. "Forget charity and dwell upon optimism. That's the one thing that Pragmatists can never master. Always willing to look for the worst, and to use awful possibilities as a scourge to beat themselves and harry everyone else. If you'd stop thinking so furiously and put your mind to controlling your metabolism, you'd be healed by now. *You* have reserves of power and ability *they* know nothing about, but sometimes it hardly shows. By now, I would have recovered completely, whereas I still see you fighting to control the pain."

"I'm not an Intel," she said, in a low tone. "I can't make the bone knit and the flesh heal by the power of will alone."

"You *can*," Salvador told her, "if only you'll seek the proper degree of self-control. Do you seriously expect to live five hundred years if you can't cope with a clean fracture of a long bone?"

"How long I might live is my own affair," she told him. "No doubt I could live forever if I had complete somatic awareness and control. But even *mensanas* can only manage seven hundred years for all their meditations and vanities."

"The quarrel is pointless," observed Salvador. "We need to remember that we need one another. There is no one to watch over us but one another."

"Is that why you carried me into Merkad?"

"That's a stupid question," he replied. He did not amplify the remark, letting her add whatever silent comment she cared to. He looked away from her, and then stood up to go to the door. He went out to talk to the crowd and investigate the troubles of those unfortunates he had not previously seen.

Teresa heard his voice as he lectured them in his own language, reciting poems and instructing them in the arts of Intel meditation. They loved the sound of what they did not understand. It was all part of the magic.

She heard other sounds, too—the sound of whispered Merkadian prayers, the sound of grateful sobbing, the sound of a harsh wind in the trees. It all mingled together into a rhythmic pattern which seemed to echo the flow of her blood in its vessels.

Salvador was right: she did have difficulty controlling the pain, and her strength of mind was far from being what it should have been. She did not know quite why, but she contemplated the possibility that having come to Earth she had become more like the people of Earth—the semi-humans who knew nothing at all of the ways that the will could use to dominate the feeble flesh. It was a dreadful thought, that she might change into one of them, dragged back from the peak of Tanagarian attainment into the morass of indomitable pain and decay.

She felt—though in truth she had no real need to feel it—that she was growing further apart from Salvador by the

minute. The people outside believed that his torn robe was
stained with his own blood—that knives had been driven into
his body and that he had survived by means of a special dis-
pensation from heaven itself. She could almost believe that it
was true herself. He seemed so little troubled by the demands
that his terrible journey across the fells of the Kezula had
made upon him that anything seemed possible. He was
uncorrupted and incorruptible, whereas she seemed to be
slowly losing command of her own identity.

Was it true, she wondered, what Cheron Felix had said
about the dreams that had been forced into his head? Had he
been changed, in the very roots of his soul? And she too,
though she had not known it until now? But not Salvador.
Never Salvador, the creature of intellect, whose flesh was a
mere convenience, inessential to his being.

When he came back, she said: "Beware of beginning to believe them. Don't go too far in accepting what they want to
make of you."

Salvador laughed, as she had known he would.

15

In Asdar, the Tanagarians discovered more wonders to be-
hold, though no man of Earth would have counted them
more than the common coin of life. Here they were privileged to observe, in minutest detail, the squalor of city pov-
erty; huddled buildings crowded with people of all ages, from
those just born to those on the lip of the grave; black streets
sweltering in the evening heat, embalmed in filth. The eyes of
their companions passed blankly over such sights, skimming
the streets for lighted places where there was the sound of
music: the soft fluting of Dahra itself or the more raucous
and insistent surge of Merkadian rhythms, and sometimes the
bells and drumbeats of Kyad. To Midas and Mondo, the
slums of Asdar consisted of an ocean of gray shadows from

which these cells of light and life shone so brightly as to be the only things that really existed. Cheron Felix, Vito Talvar, and Sarid Jerome lacked such skill in selective perception, and they saw a much more chaotic picture.

Boys like those who had sold fruit along the road to and from Talos here sold their sisters. The uniform of Macaria attracted flocks of beggars pleading for the price of a loaf of bread or a bottle of cheap wine, and also attracted torrents of abuse from local bravos and hagwives. Many of the children were suffering from obvious malnutrition, and the disfigurements of disease were commonplace. Most of the streets had but one water supply point: a pair of taps sited at a junction, one delivering fresh water for drinking (though only for a few hours each day), the other salt water for washing (whenever the tide was in).

Spektros took pride in telling all the barbarians entrusted to his tender care that Asdar was one of the most prosperous cities in the world, and that it would make the fortune of the Dahran nation.

The army mounted patrols through the streets of the district in which the barracks stood. At first, the Tanagarians could not perceive the sense in this, but after their first evening tour of duty they began to appreciate the reasoning. The main functions of the patrols were two: on the one hand, to protect other soldiers from the populace; and on the other hand, to protect the populace from the soldiers. Wherever the soldiers chose to go when they were off-duty (and there were few places where they would tolerate being denied entry) disharmony followed, and violence. The hatred which the troopers felt for the local people arose partly from scorn, but principally by simple reciprocation of the hostility which greeted them. That hostility was more difficult to understand, but any rational element within it was redundant. Its chief source was the fact that Macaria's army provided ready-made scapegoats which became the targets of all the resentments and frustrations, fears and pains that plagued the Asdarians. These were people whose life was illimitably bitter, and who needed more than anything else someone or something they could *blame* for their plight. Any actual role the army may have played in creating their situation was quite irrelevant; the crucial fact was simply that the army was *there*.

The instructions given to patrols were simple enough:

Don't kill anyone; at least, not in public; and if it *is* imperative to kill, try to stick to Kyadians and Merkadians. With the crimes perpetrated by the populace against one another the troopers were not to be concerned. The policing of the district (or lack of it) was entirely the affair of the local authorities, except where issues involving the army were concerned.

On the third evening, Midas volunteered to show the Tanagarians the sights of Asdar. They had not been unduly impressed by his conducted tour of Talos (he had, of course, never been in Asdar before either), and were further disposed to hesitate by what they had seen on a three-hour tour of duty on the streets the previous night. Midas had to explain to them that it was precisely *because* the situation was as it was that every man had a duty to himself to go into the dockland. It was a kind of challenge, which a real man had to accept. Certainly, they might be attacked, and certainly they would not be permitted to take guns with them, but that was all part of the game. He had to explain to them that the way the game was played and understood meant that every soldier of Macaria who stayed in the barracks to play dice instead of strutting about the streets where he was most unwelcome counted as a small victory for the slum dwellers, while everyone who took up the challenge contributed in some small measure to the honor of the army. (He also explained hastily that this was *not* the same thing as *Macaria's* honor, but rather the honor of free men temporarily and unjustly oppressed by Macaria.)

Despite the many weaknesses in this argument, Cheron, Sarid, and Talvar allowed themselves to be persuaded.

Instead of heading west toward the center of the city, Midas led them north and east, searching for particular drinking dens which he had heard about from troopers stationed in the barracks for some time. Characteristically, he failed to find them. When they came to a wider thoroughfare, running parallel with the docks, lit by the bright windows of hundreds of shops, Midas was outvoted on the matter of the next step to be taken, and Sarid Jerome led the group along this road. Midas rapidly accepted the fact, and took up the pose of an expert on Asdarian affairs of trade.

On this street, Midas assured him, it was possible to buy virtually anything that a man of Earth could possess, if one only had the price. Many of the shops might be dingy, their proprietors wearing several layers of grime and patched clothing, but to some extent this was mere disguise. The ships that discharged their cargoes a few hundred meters to the south brought in far more than the goods listed on their manifests, and this street was the medium by which all such illegal imports were distributed.

Cheron, generously, decided to believe as much as half of what Midas was saying, for the street was, indeed, a remarkable one. Among the goods on display were exotic foodstuffs, dozens of different kinds of cloth, shoes, dyes, cage-birds, perfumes, furniture, carved figurines, tea, coffee, tobacco, opiates, hallucinogens, poisons, seeds, maps, printed books, icons, scissors, knives, pots, pans, jewelry, and most particularly magical charms and potions of every kind. If the patter of the storekeepers was to be believed, a man with resources far less great than theirs could have bought enough magic to assure himself long life, miraculous sexual potency, great wealth, and instant death to all his enemies. Had these claims amounted to anything at all, however, Cheron and his companions would have been dead before setting foot on the street from the curses that had been aimed at them while they walked through darker alleyways.

The shops that interested Sarid most were those selling maps and books, and here he spent some time, inspecting the stock while Midas served the usual function of distracting the shopkeeper's attention by attempting to set up an imaginary deal in Merkadian treasure maps which were far better than those the proprietor had in stock because they revealed the sites of lost cities of the ancient world which the Macarians would love to loot themselves, and whose booty could be sold to Macarian scholars for fabulous prices. The proprietor would not be drawn, though he seemed good-tempered enough. He probably added Midas's story to his own resources of persuasion. Cheron, listening to some of the dialogue (conducted in Merkadian, which the proprietor had to know because virtually all his books were printed in either Merkadian or Macarian), found that his amusement was doubled by the realization that both men were entirely skeptical about what they considered to be Macarian mythology. Neither of them believed in the treasure about which they were talking.

Sarid bought a Merkadian book which claimed to be a history of the world. It was offered cheaply, as a book of limited interest. There were few enough literate men even in Merkad who could have made use of it. Most of the books in stock were religious texts and books of magic, and the vast majority were no more than folded sheets of paper or pamphlets. Far more expensive were the maps and charts showing various parts of the Sea of Hamad and all the surrounding nations. For interest's sake, Sarid asked for material concerning Khepra, but the shopkeeper had no Khepran books and the maps he offered were unsatisfactory, almost all being of Kyadian origin. Cheron eventually bought a map of Dahra and Sarid one on a much smaller scale that showed all of the Sea of Hamad. They were drawn on cloth which could be rolled or wrapped, and though the colored inks were poor in quality a good deal of care appeared to have been taken to assure accurate drawing.

Farther along the street they stopped at a coffee house to sample some of the produce of Kyad. Midas complained, but he was eager enough to eat, and appeared to relish the coffee well enough despite its nonalcoholic nature. By comparison with the army rations, which had now become so familiarly monotonous as to reduce eating to a natural function as tedious as pissing, the food was good and gave them pleasure in the eating. Still farther along the street, only partly out of concern for Midas, they bought bottles of wine from Ksah. They opened one immediately, and began passing it from hand to hand, drinking from the neck.

They did not know how far they had come from the barracks, but when they thought that they were not too far away they turned due south and walked back to the docks, knowing that if they walked along the wharves they would eventually find their way home.

Even in the dead of night, much of the waterfront was busy, with ships being loaded ready to take an early-morning tide and crewmen wandering to and from their berths. All the vessels were sailing ships, and all were made of wood—none of Macaria's ironclad steamships came here. The great majority of the vessels were quite small—less than eighty meters from stem to stern—and had only one mast. They were wide in the belly and must have been very slow. Pirates would

have found them extremely easy prey, but for the most part
they would be too insignificant to bother with.

Eventually, the four troopers found themselves crossing a
dark and empty dock, with warehouses looming on the right.
Cheron was struck by the sudden remoteness of the sounds
that carried across the water from the active wharves. It was
here, taking advantage of the conditions, that the attackers
came for them.

Four men slipped out of the shadows to form a cordon
across the dock, blocking their way. Cheron heard at least
two more move behind, and there might have been as many
as nine in all. There were knives glittering in their hands,
catching the moonlight. All Cheron and his companions were
carrying were the bottles of wine and Sarid's book.

"We want the moneybelts," said one of the men in front.
"Give us, and you live." He spoke in Dahran, but he spoke
that as a foreigner would. He was Kyadian. Probably, all or
most of his companions were also Kyadians, and probably all
from the south as none appeared to know Merkadian—a language the troopers would have been far more likely to understand.

"Cheron," said Sarid, softly—in his own language—"I will
go forward; you guard our rear. Vito, look to the side." He
had no time to give instructions to Midas, for though the
thieves did not know what was being said they readily picked
up the implication that their prey did not intend to cooperate.
They came in, knives poised.

Cheron wheeled, and lashed out at the man who was already leaping for his back. The full bottle of wine that he
was carrying smashed into the attacker's face, splintering with
the force of the blow. The brittle glass shattered easily, and
its shards cut the knife man's face to ribbons. The force of
the blow was enough to break his nose, and he staggered
back as if blinded. Cheron kicked the knife out of another attacker's fist and rammed what was left of the bottle into his
face. The bottle had broken so thoroughly that only the neck
remained, and the edge of the glass did no more than rip out
the man's right cheek, but again the force of the blow was far
greater than anything he had previously encountered, and he
was bowled over by it. Cheron went after him and sent a
vicious kick into his back, just above the hip while he was

turning. The attacker was sent sprawling and screaming, and lost all interest in the battle.

The attack which Sarid had to cope with was far more coordinated, the four men coming in more or less together. However, it was with Sarid that Midas took up his stance. The little man slipped under a groping knife and whipped the toe of his boot into his opponent's groin. The Kyadian collapsed, and Midas collected his knife with alacrity. With the knife in one hand and a half-empty bottle in the other he faced another man, weaving warily around so that his back was well-covered by Vito Talvar.

Sarid, meanwhile, had dropped both the book and his own bottle, and grabbed for the wrists of the men who came to stab him. He was too slow, and one of them slashed his right forearm, though the other's thrust was knocked away. With a cry of rage, he hurled himself forward, cannoning into both of his assailants. A blade raked his forehead above the left eyebrow, but one man spun away, winded, and the other was whirled around as Sarid grabbed the back of his shirt collar. Sarid moved smoothly into one of the holds programmed into his brain and broke the man's neck. He continued to hold up the limp body as a shield, and turned to help Vito Talvar.

Talvar was also cut across the back of one of his hands, but he had put one man out of action with a kick to the inside of the knee, and he was now taunting another to come and attack him. When the would-be assassin saw Sarid join the blond man, though, he decided that it was time to go, and set off at a panic-stricken run. The man Midas was facing— the last of the remainder still to be standing up—followed him with alacrity.

Cheron's two opponents were moaning piteously. Cheron turned to Sarid, seeking guidance, but Sarid was already striding toward the edge of the dock to hurl his useless burden into the black water. Vito Talvar wrenched his remaining assailant to his feet, and dragged him limping to the edge, then kicked him over into the water. He came back to collect the man Midas had kicked in the groin. Midas gave the knife in his hand a speculative stare, but in the end he simply slipped it into his belt, and took a long drink from the bottle in his other hand. He had managed to carry it through the fight without spilling more than a few drops.

Cheron disarmed the two men he had dealt with. The man

nursing his kidney got to his feet and staggered off. Cheron let him go. The man whose face was now a mask of blood was unconscious, and Cheron let him lie.

"The cost of coffee from Kyad," observed Midas, pointing to Sarid's bloodied head. "That's when they saw that you have money. I knew it was a mistake, but no one listens."

"Shut up," said Sarid, brusquely. He began to roll back his sleeve. Then he clenched his fist and stared hard at the long cut, holding his breath. With his left hand he stroked the lacerated flesh. After a moment, he released his breath and nodded. He touched the cut on his forehead, and made a dismissive gesture.

"Under control?" asked Cheron.

"Nothing," he replied.

Vito Talvar hardly needed to withdraw his cuff to see the extent of his own injury. It looked superficial but in fact two of the tendons connecting the fingers to the wrist had been nicked. His face was more white than usual.

"Hold the blood flow!" commanded Sarid. "Take control and suppress the pain. Quite still—concentrate."

Talvar was already trying to do all this, but the words helped by focusing his thoughts. Cheron stood quietly, waiting, while Midas looked on uneasily and took another swig from the bottle.

An Intel could probably have closed the cut and repaired the internal tissue damage within minutes, but it took all Vito Talvar's skill to slow down the firing of the neurons and form the blood clot so as to mask the affected sites from infection. Sarid, whose performance was more assured, would be none the worse for the encounter by the next day, but it might well take Talvar a week to heal completely.

When what could be done had been done, Sarid observed: "My sleeve's slit. I'll have to mend it. Failing to protect Macarian property is dereliction of duty."

Midas went over to peer down at the prostrate form on the quay.

"Pity about the bottle," he said.

It was Midas who explained to the sergeant of the guard at the barracks that Sarid and Talvar had accidentally walked into some fishing tackle on the wharf and had been cut by a gaffe and a large steel hook respectively. The sergeant confiscated the knife that had no right to be in Midas's belt, and promised to report the incident to Donsella exactly as it had happened, taking leave to hope that the overlarge feet of the Macarians had not torn the fishing nets *too* badly. Midas reassured him that they had been old and decrepit nets of foreign manufacture. Back in the bunk room he told a differ-ent story, in which the number of the thieves varied between twenty and thirty. Cheron knew him well enough by now to know that the inconsistency was deliberate, to color the lie and make it more amusing. He let the others believe that the truth might be far more trivial than in fact it was, for the very good reason that he did not want it too widely known that his friends had riches enough to attract robbers in such profusion.

16

The next time that Midas and the Tanagarians had an eve-ning off duty they stayed in the barracks. Midas did not con-sider it necessary to remind them of their duty to participate in the deadly game fought out between the army and the townspeople, possibly because he felt that he and they had made an adequate contribution already, but more probably because he had borrowed enough money from Vito Talvar to buy himself into a gambling game which promised to be more profitable and less risky.

Talvar went to watch him play, and after watching the game for a little while joined in himself. With the exception of Midas and one other Merkadian the players were prepared to bet at atrociously long odds in the belief that if fortune or their various gods were to smile on them they would inevi-tably win, and that if they lost it was the same gods (or pos-sibly others) who were to blame. There were no Macarians in the game, and no one at all—until Talvar joined in—who un-derstood the rudiments of probability theory. Even Midas ap-peared to adhere strictly to the prevailing opinion that

winning was determined entirely by supernatural factors beyond control or strategy, but he clearly had an instinct for
the odds that most of the others lacked. Talvar was sensible
enough to win modestly, and left the more spectacular *coups*
to Midas. The Tanagarian withdrew from the game after an
hour and a half because it was too easy. Once he had mastered the basic strategy it became a purely mechanical operation. Midas paid him back the money he had borrowed from
his winnings, and made an elaborate speech about the gods
favoring heroes and rewarding the brave men who had
battled against Kyadian magicians and cannibals. The little
man did not believe it, of course, but on the other hand he
did not quite *disbelieve* it either. The winnings, after all, were
there in his hand, and who was he to say that one explanation was not as good as another?

In the meantime, Sarid Jerome was working his way slowly
through the Merkadian history which he had bought. It was
not quite history in *his* understanding of the word, but it was
no less interesting in consequence. It was a summary of various oral traditions relating to the past, and was primarily
concerned with picking out the authentic tradition. Its case
was carefully argued, but the value of an argument was always assessed according to the authority of those who em-
braced the views in question, and how closely the views fit in
with other arguments advanced by unimpeachable authorities.
The reasoning was often quite clever, but was used only to
demonstrate that certain beliefs had corollaries inconsistent
with those authorities whose pronouncements could be taken
for granted, while others were not. Because of this, whole
sections of the book became, in Sarid's eyes, quite devoid of
sense, being devoted to the careful demonstration of "truths"
which he knew to be quite blatantly false.

The religious doctrines that lay behind the historical myths
in question belonged to a rather pessimistic sect of the Merkadian faith. The underlying theme of the book was the fall
of man from a state of perfection enjoyed in an imaginary
Golden Age to his present state of utter degradation. It was
obvious that the author considered "man" to be virtually
synonymous with "Merkad," and the various misfortunes suffered by Merkad in its periodic struggle against Macaria were
seen as punishments inflicted by various supernatural agen-
cies.

The text of the book would have seemed much more reasonable and significant had it been possible for Sarid to read in the myth of a lost Golden Age a metaphorical account of the destruction of ancient civilization before the Upheaval. It was, however, difficult to find any supplementary material supporting the notion that the mythology was a metaphorical representation of real events. It seemed that Merkad's mythology, at least in this version, could not be read simply as a garbled version of actual Earth history, but seemed more as if it had been created in an utterly idiosyncratic manner. Its vision of the Golden Age was Arcadian in character, and the envisaged perfection seemed to be a supernatural harmony with nature rather than technological potency. The basic image of the good life was dominated by pseudo-ecological mysticism. The kind of attitude personified by the Macarians —the drive to control the natural world and produce powerful instruments of domination—was stigmatized as inherently diabolical, as well as being condemned as ultimately futile.

Sarid might have been driven to the conclusion that Merkadian mythology had somehow missed out on the ancient world's brief period of civilization and recapitulated instead the oral traditions of *that* world's antiquity—the Eden myth itself—had it not been for the fact that the reasons given for the fall of man were strikingly different from the reasons attributed to the original fall of Adam. In a sense, this was surprising, for Sarid's own "mythology" relating to the destruction of the ancient Earth, handed down complete with appropriate value judgments from the spaceborne generations who had brought the *Marco Polo* to Tanagar, readily invited allegorical representation in terms of too great a desire to feed from the Tree of Knowledge. In Merkadian mythology it was not knowledge—not even the limited knowledge of good and evil—which had been responsible for the original deterioration of the human condition, but rather a loss of faith. What had afflicted the ancestors of the modern Merkadians, according to this author, was a deepening sense of loneliness which had led them to the supposition that there was no authentic order in the universe, no plan in history, no governing force determining the collective future of the race. Instead, the universe had come to seem uncertain and unreliable—a war-torn battleground where the phantom armies still contended in a conflict that had lost its meaning. Alienated

from God by their failure to trust in him, men had lost the
favor of God—thus, ironically, bringing about a state of
affairs not unlike that which had come to seem the more accurate state of reality. The author of the book declared his full
confidence in the belief that man could win back the favor of
God by repenting this heresy and reaffirming faith in the genuine truth, but some of his digressions awakened a suspicion
in Sarid's mind that the author was by no means free of these
kinds of doubt himself. In particular, he brought the full
weight of his sophistry to bear on the question of whether it
might not make better sense tactically for individual men, instead of courting the favor of God himself, to try to win the
favor of less powerful and less reliable spirits which, by virtue of their relative insignificance, might have more time and
energy to spare in looking after human beings. The latter
course he condemned, inevitably, as a wicked heresy, but
there seemed no doubt that he considered it a possible and viable strategy—seeming to imply that he shared (covertly, at
least) the notion of the universe as a place where one could
not be sufficiently certain of the rewards of virtue to steer a
confident course through the sea of everyday moral dilem-
mas.

In summary, Sarid concluded, the Merkadians attributed
their historical misfortunes (which were probably real
enough) to their own inability to believe in the supremacy
and generosity of God. This cast new light on the cynicism
and inventiveness of men like Midas, but had little to say—so
far as Sarid could see—about the way the new world worked,
and how closely its development had paralleled that of the
first civilizations. What Sarid had been hoping for was a better understanding of the present historical predicament of the
world in which he found himself, but in those terms the book
had little to offer. What it did give him was an insight into
the psychology of one of the new races of man, though he
had no idea how far this insight might be generalized.

When he had finished the book, he gave it to Midas, but it
was some time later that he first found an opportunity to ask
the Merkadian about the ideas it contained.

"Much of it is true, of course," he told Sarid. "But not every man can live according to the book. Indeed, that is one
of the things the book claims, so that if everyone *were* able to
do what this man says we should, then the book would no

longer be true, and there would be no reason for doing it. By following my own way, I am helping to maintain the truth."

"That hardly makes sense," said Sarid.

"That is exactly the point," answered Midas. "We Merkadians realize that it is unreasonable and unproductive to *expect* the world to make sense. That is why we are so wise in comparison to the Macarians, who claim that the world makes much more sense than it does."

"Their faith in the order of nature and control achieved through knowledge seems to justify itself well enough in the things they can make," said Sarid.

"It matters not at all," said Midas dismissively. "Machines and better guns are of no *real* importance in the scheme of things. In the end, Macaria will fall and Merkad will rise. Then Merkad, no doubt, will fall again as the people lack the faith to sustain it."

"If the Golden Age is lost in the past," said Sarid, dryly, "there seems little hope for the future. Can things only get worse?"

"What do *I* care?" asked Midas. "The future is of no interest to me except for the years I have to live there, and the fight my sons will endure for Merkad's sake."

"*Have* you any sons?" asked the Tanagarian.

"No," answered the Merkadian cheerfully. "None that I know of."

There seemed no point in continuing the inquisition. If Midas felt any inner need to make his arguments coherent and consistent, it certainly failed to manifest itself in his speeches. He seemed to have long since lost any loyalty to the truth that had been forced into him in infancy, and he did not care enough for introspection to get to know his own motives and feelings in the way that was almost obsessive for a man like Sarid Jerome.

17

Salvador's reputation preceded them along the path which they took. Inevitably, it grew. He was credited with miracles, and was given the hero's role in anecdotes whose character was suspiciously similar to long-standing elements of local folklore. At first, when Teresa heard these tales being whispered, her reaction was one of muted anger: a horror of untruth engendering a righteous fury against those who collaborated in spinning out the fabric of the lie. She did not confide this feeling to Salvador, who would have laughed, both at the nature of the emotion and the fact that she felt it at all. In time, she learned to accept the fruits of her eavesdropping in the right spirit—one of detached amusement. She came to understand that in these men and women there was no greater appetite than hunger for the extraordinary. The poorer and more desperate they were the greater was their longing for miracles. They needed to believe that the universe was continually subject to eruptions of irrationality and random metamorphoses of fortune, for the light of reason had nothing to show them but their own unacceptable hopelessness.

The new prophet gathered about himself an entourage—not by strategy, but simply because he could not get rid of them. They insisted on following him, offering him frequent affirmations of undying loyalty. Their dependence on his good will was so obvious that Salvador would not withhold it; though Teresa often thought that he was not sufficiently eager to do so. In his way, he reveled in adoration. Here, indeed, he found something that Tanagar had never given him—proper appreciation of the rigors of his life-style. On Tanagar, the asceticism of Intellectuals was taken for granted, but here it was a marvel in iteself.

Teresa never grew to love these loyal followers, but she be-

gan to appreciate that there were advantages in their presence
when they began to organize such matters as the food supply,
and began to make sure that the pressure on Salvador's time
and energy did not become unreasonable. Some of them, undoubtedly, made a certain amount of money taking bribes to
arrange interviews with the healer, but they seemed to be neither unreasonable nor brutal in their methods. They took
money only from those who could pay, added most of it to
the collective purse, and turned away no one who was in genuine need. When their actions did create a sense of grievance
they settled the matter with moderate efficiency—when they
were violent, they were neatly and clinically violent. How it
was that this kind of expertise came so readily upon men
whose previous work had been menial Teresa could not quite
understand, but she realized that Merkad was a country
where sixpenny messiahs thrived, and where "everyone"
knew, at least to some extent, what kind of behavior was expected of him and his disciples. However vague it might be
there was nevertheless a script with which the people they
met were already familiar. The only ones who were completely ignorant of it were Salvador and Teresa, but it was
flexible enough to carry them without their having to make
any substantial contribution beyond the obvious.

Salvador had been a miracle worker for more than ten
days before anyone tried to assassinate him, and the assassin
became the first man to die as a result of entangling his affairs with those of the healer. One of the loyal followers, a
man named Mihiel, took a bullet in the thigh while disarming
the man, and his prestige was so wonderfully advanced that
he became thereafter a chief among the disciples. Salvador
removed the bullet, operating with the aid of a local anesthetic, and made sure the wound would stay free of infection.
Mihiel was soon able to walk again, and so impressed Salvador with his strength of will that Salvador began teaching
him the elements of self-control. Mihiel was twenty years too
old for the teaching to have any powerful effect on the integrity of body and mind, but he soon learned to cultivate a
light trance state and claimed some success with biofeedback
intervention in the nervous and hormonal systems.

At first, Salvador could not understand why anyone should
want to kill him, and could only suppose that he or his followers had unwittingly given the man cause for bitter resent-

ment. However, Mihiel was eventually able to explain that at least some Merkadians believed in the transfer of supernatural virtue, either by a kind of "psychic osmosis" by which Mihiel and the other disciples would gradually absorb some of Salvador's healing power, or by a process of "charismatic usurpation" by which a man could take on some of the traits of someone he had killed. Mihiel apparently considered that the assassin had been extremely antisocial in his design, but he could also see the purpose in his action. The Merkadian explained that the assassin would probably have inherited only such power as would free himself from disease, and not the power to cure others. What the assassin had tried to do was evil because it was selfish, but it was not an essentially stupid or irrational act.

Knowing that Mihiel thought along these lines made Teresa distinctly uneasy, but Salvador seemed unworried by the fact that he might well become a target again.

One thing that the followers found distinctly odd about Salvador—the one point where his failure to comply with the stereotype actually became puzzling in their eyes—was his reluctance to sermonize. He made no statements concerning the relationship of God and man, nor was he given to repeating and reinforcing moral dogmas. When asked questions about doctrine (often in the interests of recruiting his opinion to one side or the other in a sectarian dispute) he would evade them, and was frequently dismissive to the point of manifest heresy. He was, in fact, so reluctant to mention God that some of his followers took to speaking of him as the man who healed "by the name of the unnamed God"—a neat and rather ingenious circumlocution. Though Salvador was not at first aware of the fact, he was rather fortunate that he had taken up his trade in Merkad, among the people of the lost faith, where his attitude was far more acceptable than it would have been in a nation as jealous of its deity as Macaria.

Inevitably, they met other priests, both itinerant and settled. The former offered no challenge, and seemed quite uninterested in communication. None of them joined Salvador's retinue, or exhibited any desire to do so. Mihiel spoke to one or two of them, and ordered his compatriots to give them food and money. Diplomatic relations were not so easy, however, with resident priests who had charge of the spiritual welfare of particular settlements (and who depended on the settlements for their own subsistence). In a small town called Zedad Salvador's followers arrived somewhat in the manner of a circus, partly because three men and a woman from the town had traveled overland in search of the preacher and were now coming home as his disciples. The sick people of the town, encouraged by the involvement of their neighbors, rushed to Salvador's tent (he had acquired sufficient apparatus to make his traveling more comfortable) with more than the usual enthusiasm. The local priest, though he said nothing that was obviously hostile, began to drop hints about false prophets, and began rumor-mongering on the subject of sorcery.

Mihiel brought this problem not to Salvador but to Teresa, for reasons she could not quite fathom. Either he did not want to trouble the prophet with such a problem or he considered that it was Teresa's duty to deal with such affairs. After some discussion, Mihiel suggested that the best solution might be for Salvador to pray in the church supervised by the local priest, and to perform some kind of ritual transferring a little of his power to its stones. If the priest were to react by denouncing Salvador as a false prophet, he would be sacrificing a useful spiritual investment. Teresa put the matter to Salvador, and after a show of reluctance he agreed to do it. He carried off the performance well—so well that Teresa was impressed by the relish he took in playing his role.

"You were obviously born out of place," she told him that night. "This is your true identity—the man who works miracles in the name of the unnamed God. You're already well on your way to becoming a cult. You could become a whole religion—the founding father of a new system of thought. Whatever you expected Jerome and the Hedonists to do, you could do a hundred times more effectively. The failure of the experiment has put you into a unique position. . . . a position far more powerful than anything envisaged in the original experimental design. If you were to put your heart and soul into it, you could become the new world's Christ, or its Muhammad."

She was not entirely serious in saying it, but it was not just mockery. In a curious sense, she felt as though she were *tempting* him.

"What would happen to you?" he asked innocently.

"You could tell me where the base is. I'd make it on my own, inform the personnel there what you intended to do, and help them keep track of you."

"I couldn't possibly let you cross Macaria alone. It would be too dangerous."

"Because I'm a woman?"

"Because you're a Pragmatist. You act too quickly for your own good, and you give far too much weight to immediate objectives rather than long-range goals. Together, we balance one another well enough. Separated, we'd find things difficult."

She frowned, not knowing whether he meant what he said or whether he was simply playing with her.

"I suppose that it has occurred to you," she said, "that your loyal disciples aren't going to take too kindly to your deserting them. At present, we're heading north with a lot of Merkad in front of us. What happens when we get near to the coast, and you want to bid them a fond farewell?"

"Do you think I can't handle that?" asked Salvador. "I think you may be misunderstanding the kind of hopes they entertain. Miracle workers are essentially ephemeral. They come and they go. It has to be that way, in order that their reputations can be sustained. If they were around for too long, people would begin to notice that they hadn't really *achieved* very much. Then again, Mihiel is almost ready to take over his own independent role."

"As Simon Peter to your Christ? I hadn't considered, of course, that you might have *already* laid the foundations of a new religion."

Salvador shook his head. "If there's to be a new cult," he said, "it won't be of my making, even if I remain its figurehead. Religious beliefs may have far more power to determine how people live than scientific ones, but their effect on the course of history is far less than appearances might suggest. What alters the course of history is discovery and technology. If any man is to make a substantial contribution to the future of this new civilization then he must do it through Macaria, not Merkad. Messiahs, in the long run, have little to contribute to the pattern of progress, precisely because an essential part of progress is winning freedom from the prison of their arbitrary ideas. The kind of stable society that results from religious tyranny is a fake, because it depends on deception and faith. Genuine stability, of the kind Tanagar discovered, depends on knowledge and doubt. In the long run, all religious tyrannies fail, because they have no armor against skepticism and no conclusive arguments by which to confound opposing ideas. You can't win a war of ideas simply by burning heretics. If I wanted to take the place of Sarid Jerome in my experiment in history, this would be the last place I'd start. Fortunately, I don't have the slightest interest in taking his place, and it would be an unnecessary complication if I did. Sarid Jerome, as far as we know, is still able to take his own place as the focal point of the project, albeit with much less assistance than I had planned to provide him with. He's a resourceful man—I don't think the game's lost yet."

"We haven't heard anything of him."

"Why should we? Merkad's a large nation. In any case, my presumption was that he would settle in Dahra. It will be much easier for him to establish an identity there, and to become powerful. In Dahra, he's a foreigner in a country that's effectively run and owned by foreigners. There's room for him to work there that would be difficult to find in Macaria. He needs time to secure an economic base, and time to acquire the trappings of what passes for scholarship in this world. He won't be ready to go to Macaria for twenty years—but when he does go, he'll have the equipment he needs to make a difference to the rate at which the indigenous scholars are assimilating the knowledge of the ancient world. We'll hear nothing of Sarid Jerome for a long time yet."

"And suppose *he* hears something of *us*? That could interfere with your careful planning, couldn't it?"

Salvador shrugged. "What could he hear of us? He might hear about a new Merkadian prophet, but even that's unlikely, in that our reputation hardly extends beyond the rural areas. There's a very strong possibility that he doesn't know that the ship crashed, and even if he does know it, he must assume that you and I are dead. You're inventing problems to stir your own adrenalin. Worry is a bad habit—it may have some instrumental value to primitives like these Merkadians, but it's a poor tool for Tangarians. Even Pragmatists."

"Thank you," she said. "I'll remember."

"Don't be too impatient," he told her. "We'll get to the coast, eventually. Then we'll cross the land bridge—or take an illegal trip in a small fishing boat. Then we cross Macaria. It's all going to take time. There's no way to hurry it, at least while we maintain our present roles. Wherever we are, we have to put safety ahead of speed. We'll get there in the end."

"As long as you're sure that our immediate and only objective is to reach the base," she said, in reply. "I only worry about one thing, and that's being entangled in some crazy Intel game. I don't want you to lose yourself in your own experiment, if it means losing me too. All you have to do is tell me—I can make it on my own, if I have to."

He laughed, and said: "You won't have to. Depend on that."

18

The night before they were due to embark, all of Donsella ti Ria's company were given leave. They wandered into the city for a final taste of civilization, and to make the most of it they made their way in small groups to the central district, which lay some distance to the west of the barracks. Midas, as usual, attached himself to the Tanagarians, but they no longer had any need to suspect his motives. He was no longer a parasite since he discovered his source of easy income. He had money enough to get quite extravagantly drunk, and this seemed to be his intention. For once his errant instincts did not betray him and he was able to lead them to a house of entertainment considerably more salubrious than those which huddled around the barracks whose proprietors were nevertheless willing to accommodate soldiers of Macaria provided that they had money. He found, however, that his companions were less than wholly devoted to the business at hand.

"This is your last opportunity for a long time," he reminded them. "In the settlements, there will be nothing to spend your money on but the essentials of life. This is your last chance to buy a little luxury, and you would be well advised to take it. Luxury is an undervalued commodity, despite the fact that it is so expensive."

"I can't help feeling," said Vito Talvar, "that there's a hint of 'Eat, drink, and be merry, for tomorrow we die' about this occasion. I have nothing against luxury, but I resent the idea that the next few hours might represent a lifetime's ration."

"What Midas is trying to point out," said Cheron, "is that the alternative might be to go without a ration altogether. We may all return here in six months—but we may not."

"For someone who understands it so well," replied Talvar, "you're remarkably restrained in your own conduct. What about you, Sarid? Are you still planning furiously away, pretending to be an Intel so successfully that you never actually manage to lift a finger?"

"If you have any plans for immediate and effective action," suggested Sarid, "then put them forward. If not, then take the advice you're being offered from all sides. Remember your duty as a Hedonist."

"The trouble with foreigners," said Midas, "is that they have no understanding of life. I know that you have spent much of your lives in the frozen forests of the far north, that you have no gods to appeal to for comfort, and that you come from a race which eats the children of men for amusement, but you must surely be under some terrible curse that makes you mad and perpetually angry. Your faces are like stone, and your flesh too, for you wipe away wounds with your shirt-sleeves, but your stomachs must be leather sacks full of jagged stones. I have tried to educate you out of your barbarian ways, but I am on the verge of despair. If it were not for my sense of duty I would wash my hands of you."

"You're too kind," murmured Sarid sarcastically. "If only you knew the magnitude of the curse that has been laid upon us. . . ." He left the end of the sentence dangling, but Midas was too old a hand to be drawn.

"You do not have to tell me," said the Merkadian. "I am not a dog cast out by donkeys to desert my friends because they have demons for enemies. Do I not already know that you are half-demon yourselves, and probably grew so large by eating the flesh of human children—which is probably the way that Mondo grew also? I know that you come from a world where there is no color, for everything is black or white, but I wish you were not quite so black and white yourselves. You are in my world now, and you should copy me in learning how to live in it."

"We must be making progress," said Cheron. "I can remember the time when we were all demon. Now it is only half. But we have never tasted human flesh and we have no demons for enemies."

Midas leaned across the table, and said in a confidential whisper: "There are no demons, my friend. Not one, in the whole world. But the world behaves as if there were, and so do you."

His eyes challenged the Tanagarians, their penetrating gaze sliding from one to another.

"You're a clever man, Midas," said Cheron. "I think that what you say is true." It was an awkward sentiment, awkwardly voiced, but Cheron was sincere.

"I will tell you a secret," said Midas. "We will not die in the hot land across the sea. The others may die, but we will not. The magic of the forest demons will hurt our fellow men, but it will not hurt us. There is not a man among them who does not carry an amulet or a bag of charms, and they do not realize that they make themselves victims by doing so. A man who puts his faith in charms must admit that they may be overwhelmed by other charms. The demons of the forest have powerful magic and men like Qapel and Mondo will begin to fear that magic the moment they begin to sweat in the forest. But you and I know that the forces of nature are not so easily controlled. The demons, or whatever exists in their place, are not biddable. We know that of ourselves, and of our enemies too. We must not speak it too loudly, because it is a truth that needs concealment in order to flourish, but it is so. We are all strong now, and we will be strong in the forest. We will live. There is no need to be afraid . . . but if fear is in you, expel it now. Enjoy it, and throw it away. It will be no use to you tomorrow."

Cheron stared at him, not knowing whether it was simply one more of Midas's speeches, to be contradicted in his next statement and by the next in its turn, or whether there really was a fugitive sincerity lurking deep in the man's complex personality, exposing itself for momentary inspection. Either way, there was a certain amount of sense in what the Merkadian said.

Midas nodded, apparently satisfied by the silence.

"Mondo will die," he added softly. "It is a pity, but it is true. He is a bad man—a worse man than I by far, but it is still a pity. The Macarians picked him because he could fight, but the ability to fight is only one small part of the price of survival."

"Why were you in jail in Sau?" asked Sarid Jerome.

Midas spread his arms wide. "It was not my fault," he said, his voice resuming its normal tone. "It was what any man would have done—I was made mad by rage and anguish. It was a crime of passion, and only prejudice against a foreigner made them give me such a sentence."

"Where we come from," said Sarid, "it is crimes of passion which are most heavily punished. A man might go free if he could show that he killed for a purpose, and that having achieved his object he would be unlikely ever to kill again. He would be forced to make reparation, but he would not be imprisoned. To give way to anger or anguish would be different, for that kind of failure might be repeated again and again and again."

Midas laughed in mock delight. "What can you expect from barbarians?" he asked. "No wonder you eat your own children. You are so very fortunate to know me, and to have the opportunity of learning how it is that a civilized man behaves!"

The Merkadian proceeded to give a demonstration of civilized behavior that made the Tanagarians wonder whether they could ever aspire to such heights of achievement. In his enthusiasm, he exceeded his capacity for pleasure before his schemes got past their earliest stage, and he passed out at the table.

"Should we take him back?" asked Cheron.

"Hardly," said Sarid. "He would be disappointed in himself, and even more disappointed in us. I think he would prefer that we did his pleasure-seeking for him. For me, of course, it would be a sacrifice, but I am surprised by *your* lack of enthusiasm."

"Somehow," said Vito Talvar, "it is not the same. The joys of intoxication depend far more on the context than on the process. I would not care to trust the euphorics that are on sale hereabouts, and I doubt if the women have the skill in sexual performance that Cheron and I would require. You, Sarid, would appreciate none of this, but you must remember that *we* are connoisseurs of Hedonism, not insensitive jeckles blowing the inhibitions out of our skulls. It's you that should be able to make yourself at home here, not us. I dare say that we could find you a mask if we were to try. Then *your* opportunity would be complete."

The only sign of anger that Sarid permitted his face to show was a slight curling of the lip. He opened his mouth to reply, but Cheron interrupted him by banging his glass down hard on the table. Having claimed their attention, he said: "It would be futile to maintain the pretense that we are still what we once were. It is not inherent in human nature that some men should be Pragmatists and some Hedonists, and that some Pragmatists should occasionally lapse from their ordinary conduct. Look around you now, and see if you can point to any man here and say: 'That is a Prag' or 'That is a sensual.' The division of men into these types is a social convenience which has meaning only in the society which generated it. We are on the Motherworld now, and we are simply men. There is nothing absurd, *here*, in the claim that Midas made to be called a civilized man. If we persist in the delusion that we can maintain our old identities in such a vastly changed world then we are mad—as, indeed, we will seem to its inhabitants."

Sarid hesitated a moment, and then nodded. "You're right," he said. "We're a long way from Tanagar, and we're out of Salvador's experiment too. It's clear enough now why he brought us here, and it's equally clear that his plans went awry the moment we made contact with another human being. He didn't anticipate our being drafted into the army. He expected that we could be free in Dahra to do whatever we wanted to. He was wrong—the Motherworld has taken us over and is using us as it will. We have to adapt to that."

He put down his own glass, and rose to his feet without another word. He went to the far side of the room, where groups of prostitutes were seated, laughing and talking. He approached one such group, interrupted the conversation, and in the space of five minutes he disappeared into a warren of corridors at the back of the hall, conducted by one of the girls.

Vito Talvar looked positively aghast. Cheron could easily understand why. The suppression and control of sexual arousal was one of the most fundamental techniques learned by all Tanagarians in youth. Full conscious control of such arousal was held to be a prerequisite of proper sexual relations. If there was one thing more than any other which set the Tanagarians apart from their fellow soldiers it was this most simple of things. The inability of Motherworld men to control their erections was, to the Tanagarians, both absurd and unhealthy—a sign of childishness or depravity. The strategies adopted by the whores to cater to this situation—the use of cosmetics and perfumes to construct a shabby and arbitrary vocabulary of signals—seemed to Cheron and the others to be rather revolting. The absence in the behavior of Earth women of the conventions which regulated sexual conduct on Tanagar redoubled the implicit unattractiveness of the prospect of intercourse with them.

Cheron's immediate reaction to Sarid's action was—as he realized almost immediately—precisely the same as Talvar's. It could only appear to be a particularly degraded form of jeckling. Talvar remained with that belief, however, while Cheron quickly abandoned it in favor of an attempt to see the gesture as it really was: a kind of renunciation of the cultural legacy of Tanagar, and an acceptance of Earthly identity.

The moment he saw things that way, he realized that the logical course for him to follow was an identical one, but of course he hesitated.

It's all right for a Prag, he found himself thinking. *A man of purpose and determination. But what about a poor weak sensual, who can only think of sex in terms of pleasure?*

He knew as he sat still, staring at the table, that Vito Talvar would stay exactly where he was. Nothing would persuade him that anything at all could be achieved by buying the favors of a Dahran whore—or, indeed, establishing any kind of sexual relationship with any other man or woman of Earth. His Hedonism was devout enough to keep him celibate for the rest of his life.

It's too much all at once, thought Cheron. *For all my good intentions, I have to take such things slowly. I can't adopt the crazy ways of the Motherworld just like that. It takes time.*

Such doubts, however, conflicted with a genuine admiration for Sarid's gesture, and the ironic knowledge that both he and Vito Talvar had been completely upstaged.

He poured himself a drink from the almost-empty bottle, and swallowed it in a single draught. The way it seized his throat brought tears to his eyes.

He stood up and said: "Look after Midas. I daresay I won't be long."

After such a declaration, there could be no turning back.

19

The room to which the whore conducted Cheron was just a tiny cubicle containing a bed with a thick, soft mattress, a stool, and a small table. There were two ragged cushions stood on end on the tabletop, resting against the whitewashed plaster of the back wall. There was also a douching apparatus. The room was saturated by the odor of perfume, but underneath the sickliness there was a sharper smell of semen.

The girl was probably no more than sixteen or seventeen. She was small, even by the standards of Dahra. Her skin was a pleasant, even brown, and she had wisely refrained from altering her complexion to make it seem lighter. Her hair was long and glossy. The main reason he had selected her was because her teeth were white and healthy.

She disrobed with practiced ease and lay down, spreading her legs. She kept her gaze on his face while he undressed, but said nothing at all, perhaps assuming that he would not understand her language. Cheron was slow in removing his trousers, but she did not seem impatient.

He was surprised to find that she put on a show of being excited, though she switched it on so abruptly that he knew it for a much-rehearsed performance. He knew that if he closed his eyes he could imagine himself elsewhere, operating under very different circumstances, but he felt that to do so would somehow be cheating. He kept his eyes open, and tried to fix everything in his consciousness, seeking some kind of authentic aesthetic response in the novelty of the situation and its exotic quality.

Killing he had found easy, but he had been prepared for that. This he found alien, but he was relieved when he discovered that it was, in fact, possible. In response to her urging he brought himself to orgasm quickly, and withdrew immediately. She had taken her eyes away from his face now, and she did not look at him again. He left the room, having nothing else to say or do. He had paid her, of course, in advance.

He walked steadily back to his table. His emotions were mixed, but he had the satisfaction of knowing that he was presenting the outward appearance of being completely in control.

Sarid had not yet returned. Apparently, he was taking the whole thing more seriously.

For several seconds, Talvar doubted that the implications of what he had seen were true. Cheron watched the blond man toy with the idea that it had all been a joke. Then, he saw Talvar abandon that hopeful pretense.

"I don't understand," said Talvar. "I just don't see why."

"It was necessary," said Cheron.

"Did you enjoy it?"

"No. The pleasure they derive from it isn't the same as the pleasure we derive from it. It means something very different."

"Yes," said Talvar. "I know."

"I didn't do it for pleasure," said Cheron. "That wasn't the reason. I did it for a purpose. I'm a different kind of man from Midas, and I always will be. I can't change the abilities I have no matter how far I go in acquiring new ones. But I live in Midas's world."

"So do I," the blond man said, "but if I lived in a cave I'd be a man living in a cave. I wouldn't feel it incumbent upon me to hang upside down by my toes while I slept because the cave was inhabited by bats."

"Nor would I," said Cheron. "But we're not living in a cave. We're living in a society of men. There's all the difference in the world."

"Not to me," said Vito Talvar. "Nothing in the world is going to turn me into something like *that*." Significantly, though, it was not at Midas that he pointed but another soldier at another table.

Cheron saw Sarid approaching then, and broke off the exchange by turning to face him. He noticed that another man was approaching too—the Khepran Baya-undi. Sarid's path and that of the black man intersected a few strides from the table, and the two arrived together, though Sarid seemed slightly surprised to find himself so suddenly accompanied.

"What do you want?" he asked, a little more brusquely than was necessary.

Baya-undi ignored the impoliteness, and said: "It is necessary that I speak with you."

Sarid shrugged, and indicated that Baya-undi should take the chair which he had previously used. He found himself another one and brought it to the table.

Once Sarid was seated Baya-undi assumed a conspiratorial air and said: "Tomorrow we set sail from the main harbor. It is likely that we will never return."

"I don't know," said Sarid, reasonably. "Things in the Bela settlements can't be as bad as rumor paints them. If they were, the Macarians would be in full retreat, not sending for a few thousand reinforcements."

"You owe no more allegiance to Macaria than I do," said Baya-undi, unperturbed by the contradiction.

"True," said Sarid.

"We do not have to take that ship," said the black man. "There is another that will take us. To Kyad, and far along the coast. From Kyad, it would not be too difficult to reach Khepra."

"Three things occur to me," said Sarid levelly. "Firstly, the Macarians have a reputation for pursuing deserters, and their ships are far faster than any Kyadian vessel. Secondly, I have no good reason for putting my trust in Kyadian seamen, and have already encountered some who have made me suspicious of the species. Thirdly, I do not want to go to Khepra."

"The Macarians cannot search every ship that leaves Asdar," said Baya-undi. "It would be absurd of them to try. The men of Kyad are trustworthy enough, if you know how to deal with them, which I do. And Khepra, believe me, is the one place on Earth that is worth living in. It is the only truly civilized nation."

"We've heard the last part before," said Vito Talvar. "I think Sarid might be a little hasty. If the alternative is between the Bela and Khepra, *I* might want to go to Khepra. But I share his anxieties about those who might be our hosts for the voyage."

Sarid did not show his displeasure, and Baya-undi took this, incorrectly, as a sign of irresolution. He tried to move even closer, his elbows creeping across the table. "If it were only one man," he said, "I would not trust them either. One deserter makes easy prey. But a vessel such as the one I have in mind does not carry a large crew. If their passengers were four strong men, armed with good weapons, the passengers would have little to fear."

"Except poison," said Vito Talvar. "But aren't you forgetting that we don't have our weapons?"

"We must go back to the barracks this evening, and slip out over the wall—with our guns—before dawn. It can be done. I have studied the problem."

Talvar opened his mouth to speak again, but Sarid Jerome silenced him with a gesture.

"I have studied the problem too," he said. "We owe Macaria nothing, as you have suggested. If desertion offered us a way out of our predicament, we might take it. I do not think that we would need your help, even to act as a go-between to fix us a passage on a Kyadian ship. However, desertion seems to me to be a very poor risk. It offers a greater chance of getting killed than going to the Bela, and even if we got away, we would have to go somewhere like Khepra. I do not want to go to Khepra."

"In Khepra you would not have to fight. Khepra is a nation where men may live peacefully."

"I wonder why you ever left it," said Sarid, amicably. "I wonder why a man such as you—obviously a man of means and intelligence—should leave the last outpost of civilization to visit a place like Dahra."

Baya-undi shrugged. "Sometimes," he said, " a man's duty takes him far from home. Khepra knows that she is not alone in the world. She has her traders. It is necessary that she should acquaint herself with the way of things in the greater world."

"To put it another way," said Sarid, "you were a spy, collecting information on Macaria's activities."

The black man made a gesture of injured innocence. "I sought to know nothing that is secret. I wished to know only what any street-trader in Sau would know. The Macarians had no possible cause to object to my investigations. They seized me illegally. They seized you also; I know it. We would all like to return home, but if you cannot return home, why not go to a place where you will be received as honored guests rather than a place where you are sent to fight savages for an alien power?"

"It all depends," said Sarid, "on one's long-range plans. We will not be in the army all our lives. And the army is one way by which a man—even a foreigner—might seek to advance himself in Macarian society. Ultimately, *our* destiny is to go to Macaria. I do not know which is the one authentic kind of civilization, but I know which kind I find most attractive. The future of this world belongs to Macaria and to no one else. I cannot see any way that desertion to Khepra would fit in with our plans. That is all there is to say."

Baya-undi looked at Cheron, and then at Vito Talvar. "Does this man speak for you all?" he asked, with a contemptuous flick of the finger in Sarid's direction.

Talvar hesitated, but then said: "He does."

The black man did not bother to get a second opinion from Cheron Felix. "Well then," he said. "It is settled. We go to the Bela. I wish that I could find the prospect as inviting as you seem to do."

"No one will interfere with *your* plans," said Sarid quietly. "Go to Khepra, if that is what you want."

Baya-undi arched an eyebrow. "Alone?" he said. "I would not be so foolish. Four men might do it. One cannot."

"You might find other partners," observed Cheron.

The Khepran laughed. "It would be dangerous enough to take ship with Kyadian cutthroats. It would be twice as dangerous to take Merkadian cutthroats as allies. You are the only men I would trust."

"That seems very generous," said Sarid, "considering that we are as different from you as any men in the world."

"You may be white giants from the snowlands," said Baya-undi, "but you are civilized men. In your hearts, that is. You do not act like barbarians and you do not think like bar-

barians. I have seen this. There is something in you that re-
minds me just a little of the men of my homeland. If your
skins were black I would take you for members of a noble
house. I could count you as friends, and that is something I
could say to no other white man or brown man in the
world."

"That's quite a compliment," said Vito Talvar, breaking
the silence which formed because Sarid appeared to be giving
the statement very careful thought.

"Yes it is," agreed Baya-undi. "It certainly is."

20

Teresa Janeat unfolded the sketch map on the groundsheet
and stabbed a finger at the region of wilderness to the west of
the blot that was Naryn, the third city of Merkad.

"We're on the southern fringe of it," she said. "The desert
to the north is virtually uninhabited, and won't be easy to
cross, but a straight route will bring us to the fishing ports on
the bitter sea. The alternative is to skirt Naryn and head up
toward the land bridge. The difficulty there is that the region
between Naryn and Ophidion is densely populated and considerably richer than the regions we've traversed so far. If we
could abandon our present identities, that's the way I'd
choose. That's the way our followers want us to go *in* our
present identities—either that or to the east. This is the moment of decision."

"It shouldn't be too hard for us to present our loyal followers with a reason for our going on into the desert—alone,"
said Salvador.

"Suppose it doesn't work?" asked Teresa.

"It will," replied the Intellectual.

"You'd better put that to the test some time within the
next twenty-four hours," said Teresa dryly. "We've gathered
too large a crowd here already. They've been coming from

Naryn itself. That's too much attention for us to attract.
There's likely to be trouble. We could try slipping away in the
early hours instead."

"I don't think so," replied Salvador.

"There's a precedent, of course," said the woman. "Not
one that *they* know about, but one I'm sure you'll have in
mind. Christ went into the wilderness for forty days and forty
nights."

"We won't be there for quite that long," Salvador assured
her.

"As long as we remember to beware of temptation," she
answered. He smiled, not bothering to retaliate, accepting the
fact that it was a declaration of submission to his plans.

Teresa folded the map and slipped it into a goatskin wallet
by the side of her pillow. She stepped outside into the gathering twilight, breathing deeply. The breeze, blowing from the
south, was strong enough to feel cool on her skin. The disciples were stacking bundles of twigs, ready to start the fires
that would burn all night, around which the faithful would lie
down to sleep. Her gaze traveled past the crowd, most of
whom were unfamiliar to her. Deliberately, she did not meet
the hundreds of inquiring eyes that fixed upon her as she
emerged from the tent. She could not abide the eagerness of
the miracle-hungry stares. Instead she looked out across derelict plain, toward Naryn, which sheltered several kilometers
beyond the horizon. There were still travelers picking their
way across country, in ones and twos. If they continued to
arrive through the night—and she knew no reason why they
should not—there might be a thousand people gathered
around the campfires by morning.

It was too many; *far* too many.

Something far away on the horizon caught her eyes, and
she squinted, trying to make it clearer.

It was a cloud of dust. She knew that it was not raised by
sandaled feet.

She ducked quickly back into the tent. "Salvador!" she said
urgently. "Mounted men—a good many of them."

The Intellectual looked up, his face set like mahogany.
"From Naryn?" he asked.

She frowned. "Not quite the right direction," she said.
"From the west, all right, but from somewhat south of
Naryn, unless they've followed a curved route."

He stood up, and came with her to the flap of the tent. He lifted it, and crouched to peer through, but did not step outside. The angle did not permit him to see anything. Teresa called Mihiel, and pointed out the approaching riders.

"Who are they?" she demanded.

The limping man shook his head. "Wait and see," he said uneasily.

"Get our things together," murmured Salvador, in Tanagarian. "And get out the dark clothes you acquired. We may need them. Make them up into bundles." To Mihiel, in Merkadian, he said: "If there is to be trouble, do not take too many risks. We may need help, but I want no one to be hurt on our account."

Teresa had already gone past him into the tent, but when she heard what he said to Mihiel she turned.

"What's the point of that?" she asked.

"I meant exactly what I said," Salvador told her. "If the Macarians are coming, I don't want a pitched battle—but we may need help to secure our escape. We can't afford to be taken."

She said nothing, but got to work gathering together the things they would need if they had to run. Salvador made not the slightest sound, but stood by the tent flap waiting for the riders to come within sight.

When she joined him again, he said: "They're not Macarians."

Most of the riders halted beyond the limits of the area marked out by Salvador's followers. Only three urged their mounts to thread a winding path through the silent crowd. The disciples watched the riders carefully. No one was asleep, and the signs of exhaustion were no longer evident on their faces.

Salvador finally emerged from the tent, to stand before it in the same bloodstained robe that he had worn when he carried Teresa Janeat into the small village near the border with the Kezula. The hem came only halfway down the thigh, leaving most of his long legs bare.

The leading rider dismounted twelve meters away, and held out his arms in greeting. His belt held both a dagger and a pistol, and around his shoulder was a bandolier filled with rifle cartridges, designed for the Macarian weapon that rested in a holster slung from his saddle. He was big by the standards of his people, but not nearly so tall as Salvador. His two companions, who remained on their horses, were also heavily armed.

"I greet you," said the leader. "I am Daran, though my men call me by the name Machado. I am the most devoted of your followers. Perhaps you have heard of me?"

While he made this speech the man was approaching, and when he finished he was close enough to try to enfold Salvador in a fond embrace. Salvador, however, stayed this gesture of brotherly affection by extending his arm.

"I do not know you," said Salvador.

"No matter," said the other. "I have come to save your life, and help you in your holy work."

The fires were being lighted now as the twilight dwindled and darkness descended. The wind seemed to have become noticeably cooler.

"To save my life?" asked Salvador. His voice was confident, and he was projecting it well. Almost everyone in the camp could hear what was being said, but while Machado seemed to be shouting Salvador did not.

"There have been riots in Naryn," said Machado. "The people of Merkad took to the streets to demonstrate their feelings for the Macarian overlords and their traitorous collaborators. They called your name in every street of the city. There has been an assassination in Zedad, and there too your name is called. I have brought my men to guard you on the road to Naryn. Your followers await you there in their thousands. With God's help, you and I might take the city this night."

"How many men do you have?" asked Salvador evenly.

"I have forty here," Machado announced, "but I have ten thousand or more in Naryn who will come to you if you ride beside me."

"I think you are an outlaw," said Salvador. "I think that you are the chief of an army of thieves. Why should I lead you to loot Naryn?"

Machado's expression, which had been radiating good will, suddenly went bleak. "We are freedom fighters," he declared, loudly. "Loyal soldiers of Merkad. Certainly we are outlaws, because Merkad is ruled by the forces of Macaria, and Macaria makes the law. Only traitors to Merkad hold to that law, and it is that law which has reduced the honest men

gathered here to wretchedness and desperation. You love
them, and so do I—we are one, though you are a holy man
and I am a warrior. Your followers in Naryn are crying out
for you. If you refuse to go to them, they will be lost. Will
these men gathered here permit this? It is *their* will that demands that you should ride, and they will be proud to follow,
no matter how tired they may be. Am I not right?"

His voice had risen in a crescendo, and as he spoke the final words he turned to the crowd, fully two-thirds of whom
must have set out from Naryn during the day. Several voices
made enthusiastic reply, and there was a ragged echo of assent. Many of those who remained silent must have felt themselves to be in a tiny minority.

"I am a healer and a holy man," said Salvador. "I do not
make war. I have no followers among men who carry guns.
It is nearly time for me to go away, to leave this land forever. My road does not lead to Naryn, and neither should
yours. Go back to the hills in the southwest, and leave me to
do *my* work."

The trouble is, thought Teresa as she watched, *that the
prophets of Merkad are not noted for counsels of peace.*

"You are a holy man," replied Machado, "but I am also a
holy man, in my way. I carry a gun, but a gun which does
the work of the true God. Though many others have turned
away, my faith remains strong, and I will fight for that faith
against the false God of Macaria. No true holy man could do
otherwise. You are a strong man, my friend, and I offer *you*
the gun, to use against the false God and his armies. Will you
do it?"

"I will not," said Salvador flatly.

There was murmuring in the crowd now that would not die
down.

"You fool," muttered Teresa. "You're losing them. He
knows what he's about better than you do."

Salvador must have heard the words, but he ignored them.
He stretched out a bony hand toward his challenger.

"I will not take your gun," he said, "but will you give me
your knife?"

Machado hesitated for a moment, and then took the dagger from his belt and handed it over. Its blade was some
twenty centimeters long and three wide, though it tapered

toward the point. It was sharpened along each edge, and was perhaps half a centimeter thick at the rib.

Salvador held it up, so that it caught the firelight. There was still enough light in the gathering dusk for the crowd to know what it was.

"I am a holy man," said Salvador. "You say that you, too, are a man of God. I say that you are a liar. I think that we should put the matter to the test. We will see who can demonstrate his godliness."

Salvador pulled back the tattered sleeve of his robe, exposing the length of his left arm. Slowly, he drew the point of the knife along it, from the wrist to the elbow, drawing a long trail of blood. Then he reversed the knife and retraced the cut with the hilt. He took a cloth from his pocket, and wiped away the blood. Then he extended the arm to Machado.

"Am I not healed?" he asked.

Machado, fearing an invitation to do likewise, said: "It is a trick."

"He says that it is a trick," said Salvador clearly. "He says that I have no healing power. He says that I am not a holy man."

Machado saw the danger, and opened his mouth to change the ground of his argument. Salvador did not give him the chance.

"Perhaps it is a trick," said the Intellectual. "Perhaps it was nothing. You are not children to be startled by children's tricks."

As he spoke the final sentence he held his arm straight out, fist clenched, with the heel of the hand facing upward. Slowly, he brought the dagger down vertically, so that the point went into the flesh halfway between wrist and elbow. The blade was parallel to the length of the arm. He pushed the blade in, and kept pushing until it emerged from the other side of the arm. When he was done, the knife was buried to the hilt, and blood was seeping down the blade. He let three or four drops fall from the point, and then he slowly withdrew the weapon. Then he held his arm vertically above his head. The wound was visible, but it did not bleed.

Salvador threw the dagger to the ground, so that it stuck in the soft soil. With his fingers he rubbed the wound, and when he took them away, there was nothing. It was as if the dagger had never been passed through the flesh.

Machado said nothing now.

"Bring me a brand from the fire!" Salvador commanded. Mihiel moved to comply with the request, and brought a length of wood whose tip was burning. Salvador laid the burning tip on his arm, and then bent down to touch the white flesh on top of his feet. Slipping off his sandals, he stroked the sole of each foot in turn. Then, without warning, he tossed the brand to Machado, making it turn cartwheels in the air as it flew. Machado did not try to catch it, but dodged as it flew close to his face.

"I am a healer and a holy man," said Salvador gently but clearly enough to be heard. "I speak with the voice of God. I say that your voice makes false claims. I say that you have no right to make yourself heard."

Machado drew the pistol from his belt.

Salvador spread his arms wide. "Perhaps you can kill me," he said. "But if you do, you are revealed for what you are, and you stand outside the law of God as well as the law of Merkad."

Machado put the weapon away, without pointing it at anyone. He looked at Salvador with fearful resentment.

"Pick up your knife," said the prophet, "and go."

Machado did as he was told.

Salvador turned quickly to Teresa. "Get the bundles," he told her. "If half of what he says about events in Naryn is true, they'll come to arrest us before morning. We go now."

Teresa's gaze flicked past him, to scan the firelit assembly.

"What about them?" she demanded.

"There'll never be a better time," he answered. "At this moment, I could tell them *anything*. Anything at all."

She shook her head, almost imperceptibly, and went into the tent to collect such belongings as they could conveniently carry.

Meanwhile, Cyrias Salvador, a healer and holy man of the conquered race of Merkad, began to offer the fondest of farewells to the people who had chosen him as their spiritual leader.

He did not disappoint them.

21

Their journey across the Sea of Hamad took Cheron and his companions nearly four days. The ship that carried them could maintain an average speed of little more than two hundred kilometers a day unless the weather was particularly fair, allowing her sails to relieve the boilers of much of their work. Compared with the Kyadian ships and the Dahran fishing vessels Cheron had previously seen, the steamship was an impressive symbol of material progress, but Sarid was unimpressed by her engine room and by her single-screw propeller. Corporal Spektros, on being acquainted with this opinion, was quick to assure everyone that the ship was already out of date by Macarians' standards, but could not easily be replaced because the Sea of Hamad was landlocked. The oceangoing ships being built in Vondrel and Volokon were much more impressive, and once canals had been built to connect the Bitter Sea to the Calm Sea and the Calm Sea to the Western Ocean—thus giving Macaria's chief ports of Solis and Armata a sea route to the world at large—much more might yet be accomplished.

The journey across the sea was infinitely tedious for the passengers. Their quarters were cramped, allowing each man little more than a bunk and a place to stand, and the deck seemed almost as crowded when they were assembled there. The men who became seasick were a miserable embarrassment to themselves and everyone else; the men who did not were soon bored. The only ones who were reasonably content were the hardened gamblers, who required of life nothing more than a space to squat and throw their various species of dice.

The crew of the vessel were a mixed collection, mostly Dahrans and Merkadians, but with a few Macarians brought south because of their experience with steamships. There

were also two Camelonians, who had first sailed from the
port to which Sarid Jerome had once claimed to belong, but
no one now remembered that claim, and it probably would
not have mattered if they had. The Tanagarians were accepted now, and no one cared any longer where they had
come from.

The food which the soldiers were given on the ship was noticeably worse than the fare they had received on land. It was
the same kind, but the meat was of poorer quality and it was
less competently cooked. A further drop in quality once the
company reached the Bela settlements was predicted, but
there was no reason for the conviction. It was simply a part
of the doleful grumbling brought forth by the conditions of
the voyage.

For the first time, the three Tanagarians began to weary
significantly of one another's company. Vito Talvar joined the
gamblers, and Cheron began to find Sarid Jerome withdrawn
and uncommunicative. By the same token, Sarid found
Cheron's everpresence tiresome and his conversation irritating.
The only other man either of them felt comfortable with was
Midas, but he was involved with the dice game, and so Sarid
began to prefer his own company, and would sit or stand
apart from the others, while Cheron talked more frequently
to Qapel and to Baya-undi—though always separately, for the
two had no interest in or liking for one another. Baya-undi
was the more intriguing, but when personal matters were discussed he was extremely reserved—in the culture from which
he came, apparently, it was not customary to talk about
oneself or to ask personal questions. He would talk about
Khepra, but only in the abstract; about his own life there he
was conspicuously reticent. Qapel, by contrast, had no topics
of conversation outside his own life and that of his erstwhile
neighbors. He was illiterate and uneducated, and had only the
vaguest idea of what existed beyond the horizons of his own
experience. Cheron, for want of anything better to occupy his
time, took over the language lessons which Vito Talvar had
started and then abandoned, and made considerable improve-
ments in Qapel's handling of the Macarian language. He also
began to tell the Dahran something about the history of the
world—the true history which both Midas and Baya-undi had
rejected as a myth. Qapel listened attentively enough, but

Cheron was never quite sure whether he believed any of it or not.

They finally reached the southern shore of Hamad in the early hours of the morning, well before dawn. They were transferred to the shore in small boats, and hustled through the darkness into ill-lit wooden bunkhouses where they were allowed to return to sleep. No allowance was made for the disturbance, however, when they were roused next morning at the customary time.

They were in a wooden fort of no great size, situated on an island in the estuary of the great river. The island had been cleared of all but a few trees and most of the land around the fort had been divided into plots and planted with vegetables of various kinds. There were two or three clusters of buildings on the southern half of the island; the fort faced north and overlooked the harbor. There was a small fleet of fishing vessels in the harbor, but these were operated by the army; there was no native population. The only people on the island who were not military personnel were a handful of Macarian agricultural scientists and their assistants—all the settlers were on the mainland.

The island was several hundred meters from the shore, and even from the highest point very little could be seen of the settlements. Inland, where the land rose from the coastal plain, there was nothing visible except an infinite wall of bright green—the fringe of the Great Equatorial Forest. Cheron, after listening to so much talk about the forest and its evils, was disappointed to find that it did not extend all the way to the very edge of the sea, and that it seemed so very placid.

After a certain amount of obligatory parading and drilling, and the morning meal—which was light on meat but otherwise quite adequate—the new company received a lecture from the commandant of the fort. The subject was the rigors of life on the Bela. The commandant was clearly a man whose outlook on life was more than usually bleak, and he promised the company that if the forest did not kill at least half of them, then the heat would probably drive them mad. He warned them not to underestimate the forest savages, who were clever fighters despite being dwarfs who could not walk or stand upright like real men. Then, however, he went on to talk about the vital importance of the work that Macaria was doing here—not, of course, simply for Macaria but for the whole world. The establishment of the colonies was vital, he assured them, to the future of the entire human race. It was an important step on the way to the eradication of barbarism and the conquest of hunger.

When he had finished, junior officers took over to offer more detailed advice on the strategies required in order to survive and stay healthy "up the river." Cheron quickly gathered that they would not be spending much time in the pleasant and peaceful farming communities on the edge of the forest, but would instead be hastened forward to join the advance guard of Macaria's attempt to take civilization into the very depths of this hostile land.

Midas, of course, soaked up all the rumors in the fort within twenty-four hours of his arrival, and passed them on with alacrity.

"The fighting is up river," he explained to Cheron and Vito Talvar. "The Macarians have tried to establish a chain of lumber camps, for cutting the great trees. The plan is to float the logs down the river to sawmills which will produce building materials, paper mills, and distilling plants which will produce charcoal and alcohol. They cannot take the greatest trees, of course, because they are far too big. Men talk about trees a kilometer high and ten thousand years old, but you know how men talk . . . I would not call them liars, but for myself I will only say that the trees are very big until I see them with my own eyes. Anyhow, the logging camps are close to the river, where the greatest trees do not grow—what the men are felling are much smaller individuals. They are clearing land as fast as they can, using tractors and chain saws, building fires to take care of the waste foliage. They build for themselves, of course, as they go. On the neck of the forest it is no more than the tiniest flea bite—they have done nothing. Maybe they have started one or two small forest fires, and they hunt through the parts of the forest that are not too dark or dense, but really they have done nothing. None of the areas they have invaded are within fifty kilometers of places where the forest demons live, and yet the demons have come from the greater forest to attack camps—not once or twice but dozens of times. They are difficult to kill, because even though they have no proper feet they scuttle over the ground like brown spiders, carrying

blowguns and sometimes bows. Their darts and arrows are always poisoned, and they make men terribly ill even when
they do not kill them.

"At first, only a few soldiers went to each camp, but now
we go in companies, to build and defend stockades, to burn
out sections of land and dig ditches to make moats of river
water . . . and, of course, to fight. Now, the demons are beginning to attack the farmland and the factories which are
processing the wood. It seems they are not prepared to share
their continent, and are trying to force Macaria back into
the sea. No matter how clever they are, they are very foolish.
In the long run, they cannot endure against guns—for themselves, they do not seem to understand the use of fire. No one
knows their language, and they die very quickly if captured,
no matter how much care is taken to keep them alive. Once
they lose their magic, they are not so fearsome. On the other
hand, there are very many more of them than there are of us,
and if they persist in trying to destroy us . . . well, my
friends, we have come too early in the day. It will not be tomorrow that this war is won. Not for many years. It will not
be so easy to stay alive for the time this first wave of attacks
lasts. I would not care to say when things will settle down.
We may have to kill a great many of the little brown ones in
order to persuade them that we deserve to be let alone, or
even treated with respect."

This diagnosis of the situation proved to be more or less
correct. The fort's complement was already depleted, and
Donsella's company was not intended to restore its strength.
The next day the greater part of the force was transferred to
two riverboats—wide-bellied barges used to transport food
and goods between the farmland and the factories which
were supposed to be processing the lumber floated down the
river. Beyond them, the river was, of course, unnavigable,
and further progress would have to be made on foot, along
trails cut through the vegetation on either bank.

The river was bounded by curtains of green: the slow-mov-
ing shallows supported dense beds of reed, while the trees
that grew close to the bank were festooned with creepers. The
everpresence of the creepers made it difficult for the trees to
build up their own bulk, and for the most part they were thin
in the trunk, and rarely stood straight.

Near the coast the river was very wide, and the shallows

were extensive, frequently interrupted by mudbanks that loomed out of the water as the tide went out. The mudbanks and the reed beds were teeming with life—there were great flocks of wading birds, basking crocodiles, and clouds of insects. Rafts of water lilies drifted in the deeper water, providing unsteady footing for slender lizards and croaking frogs, which competed with darting flycatchers for the insects.

As the tide ebbed the riverboats were forced farther away from the bank, but they still passed close to wooden piers that jutted from the shore into the deep water, from which children waved to them as they passed. The children seemed cheerful enough, but this region was a long way from the heart of the forest, and no raiders had come so far as yet.

By the time the sun had risen to its zenith the Bela's banks had crept in on either side of the boats, so that they now seemed to be making their way along a green corridor, with sheer walls rising to either side. The neat arrays of huts that they passed occasionally were now invariably protected by wooden palisades, even though the cultivated fields extended for several kilometers outside the walls before the boundaries that marked the domain of the forest.

The boats stopped three times to unload items of cargo, though their holds had not been loaded to any appreciable degree. They would be much fuller when they came back downriver again, assuming that work had not come to a total standstill at the lagoons above the dams which the Macarians had built to facilitate their work.

In the afternoon, the heat became oppressive and the soldiers lethargic. They sat or sprawled on the decks of the boats, too enervated even to gamble. The birds had long since lost their appeal as a spectacle and the insects had become a nuisance.

Sarid and Cheron were sitting in the bow of the second boat when Baya-undi sought them out. He assumed his conspiratorial air as he squatted down beside them, and they knew what he was going to say before he opened his mouth.

"I have an idea," he began.

"Have you?" asked Sarid dispiritedly.

"If we were to strike out on our own *here*, there would be no possibility whatever of the Macarians giving chase. To live off the forest would not be difficult, and within three days we could be back on the coastal strip. Khepra is really no further from here than from Asdar, and the people of Yezirah are more peacefully inclined than the men of Kyad."

"In that case," said Sarid, "we wish you the best of luck."

"You do not want to come with me?"

"No."

"Why not? I know that you do not want to go to Khepra, but do you really want to go on upriver now that you know what we have to face? How much of this do you need to see?"

"I've seen a map," said Sarid. "Cheron has it in one of his pockets. The Sea of Hamad curves around, and stands both north and east of us. To reach Yezirah we would have to go around it. It is a very long way, and the forest is presumably full of small brown savages. I think that you should go alone. They probably would not bother a lone man. There are, of course, snakes and leeches and a few predatory animals, but they will probably keep their distance. You will not worry about the walk being so long, as it will take you home. For myself, I have not the stomach for it. Leave me to my fate, I beg you."

Baya-undi gave up the struggle, and laid his head back against the rail that guarded the bow. He looked back over Sarid's head to the bridge of the boat, such as it was, where the captain watched the stern of the first boat with stony-faced concentration, smoking a thin cigar.

"Your pale skin will burn," prophesied Baya-undi. "It will become diseased."

"We're almost as brown as Merkadians now," observed Cheron. "We'll get darker still, if need be. We'll outlive you, even if your charms hold all the misfortune in the world at bay."

Baya-undi touched the amulet that he was wearing around his neck. The rim of it showed above the neck of his undershirt. He smiled, showing his white teeth. "A Khepran does not put *too* much faith in his own magic," he said. "We do not spurn its protection, but we know better than to depend on it entirely. Magic can always be set aside by other magic, and frequently is. *You* know that."

"It seems that everyone knows it," answered Sarid, "but it prevents no one from carrying charms and medicines, and with every night that passes I hear whispered incantations that are surely not prayers to Macaria's God."

"The wise man takes advantage of everything that may help him," observed the Khepran. "Even if his spells are worthless, they cost little in time and effort. *Some* of them are bound to be effective, if a man had enough. You carry your own medicines in your leather belts—I am certain that you would not rely on the army's surgeons if you were to fall ill."

"No," said Cheron amiably. "We would not."

"Such is life," said Baya-undi. "We are surrounded by infinite seas of uncertainty, and each man must make his way as best he can. No man can travel safely alone."

Sarid laughed, but without malice. Baya-undi hesitated only a moment, and then he laughed too.

22

When the boats turned north again, leaving the company to continue southward on foot, it was almost a relief so far as the Tanagarians were concerned. Seven days of virtual inactivity had put a considerable taxation upon their patience and spirit. Boredom was something entirely alien to them—or, at least, the boredom of inactivity and waiting. It was not a problem they had learned to cope with in their previous lives, and the one set of memories which it could recall was that pertaining to their time aboard another ship: the starship *Sabreur*. The analogies that were easy to draw did not help them to feel any better about their long haul across the sea and up the Bela. Marching along the rough-hewn trail was by no means exciting, but it allowed them to use their limbs and muscles. Tedium is much easier to accommodate, they found, when one's body is active.

According to Spektros, the intention was that they should march southward in three day-long stages, staying each night in encampments set up as relay stations. As things turned out, however, these plans had to be hastily revised. When they reached the first relay station, a mere day's march from the slowly growing town surrounding the flooded valley above the first of Macaria's dams, they found it deserted. There should have been a dozen men stationed there, but there was no one.

Captain Donsella ti Ria immediately went into a huddle with his junior officers, but such decisions as they made were not communicated to the men, who slept uneasily that night in the bunks that had been made ready for them. Not until morning were they informed that the company would be divided. One party would return to the dam in order to transmit the news back down the river. One party would replace the vanished garrison, while the third would press on as planned, hoping that the next post upriver would be safe. The captain permitted the men to draw lots in order to determine the composition of each party, as it was obvious that considerable risks were involved.

As luck would have it, the Tanagarians found themselves split up. Sarid Jerome was attached to the party returning downriver. With him was Baya-undi. Vito Talvar and Cheron Felix were with the largest party—the one detailed to go forward. So were Midas, Mondo, and Qapel. Donsella himself would lead this force, and Corporal Spektros was appointed to go with it, as well as both the company's sergeants.

"The thing is," Spektros explained to Cheron, "that it's as easy for the savages to attack a post like this as it is for them to attack upriver. The forest's as dense to the east as to the south. *We* only move up and down the river, but *they* don't. It may be—it almost certainly will be—that we'll find the next post fully manned. There's no reason yet to suppose otherwise."

"I suppose the post must have been overrun," said Cheron. "There's no other explanation for the absence of the men?"

"Hardly," said Spektros. "What the savages have done with the bodies, I don't know. They always take back their own, if they can. Perhaps they threw the others into the river, or dragged them off into the forest depths. We're very close to the forest now—the *real* forest, not the jumble of saplings you see around you. Those trees that you see in the east are nothing—barely adequate to mask the real giants that lie beyond. If you were to walk due east in a straight line you'd find yourself in a different world before you'd gone five kilom-

eters. If you *could* go five kilometers in a straight line,
which I doubt."

Despite the corporal's reassurances that all would probably
be well, Cheron was nevertheless certain that the Macarian
would far rather have accompanied Sarid and Baya-undi
downriver. They, no doubt, would return this way in time,
but the opportunity to withdraw even temporarily from the
anxious situation seemed enviable.

Cheron was surprised to find that the prospect of parting
from the Pragmatist did not cause him as much worry as it
might have. There was not much time for anguished farewells, but when the time came for their ways to part Cheron
found it quite easy to maintain the appropriate degree of control.

Sarid touched him on the shoulder, and said: "We'll no
doubt meet again in a few days." Cheron merely nodded, and
did not reciprocate the gesture. It was the same with Vito
Talvar.

However, once Sarid had gone, Talvar turned to Cheron
and said: "For a Pragmatist, he wasn't so bad. Mad, of
course, but he wouldn't be here if he wasn't."

"We'll have to make our own plans now," said Cheron.
"As well as doing our own Intel work."

Talvar laughed. "I've been making *my* plans since we were
dumped," he said. "I wasn't ever going to take orders from
Sarid."

Cheron did not bother to question the statement, but it did
not occur to him to take it seriously. It was simply the kind
of thing that people were liable to say in the kind of circumstances in which they now found themselves.

When they began to march south again, Cheron found
himself paired with Midas.

"They weren't *all* killed," Midas informed him. "They
should have had a small boat—you must have seen the jetty.
It's not worth keeping large boats south of the dam while
they're floating all kinds of rubbish downriver, but they'll
have had a rowboat. I think they came under attack and ran.
Probably Dahrans."

Cheron, meanwhile, scanned the foliage to their left, wondering how many places there might be along the trail where
an ambush could easily be set. There were relatively few
large trees this close to the river, because floodwater some-

times covered this area, but what Spektros had said was true. The *real* forest was not far away, hiding behind the serried ranks of smaller, less awesome growths. Even as things were, a day's march might take them past a thousand trees from which a sniper with a bow might loose an arrow off at the party without exposing himself to any undue risk.

The day, though, passed entirely without incident. They saw not the slightest sign of the forest savages—nor, indeed, any other mammal of significant size. There were only the bright birds and the croaking frogs, and lizards skipping up and down the tree trunks in search of beetles and ticks. The next stockade proved to be fully manned, and Spektros spent the period of the evening meal informing everyone in the party that he had been right and had told them so. No one objected to his boasting; they were all pleased to discover that he was right. The main part of the company went to their beds quite contented, reassured that life along the Bela was not quite as hazardous as they had begun to believe.

They were still in their beds when the savages mounted their attack, an hour before dawn.

23

Cyriac Salvador tipped back the brim of his hat when Teresa's shadow fell across his body. She was dusting sand from her hands and sleeves, and he had to turn his head away when a few drifting motes stung his eyes. She had just scrambled down the rocks that hid and protected the water hole, and which provided a temporary refuge from the noonday sun.

"He's still coming," she said. "Just one man, and a mule. I think it's a mule—it may be a donkey."

"It hardly seems to matter," said Salvador levelly. "He's not necessarily following us, you know. Insofar as there *is* a road across the desert, this is it. It may not look like much to us, but it means a lot to the people who occasionally wander across the wilderness. If only camels had survived the upheaval, this would be the perfect territory for them. Not exactly the Sahara, of course, but *something*. Actually, though, I suppose it *is* a bit of the Sahara in a way, even though there was fertile land here for a couple of thousand years after the inundation. Perhaps it will grow again—the desert reasserting its authority and claiming all the land over which it held dominion in the days of the ancient civilizations."

"We're too far north," said Teresa tersely. "The spot where we now stand was under the sea, I think. Four-fifths of Merkad was part of the Mediterranean seabed. That's why they never developed archaeology, though their culture is probably as old as Macaria's. Nothing much to dig up."

"You take things a little too literally," said Salvador, with the ghost of an affected sigh. "That's a fault I had previously met only in Intellectuals."

"Perhaps your circle of friends was too limited," she told him. "However, the question is: do we wait for him, or do we keep one stage ahead of him?"

"He may be desperate enough to walk through the desert at noonday," replied Salvador, "but I see no reason to copy him. We have no need to be afraid of him, whoever he is, and if he wants to catch up with us—let him."

He retired once more beneath the wide brim of his hat, and edged himself back to take what cover there was in the cleft between the rocks. Teresa sat down by the water's edge, and moistened a cloth, which she then began to dab over her face and neck.

"We should have got mules," she said. "This is no country for walking."

"The opportunity did not readily present itself," Salvador pointed out. "When a holy man tells his disciples that he is going into the desert to fast and to put himself to the test, it is hardly appropriate for him to start inquiring where he can buy a pair of mules."

"It's a long time since we ceased to be holy men and became ordinary travelers," she said.

"No," he corrected her. "It only *seems* to be a long time. You live too much in the present, and are too fully conscious of your surroundings. You suffer too much. With better con-

trol, the desert would not disturb you. You would be better
able to appreciate the silence and the emptiness. It is an ex-
cellent place for a holy man to take himself apart for meditation."

"Salvador," she said patiently. "You're *not* a holy man."
She knew that he was teasing her, but still she could not let it
pass. "Anyhow," she went on, "the sooner we're out of this,
the better. Nothing else can be as bad."

"Pragmatism breeds impatience," observed Salvador. "The
trouble with allowing yourself to become obsessed with goals
is that no matter where you are you want to be somewhere
else, and no matter how fast you go you want to go faster. I
realize that it's as much a matter of metabolism as psychology, but metabolism can be controlled. Empty time is not
wasted time, unless you make it so."

To this she did not reply, knowing that nothing she could
say would achieve anything except to make him go on longer
with his catalog of homilies. She rebound the cloth around
the lower part of her face, to keep the sand from her mouth
and nose. It was still wet, but it would dry off in minutes in
the hot air.

She walked back from the mudhole to squat in the shade
of a bulbous cactus, and cursed the lack of trees. She wondered whether the date palm had gone the way of the camel,
and decided that it may well have. This part of the world had
suffered far greater changes than most in the cataclysm which
had put an end to the ancient civilizations, and the ecology of
the region had been dramatically transformed.

Nearly an hour passed before the other traveler finally
reached the mudhole—he had been walking very slowly. He
was leading the mule by a leather halter, and both man and
animal seemed to be on the point of dropping. As he made
his way between the rocks and down to the murky pool he
saw them both waiting, and literally reeled when the surprise
stopped him in his tracks. He fell to his knees. Both Salvador
and Teresa got up to help him, but it was not until they took
away the hood that covered everything but his eyes that they
realized who he was.

"Mihiel," said Salvador. "I should have known."

Mihiel was unable to reply, for the moment. Teresa took
the cloth away from her face, and wet it again in the turbid

water of the pool. Then she pressed it to Mihiel's face, and squeezed a few drops between his lips.

"A loyal disciple," said Teresa dryly, "should do what his master tells him. Anyhow, I thought you said he was about ready to strike out on his own behalf."

Mihiel opened his mouth, but his lips were cracked and whatever he began to say was unintelligible.

Teresa turned away to see to the mule, but it had found its own way to the edge of the pool, and was placidly ducking its head, up to its ankles in loose mud.

When Mihiel was finally able to make himself understood, he said: "I knew that I must follow. There is so much to learn."

Salvador nodded, and it was this assent rather than the statement that provoked Teresa to reply.

"Look, Mihiel," she said, pointing to Salvador's garb, "he's not a priest. We're not holy men. *I*'m not even a man—I'm a woman. We stole the bloodstained robes from dead men. We're just travelers, trying to get safely to Macaria. Do you understand me? We are *not* holy men."

All Mihiel said was: "I have seen."

"It was the final act that did it," said Salvador, in his own language. "It impressed Machado, and it impressed Mihiel too. I was teaching him the elements of control. He thinks he might be able to learn enough to do what I did."

"Don't you think you'd better explain to him," said Teresa, quietly. "Don't you think that you'd better tell him that he's all but killed himself for nothing? Tell him what the difference is between a light trance state and sufficient cellular control to push knives through your arm. Tell him that he missed out on two years of drug treatment and twenty years of training. Tell him that even *I* can't do what you did, though I have ten times the ability he can cultivate. And tell him that you're not a holy man. Or does it make you feel good to have your own little band of worshipers—even a band of one?"

"I don't think you're looking at this intelligently," said Salvador quietly.

Teresa made a derisive gesture and turned away.

Mihiel tried to say something more, but Salvador touched his lips to soothe him into silence.

Later, after Salvador had rigged up a makeshift awning to

provide shade, and Mihiel had gone to sleep, Teresa said: "I suppose you intend taking him with us?"

"What else can we do?" asked Salvador. "I suppose you'd like to leave him here to die?"

"He'll slow us down."

"Perhaps. But once we reach the coast, he might be useful to us. He's in a better position than we are to persuade the captain of some fishing boat to take us to Macaria."

"He'll want to come with us."

"So what? There are thousands of Merkadians in the ports of Macaria. Armata is probably the most cosmopolitan city in the world. He'll attract far less attention than we will—he'll be able to move about the streets more freely than us. We may need him."

"Provided that you can persuade him that anything we need to do is just one more way of serving the unnamed God."

Salvador shrugged. "What do *you* propose we do?"

"Leave him," she said. "He won't die. Tell him to go back the way he came. Command him, in the name of the unnamed God."

Salvador shook his head. "He won't make it, even if he could be persuaded to go. I can't leave him any more than I could leave you when you broke your leg."

"You needed me."

"I need him. *We* need him. Let's not be so parsimonious with our needs that we can't justify saving his life. Need is easy enough to find, if it suits you. Even a Pragmatist must appreciate that. Even a misanthropic Pragmatist."

"Are you sure that you don't just get an illicit thrill out of the prospect of having a slavish disciple licking your heels?"

"Don't be so stupid," said Salvador tersely. He paused for a moment, then added: "Anyhow, he's very kindly brought us a mule. Surely even you can be grateful for that."

She sighed, and then gestured briefly with her hands. "All right," she said. "I'm sorry. There's nothing else we can do, and he may be useful. It's just that I like to keep things simple. All I want to do is to get to the base. I didn't like him when he was heading your circus troupe, and I don't like him now—I thought all that was behind us. But I suppose it doesn't matter—just so long as you can handle him. He *will* slow us down, though, with that damned limp."

"I wouldn't worry about it," said Salvador. "You've done a lot of limping yourself. Someday soon, it might be my turn."

She spared him a bitter smile on account of that remark—but not until his back was turned and he was ducking back beneath the awning to share the shade with his most loyal of disciples.

24

———————

Cheron was roused by the sound of a shot, followed immediately by the yelling of one of the sergeants. He slid quickly from the folds of his blanket and groped for the rifle he had laid down beside the bunk. He was fully dressed apart from his jacket, and he did not wait to put that on. Spektros was running along the line of bunks while the man nearest the door turned up the lamp. Cheron stumbled toward the door of the barrack room, catching a batch of ammunition clips thrown at him by the sergeant. He loaded the rifle before launching himself out into the compound.

Donsella ti Ria shouted to the emerging men to get to the wall, and Cheron ran across the open space, leaping onto the platform that would allow him to fire over the palisade. He found himself beside Qapel, who had been standing guard. The Dahran was sighting along the barrel of his rifle, moving it uneasily from side to side. Cheron looked out over the area that had been stripped of cover, but could see nothing.

"Where are they?" he demanded.

"In the trees," said Qapel. "They have to come out to fire. Their bows have no range. Watch for them scuttling like great spiders."

"I can't see a thing," answered Cheron. There was no moon, and the starlight hardly illuminated the ground at all. As he spoke, though, a bundle of burning rags that had been soaked in some kind of vegetable oil was sent soaring over the fence to land fifteen meters away. The flame created by the evaporating oil as it burned was yellow and smoky, but it gave enough light for him to see a dark shadow move back toward the trees—looking for all the world, as Qapel had said, like a huge furry spider.

Qapel fired at the swift-moving shape, but missed. More rag bundles were thrown out. Each one, Cheron knew, would burn for thirty minutes or so. He wondered how long it would be until dawn.

"Ammunition?" asked the Dahran.

Cheron was still clutching three spare clips. He gave the Dahran one of them. Behind him, Donsella was bawling encouragement to the last men to turn out, reminding them that there were twice as many men and more than the savages had expected to find, and that this time they would be beaten off. Cheron was not so sure. He saw shadows moving behind the firelight, and fired at them. In the uncertain light it was difficult to pick a target, and the shadows moved so quickly, hugging the ground. Despite the fact that the ground had been cleared it was far from flat—there were sawn-off tree trunks and root ridges in abundance. They could not have given adequate shelter to an ordinary man—not even a man the size of Midas or Qapel—but the savages hugged the ground so closely that the sea of ridges seemed to soak them up. They were moving on all fours, heads held low, and the firelight did not reflect from their furry hides—only from their large eyes. It was obvious that the forest people were far better equipped than humans for night vision.

A slender arrow ricocheted off the top of the fence by Cheron's elbow, and Cheron realized that in spite of the flares they could get close enough to shoot. He also realized that without his thick jacket a poisoned arrow or dart would go through his shirt with ease. He cursed himself for his impatience, noting that Mondo, farther down the line, had paused long enough to dress properly, but it was too late now to return. The shadows were moving again, in bewildering profusion, and he had to shoot at them. As he went through the full clip he saw only one of the strange silhouettes fall back. He reloaded, and heard the click of another arrow rebounding from the wall close at hand. The missiles did not seem to have much force behind them, but if all they needed to do was scratch the skin, they probably did not need it. He tried to duck down a little lower, almost going down to his knees in order to keep his bulky shoulders out of sight. He tried to calculate how much more of a target he was than Qapel, who had almost to stand on tiptoe to fire over the wall.

The order came to fix bayonets, which he did with trained efficiency while Qapel continued to give covering fire. As soon as the bayonet was in place he was forced to stab at something which hurtled over the wall, having scaled it without the slightest difficulty. He felt the blade go home into flesh, but the forest man was already moving away, rolling like an acrobat. Cheron shot the creature, and watched it roll over twice more before he was sure that it had, in fact, been killed. As he turned back to his post he saw that other shadows were already inside the stockade, and that men backed up against the barrack-room wall were trying to stab them. He watched one blown down by a bullet from the captain's pistol. The attackers had no knives, but did not refrain from hand-to-hand combat.

Cheron leapt down from the platform and went down on one knee, scanning the top of the fence and hoping to shoot the attackers down as they came over it. Two shots—both unsuccessful—proved to him that it could not be done; they were too quick. He began to fall back toward the barrack room, and yelled to Qapel to follow him, but Qapel was already wrestling with one of the savages. Cheron had to stab with his own bayonet as one of the little men tried to drag him down. He tried to get back to the door of the lighted bunkroom, but realized that the building was going up in flames. The lamps inside had been torn down and their fuel scattered everywhere. Whether it had been done by accident or whether one of the savages had got inside there was no way to tell.

He reversed the rifle in his grip, knowing that he had fired the last cartridge in the clip and having no time to reload. He wrenched the bayonet off to use as a dagger in his right hand, while he whirled the gun as if it were a club in his left. He knocked one of the savages away, but he knew that such victories could only be momentary—he was no longer in a position to do any real damage. He stopped them when they grabbed for his legs or jumped at his face, but he could no longer hurt them with the rifle. He realized that his hands were probably more effective weapons in this kind of fight than the blade he was carrying, and he dropped both the bayonet and the gun. He slipped into a crouch, ready to face any assailant and grapple with him, breaking his bones with practiced ease. With the light of the blazing building sending dancing shadows everywhere, and the heat blistering his back, it was easy enough to imagine himself in a tortured dream, ready to kill and kill again with crazy efficiency.

He never saw the missile which struck him down—it was probably no more than a tiny dart. He did not even feel the prick as it penetrated his skin, but reeled instead under the purely psychic impact of synesthetic flashes which confused his vision. He fought to keep control of his senses, but felt himself losing his balance and slipping sideways.

Control! he commanded, trying desperately to rally his metabolism to fight against the drug that had entered his veins. He did, indeed, manage to take control, and brought himself back upright, feeling a triumphant surge of adrenalin. Then he was losing again, letting go. Whether he had been hit a second time he did not know; he just knew that control was gone and that all possible hope of control was lost. Acceptance of that fact, in the last dying seconds of consciousness, was almost a relief.

For the last fading moment, it was as though he were back aboard the *Sabreur*, and the poisoned dreams were letting him free at last.

Part Three

THE COST
OF PROGRESS

1

As the small fishing boat tossed on the waves of the Bitter Sea, Teresa Janeat had to fight hard to balance the ladle of fresh water which she lifted to her lips. She managed not to spill too much before passing it on to Cyriac Salvador. As Salvador passed it in his turn to Mihiel, the sailor who had brought the bucket looked down at them with frank animosity. He was little more than a boy—perhaps fifteen or sixteen years old. Mihiel gave him back the ladle with a brief word of thanks.

"What's the matter with him?" asked Teresa, as the boy walked back along the deck, keeping his balance skillfully despite having to carry the bucket.

"He thinks you're Macarians," said Mihiel. "When I paid for the passages, I did not mention that you were not . . . like me. To him, all foreigners are Macarians. I could not tell the owner that you are healers and men of god."

"What *did* you tell him?" asked Teresa.

"I told him not to ask questions. He and his crew will reach their own conclusions. I think they will decide that you are criminals trying to reenter Macaria illegally. Do you want me to tell him some story that he will believe—something that might give him a good opinion of you?"

"There's no need," said Salvador. "Lies multiply well enough on their own. When people find that their own conclusions are wrong, they shrug their shoulders—they cannot blame themselves. When they find that they have been deceived—it is an irritation that sometimes makes them act. Let's not complicate our affairs too much. I want the captain to forget us as soon as we set foot on the shore to the east of Armata."

Mihiel—who was not much older than the boy who had brought them water, and who might have been his brother or

163

cousin as far as appearances were concerned—turned his head to look back over the stern at the bubbling wake left by the wind-driven boat.

"Is that why you have not told *me* why you are going to Macaria?" he asked.

"No," said Salvador. "I have not told you because you would not believe me."

"I would believe anything that you say."

"I am not a holy man. I am only a man. What I did in Merkad I did for the sake of expediency."

Mihiel shook his head.

"You see," said Salvador, not unkindly, "there are things I say that you cannot believe. You could not accept *my* reasons—you will only accept the unknown reasons of an unnamed God. Why not? Perhaps it *is* the unnamed God that is guiding us all to the mountains in the far north of Macaria. If that is so, then I know His reasons no better than you. The reasons that I think are mine are no more than illusions, which I cannot penetrate—merely His devices to ensure that I do what it is in His mind that I should do. If that is the case, what does it matter what I think? Whatever I tell you, the truth remains the truth."

"You are playing with me," accused the Merkadian. "You are twisting me in a knot of words."

"Yes I am," said Salvador. "And I am sorry. Believe me."

"This game-playing is pointless," said Teresa. "What interests me is what you propose to do when we get to Macaria. It will not be so easy to travel there without attracting attention. The gulf between the towns and the villages is not so great. The law does not lose its effectiveness beyond city boundaries."

"Precisely *because* things are better ordered," replied Salvador, "it may be easier to get by without documents. In Merkad, we could not have gone into a city or passed by any kind of Macarian post without being asked to show papers of identification. In Macaria, we might avoid that. However, it would be safer to obtain papers if we can. Once we have them, it will be much easier to make traveling arrangements. I think that we have sufficient cash in hand to make ourselves reasonably comfortable. Our journey through Merkad has been remarkably inexpensive—at least until we had to pay for this illicit passage across the Bitter Sea."

"How do you propose to get papers of identification?" asked Teresa.

"Macaria is full of Merkadian laborers," said Salvador. "Especially the strip along the coast from the land bridge to the region east of Armata."

"You're not suggesting that we try to pass for Merkadians? Extraordinary Merkadians we have been, but ordinary Merkadians we could never be."

"You're interrupting me," said Salvador silkily. "I do not propose that we should pretend to be Merkadians. I think we would be more convincing as northerners, from one of the less notable provinces. The significance of the fact that there are so many Merkadians on the far shore is precisely that Mihiel had no difficulty in arranging this passage for us, and there must have been a hundred like him making similar crossings this month. There must be some means whereby they can equip *themselves* with some kind of documentation when they enter the country illegally. A thriving industry in forgery, which probably caters not only to Merkadians but also men of Assiah, Surya, and Kalispera. Mihiel, with a little help from the captain, and our reserves of money, can almost certainly locate someone who is willing to provide us with documentation enough for our purposes."

"And then?" asked Teresa.

"Then," said Salvador, "we catch a train."

"A train?"

"A locomotive that runs on tracks. Driven by steam power, fuelled by charcoal briquettes. Macaria is a civilized country, if you remember. We catch one train into the center of Armata; we change; and we go north to Galehalt in the mountains. After that, we will have to make our own way again, but we will have covered seven-eighths of the distance in reasonable comfort."

"You don't think we'd attract suspicion, traveling on a train? Two tall foreigners and one small Merkadian, riding a railroad for more than a thousand kilometers."

"In Macaria," said Salvador evenly, "*everyone* travels by train. We shall not go first class, and we need not attract attention. Macaria is the center of the world—the most active nation on Earth. There is nothing remarkable there about the sight of foreigners, not even in railway carriages. We would attract far more attention, I feel sure, if we tried to do as we did in Merkad and keep to the less populated areas, carefully avoiding the good roads. *That* kind of behavior would attract suspicion in Macaria."

Teresa looked sideways at Mihiel, then returned her gaze to Salvador.

"This scheme is recent, I suppose," she said.

"I settled upon it this morning," agreed Salvador.

"You seem very sure that we can get forged documents. Suppose we can't. Or suppose we can but they aren't good enough. What happens to us if we're arrested?"

"We serve our sentences, and then resume our journey. I doubt that anything too terrible will happen to us—not in Macaria. It is a civilized nation. Indeed, I had seriously considered the alternative scheme of simply approaching the proper authorities and asking to be provided with wholly legitimate documents, risking the possible consequences. On the whole, though, I think my present intentions represent the preferable choice. The worst of the journey is over, now. We are in less danger of our lives on Macarian soil than we have been in Merkad despite the privileges we enjoyed because of our imposture."

"It seems dangerous to me," she said. "But at least it's direct." She sounded uncertain.

"It's perfect," Salvador assured her. "Not in the sense that it cannot fail, but in the sense that it achieves a good balance between safety and convenience. Had you thought of it yourself, you would have considered it brilliant."

"And what happens to *him*?" asked Teresa, who customarily referred to Mihiel in the third person, except when she addressed him directly.

"He will come with us," said Salvador. "As long as he desires to do so."

"*All* the way?"

Salvador nodded.

Teresa looked at Mihiel, who was watching her uneasily. "You would be well advised to end this comedy now," she told him. "Go home to Merkad once you have seen us safe on the farther shore. There's no more benefit that you can possibly receive from this association."

She was aware even as she said it that she was not using words that he could readily understand, and she already knew full well that he was at his most intractable when understanding was just beyond his grasp.

"My place is with you," he said, speaking to Salvador, not to Teresa.

"Perhaps it is," answered Salvador.

Switching to her own language, Teresa said: "He isn't going to feel that way when he's finally confronted by the truth, is he?"

"That depends," answered Salvador, "on how ready he is to accept miracles. He's eager to learn, though he hasn't yet got it into his skull that what there is to be learned isn't at all what he believes it to be. It will be interesting to see what happens as he finally comes to accept that. He *will* learn, you see. He must. It's the cost of progress."

"Yes," she said. "I know."

2

As Cheron came slowly back to consciousness he could not help recalling the other awakening, when the pain had filled his being and he had felt himself burning. The images that floated unbidden in his mind now, though, recalled a past that he had not possessed at that time. They came from a time much closer to the life he had lived during his first existence, which was buried now beneath eight thousand years of oblivion. The "I" that struggled to assert itself now was that of a man hatched from a metal womb and born into the world called Earth; the world called *Motherworld*.

I am Cheron Felix, he thought, *soldier of Macaria.*

Memories of the battle fluttered briefly in the borderlands of his consciousness, and he remembered falling into unconsciousness. The memories slowly dissolved into an awareness of his present situation.

His hands were tied behind his back, and his arms were aching with the strain. His head was throbbing, and his eyes

seemed sticky, so that opening them was an effort. When he
did get them open he was dazzled by the light that was only
partially obscured by a frail canopy of green. He was lying
on his back, looking up into the foliage of a slender-boughed
tree. He twisted to look about him, and saw the bloodied face
of Midas a few centimeters from his own. The Merkadian
had been laid out beside him on a cushion of green moss,
though on his side rather than on his back. At first, the Merkadian seemed to be dead, but after a moment or two Cheron
felt the soft current of his breath.

Cheron rolled over the other way, but had to twist himself
about somewhat before he saw the other bodies stretched out
by his feet. There were two: the nearer was Qapel, and beyond him was Vito Talvar. He struggled to sit up, and eventually managed it. They had been set down in a small
clearing, surrounded by trees. The trees were not tall, suggesting that they were not far from the riverbank, but when he
strained his ears to listen for the sound of the water he could
hear nothing. He wondered how far the little forest men
could have dragged his body, and those of his companions.
Midas and Qapel might have been easy enough to move, but
Vito and he probably weighed as much as three or four of
the forest men. Possibly, the stockade was no more than a
hundred meters away. At first, the thought encouraged him,
but then he realized how meaningless it was. How could the
stockade represent safety, when every man in it might be
dead?

He wondered, briefly, whether the garrison might have
taken to the river, as Midas had suspected the other of doing,
abandoning the men already stricken, thinking them dead.

Why am I not dead? he wondered.

Clearly, the poison which the forest savages used to make
their arrows and darts more effective was not as deadly as
rumor would have it. He felt sick, and a little dizzy, but in
no danger of imminent death. Of course, he was much bigger
than an average man, and probably had a far stronger consti-
tution, but Midas seemed to be alive despite a bad wound on
his head.

It took him a few minutes to wriggle into a position from
which he could ascertain that Qapel too was only unconscious. Vito Talvar was also alive. Having made certain of
this, Cheron began to work on the cords binding his wrists

and ankles, but they were well tied. Before he had made any real progress in loosening them, Vito Talvar began to come around.

Cheron waited for him to recover sufficiently to notice that he was not alone. Once he knew there was an audience, Talvar allowed himself the luxury of a theatrical groan.

"For a man who once thought that he had only one life to lead, and who now finds himself embarked upon his third, you don't sound very thankful," said Cheron.

"Life," answered Talvar, "is overrated."

. "Console yourself," advised Cheron. "After all, it's all profit."

"I was hit by an arrow," said the blond man. "Like a hero, I continued to fight. I was magnificent, I think. But eventually I simply fell over. Not poison after all, it seems."

"Weak poison," said Cheron. "We appear to have been made prisoner."

"I had noticed," muttered Talvar, pulling experimentally at his bonds. "What worries me is why."

"If Midas were awake he'd no doubt have a dozen theories, all unpleasant. He'd be imagining the savages bearing us back to the treetops of the great forest giants, to their own world—either to serve as slaves or to provide hours of innocent and leisurely amusement in being tortured to death."

"You, of course, have a more comforting theory?"

"Actually," said Cheron, "no."

"I have. It is simply one more move in the foul game that fate is playing with us. One more little joke."

"I doubt that it's part of Salvador's plan, at any rate," said Cheron dryly. "Sarid will have to carry that alone, now, if it's ever going to amount to anything at all. Poor Salvador."

Vito Talvar considered this statement for a moment, and then said: "We're still being observed."

"By whom?" asked Cheron.

"By Salvador and his friends, of course. The experiment. They implanted something in our skulls—some kind of apparatus to relay information. If they want us out of here . . . perhaps they could get us out. After all, we're valuable. You don't ship men across interstellar distances just to lose them casually, do you? There may be hope for us yet."

Cheron looked around, at the slanting trees and the flowering plants that grew where the sunlight angled down between their crowns, his eyes following a dragonfly that arrowed across the clearing, possibly heading for the river.

"You think so?" he said, feeling far from convinced.

"No," said Talvar. "Not really. It wouldn't be Intel style, would it—zooming down from the satellite, guns blazing, to pluck their faithful servants from the jaws of an ugly death. Sarid might. Not Salvador, nor anyone like him. Nor the woman—the people that interstellar recruit can hardly be chosen for their compassion and gregariousness, can they?"

While he was speaking, he nudged Qapel gently with his toes, trying to rouse the Dahran from his unnatural sleep. Cheron resumed the struggle against the cords, and made a little headway in the attempt to work his right hand free.

Qapel began to come around. His first words were: "They told me when I left my village that I was a fool. At least my brother is spared."

"You're not dead yet," Cheron informed him.

"I am in the hands of demons," replied Qapel. "What is the difference. I am hurting."

"They didn't drag us here and tie us up without a reason," said Cheron, as much for his own benefit as for Qapel's. "Their intention, at least for the moment, is to keep us alive."

"What I want to know," muttered Vito Talvar, "is where they are now. And what they're doing. Why *us*, do you think?"

"Perhaps we are the only ones who lived," said Cheron. "But more likely, we are the only living men who did not take to the water. I doubt if the forest men can swim. We four were unlucky enough to be taken out of the fight early, but lucky enough to be taken out without being killed. I doubt very much whether they selected us for some mysterious privilege."

His right hand came free at last, and he quickly disentangled his left. He began picking at the cords around his ankles, cursing his lack of a knife.

"Never mind that," said Vito Talvar. "Free my hands, then Qapel's. That way we can *all* work at untying further knots."

Cheron saw the sense of this and began to wrestle with Talvar's bonds, disregarding the blond man's impatient twitches as best he could.

"Which way is the river?" demanded Talvar. "If we can get to it. . . ."

"The sun is moving westward in the sky," said Cheron. "The shadows will point west if they are shortening, east if they are lengthening. We must still be on the east bank of the river."

"We can't sit still and wait to see how the shadows move," complained Qapel, impatient to have Cheron make a start on releasing him.

"We can always guess," said Cheron. "And if we're wrong, we'll find out soon enough and turn back."

Bent over his task, he did not notice that it was already too late. He did not know it until Vito Talvar wrenched his hands free and indicated that he should turn around. He did so, and saw the men of the forest clearly for the first time.

They seemed as much ape as man. Had they extended themselves to their full height they might have measured a meter and a half from top to toe, but their spines were curved, and in fact they crouched humpbacked and bent-legged. Nevertheless, they were bigger than Cheron had judged them to be when they had been mere shadows in the firelight. Their chests were burly, their legs strong and their heads large. They were not, as rumor had it, four-handed—the feet still took much of the burden of support and were far more massive than the hands, but the toes were long and supple, obviously geared for gripping and for a certain degree of manipulative ability. Though they wore no beards—their dark brown faces were naked and the skin seemed to have the texture of polished wood—they were rather hairy. In front the hair was pale and downy, gray and yellow streaks fading into one another, but across their backs and around their limbs the hair was much coarser and its color darker, dappled brown and gray-green. The patterns of their coats varied, individualizing them. The hair on their heads was daubed with some kind of pigment; sometimes red, sometimes yellow, and once black.

The savages were crouching on the ground at the edge of the clearing, scorning the thin branches of the awkward trees that surrounded it.

As Cheron turned away from Vito Talvar, coming into a kneeling position, one of the savages threw something at him—or, at least, *to* him. He flinched reflexively, but the bundle came apart as it landed close to his hand, and he saw

with surprise that it was an army jacket. In fact, as he found
on closer inspection, it was *his* jacket.

The savages swung their long arms almost as if they were
trying to stone the group of prisoners to death, but what they
lobbed into the clearing was an assortment of kitbags, sleeping blankets, water bottles, bandages, bowls, and spoons.
Some of the apemen came forward—though tentatively—to
lay down other gifts—bread, some dry biscuits, some preserv-
atives in screw-top jars. Then they retired and stood watching.

Cheron finished releasing Vito Talvar, and then freed his
ankles while Talvar released Qapel's hands. Then he went to
look at Midas, and found that the little Merkadian was more
badly hurt than he had seemed.

"I think they're planning a journey," said Vito Talvar, in
his own language.

Cheron replied in Dahran, for Qapel's sake: "They seem to
be seeing to it that we're well provided for." He picked up his
jacket and put it on.

One of the forest men—the one with the black-painted
crown—signaled with his hands that the prisoners were to
gather up the other equipment. Talvar and Qapel began to
comply, while Cheron untied Midas. Finally, Cheron stood
up and began to inform the apemen in sign language that
Midas would have to be carried. At first, he thought they did
not understand, and he tried ever-more elaborate pantomimes
involving imaginary stretchers. He mimed the business of
skinning saplings to make poles, but they did not seem
impressed by the notion of providing him with a knife. In the
end, they made placatory gestures, and after a delay of some
minutes they produced the makeshift stretcher themselves,
having found poles among the wreckage of the stockade and
its buildings—or so it seemed.

"I'm going to dress that head wound," Cheron told his
companions. "The stuff in my belt should sterilize the bandage and prevent infection. There's not much else I can do,
except give him something to control the pain if he wakes up.
I don't think he can have been hit by a dart—he's just been
knocked unconscious. I only hope his skull isn't fractured."

"I think they're inviting us to move," said Talvar.

"Tell them to wait," Cheron instructed him. He did not
bother to look up to watch the blond man attempting to con-
vey this message to their captors. When he had finished, he

and Qapel eased their stricken comrade onto the stretcher. Qapel moved to pick up one end, but Cheron waved him back.

"Vito," he said. The blond man took up one of the packs, and then took the head of the stretcher. When they were all set, they looked again at the black-capped savage, who made clucking noises that may have indicated satisfaction and pointed with a stabbing finger, insistently.

"Which direction is that?" asked Vito Talvar. "I haven't been watching the shadows."

"Neither have I," replied Cheron Felix. "But I wouldn't mind taking long odds that it's east."

3

The cell was some three meters by two. Its walls were made of ill-fitting wooden planks and its floor was dirt. It would not have held a determined prisoner for three days, but the overwhelming probability was that no one had ever tried to get out of it. There was nowhere to go. Outside the cell there was the fort; the fort was on an island; the island was in the estuary of the Bela river. Anyone placed in the cell had little alternative but to accept his situation. The worst of it was the smell; the sanitary arrangements were distinctly primitive.

Baya-undi lay back on his bunk, staring up at the small skylight set in the slanting ceiling.

"I do not understand it," he said. "It's utterly unjust. We have done nothing."

"Things could be worse," said Sarid Jerome. "Rumor has it that the savages took full advantage of the new moon. I don't know how the rest of the company fared, but I suspect many of them would be glad to trade places with us . . . if they were able to be glad about anything at all."

"But it makes no sense! Why have they taken us away from the others? What do they intend to do to us? It is madness."

"It's no use asking me," said Sarid. "Perhaps they have discovered that you and I were, after all, illegally inducted. Perhaps they intend to set us free, and return us to our homelands." His voice was level, but even Baya-undi appreciated that he was being rather bitterly sarcastic.

"They should have told us why," said the black man. "We should not be treated in this way by supposedly civilized men."

"They didn't *know* why," said Sarid tiredly. "Some kind of signal came through. I think they may have a crude radio link with Asdar. Anyhow, they were told to hold us. Maybe a messenger came through on the last boat, and we're being held for someone coming in on the next. They're not being malicious—they're just following their orders."

Baya-undi was silent for some minutes, and then said: "I suppose that you know of no reason why this might have happened?"

Sarid sat up on his own bunk in order to look his companion in the eye. "Do *you*?" he countered.

"Of course not. Except. . . ."

"Except that we talked about desertion," Sarid finished for him. "My friend, *everyone* talks about desertion. It is a perennial topic of conversation. If they were to arrest everyone who discussed the possibility there would be two hundred men in this cell, and not just two. Unless, of course, you did something more than talk, back in Asdar?"

"I did nothing," said Baya-undi. "Nothing at all."

"In that case," said the Tanagarian, "it's clearly a case of mistaken identity. It was some other northern giant and some other Khepran spy they wanted." In his head, however, he was carrying on a much fiercer argument. There was no reason, so far as he could see, that any mutual act committed by himself and Baya-undi could be responsible for their arrest. Clearly, mistaken identity was entirely out of the question. Therefore, it had to be *either* himself *or* Baya-undi who was wanted, and for some reason they had both been taken in. If it was Baya-undi who was the object of the move, then the charge to be laid was presumably to do with Baya-undi's information-gathering activities in Sau. But if the object of the arrest was himself . . . what could possibly have happened?

Had the other Hedonists landed in Dahra after all—and had they managed to organize themselves without falling prey to the Macarian recruitment drive? Were *they*, in some way, behind this? If so, how? If not, who . . . ?

He knew that the only way to cope with these questions was to be patient, but it was not his way to be patient. Imprisonment was, for a man such as he, the ultimate irritation. It forbade action, and while he did not know the reasons for it, it precluded constructive thought.

He propped an elbow up upon his knee, and rested his chin on the heel of his hand pensively.

"Baya-undi," he said finally.

"Yes?"

"There's a rat under your bed. I think you should move your boots."

4

Mihiel handed the bundle to Teresa Janeat, and watched her unpack it. She held up a pair of trousers, looking critically at their length.

"They're only a little too small," said the Merkadian. "They're not new, of course, but they're clean. You won't look out of place in them. I think you can still pass as a man, easily enough."

"Did you have any trouble?" asked Salvador.

"No," said Mihiel. "There are a great many Merkadians here. There's a kind of loyalty that arises out of the fact that they're on alien soil, plundering from the Macarians in partial reparation for all the political crimes of history. I have Macarian money, too—but only a little. You didn't give me much to change."

"What about the documents?"

"We'll have to collect them. They're being prepared—you'll have a chance to look them over before parting with the gold. They'll provide more Macarian script, too, in return for the rest of the coin."

"You didn't tell them how much coin we have?" asked Teresa.

"I had to tell them that you had enough," Mihiel replied, coolly. "I was vague enough about the currency exchange."

"You think these men are trustworthy?" asked Salvador.

"I think so."

"How much of their trust is founded in this loyalty among Merkadians?"

Mihiel shrugged. "They know that you are not from Merkad," he said. "I told them that your own nation had much in common with ours—that your people had been treated as mine had. They know nothing of the barbarian territories beyond the northern mountains, but I think they accepted my word."

"You can't depend on that," said Teresa, in Tanagarian. "He's a peasant, in their eyes—they'd slit his throat as readily as ours. They're taking us all for a ride. We have no guns, remember."

Salvador did not respond. Instead, he continued the conversation with Mihiel, in Merkadian. "Where do we have to go?"

"To a warehouse, not unlike this one," said Mihiel. "There's a small office, where a great deal of paperwork is done. The warehouse was busy while I was there, but it will be empty now that darkness has come. If they intend to rob us . . . well, the opportunity is there. I could not ask for a safer meeting place, however, for that would have betrayed a lack of trust, and that might have led them to plan theft if they did not intend it already. We do not have to go. We could leave now, and trust to good fortune."

"That might be a good idea," said Teresa, speaking now so that Mihiel could understand her.

"No," said Salvador. "We'll get the papers."

He took from the bundle the clothes that Mihiel had obtained for him, and he began to change. Teresa, after a moment's hesitation, did likewise. She was not unduly displeased. At least they were grasping the nettle—deciding what was necessary and going for it, in a straightforward manner. Secretly, she liked the notion of the train journey. As Salvador had said, if it had been her own plan she would have tolerated no others.

They had taken up temporary lodgings on the top floor of a warehouse that was not currently in use. Salvador had picked the lock on the main door, and as yet no one had tried to move in with them. The room they were in had no windows, and the light of their candles did not betray their presence to anyone outside.

When they had finished dressing, Mihiel said: "We have more than an hour to wait. I will know the time from the stars. It is not far."

"We will spend the time in learning," said Salvador.

Teresa made a small sound to signify disgust.

Salvador turned his pale eyes toward her, and said, "You would be welcome to join us. Practice in mental discipline is valuable for everyone. You are neglecting your own mental fitness deliberately, as some kind of gesture of defiance. That is not intelligent."

"I'll look after my own mind," she said. "I'm going down to the dock." She went out of the room and descended to the lower floor, leaving Salvador to continue his experiment in human engineering. She knew that it was not going well. Without the drugs given to Tanagarians in infancy to enhance the development of the nervous system, the boy must lack much of the physical resources necessary to cultivate even the degree of control that Hedonists possessed. There was no question of the Merkadian developing the potential longevity of the Tanagarians. At best he would learn to control a few bodily processes that were at present involuntary, and would learn to dominate the workings of his glands a little more than he could at present. Trance states and calm of mind he already had mastered, but they were the most superficial of tricks in ordinary circumstances, when external stimuli made no powerful claims on the attention and the adrenal glands. He already believed—and Salvador had not disabused him of the notion—that the trance itself was a kind of communication, the opening of barriers that had hitherto kept him hidden from the touch of God's breath. For Mihiel, that was an easy thing to believe.

She paused on the concrete apron before the warehouse, but there was no one about, so she walked down to the quay. The tide was out, and some thirty meters of silt was exposed at the seawall, but the quay still extended more than a hundred and forty meters into the quiet sea. A few sluggish waves hissed and rustled as they rolled over, but there was very little wind.

What Salvador had said to her before she left was, she realized, more true than she had allowed herself to see at the time. She was, at this moment, physically weaker than she had ever been before. Had she not been able to blank out the pain she would have been plagued by a constant ache in her leg, which had never fully recovered from the injury she had sustained in the Kezula. She should have been able to restore the damaged tissues to health, but her battle with the constant strain imposed by the long journey had never been fully won. Even leaving aside the leg injury, she had not been able to sustain herself against the rigors of recent existence as well as she should. She had bought too much temporary relief with endorphin, and now she was in a perpetual state of semi-anesthetization. Her reflexes were slow, her very thoughts seemed reluctant.

I am not fitted for this life, she told herself. *I am not made of the same frail flesh as these ephemeral men of Earth, and yet I suffer from the impositions of this vile environment. Earth is dragging me down, and I am slowly becoming its creature. If only I could discover what goes on behind the mask that Salvador wears instead of a face. I would dearly love to know whether he really has the strength to remain inviolate.*

It had never occurred to her before how much the gifts of Tanagarian civilization actually depended on the matrix of that civilization, despite the fact that they seemed quite independent of it. She wondered how much this experience might steal from her lifespan, and how rapidly she could properly restore herself once she reached the base in the northern forest.

She could not help but think about Mihiel, and his attempt to learn from Cyriac Salvador something of what he considered to be the basic equipment of a God-favored man. She felt that she understood his motives well enough, and Salvador's at least in part, but what fascinated her in the situation was its tragic absurdity. Though she might degenerate, in time, into such a creature as Earth might have birthed, no men of Earth—even in the security of the Tanagarian base or

the satellite—could ever hope to become more than the palest
imitation of a Tanagarian. It was not simply a matter of the
physical equipment and the early training, but also of the
knowledge and the habits. Not knowledge in the Intel sense
of system after system of integrated theory and data, but
knowledge in the sense of self-confidence and psychological
adjustment to the reality of things. A Merkadian might be
perfectly at home in Merkad, but he could never be at home
in the *universe*, as a Tanagarian was.

Or claimed to be.

The qualification that rose unbidden in her mind startled
her slightly. The notion that her intellectual and imaginative
horizons—even Salvador's—might seem from some other
point of view just as limited and stupid as Mihiel's was not
actually horrifying—it was not even unpleasant, if one had
any sense of irony at all—but it was strange. It was not the
kind of idea that was readily thinkable, let alone the kind of
thought that might sidle out of an unsuspected crack in her
self-consciousness.

It is not merely Mihiel, she thought, *but the whole of
Earth that is limited. And not just now, but forever. No matter how ingenious the Macarians may be, they can never
reconstitute the technology of ancient Earth. Their industrial
revolution will peak much earlier, will fail to deliver all that
the old books promise them. They lack the power, in the
broadest possible sense of the term. They can never make
that crucial metamorphosis that will allow them to become
Tanagarians. Not, at least, if they are left to develop themselves, with or without the help of men from the vaults. It is
not Tanagarian intelligence that they need to help them over
the hurdle, but Tanagarian starships. Without those, they are
confined by their resources, and they will never be able to
build their own.*

There was no thought in this reverie that she had not previously entertained, but now it pointed, uncertainly, to a new
concluding notion . . . a new question.

What, then, might they become instead?

She wondered whether the question had occurred to Salvador, and—if so—what his attitude might be to the range of
imaginable answers.

She stared down at the impenetrable water for a few
minutes longer, and then began to walk slowly back to the

warehouse, where she met Salvador and Mihiel making their way down the wooden staircase.

"I haven't been away as long as that," she said.

"No," answered Salvador, "but I do not think it will do any harm to be early at our destination. I will not mind waiting if our papers are not quite ready, and it will give us a chance to size up the situation."

She fell into step, and Mihiel led the trio through the warren of side streets behind the docks. Occasionally, as they walked by, people would stop to stare because of their tallness, but no one spoke to them or seemed unduly disturbed by the sight of them.

Their destination proved to be less than twenty minutes away. It was, as Mihiel had said, a back-street warehouse set at the end of a cul-de-sac. There were stables beside it, and the heavy breathing of horses was the only sound they could hear as Mihiel knocked on the door panel cut into the tall gateway of the warehouse. After a brief exchange of whispers they were admitted.

Unlike the warehouse where they had rested since the afternoon, this one was piled high with crates, and there were men repackaging goods in a lighted enclave in the rear. They did not get a chance to see what kind of goods were being handled, though, for they were taken by the man who had admitted them to a small office, also lighted, which was in the corner behind the gates.

Inside, there was a man working at a desk, in the light cast by an oil lamp. He was smoking a pipe with a slender stem and a round bowl. He did not look up for several seconds after they had entered.

He said: "You're early," and then leaned back in his chair to subject Salvador and Teresa to a searching examination.

"Northerners," he said finally. "From Axrig. At least, that's where you're from *now*. Axrig." He stabbed a finger at the documents scattered on his desk. The desk was extremely untidy, littered with papers, inkstands and various kinds of stamp-blocks.

"The papers are ready?" asked Salvador.

"Just," agreed the other man. His voice was slow and grating, and his eyes had not lost their calculating stare. "You have the money?"

Salvador nodded. He had already transferred a good deal

of coin from the money belts which he wore to his pockets. He now brought forth a small pouch containing gold coins. Their apparent origins were various, but it was their content that mattered, not their ornamentation.

The man with the pipe accepted the bag, and spilled the coins onto his desk. He picked up three in turn, weighing them in his palm. Finally, he settled on one and held it up.

"Where did you get this?" he asked.

"Does it matter?" asked Salvador.

"Dahra has been debasing its gold coinage gradually for the last forty years," he said. "Bankers and Macarians—and anyone else with any sense—started hoarding these a generation ago. There's nothing like them in circulation now. What are men from the northern forests doing in company with Merkadian southerners, crossing the Bitter Sea in fishing craft?"

"If what you say is true," said Salvador, equably, "you should be glad to get the coin."

"If?"

"I don't doubt that it is," Salvador reassured him.

"Do you have more of this?"

Salvador shook his head. "Not here."

"Where?"

"Farther than you'd care to go. I have a few extra ounces that I should trade for Macarian paper money. That's all I'm carrying."

As he said it, Salvador took a few more coins from another pocket.

Teresa began to grow anxious. She and Salvador had two money belts each. They were wearing them. This would not have been obvious in the loose-fitting clothes that they had previously adopted, but now that they were in Macarian dress the bulge at Salvador's waist was quite noticeable.

"We will take the papers now," said Salvador softly.

The Merkadian shrugged, and began to gather the materials on the desk, sorting out half a dozen sheets of paper and some pieces of folded card.

"The certificates are given in the name of an obscure local parliament in the north," he said. "They'll pass anywhere except the region itself. The countersignatures aren't forgeries, but no one you meet is likely to have seen the real signatures of the noble gentlemen in question. They don't give you any authority, so don't try ordering anyone about. They give you permission to go just about anywhere except sites and premises controlled by the College, but don't push your luck anywhere that you're clearly not wanted."

Salvador read over the papers carefully, taking several minutes to do so. The Merkadian watched him, frowning.

"The boy said you could read," he murmured. "You know, I think I'd like some evidence of your *real* identity. I don't know of anywhere you could have got those coins, except perhaps from a Macarian bank. You didn't get them in Dahra, but maybe someone wants us to think that you did."

Salvador met his hostile stare quite casually. "You think we're agents of the police?" he asked.

"It's not true," said Mihiel quickly. "They are men of God—healers and holy men."

It was perhaps the worst thing he could have said. It was far too obviously absurd.

"Search them," ordered the man with the pipe. Teresa felt the hands of the man who had brought them to the room touch her waist and move upward. They were already aware of the belts, and they would soon be apprised of the fact that she, at least, was not presenting her true appearance to the world.

She turned quickly and smashed the edge of her hand into the man's throat. He was taken completely by surprise, and was unable to make any evasive action. He was hurled back into the edge of the open door, gasping horribly.

The door was slammed shut as he fell, and his body blocked it. Teresa had to stoop to grip him by the shoulders and pull him aside, but already there was someone else in the shadows beyond, trying to push as she pulled.

The man with the pipe brought his right hand up from his lap, where he had carelessly laid it to rest. It was holding a pistol. He had presumably intended to use this simply to cover his guests while they were searched, but Teresa's action had taken him by surprise too. He fired, without taking proper aim. The bullet went past Salvador's ear as he ducked away from it.

Mihiel leapt over the desk and launched himself upon his seated countryman. The chair went over backwards, and the two Merkadians were tumbled to the floor in an untidy heap.

The gun went off again, but neither Teresa nor Salvador was in a position to see the result.

The first man who came through the door was large, but his bulk was mostly fat. He was wielding an iron crowbar, and tried to chop this across Teresa's face. She ducked under the sweeping arm and launched herself forward to butt the man in his midriff, sending him staggering back into the others who were trying to follow him through the narrow doorway. Teresa went after him, and Salvador—seeing how heavily she was outnumbered, followed her.

The fat man finally sat down, and one of the others got past him, wielding a thick shaft of wood a meter-forty long and six centimeters in diameter. Teresa grabbed it as it whistled through the air toward her, and twisted, using its momentum to jerk the man off balance. When he recovered, *she* had the club, and she fractured his skull with it.

Salvador kicked a knife out of one man's hand, and stabbed a thumb into someone else's eye.

A stack of boxes toppled over on top of Teresa, knocking her to the floor, but she was able to roll out of the way of the assault which followed. A man with a knife left off threatening Salvador to stab at her, but a kick from the Intellectual took him at the base of his spine and he sprawled over her instead. She broke his arm, took the knife from his nerveless fingers, and shoved the blade into the side of his neck. Someone fired a pistol at her, but the bullet hit the body of the knifeman. By the time she extricated herself Salvador had put the gunman out of action.

Teresa dived for the gun that clattered on the stone floor, and snatched it up in time to see the man with the pipe, risen now from behind his desk, taking aim at Salvador's back. She put a bullet into his face, and his own shot went wild. When she turned to find more targets, she could see only fallen men. Three were still able to crawl, and she took careful aim at one of them.

"Wait!" said Salvador.

She hesitated—and then, having hesitated, obeyed.

Salvador surveyed the carnage left by her assaults, and compared it with the results of his own.

"You appear to have learned your methods very thoroughly," he observed.

"It's easy," she said, "once you get the hang of it." As she looked at the blood flooding out of the neck of the man she had stabbed, she realized that she spoke the exact truth. It was *so* easy.

Salvador went back into the office, and stepped behind the desk.

"Come *on*," she said. "We've got the papers. We have to get out of here before the shots bring a mob with the police in tow."

But Salvador was standing quite still, looking down at something behind the desk, and seemed not to have heard. She realized that it must be Mihiel, and that he must be dead.

"There isn't *time!*" she shouted, and her voice rose so steeply that the final word was almost a screech.

Already there were noises in the street, and the horses next door had begun to whinny in gathering panic.

By the time the vanguard of the crowd arrived, however, the Intellectual and the Pragmatist had made their escape through the back of the warehouse, taking with them their forged papers, their gold, and a revolver that still contained three live cartridges.

5

At first, the trek through the forest was not too different from the journey upriver that had brought the company southward from the dam. The trees were dense, but the bright sunlight burst through the canopy in a thousand radiant beams that were forever shifting and blinking as the leaves fluttered in the breeze. The ground was covered with plants whose rubbery leaves hugged the ground, and with carpets of green florets whose nectar attracted hordes of humming insects.

They took turns carrying the stretcher on which Midas lay, though Qapel took only brief spells. The weight tired him far more than Cheron and Talvar, but he insisted on sharing the work. Occasionally the undergrowth was dense enough to cause them problems, but for the most part the forest men guided them by a winding route that was easy enough to follow. Only two or three of the apemen were with them at any one time, and frequently only one. They too, it seemed, took turns in this onerous duty. They did not like to walk. Wherever the others went, Cheron felt sure they were following a course much more attractive to their own way of thinking.

As the day wore on, however, the forest changed, as they knew it would. The trees grew steadily larger—thicker in the trunk and much taller. They grew further apart, but the amount of sunlight that evaded their crowns grew less and less, for the boughs grew more widely and the foliage much more densely. The low boughs retreated to form a kind of ceiling twenty meters above their heads, and soon the boughs that they could see were almost all gnarled and bare and all but dead, their functions having passed to successors much higher in the canopy. Without light to support them, the green plants disappeared from the ground, leaving only saprophytes to plunder the rich humus—white and yellow fungi, often grotesque and ugly, which were in their turn the food of insects and small animals equally bizarre. It was not too difficult for Cheron to imagine that the whole stratum that contained them was a kind of graveyard, haunted rather than lived in by pale, cold things.

For a while, their way was illuminated dimly by a feeble gleam from areas in the canopy which were not so much transparent as translucent, but eventually Cheron paused to light a lantern. By this time they had only one attendant, who never touched the ground with his hands or feet but moved instead on the lower boughs, looking down at them and occasionally signaling the way to them with urgent jabbing motions. His companions, no doubt, were able to keep much closer to the sun.

"How much oil do we have for the lantern?" asked Cheron of Qapel, who had taken an inventory of the supplies the forest men had given them.

"Enough for forty hours," replied the Dahran. "Less than two days if we let it burn while we sleep. Three if we use it only while we move."

"That sets the limit on our journey, then," said Talvar.

"We may hope so," said Cheron, dryly. "But let's not take it as a guarantee."

The prospect of having to walk through this Stygian underworld without a lantern was disturbing, but the prospect of having to walk through it at all for days on end was disturbing enough in itself, and they did not dwell too much upon the more frightening possibility.

By the time they stopped to rest and eat, Cheron could no longer estimate what time of day or night it might be. They had surely walked for several hours, but he had not been sure what time of day it was when they set off. The sun had been high, but whether it had been late morning or early afternoon he had not bothered to ascertain. He knew that from now on the cycle of night and day might mean very little.

Strangely, for a land of eternal night the forest floor was not particularly cold. The temperature had dropped considerably lower during one or two of the nights they had spent in Dahra, though only for a few hours. Here, such heat as there was did not leach away, either into the ground or up into the atmosphere. Perhaps the forest regulated it in some manner.

To supplement the meal they made from the supplies provided at the start of their journey the forest men brought them fruit. Midas finally came around, and was able to sip a little water, but he was weak and very ill, and could not manage a coherent sentence. They wrapped an extra blanket around him to make sure that he stayed warm.

"If we could make a fire," said Qapel, "we might make a soup of some kind."

"We have been eating soup twice a day since time immemorial," said Vito Talvar. "I can no longer remember a time when I did not live exclusively on soup. Rejoice that at last we have a change. At this stage, any change should be hailed as a new joy. We may not have much to be joyful about in this place. I am sorry now that I ever suggested that hell might be anything but darkness, where there is nothing to walk on but the substance of decay, and where everything is either dead or vile. Obviously, I am being punished now for having complained too much in the past. No doubt I will have ample opportunity to scream my sorrow at the empty sky, after we all go mad."

"Perhaps we can make a fire when we rest tonight," said Cheron. "When I made a move to unpack and pitch the tent,

our guardian signaled furiously, so I think we have much farther to go before we rest for any length of time. At least the
walking is easy now that there are no creepers to tangle our
feet, and no stinging insects to add to the miseries of sweltering heat."

"No indeed," said Talvar. "Perhaps, then, this is paradise
and a just reward for all the prayers we offered when the
sweat stood on our faces and the insects swarmed around our
lips and eyes."

"Where can they possibly be taking us?" asked Qapel,
whose mind was perpetually grappling with immediate problems, and shunned the flights of fancy that decorated the
thoughts of Vito Talvar and Midas. The fact that the questions he asked were unanswerable did not inhibit him from
dwelling obsessively upon them.

"They must have a good reason," said Cheron. "They're
taking far too much trouble for any trivial purpose. We're
slowing them down, and causing them to descend regularly,
one by one, to this wilderness which is surely hell to *them* as
much as it is to us. If our journey is to be long, it will be
arduous, and no less so for them than for us."

"What manner of creatures are they?" asked Vito Talvar.
"They seem neither animals nor men. Are they the descendants of human beings or of apes? How can they have
changed so much—whatever they are—in the time that has
passed since the upheaval? There was nothing like them in
the old world."

"There was nothing like the forest, either," said Cheron.
"A tree is a tree, but what we have here is a community of
trees that creates an environment that the Earth has not previously known. The old world had rain forests, but not like
this. If this land was irradiated in the atom wars, then such
plant life as survived might have been changed drastically by
mutation and selection, but I cannot help but find this place
strange and unnatural."

"At least we live," said Qapel, turning from contemplating
mysteries to counting his blessings. "In the moment when I
was struck down I expected never to rise. I would have said
my death prayer if I could."

."Were you hit by a dart?" asked Cheron.

"Grazed by an arrow, I think," replied the Dahran. "The
back of my hand is scratched, though not deeply. It was not

fired at me—it was held by one of the demons when he jumped on me."

"I think they intended to take prisoners," said Cheron. "Perhaps their weapons were anointed with something other than their customary poison, or they diluted the poison so that it would not kill. All of this has been deliberate."

"Including the selection?" said Talvar, waving his hand to indicate the present company.

"That would be to take the conspiracy to absurd lengths," said Cheron. "No, they simply wanted prisoners, to take into the heartland of the forest. Perhaps we are curiosities, destined to be caged in some distant place where the savages have never seen an upright man, and never before suspected that any such existed. Our captors may have been called liars for telling tales of their battles against alien invaders, and we are to be their living proof."

"I think I like that idea better than the one about being taken back home to be tortured to death, but I still don't like it much. Do you suppose there's any chance of our escaping?"

"Every chance," said Cheron. "There's also every chance that we'd never find our way out of here. In fact, I'd say that our chances of survival are entirely dependent on the good will of our hosts."

"That," said Talvar, "is exactly what I'm afraid of."

6

———

Sarid Jerome and Baya-undi came out of the bathhouse dripping water, and were handed towels. Clean uniforms and undershirts were waiting for them when they finished. Sarid noticed without surprise that his money belt had disappeared. At the moment of arrest his person and property had ceased to be sacred.

While they dressed they were attended by a guard carrying

a rifle, but his presence was largely symbolic. He stared studiously out to sea, knowing full well that there was no possibility of his charges attempting escape.

They had bathed, of course, in salt water which had been pumped directly from the ocean and coarsely filtered. Macarian sea soap was not terribly efficient, but Sarid still felt clean and refreshed by comparison with the way a night in the cells had left him.

"I take it," he said to the guard, "that the man who has ordered us to be arrested came in on this morning's steamer?"

"I don't know," replied the guard, as instinctively uncommunicative as all of his species. He saw that his charges had finished their preparations, and indicated that they should begin to move back to the gatehouse, where a sergeant was waiting to conduct them to their rendezvous in a proper military fashion.

They were marched across the drill-square and taken into the building which housed the commandant's quarters and most of the offices occupied by his staff. They were taken into one of the offices, whose design seemed to Sarid strikingly similar to the first room which he had seen on the Motherworld—the office in the barrack house on the road south of Sau, where he had been inducted into the army. The man sitting behind the desk, however, did not have his feet on the table, and he rose when Baya-undi and Sarid were shown in. He indicated that they should be seated, and did not resume his own seat until they were.

Sarid noticed that on the desk in front of him was the money belt which had been taken from him and the bag of personal possessions that had been taken from Baya-undi.

"What are your names?" asked their interlocutor. He was a man in his late thirties or early forties, looking not unlike Captain Donsella ti Ria, though he was not in uniform. His hair was light brown and his skin was pale, hardly tanned at all by the sun. He was obviously Macarian, and had not been long in the south.

When Sarid and Baya-undi had given their names, he asked: "And what are your nations?"

"Khepra," replied the black man.

"Camelon," said Sarid, after a slight hesitation.

"I think that one of you, at least—and perhaps the other too —is lying," said the man at the desk. When this statement brought no immediate response, he said: "My name, by the way, is Toran Zeyer. I'm a member of the College of Archaeologists, based in Solis."

He opened two of the pouches in the money belt, and pulled out a gold coin and one of the small phials containing a colorless liquid.

"This coin is curious," he said. "Even with a primitive balance I can detect that its weight is wrong. If it is gold, it is too pure. If some other metal is inside the plating, it is counterfeit. The phial—and all the others with it—is unremarkable, but the medicines in them do not have the appearance of the charms that are usually found in such things. There is nothing with a strong smell, and I recognize none of the herbs and potions which are popularly rumored to be effective in combating magic and disease."

"What does that signify?" asked Sarid.

"Hardly anything. *Your* charms" (he was speaking now to Baya-undi) "are much more conventional. In a way, almost *too* conventional, for a man who comes from Khepra. They are almost all of Dahran and Kyadian origin."

Baya-undi shrugged. "In foreign places," he said, "one uses the methods that are effective there. In Dahra I needed no wards against Khepran magic. Nor do I need such things in Khepra, where evil magic is far less often practiced than in Dahra."

"Quite so," said Zeyer. "There is nothing here which offers any clear testimony at all as to your origins, but by the same token it cannot tell me that your stories are false. Nevertheless, I believe that one of you is not from the nation you have given as your own—and, in fact, is from no other nation on the face of this world. One of you, at least, is from a world that circles another star. And since you are both indubitably human, I think that the man in question is probably descended from the people who left Earth more than twenty thousand years ago, before the old world was destroyed. It would save us all a little time and trouble if one of you—or both—would care to tell me the truth."

The silence was impenetrable, as both Sarid and Baya-undi registered their astonishment. Sarid glanced sideways and suppressed an urge to laugh at the amazement of his companion, which was just about to be compounded. *Poor Baya-*

undi! he thought. *A man who does not believe that there ever was an old world!*

"How did you know?" he said, as levelly as he could.

Zeyer turned his blue eyes to stare at Sarid. "We are not fools," he said. "You must have realized that we would find the crashed ship, and that when we found it we would know it for what it was. It came down in Merkad, near the border with the Kezula—shattered by the impact but certainly not obliterated."

Sarid shook his head slowly. "I didn't know that it had crashed," he whispered. "We were dropped in Dahra. Cheron said that he saw a flash, but we had no way of knowing the ship came down."

"We?" said Zeyer, his glance flashing swiftly to Baya-undi.

Sarid sighed. "Not him," he said. "He really *is* from Khepra, unless he's a Kyadian with delusions of grandeur. I had two companions. They're still upriver."

"Cheron Felix and Vito Talvar?"

"That's right."

"There were no others?"

"There were supposed to be. There were twenty of us aboard the ship. I've seen and heard nothing whatsoever of the others. It looks as if none of them made it. Unless they're in the Kezula, living wild."

Zeyer looked down for a moment, then lifted his eyes again to look at Sarid. His face was set hard, but there was a burning curiosity in those eyes.

"A report came in this morning," he said. "Your company was attacked at the post where it paused for the night. About half the men escaped down the river. Neither Cheron Felix nor Vito Talvar was among them."

Sarid digested the information but said nothing. He kept the muscles of his face under strict control. The table of temptations said nothing about sorrow, or even grief, but the table of the virtues stressed authority, calm, and above all else, control. Sarid Jerome had never made a fetish out of being a virtuous man, but there were moments when virtue is a necessity.

"It seems, then," said Zeyer slowly, "that you're alone."

"Quite alone," agreed Sarid. *Except*, he added silently, *for the eavesdroppers in the sky.*

"The news from upriver isn't very definite," said the Macarian, "but men who fall victim to the savages never reappear. Any hope there might be is very slender."

"Yes," said Sarid. "I know. And if any of the others got out before the ship began to malfunction, they'd have got out of the Kezula as quickly as possible, into Merkad or Dahra. They were on the edge—they couldn't have crossed the mountains into Kyad."

"My colleagues are making investigations in the territory surrounding Sau and that around Zedad. If there's anyone else, we'll find them. If not . . . then I'm all the more glad that you came back down the river in one piece. You must explain to me, among other things, just why you were going up the river in the first place."

Sarid opened his mouth to reply, but Toran Zeyer waved him into silence. The Macarian stood up, and went to the door. He opened it, and informed the waiting sergeant that Baya-undi could be returned to normal duties within the fort.

When the black man had gone, Zeyer returned to his seat. From a cupboard set in the wing of the desk he produced a bottle of wine and two glasses. He poured out two measures and passed one over to Sarid Jerome.

"We'll return on the steamship," he said. "We must get back to Macaria as soon as possible. To Solis first, and then to Armata. But first, Sarid Jerome, you must tell me. . . .

"Who are you? And why are you here?"

7

My name is Sarid Jerome (said Sarid), and I am a Pragmatist. It will take a long time to make you understand all that that word implies. If you know it at all, you will know it in a way that is devoid of the greater part of the meaning it carries on Tanagar.

Tanagar is the name of my world.

I think that even to explain the way that I describe myself,

and what I mean when I speak the name of Tanagar, I will
have to tell you something about our ancient history.
Strangely, it is a subject which I do not know a great deal
about. By Tanagar's standards I am an incompletely educated
man. You will understand that, I think. Your own society is
becoming more complex, and if I were to take a man from
Macaria—not the worst of your citizens, but an ordinary, intelligent man who has some useful role to perform—there
would be little chance of his being able to tell me everything
about Macaria that is known. Even among our Intellectuals—that word, too, has a special meaning—there is none
who knows everything that is known. There is a division of
labor among them as there is between all individuals, and to
recover *all* of the knowledge that Tanagar possesses you
would need a very large library and a great number of human beings.

Our ancestors left Earth in a starship named the *Marco
Polo.* There were other starships, but I know none of their
names and as far as we know they all perished somewhere in
the depths of space. The *Marco Polo* wandered through the
darkness in search of a habitable planet for a *long* time—far
longer than anyone had anticipated. The original generation
would not have expected to find a world in the course of
their own lifetime, but they must have entertained hopes on
behalf of their children and their grandchildren. Mathe-
matical calculations would have assured them that the probability of finding a world so soon was very small, but there are
few people who can see beyond their own personal horizons
in time, let alone those of their descendants. Every generation
born aboard the starship must have hoped, for its children if
not for itself. The end of the journey might have been only
fifty or a hundred years away—a generation then was what
you mean by a generation—and there was *always* hope, *always* anticipation. This, I think, was important. In fact, the
voyage of the *Marco Polo* lasted several thousand years. (I
am deliberately vague because time, for the inhabitants of the
ship, was slowed down a little relative to the time passing
here on Earth—or on Tanagar. Much of the time they were
accelerating from velocities well below light speed, or decelerating to them, but over the centuries the time dilatation
would have become important.)

Another thing which was important, if we are to understand the history of Tanagar and its founders, was the character of the Earthly society which they came from. You already know a good deal about that world by virtue of having dug what is left of it out of the soil. I don't know how complete your picture is, and you may know more than I do. What I know, however, is precisely what the starborne generations thought to be crucially significant.

I know that the *Marco Polo* left Earth after three centuries of rapid technological progress. From the building of steamships and railway engines not very different from those which you have today, to the building of starships like the *Marco Polo*, there was a time gap of no more than three hundred and thirty years. Perhaps eleven generations, though we may call it ten or fifteen if you wish. Those generations were crowded with change in almost every aspect of life, and through them all the pace of change continued to accelerate. In the beginning of the period, the prospect of material and mechanical progress was one which aroused tremendous optimism and confidence in the future. At the end of the period, the same notion was regarded almost with terror, and it was held that progress had destroyed the world, destroyed mankind, and destroyed everything that made life worth living.

In every one of those eleven generations there was a war. Usually, there were three wars, or four. In the beginning, they were small wars, but with technological expertise there grew the ability to make war more effectively, and on a much larger scale. Communications reduced the effective size of the political community that was the world to the point where wars, when they broke out, were likely to affect every last corner of the globe in one way or another, whether there were bombs falling there or not. The bombs that did fall grew in destructive power enormously, and the aftereffects of their use became appalling to contemplate. The world we are now in, I suppose, is the eventual product of those aftereffects, and if the first generation born aboard the *Marco Polo* could have seen this world they would have been triply appalled. They would have been distressed by the way things *are*, doubly distressed by an account of its history, and triply depressed by the pattern of development which suggests the kind of future it will have. For this world, as you no doubt know, is once again in the grip of material and technological progress . . . except that this time, there will be no starships.

Macarian technology will peak before another *Marco Polo* can be built. Whether it will peak before the world is provided with the means for its second self-destruction, however, is more open to question.

The point I am trying to make here, though, is not a point about *your* world, but a point about *theirs* . . . about the world they created aboard the starship. The starship, in a sense, *was* a world. It was a tiny world, but a world nevertheless. It was a metal shell containing a stable ecosystem, potentially capable of going on forever through the wilderness of space. That is perhaps as well, in view of the fact that it very nearly *did* have to go on forever. But the starship was a much more *controllable* world than Earth. Its physical processes were much more carefully regulated—as an environment it was much more completely *known*. Every detail of its delicate balance was appreciated, every aspect of its complex chain of dependencies was under constant check and supervision. There were a million things that might go wrong at any moment, but the people knew about them all, and were vigilant.

The social world of the *Marco Polo* was controllable too. There were three thousand people on board, and the ship was thus somewhat larger than a village, but it was nevertheless only a small town. Perhaps no man could know all his neighbors, but he could know most of them, and it was not difficult to *get to know* any one of the remainder.

The starship community, for this reason, was capable of extreme solidarity. Not only was it capable of it, but it had every possible motive for maintaining it. The community were refugees from a world which had—as they saw it—plunged into chaos, blindly and recklessly. They were living in circumstances which demanded that they should regulate their population strictly, not just in terms of absolute numbers but in terms of roles. Every man, woman and child on board had a role to fill, and while some roles were more demanding than others and many were probably not indispensable, that seemed to the community the way things should be.

The men and women of the *Marco Polo* had to create and sustain a perfectly stable society. Their physical conditions of life were basically unchanging, and their society had to fit in with that. On top of that, however, they began the journey with the notion imprinted on their minds that change was, if not utterly evil, at least terrifyingly dangerous. Innovation, in their eyes, had destroyed their Motherworld. In their psychology, the only possible perfection lay in stability; change, no matter how promising it might seem, was threatening. Their ideal society was very much a Platonic one. (Do you have Plato? No matter.) Aboard the *Marco Polo* they established a Platonic Republic—a society designed to be secured against the very possibility of change in terms of its institutions and apparatus.

The community of the starship did not consider their social system to be Utopian—indeed, they saw Utopian dreams and ideals as contributors to the disaster which they had left behind on the Motherworld. They were suspicious of Utopianism and opposed most demands for social reform by stigmatizing them as Utopian fantasies. They considered the stability of their society to be a good in its own right—a kind of perfection in itself. They were unwilling—and perhaps unable—to discuss the problem of whether there might be alternative kinds of stability, for such questions could only become meaningful if they allowed the possibility of instituting social change in order to get from one state to another.

Two more general points need to be made in this connection. Firstly, the community did not see their situation as a sterile one, in the way that their ancestors might have considered it. This was not, you will remember, a society without a future, nor a society whose future could only be identical to its present. Every generation hoped for a kind of salvation which would occur, if not in the immediate future, at least in the foreseeable future. The stable society of the ship was a means as well as an end. Secondly—and this point is intimately related to the first—the community did not altogether abandon the mythology of progress. What they desired was *social* stability, what they opposed was *social* change, and the progress which terrified them was *material* and *technological* progress. They were not opposed to the growth of knowledge—how could they be, when their whole way of life was dependent upon total knowledge of their situation? Knowledge in itself, and in certain kinds of instrumental value, they held to be good, and they intended to make full use of their abilities to pursue further knowledge. The limitations they wanted to place were upon the *use* of knowledge—or, to be precise, certain kinds of use. Nor were they opposed to psychological changes. As well as the growth of knowledge they were committed to the growth of individual personality. Indeed, the chief purpose of the society they designed was to allow and encourage individual people to develop as they could and might into healthy, happy human beings. One of the main indictments they made of the society they left behind was precisely that it had *not* permitted this to happen. They were, in consequence, committed to an ideal of *moral* progress. They envisaged a pattern of social institutions which would be rigid, but considered that within those institutions—for this is what the institutions would be designed to do—individuals might become better people, from one year to the next and from one generation to the next.

These goals and commitments had several necessary consequences in the way that the starship society was organized. One consequence has to do with the growth of knowledge. There was already, in the Motherworld's societies, a class or caste of individuals whose primary role was to hold in trust and elaborate knowledge. I imagine that there is such a caste in Macaria today, gathered about the College of Archaeology, and I am sure that you will understand what I mean. Aboard the *Marco Polo* this class became much more distinct, for two primary reasons. Firstly, because the number of people aboard the ship was so limited, the responsibility of possessing knowledge became a much more important one. The ship's data banks, of course, carried virtually all of the Motherworld's knowledge, but the availability of data is not all that is involved in the maintenance of a knowledgeable culture. *Knowing* is far more than possessing a book or a tape, and the possession of knowledge in the form of a library of some kind is a very poor substitute for the possession of knowledge in the form of memory, expertise, and understanding. Data banks contain knowledge, but they do not *know* . . . and they surely do not *understand*. There was, therefore, a corps of men and women aboard the *Marco Polo* whose responsibility was to keep secure man's dominion over his own knowledge: all the knowledge that was not involved in the business of running the ship; all the knowledge that was not immediately applicable. This was not work that could be divided between the entire ship's complement, partly because some people filled roles which would have made this kind of accessory work too difficult, partly because some

people were simply not suited to it, but mainly because neither knowing nor understanding is something that can simply
be sliced up like a cake and shared in like manner.

The second reason for the appearance of the distinct caste
of Intellectuals was that these people now had a second dimension of responsibility. They were not only the society's
knowers, but also the ones who had to arbitrate concerning
the proper uses of knowledge. They were the people responsible for the disconnection of knowledge and technology. It was
not enough that they should know and understand—they
must also *control* knowledge and understanding in its social
uses and implications. The twin demands of maintaining the
growth of knowledge while keeping material and technological progress in a straitjacket necessitated the establishment of
a system wherein knowledge could be held esoterically. The
Intellectuals were required to know, and to control the dispersion of knowledge among themselves and others.

In saying that the caste of Intellectuals became distinct, I
do not mean to imply that those who were not Intellectuals
aboard the *Marco Polo* were without knowledge, nor that
they were deliberately discouraged from learning. All I mean
is that outside that caste of Intellectuals it was no one's *sworn
duty* to cultivate knowledge, and that there were certain items
of knowledge—whose removal from availability still left a
vast reservoir that no one mind or lifetime could hope to ex-
haust—which were confined. I am not a knowledgeable man,
though I hope I am not ignorant, but the important thing is
that it is not simply the lack of knowledge which sets me
aside from the Intellectuals. I could spend my lifetime in
study, if I wished, and cultivate expertise in a dozen different
fields, obtain free access to research facilities, make new discoveries . . . and still I would not be an Intellectual. To be
an Intellectual is different from making a hobby of self-culti-
vation or scientific research. To be an Intellectual is to have a
duty to perform certain intellectual tasks, and to be dominated
by that duty in every aspect of one's life. At the same time,
however, it is unlikely, given our educational system, that a
man who *did* want to spend his lifetime in study and make
new discoveries would be left to do so on an *ad hoc* basis
unless he so lacked discipline that he could not possibly become an Intellectual—in which case, so we are told, it would

be extremely unlikely that he ever *would* make any real contribution to the storehouse of knowledge. But I digress. . . .

It will be immediately obvious that the Intellectuals became the central political authority aboard the *Marco Polo*. The responsibility to determine the social uses of knowledge became virtually synonymous with the responsibility of social control and the maintenance of social order. The ship's society was democratic, but the real power was vested in the Intellectuals, for their duty was in itself a kind of power, as all duty is. The governing body of the ship was a Parliament of no fixed size, headed by an executive president. The Parliament, by majority decision, could co-opt anyone or drop anyone, and anyone else could be elected or dropped by petition of the populace—in fact, by a quota somewhat less than a majority. Members of the Parliament involved in particular executive decisions routinely sought endorsement by petition. In practice, the Parliament always had more members than it needed, and never worked as efficiently as it should, simply because of the generosity of people in and out of it, who were far more eager to co-opt new members than to banish old ones. This was never seen as a disadvantage—efficiency in making decisions was not regarded as a matter of high priority. The Intellectuals never had a majority in this Parliament, and were frequently underrepresented in strictly statistical terms, but they nevertheless controlled it. It would have been absurd, under the circumstances, for anyone but an Intellectual to be President, except in times when no decisions needed to be made and no executive was therefore required to exercise power. I presume, however, that the paradox of democracy is well-known to you.

I think it will be clear enough to you *why* the Intellectual caste developed, and how it became distinct from the remainder of the populace. It was not, of course, a hereditary caste. New recruits were selected on the basis of their aptitude for the role, in terms of intelligence, ability to learn, sense of commitment, et cetera. Candidates were selected as early as possible, and though late recruitment remained possible and some candidates were later rejected, the special training to which candidates were subjected almost invariably reinforced the kind of value priorities that were necessary and desirable. Candidates for the Intellectual class were taught to value knowledge for its own sake, to value self-discipline, and above all to value their own intellectual powers. Learning to be an Intellectual consisted far more in internalizing these values than in accumulating the knowledge that represented the resource which these vessels were intended to contain.

Because the Intellectuals selected out the children who showed spontaneous tendencies toward this pattern of values, and made no attempt to reinforce these values in individuals outside the intended Intellectual class, it was inevitable that non-Intellectuals should develop different value orientations. Because they knew exactly what they were doing, the Intellectuals began to look closely at the alternative modes of value orientation, and to consider their functionality very carefully.

It was clear to the Intellectuals—and, presumably, to everyone else—that happiness depended on the integration of an individual's desires and his or her role. In the crudest possible terms, if what a man did could not provide him with the means of getting what he wanted out of life, then he would not be content. In the view of the *Marco Polo* community, the seeds of self-destruction present in the society of the Motherworld—widespread discontent and the commitment to uncontrolled change—were direct consequences of a massive dislocation of ends and means affecting virtually all the Motherworld's societies at all levels. The desires of ordinary men had commonly been at odds—often grotesquely at odds—with the means available for their attainment. Men seemed to have been far more contented during the pre-progressive stage of social evolution, when society as a whole had not the means to provide more than a very few individuals with anything at all beyond the apparatus of simple survival. Where there was nothing to desire, apparently, people had been content to desire nothing.

I myself have never been certain of the merit of this argument. I do not believe that men were more content in the pre-progressive world. I think that they were as miserable as I would have been in their situation. I do not believe that there was much happiness about in the world at that time, and the fact that people did not notice its absence does not seem to me to be grounds for assuming its presence. However, you will have noticed by now that this commentary is not entirely complimentary. This account comes not from a fervent admirer of Tanagarian culture, but from a criminal and would-be revolutionary. This story is being told by a dissenting voice. Not, you understand, that I dissent from everything or disapprove of everything—simply that to some extent I stand on the sidelines, and am prepared to be cynical in regard to some of the developments of the society envolved aboard the *Marco Polo*, and even more cynical about succeeding events on Tanagar.

Anyhow, the Intellectuals aboard the starship saw as their principal problem in social engineering—the one fundamental achievement which would render their other aims practicable—the restoration of the integrity of desires and roles. What they wanted was to assure that every man, woman, and child aboard the ship should have the means available to fulfill such goals as he might legitimately choose for himself. It was not necessary that such fulfillment should be easy—indeed, it must not be too easy, for the instant gratification of desire kills contentment as easily as nonfulfillment—but it was necessary that the prospect of fulfillment should always be there, and that the prospect should be a realistic one. Things had to be set up so that everyone could, in the end, obtain the objects of his desire without having to make unrealistic demands upon his personal resources.

It was immediately obvious that this problem was not so much a problem in creating appropriate means as a problem in creating appropriate desires. The resources of the starship were strictly limited. There was nothing that was not measured: food, water, air, space, all kinds of possessions. Everyone knew this, and was well aware that there was no possible point in making demands that the ship's system could not fulfill. In this sense, the community of the ship was in a position which was widely seen as analogous to that of pre-progressive man. The ethos of *moderation* was already well-established. There was no possible opposition to the dominance of an ethic of self-control, by which it became unthinkable for any member of the community to demand more than the ration that was available to him. It helped, too, that in matters of food supply, water supply, and air supply a rigorous egalitarianism prevailed.

The Intellectuals did not accept that any particular *degree* of desire was already inbuilt into human beings. They accepted the necessity of desire, and the irrationality of presuming that humans could be born without inbuilt desires, but they did not admit the innate insatiability of the human organism. They did not interpret the catastrophe of the old world as a *natural* catastrophe which had come about because of a developing disjunction between the widespread perception of new possibilities for ambition which were necessarily limited in attainment to a small fraction of the ambitious. Indeed, they considered the tragedy of the old world to be very largely a matter of the deliberate *creation* of desires in large numbers of people despite the fact that the created desires were incapable of fulfillment. They did not envisage, of course, a vast conspiracy set up specifically to create unfulfillable desires, but they nevertheless contended that this was the inevitable consequence of purposive actions taken by a minority of individuals.

To reduce the argument to very crude terms, again, what the Intellectuals argued was that the capitalist ethic had destroyed the world. By the capitalist ethic they did not mean the existence of a free market, or even economic competition *per se*, but something rather more specialized. What they meant was the way that some individuals, having developed a strong interest in making other people work for them, helped to create a mythology whereby the rewards of diligent industry and hard work might be far more than they were actually likely to be; and that the same individuals, having an equally strong interest in making people buy from them the things that they made, created a corollary mythology whereby they made promises regarding the benefits to be obtained from their products which were entirely impossible of fulfillment. In brief, the Intellectuals imagined capitalism, and the progress instituted by capitalism, as a man carried by a donkey which he persuaded to move by dangling a carrot before its nose. They recognized that in parallel with this system there were others where the man used a whip instead of the carrot, but did not blame these men so much because they made less progress that way. The Intellectuals, unlike most of the social reformers of the Motherworld they had left behind them, were not particularly concerned about the question of whether the man ought to be riding the donkey at all, instead of walking on his own feet—or perhaps carrying the donkey. *Their* main concern was how the man persuaded the donkey to move, for it was this, they contended, which created the radical disjunction between desires and the means of fulfilling them. It would not have been so bad, they contended, if the man had only wanted to get to a particular destination, at which point the donkey could have the proffered carrot—the fact was that he had no destination, but simply wanted to keep moving, and under those circumstances, they thought, the carrot was just as bad as, and probably worse than, the whip.

The Intellectuals, therefore, made a close study of the kinds of desires which people seemed to have—if not inborn into them, at least inculcated easily and with no particular strategic effort. They also observed very closely the way patterns of desire seemed to develop. Their conclusions were probably quite unremarkable. What they found was that most people valued pleasure first and foremost. Supplementary patterns of desire were mainly determined by the discoveries they made about what gave them pleasure and what did not. However, they also concluded that the question could not thus be simplified into utter triviality, for they found that some people valued things other than pleasure, and that "pleasure" itself was rather too undefined as a concept.

Eventually, they began to believe—rightly or wrongly, but certainly not arbitrarily or stupidly—that they might profitably isolate three kinds of pleasure. They distinguished a relatively simple species of sensual pleasure—the pleasure of eating, of drinking, of euphoria, or orgasm . . . a kind of "pure pleasure," though that is perhaps to misrepresent it. Then they cited pleasure in *achievement*—the pleasure of making things, of accomplishment, the pleasure of successful competition. This kind of pleasure was held to be much less individual and personal, but to be connected with social prestige. Basically, individuals primarily devoted to the first kind of pleasure value experiences in their own right. Events are important to them while they are happening for the sensations they produce. Individuals devoted to the second kind of pleasure, however, assess events and situations by what comes out of them—their products and results. People whose lives seemed chiefly devoted to the first kind of pleasure the Intellectuals dubbed "Hedonists." People who seemed chiefly orientated toward the second kind, the Intellectuals dubbed "Pragmatists."

When they first made this classification, you understand, they were merely pointing to vague tendencies in human behavior. They were not contending that "Hedonists" operated in hedonistic terms all the time, or that Pragmatists were necessarily and consistently pragmatic in every endeavor. Indeed, they noted that the people who were most relentlessly pragmatic sometimes showed a tendency to switch into a hedonic mode of behavior in a rather idiosyncratic way. Instead of moving easily from one mode to the other they made the transition only with difficulty, and tended to have hedonic outbursts. Their indulgence in pleasure for its own sake frequently seemed to be frenzied, and was usually temporary, confined to particular times when it became almost ritual. This kind of syndrome eventually came to be known by terms derived from an ancient Earthly text of some kind. The pattern of behavior which was basically pragmatic, but with these occasional outbursts of hedonic indulgence was dubbed the "jeckle" pattern, and the periods of indulgence as "jeckling" or "hydeyhigh." I am uncertain of the etymology of the terms, but it is largely irrelevant.

Naturally, the Intellectuals set aside a third kind of pleasure for themselves, in that their actual role precluded them from either of those they had observed. Intellectual pleasure—pleasure gained from self-discipline and the cultivation of knowledge—was neither hedonic nor pragmatic. The intellectuals of the Motherworld, with their usual technological bias, would presumably have been Pragmatists of a sort, but pragmatism was something that the Intellectuals of the *Marco Polo* were reluctant to admit to, in that their uniqueness was vested in the dislocation of scientific inquiry from technological application. This did not, however, prevent them from taking action on the basis of these conclusions, making their work the ideological foundation stone of their redesigned society.

The stability of society, they already knew, depended largely on the division of labor and the integration of many different occupational roles. That this was not enough they considered proven by the course of various Earthly cultures. They decided that what was further required was a proper distribution of values, and proper control of that distribution. There was nothing new in the idea of fitting people to the roles for which they already had appropriate psychological proclivities. Nor was there anything new about the idea of planning the values of a society's members—providing ideas intended to make the disadvantaged content with their disadvantage, and perhaps proud of it. No one, however, had previously decided to encourage value-specialization in such a way as to create different classes within a society who filled different sets of roles and wanted different kinds of rewards.

What the Intellectuals did was to refine the value preferences which people tended to develop anyhow. The hedonistically inclined were encouraged to become specialist Hedonists—connoisseurs of Hedonism. The pragmatically inclined were encouraged to devote all their energies to pragmatic pursuits, and to despise the Hedonist way of life (as they were already inclined to do, to some extent). Jeckling was provided for in the system, too, in the establishment of rituals and institutions which allowed Pragmatists—usually donning masks—to step right out of their notional identity and take on another personality temporarily. These transitions were drug-assisted. The Intellectuals, of course, taught themselves and their new recruits to despise both Hedonism and Pragmatism as symbols of weakness and vulgarity, and to value above all things their own particular species of intellectual reward.

What they hoped to achieve as a result of this was a society where inequalities of reward could be instituted—justified by reference to kinds of work—without there being any necessity or scope for envy. Some people aboard the starship had more space than others, in different locations with different advantages. Many had personal possessions that were different in kind and quality from those provided for others. There are some commodities, as you will readily understand, that cannot be shared out equally between everyone as air and water can, and it is an extreme and stupid solution to say that whatever cannot be enjoyed by all should not be enjoyed by any. This was the problem which the Intellectuals set out to solve—and, by and large, they did it. They were able to provide each class with a reasonable sufficiency of the kind of reward its members cherished, without arousing envy in the nonrecipients. I won't say that life was entirely harmonious—indeed, there was probably a good deal of argument and hostility—but it always remained under control. Everyone could see enough of the logic of the situation to appreciate it and accept it. The *Marco Polo* could never be mistaken for Utopia, but it was a sufficiently happy ship to survive

. . . not just for two generations, or ten, or fifteen, but for more than a hundred and fifty.

And those generations grew steadily longer, because the Intellectual program of personal improvement within a stable society actually bore fruit.

8

In a sense (continued Sarid) the *Marco Polo* community designed its social institutions in much the same way that the ship itself had been designed. The ship was a machine for living in: a life-support system that would perform its function in perpetuity, just so long as people were content to exist within its limitations. The environment of the ship was above all else a *controlled* environment, minutely regulated to maintain certain optimum conditions—and yet within it there was a good deal of scope for individuality. It would be a mistake to see the ship simply as something which confined people and imprisoned them within a narrow set of circumstances. It wasn't just that, and no one regarded it in that way, because the ship was also their means of salvation. I don't mean that it simply allowed them to live whereas they would otherwise have died—I mean that *because* it maintained so carefully the fundamental conditions of life, so that everyone was adequately fed and everyone had a role to fulfill in the maintenance of life within the ship, it left room for a certain kind of freedom—a liberation of the spirit.

This may sound odd to you, because you have a different way of seeing things, but the very stability and certainty of the ship's physical provisions, far from making life regular and automatic, allowed it to become relaxed. It not only permitted but encouraged the growth of idiosyncrasy, of individualization. It allowed people to achieve and maintain recognizably distinct identities. Against an even background, the differences between people stand out far more than they do against a varied background.

It was in this way that the ship's social system became a kind of echo of its physical circumstances. The network of social institutions, too, became a machine for living in. Its keynote was always *control*—the control of the social environment through the self-control of its members. You might suppose that the result of that would be the disappearance of individuality, the reduction of social intercourse to pure mechanism, but in fact that wasn't what happened. By providing a matrix of social responsibility that everyone could depend on—the certainty that obligations would always be met, and that there would be no breakdown—the social order allowed the individuals within it to get a firm grip on their own individuality. Each one was aware of his or her uniqueness, and of the uniqueness of others, precisely *because* there was a basic constancy against which that uniqueness could stand out.

Here again, the Intellectuals made a radical break with the traditions of social reform that were present in the world they left behind them. For hundreds of years—perhaps thousands—there had been a main current in Utopian philosophy which claimed that the thing most vital to a good society was love, or fellowship, or fraternity, or comradeship. A great many would-be prophets had insisted that the one thing most important to the attainment of the good life was that one should love one's neighbors, be united with them by some essential bond of *feeling*. Many of them claimed that *all* the good society needed was this spirit of fellowship, but even those who claimed that it was not sufficient nevertheless claimed that it was necessary.

The Intellectuals, however, were suspicious of feelings. Again, this is a corollary of their own perception of themselves—of the kind of people they needed to be in order to do what they needed to do. They felt that the passions—love more than any of the others—were actually the most serious threat to social order, rather than the foundation stones of a good social order. They believed that no society at all—let alone a good one—could be founded on the demand for universal sympathy and fellowship. They appreciated what they claimed no other reformers had ever properly appreciated: the importance of the freedom *not to love*. They argued that the foundations of the good life lay not in the foolish hope that every man might somehow come to love every other, but in the provision of circumstances which assured that a man could rely upon his neighbors to fulfill their social obligations *in spite of* the fact that they did not love him.

A good society, they contended, is one that is not only good for the man who is generous, kind, and loving by inclination, but also for the man who loves no one, who is solitary and even misanthropic, and who wishes to insulate himself against the disturbing effects of his own passions and the unreasonable demands of the passions of others. A good society, they argued, should be able to accommodate individuals of many different kinds, and what it must demand of them is not that they should feel in particular ways but that *all* their feelings should be kept well enough under control not to lead them into actions liable to injure or disturb others. Their ideal republic was Platonic not only in opposing change but in treasuring calm of mind above all other social obligations. Aboard the *Marco Polo*, the one primary duty which an individual owed to his neighbors was not that he should love them, but that in all his dealings with them he should maintain calm of mind.

There grew up along with this social philosophy the means for its achievement. The Intellectuals put a great deal of effort into the development of techniques by which the mind could achieve better control over itself and over the body. They developed methods of meditation and biofeedback. They instituted education from birth in techniques of self-discipline. They found methods of enhancing the body's physical development in such a way as to permit greater conscious control—particularly a series of drugs which encouraged the development and ramification of extra nervous tissue within the body. With the aid of these drugs, and psychological training, and the moral pressure of the social group, the Intellectuals were able to achieve their ends. The people aboard the *Marco Polo* grew rapidly better able to control their nervous systems, their hormonal systems, and other tissues of their bodies.

One of the most remarkable effects of this regime was that the process of physical aging was brought under greater control. Over a number of generations people acquired the means to slow down this process and extend the term of healthy existence. More remarkable still, perhaps, was the fact that the effect was differential in terms of the three classes identified and differentiated within the society. The Intellectuals themselves were the main beneficiaries, being by far the most efficient in self-control. The life-span of an Intellectual was extended by stages to a norm of seven hundred years instead of seventy. Pragmatists commonly achieved four or five hundred, while Hedonists commonly died at two hundred, only rarely surviving to be two hundred and fifty.

That this difference should appear was perhaps not altogether surprising. That it should be so marked testifies to the success of the Intellectuals in converting vague dispositions into well-differentiated types. The Intellectuals, by definition, were those members of society best suited to the rigorous self-discipline, ascetic habits and emotional repression necessary to the attainment of the fine pitch of self-control required to extend the life-span to its fullest extent. Hedonists, again by definition, were the least suited, dependent upon the immediacy of sensory pleasure, incapable of asceticism and emotional repression. It may be worth noting that the Pragmatists, as well as being intermediate in terms of the average age attained, were also the most various, in that the distribution of levels of attainment was much less concentrated. I speak in the past tense here, because I want to emphasize later that the situation on Tanagar is not the same as that which pertained to the spaceborne generations, but virtually all the observations I have made here are also true of the present situation. I am more than two hundred years old. I do not know how much longer I have to live, but I would guess that translocation to Earth may have reduced my expectations quite considerably. I may live no longer than you, if I remain here, though I would certainly have outlived you if I had been allowed to resume my life on Tanagar.

Why do I say "resume"? Patience—all in good time.

If the *Marco Polo* were still wandering through the depths of space, searching for a habitable world, then everything there would be exactly as I have described. The community would still be three thousand strong; every man, woman, and child would have an allotted role to fill; not everyone would be perfectly happy and certainly not all of the time, but in the main, they would be content. Indeed, speaking from the Pragmatic viewpoint, I would say that the social order devised by the Intellectuals was an ideal instrument—which is not to claim that it is the only possible instrument—for assuring that the ship could continue on its way for as long as it required to fulfill its purpose and find a new home for man. The voyage might have lasted seven thousand years, or seventy thousand, or seven hundred thousand; the means would still be appropriate to the end.

In the eventuality, however, the voyage *did* end, and the Intellectuals were faced with a new problem: how to colonize the new world and develop a human community of much greater size and complexity than that of the *Marco Polo*. In point of fact, it could not have been easy to take the decision to end the journey. The mythology of the new world which the people of the ship believed in was a rather pleasant Arcadian mythology. In general, the images of the new world contained within the ship's artworks was the image of a young, unspoiled Earth, with gentle blue skies, an abundance of greenery and perhaps a little more oxygen in the air than Earth had possessed, to contribute a touch of perpetual intoxication.

Tanagar did not fit that image very well.

It had, of course, the basic qualifications: it had a nitrogen/oxygen atmosphere, a surface temperature which—in several sizeable regions—fluctuated between tolerable extremes, and there was free water at the surface. Unfortunately, it was parsimonious in supplying these necessities.

Tanagar is larger than Earth, and the acceleration due to gravity at the surface is considerably higher. The *Marco Polo* had simulated gravity with perpetual spin, but the simulated gravity was only half Earth-normal—more nearly a third the force that would have to be contended with on Tanagar. The atmosphere is denser but the percentage of oxygen is less. The partial pressure is adequate, but the atmospheric pressure taken as a whole created problems for would-be colonists. Rather more important is the fact that Tanagar's oceans are far smaller than Earth's. The surface area is greater, but the proportion of that surface covered by water is much less. For this reason, much of the land surface of Tanagar is arid desert where nothing—literally *nothing*—can live.

Life evolved on Tanagar in much the same way as it did on Earth, but the oxygen in the atmosphere, at the time of the arrival, was almost entirely the product of marine algae.

There were plants on land, and some animals too, but their range was very limited both geographically and taxonomically. The most advanced form of life on land was a species of insect, though there were very many exoskeletal species—fish—in the sea. In a way, Tanagar *was* a young Earth—but one that was too young to be very attractive, and Earthlike only in patches. It never *would* be Earthlike, except in patches. It posed tremendous problems of adaptation.

The temptation to leave Tanagar alone and go on in search of something more promising must have been great. If the decision to colonize Tanagar had been a final commitment, I think it would not have been taken. However, it was *not* an irrevocable commitment. The *Marco Polo* could pause in Tanagar's system for as long as its owners wished, and then continue. The ship itself could remain in orbit, renewing its resources with the aid of Tanagar's sun and the debris of its solar system. If, in the fulness of time, Tanagar proved too unpleasant, the ship could proceed. In the meantime, life aboard her could be maintained in the fashion it always had. A new population could be produced in order to make the attempt to establish a self-sufficient settlement on Tanagar.

I think three things were important in making the decision to stay. Firstly, the goal of creating a new human world *was* a vitally important one. It seemed wrong to pass up an opportunity because it was not ideal. The ship had been searching for a long time, and it was not difficult to imagine that it might never find another opportunity at all. Secondly, the colony would be an *experiment*—an attempt to meet a stern challenge. It would constitute a kind of test of the society which the Intellectuals had established. They felt that if the *Marco Polo* community proved adequate to the task it would somehow have proved its worthiness. If you like, you could say that the colonization of Tanagar was a test of manhood, in the broadest meaning of the word. Thirdly, Tanagar presented a curious kind of analogue of the situation of the ship. It offered small fertile islands separated by vast tracts of utterly hostile wilderness. In the beginning, at least, the colonists would have to live in metal domes, protected against the rigors of the environment. In the first instance, at least, the abodes of man would be shiplike—contrived and controlled ecosystemic enclaves. This was the kind of situation that the ship community understood.

The details of the colonizing process are largely irrelevant. The colonists found that the methods of physical control they had developed for other purposes served them well in creating beings who could live on the surface. With the aid of drugs and the fact that their bodies could be brought under much more rigorous and conscious control than those of their ancestors, the men and women of the *Marco Polo* adapted their children well enough to the environment of Tanagar. They were able to live, work, and build there.

On Tanagar itself they built analogues of the *Marco Polo*: ten in the early centuries, then forty, then a hundred and eighty. They built communities three thousand strong, encased in delicate machines.

I do not mean, of course, that the colonists lived *precisely* as their forebears had. They developed the resources outside the domes, surrounded themselves with gardens and farms, explored the deserts and the seas. In space they built stations, and more ships to explore the solar system and to facilitate better communications between the ground and the Mothership. They made use of what they had, and they adapted themselves in virtually every way to the fact that they were now living on a planet and not—or as well as—a ship. The fundamentals of their social order, however, did not change in the least. They had been built to resist change, and resist change they did. The range of activities undertaken by the community expanded vastly, but their way of organizing them did not. In fact, the reaction of the Intellectuals to the fact that circumstances had been drastically altered was not to relax the demands of the social order but rather to intensify them—to work all the harder in order to preserve them. The fact that circumstances had changed did, not unnaturally, create stresses and strains that had not previously been present, and these had to be opposed if the perfect crystalline state of the social system was to be preserved.

Preserved, of course, it *was* to be, for its stability had never been justified solely on the grounds that it was a temporary necessity occasioned by the circumstances of the journey, but also on the grounds that stability was worth preserving in its own right, as the principal duty which a society owed to its members.

It was not until the *Marco Polo* reached Tanagar that the Intellectuals began discovering traitors in our midst, and began a crusade to purge the social order of its deviants: the individuals who, for one reason or another, were incapable of maintaining the degree of self-control necessary to the maintenance of order. The Intellectuals, of course, were a humane élite. They were set against execution and imprisonment as punishments that could not be condoned by civilized society. The legal codes drawn up aboard the ship and maintained on Tanagar were very strongly biased toward reparation rather than retribution, but on Tanagar it became necessary to alter the emphasis slightly. The worst criminals—the ones whose passions seemed to threaten social order by leading to extreme breakdowns in obligation and responsibility—were actually exiled from the community. They were simply placed in suspended animation for an indefinite period. No harm was done to them; they were merely removed from the society which they threatened. It was hoped, I think, that the Intellectual Rule could be assured by this stratagem—that it would be a temporary measure, eugenic in its effects. However, the fault appeared to be an environmental one rather than a genetic one. On the *Marco Polo*, the social system devised by the Intellectuals had worked extremely well. On Tanagar, it only worked well. It was weaker, though no one was entirely sure why. For myself, I think it is simply that on Tanagar, there are horizons. Where there are horizons, there are also possibilities. Perfect contentment is not so easy to cultivate in oneself.

The *Marco Polo* never did set out again to resume its journey. It orbits Tanagar still. The phase when it was the ship's community that effectively ruled over the planet's communities has long since ended. It remains the location of the supreme Parliament, but that Parliament is dominated by the delegates of the surface communities, and it is a long time since there was a President who was not born and raised on the surface.

Interstellar travel was, however, resumed eventually. Though the Mothership remained in orbit, and nothing like her was ever built again, smaller ships were developed whose purpose was to take over the burden of exploration. These ships carry no crew, save for exceptional projects concerning other worlds. Effectively, they were probes, sent out to report back on conditions elsewhere in the galaxy. If they find another habitable world, perhaps *then* a new mothership might be built, to carry the seed of mankind to new ground, but in the meantime they send back data which is treasured and stored by the Intellectuals of Interstellar—the department which controls these projects.

In several thousand years, these probes have found no new worlds where men might live. They have, however, found one old world where men *do* live. We have, as yet, discovered no new Eden . . . but we rediscovered Earth. I say "we" here, because I am now involved in this process of rediscovery, but the Intellectuals have not seen fit to make the fact of the rediscovery public. I would have lived and died on Tanagar never knowing of it, had it not been for the fact that I took to a life of crime.

As I have said, I am a revolutionary.

I am the worst of criminals, in the eyes of the Intellectuals—and, I suppose, in the eyes of most other people too. I am an advocate of change. Not, you understand, that I am an agent of chaos—the kind of change I believe in is controlled change. I would argue that it is not too different in principle from the changes of circumstance which have overtaken the children of the *Marco Polo*, extending their numbers, their dispersion, and modifying their bodies and their ways of life. That kind of change, according to the Intellectuals, is not *really* change, though I cannot see how it can be put under the heading of growth of knowledge or moral progress. I see it as real change, and argue that there has not been enough of it. They see it as a kind of constancy, and they condemn my demands for change as something radically different and dangerous.

The details of my activities are not important, but what I tried to do was to organize a conspiracy of Pragmatists to usurp the rule of the Intellectuals, in order to return some sense of purpose to the colony on Tanagar and encourage the population to leave their metal wombs and their carefully constructed communities in order to begin the real transformation of Tanagar into a world fit for human habitation. The Intellectuals were too content to accept the situation on Tanagar, too preoccupied by the business of adapting men and not concerned enough with the business of adapting the planet. We *have* the technology required to alter the face of that world, to create a world where the possibilities of life would be so much greater—but that is not what the Intellectuals want.

You understand, I hope, that I am not *against* stability, nor would I ever argue that change *per se* is desirable. I am a Pragmatist, and I think that the only possible justification for change is that change will make things better. I think there are things to be achieved which we are too frightened to attempt, things to be built that we have convinced ourselves that we do not really want. Now that the race of man is expanding again—now there are far more than three thousand people—I think that it is no longer necessary or desirable that the Intellectuals should maintain the degree of domination that they do.

I led a *coup* which succeeded in taking over one of the domes on the surface. The success was short-lived. I was convicted of a crime of passion, and sentenced to eternal life. I was put away—forever, I thought. It had not occurred to me that Tanagar might find a use for me. I had thought that my release, if it ever was to be secured, would depend on the eventual success of the revolution which I had tried to begin. However, I was snatched back from my comfortable living death, and brought here, as a pawn in a great experiment.

You will understand that in telling you why I was brought here I am drawing inferences rather than explaining facts. Cyriac Salvador did not think it necessary or desirable to provide me with an account of his reasons—indeed, he challenged me to work them out for myself.

You have to imagine, I think, the reactions of Interstellar's Intels when they found that human life was not, after all, extinct on Mother Earth. They had not anticipated it. They had always considered that if their probes ever did find new human worlds they would be worlds seeded by starships like the *Marco Polo*. Though they had no way of calculating what such worlds would be like, they were prepared to find them in some important way enlightened: worlds whose leaders knew well enough the tragedy of the ancient world, and shared a similar understanding of its causes. They were not sufficiently narcissistic to imagine that the other starships would have duplicated their own society, but they felt confident that the same ideals would be upheld and that the social structures involved would be functionally similar. It must have come as a shock to them to find a world which had no memory whatever of the atom wars and the Age of Progress, despite the fact that it was growing up in the same place. It must have disturbed them to find a *primitive* world, harsh and brutal, divided into many camps savagely opposed to one another. I think you can appreciate what sharp contrasts they would have seen.

The problem which faced them was simple enough: what to do? What *could* they do? What did they *want* to do? The last question was probably the most important, because it was the one which was most difficult to answer. Should they attempt to act as guides, taking control of Earthly history? If so, how was it to be done, and what would be the ultimate aim? Surely not to divide up Earth's population into units of three thousand, each one equipped with a metal dome and a self-sufficient ecology! Surely not to bring the leading nations as rapidly as possible to the brink of a new Age of Progress!

I think the decision of the Intels was the simplest one they could make—and the easiest to carry out. They decided to watch, to observe, to study. They decided to treat Earth as a kind of laboratory, in which they could inspect the behavior of human beings—beings like themselves and yet *alien*. Such a response would be typical of the Intellectuals. Earth could be useful in the service of one of their ideals—the growth of knowledge. It substituted, in a way, for a wellspring they had long ago dammed up, for in stabilizing their own society they had put an end forever to social science. By stopping change they had robbed themselves forever of the opportunity of determining the mechanisms of change. Earth offered them a plurality of developing societies, and gave them an opportunity to recover what their own world could never be permitted to give them: history. Tanagar's history is thousands of years dead, buried in a past so remote that it has almost ceased to have meaning except as mythology. Earth is still living its history—perhaps reliving it.

However, the decision to observe patiently, once taken, must have been a difficult one to keep. The temptation to interfere, to experiment, if only in the smallest degree, must have been immense. They would not have seen it as temptation, of course—in their view, only passions are temptations, and intellectual curiosity is something else entirely.

They did not want to control Earthly history, partly because it would have destroyed the usefulness of Earth as a laboratory and partly because they had no goal in mind to which such control might be directed. What they *did* want to do, I think, was to accelerate it a little. They watched the emergence of Macaria as a powerful nation, and realized that in Macaria the future of the world was vested. They realized quickly that the shape of Earth's future would depend entirely on the rediscovery of the lost heritage of the ancient world—on the fruits of archaeology. This was interesting, because it promised to take the history of the *new* Earth into entirely new territory. There would be a renaissance, and a limited industrial revolution, but the new Age of Progress would be crucially limited by a lack of nonrenewable resources that the ancient civilizations had used up. On top of this, along with the scientific knowledge of the ancient world, Macaria was bound to discover what had happened to that world, and would presumably reach an understanding of *why* it had happened. For this reason, if for no other, the second history of civilization might be dramatically different from the first. As the Macarians rediscovered the past, they would also see the threat of the future, much earlier than the old world had perceived it.

This was by far the most interesting thing which, in the view of the Intellectuals, could happen on Earth. It was the one pattern which they thought it worth encouraging and assisting. Perhaps they feared that the Macarian initiative might be lost, but more likely they simply wanted to stimulate it and accelerate it for their own convenience. So they brought from the vaults a kind of catalyst—a man who might add considerably to the pace of Macaria's advancement of learning. Chance and circumstance alike had made me perfect for the role. None of their own was fitted for it, not even a well-adjusted Pragmatist . . . but a revolutionary, a believer in change, was a different kind of being altogether, in their eyes.

Salvador intended that I should establish an Earthly identity. He did not want to make me an ambassador from the stars. He wanted to slip me into the pattern of Earthly history as unobtrusively as possible. If I were ultimately to reveal my identity, of course, that would not matter, but it would be better if any revelations could be inhibited, to come later rather than sooner. He intended, of course, to provide me with nineteen allies to assist me in my cause. He did not intend the ship to crash. How much this changes things, I don't know. Salvador, of course, is dead now, but his kin are not. Earth is still a laboratory; you and I still constitute a great experiment. At this moment we are under closer observation than you imagine. That observation will continue.

It is up to us—to you and me and your superiors—to decide what we are going to make of the new situation. I dare say that there are aspects of the situation which you will find distasteful in the extreme. Remember, please, that I am not overwhelmingly delighted with my own situation. But this is where we are, and why.

This is the beginning.

9

Macaria was a land of contrasts. Though its chief towns—and especially the capital city, Armata—were huge and smoky, with little hint of green even in the derelict land, its countryside was marvelously fertile, checkered with wheat fields and orchards and huge acres planted with potatoes and beets. When Salvador and Teresa went westward into Armata the harvesting of the staple crops was just beginning, and the fields were alive with men, women, children, and horses, while horses and carts were everywhere in the lanes that divided the land. By comparison, the towns seemed slow and almost moribund—especially the suburbs. Here, the majority of the men worked indoors—and frequently their wives and children also. There were no crowds in the streets except when the shifts changed at these places of work, and the people seemed enervated instead of energized by the heat of the sun.

The chimneys to the east of Armata seemed to fill the sky with a haze that never quite dispersed. It did not hide the sun, and certainly did not mask its heat, but it turned the sun blood red for half the day as it rose and set, and painted fantastic patterns of roseate light upon the sky when thin cirrus clouds collected high above its domain. The city center basked in a more appealing light, and trees lined some of the wider streets, but even here the dirt was settling and turning all the buildings slowly black. There were far more motor vehicles on the roads, but they were mostly lorries carrying goods or public transport vehicles, and were relentlessly utilitarian in their design. Only in the occasional gaudiness of its architecture did Armata boast convincingly of luxury.

The railway station at which they arrived, on the east side of the central district, was relatively small; the more important parts of the nation were to the west and north of the capital. It was the station from which they departed again that really gave eloquent testimony to the ambitions of the nation. The passenger station had a dozen platforms and was flanked on either side by vast goods yards, which sent forth such a clamor that they seemed to be screaming for attention. Most impressive of all, however, was the fact that there was already a railway museum, where passengers could see rolling stock that had been made redundant only a decade before, and could compare the graceless engines with the best of the new locomotives.

Teresa and Salvador had no difficulty purchasing tickets. They attracted no special attention on the station—the people seemed to be far too busy to look at one another or to evince the slightest curiosity about events external to the realm of their personal affairs. They had feared pursuit after the affair in the warehouse, and could not see a policeman without falling prey to fantasies of arrest, trial, and execution for murder, but it seemed that no one was on their trail. If the survivors of the battle had given descriptions of their assailants, those descriptions had not been passed along the line as fast as the two fugitives had traveled. In all probability, the survivors had made their own escape from the scene of the crime, not wanting to be implicated at all with the kind of dealings which had turned out to be a prelude to destruction.

They traveled second class and found themselves allocated to a carriage near the rear of the train that would start them on their journey to the far north. The seats were narrow but quite well upholstered, and the carriage did not get unbearably hot by day or unbearably cold by night. It was possible to sleep on the seats in reasonable comfort, and this meant that their circumstances had improved markedly by comparison with those they had endured on the train that had brought them into the city from the east.

At first, the train stopped frequently in the outer regions of the city, and there was a constant exchange of passengers, but as time wore on the stops grew less frequent and the population of the carriage declined until it was easy to identify those who—like themselves—were long-distance travelers destined for the mountains. These individuals—almost all men—were armed with materials to keep them occupied and apparatus to keep them comfortable. As well as luggage, they had books and blankets, carved board games and cushions. Some of them were already acquainted with one another, and secured by collaboration small territories where they could spread out their possessions and endeavors. Others began to strike up conversations with carefully guarded and conventional strategies. Salvador and Teresa were sharing their particular section with a lone individual—a man of perhaps fifty years, who seemed at first too tired and dejected to attempt any kind of communication, but who fell prey in the end to the boredom of insomnia.

"Where are you bound?" he asked tentatively.

"Galehalt," Teresa told him.

"All the way," he said. "You'll find it slow going in the mountains, but not unpleasant. Exciting sometimes, but not dangerous at this time of year. I'm bound for there myself, but it's only a step on my way. I go east then, toward Pavla. Galehalt is your destination?"

"No," she said. "We go on northward."

"Beautiful country at this time of year," said the man, as if talking to himself as much as to his companions. "The forests are magnificent. Lonely, of course, except the country around the lakes—and the places where they are dragging out the bones of cities too long dead. There are whole towns full of antiquarians, now, cutting up valleys of good farmland, bringing in laborers from the south and displacing the men who work on the land. The foresters, too, are changing the face of the world. It was all so *still* in my grandfather's time, but no more. You'll not be antiquarians, I think. Foresters, perhaps? But not from the south."

"No," said Salvador, "Not from the south."

"From the west? Vondrel, perhaps?"

"That's right," agreed Salvador.

"I thought so. You have the look of the west about you, and you have plenty of forests of your own in Vondrel. I can tell that you're forest folk by your accents—they haven't been rubbed down by the towns. My name is Alaric da Lancha."

He paused expectantly. Neither Salvador nor Teresa was anxious to reply, but in the end it was Salvador who gave the pseudonyms that were written on their papers.

"Common names in Axrig," observed da Lancha. "You have relatives there, perhaps?"

"Yes," said Teresa, "we have."

"I have myself," said the old man. "You will know it from my name, which connects me to the old aristocracy. Not that the old aristocracy counts for anything anymore. The southerners have taken everything now. Still, tradition matters in Axrig, as you'll surely know. Perhaps there are friends among your relatives and mine—perhaps somewhere a link by marriage. It would be pleasant to think so. It would be more fortunate these days to have relatives in Armata, of course. Strange how that southern city has grown so rich on the knowledge of the ancient world when it did not even exist in that world. All of this pastureland was ocean then. No relics here of the old world, and yet this land feeds the men who have grown rich by virtue of such relics. An irony, I think. In these parts, they do not say that Macaria rules the world but that *Armata* rules the world, yet if territories really meant anything it would be the northern provinces who owned the legacy of ancient civilizations. Even Vondrel and Camelon, but never Armata. They say that the snow and ice of the far north still holds captive the best of the ancient world, and that it will slowly be freed as the eternal winter retreats, but I do now know what to think of that."

"It is possible," said Salvador, declining to take any initiative in guiding the exchange of views—indeed, declining to participate to any appreciable degree.

"Armata takes our children and our wealth," said da Lancha, "but somehow we hardly see them go." He stared out of the window silently for some minutes, as if trying to decide whether it was worth going on in the face of such indifference. "It is so peaceful here," he said eventually, "especially when dusk is falling, that it is almost impossible to believe that we are at war. Men whose families have worked the land

for centuries are finding their sons taking more interest in
Dahra than in the harvest. They are being enticed away by
rumors of fortunes to be made and adventures to be enjoyed.
One of my sons was killed in Merkad ten years ago, and I
have never found out why. Merkad is always troublesome,
and always has been. I would return it to the Merkadians tomorrow, if I could. It is not as if they had anything we
wanted—not even lost cities buried in the sand. Those parts
of Merkad which were not beneath the seabed were mostly
more arid than they are today. Such cities as there were in
the coastal region were poor compared to those in the north.
He was not even an officer; his name could not win him a
commission. He was a sergeant, though he expected further
promotion. I could not pay, of course. My other son is a
scholar in Galehalt. He comes back to Pavla occasionally, but
he is no digger, and does not do site work. To tell the truth, I
am not sure what he *does* do. It is not very important. At
least, it *is* important, but only as a small part of something
greater. As an individual, he is more an instrument than a
leader. You understand?"

"I understand," said Salvador dutifully. Teresa had now
lost interest, and was no longer listening to what the man was
saying.

"Our world is full of paradox," da Lancha went on. "The
real past—*our* past—is slowly being obliterated by a present
created by a different past—a past so far away that it is not
even remembered in legend. Our history is being eclipsed by
another, whose importance seems to be draining *our* past of
its significance. Traditions count for nothing any more. Armata is everything. Does this not seem strange to you? In
your own land you are more remote than we are in Pavla,
but you must see that the changes are coming, if they are not
around you already? In Vondrel, in Axrig, in the wasteland
and the forest. Does it not seem to you that there is something absurd in the dream of Armata—something unholy,
despite the careful piety of its guiding spirits?"

"It does not seem to me to be absurd," answered Salvador.
"And unholy. . . . I am not sure what it means. I do not
know what makes a man or a dream holy or unholy."

"If God had meant the ancient world to live, would he

have destroyed it?" asked da Lancha. "It seems to me that in digging it up we are undoing His work when we should be doing it."

"It was not the wrath of God that destroyed the ancient world," said Salvador. "It was the madness of men."

"I see little difference," said the Macarian. "The madness of men and the anger of God are one and the same. I have been in Armata these last three months, and I seem to see the madness that is the anger of God waiting in every shadowed alley, and in the frown of the dark clouds that gather around. Armata may yet be cursed that in learning the wisdom of the ancient world she may share its fate. We have a saying: those who find lessons in history are condemned to reenact them. When we were ignorant, perhaps we had the blessing of God."

"I cannot believe that," replied Salvador. "Knowledge is surely the greatest blessing that it is possible to receive, from the hand of God or the endeavors of man. The knowledge of what happened to the ancient world may be precisely what is needed to permit Macaria to avoid the same fate."

"The voice of Armata itself," said the old man, with a sigh. "No doubt you are right, and it is my shame that I cannot bring myself to believe in it. All life seems to me to move in cycles—the cycle of the seasons, and of the generations. I cannot help but feel that there will be a cycle of civilizations also."

"There is no reason to think so," said Salvador. "The world turns on its axis and circles the sun, but the human world is confined by no such orbit. Men are capable of finding their own destiny."

"The gospel of progress!"

Salvador raised an eyebrow quizzically, and permitted himself to smile at the irony.

"Perhaps," he said. "And why not? The word itself has no terrors. Progress, too, is whatever you care to make it. No one need be frightened by words."

"Words have changed my world," answered the old man. "They will change yours, too. Whether you fear them or not, they rule our lives."

Salvador smiled again, and looked out of the window into

Brian Stableford

the gathering gloom, reaching out to close the gap where the frame was not quite level in its bed.

"Words," he said, "will not change *my* world. I can assure you of that."

10

The floor of the forest was not sufficiently even to make traveling easy. The deep layer of organic detritus tended to fill in hollows, but even so the roots of the great trees would occasionally rear up above its surface. The humus itself varied considerably in its texture, sometimes providing a hard crust, in other places yielding beneath their tread so that they sank in several centimeters at each step—especially when they were carrying the stretcher. Sluggish streams gouged out channels as they found a meandering course through the wooden ridges. These streams usually terminated in great black pools of stagnant water which seemed to be devoid of life but which were in fact thick soups of anaerobic bacteria. The streams themselves, though clearer, were swarming with nematode worms, and the water which they drew from them had to be filtered as well as boiled.

By the end of the second day Qapel had fallen ill. His hands and feet were blistered and his skin was showing signs of some general allergic reaction. He was slightly feverish and could not keep food down. Cheron treated the skin rash with antihistamine, but could do little to combat the internal infection except to provide an antibiotic to deal with secondary infections. The Dahran was not really well enough to walk, but Midas was still in a worse state, and did not improve sufficiently to walk for short periods until the morning of the fourth day. The one cause that Cheron found for self-consolation was that after that morning both of them got a little better.

The savages would not let them halt for more than an hour

at a time except during the hours they set aside for sleeping. They allowed their prisoners to build a small fire during the hours of "night" but not during the shorter rest periods. They did, however, manage to produce each "morning" small quantities of some kind of vegetable oil which would burn in the lamps, albeit poorly. There was too much smoke, and the lampglass had to be removed for cleaning at regular intervals, but Cheron was relieved that they would not want for light. The food which the apemen provided was no more various—and probably less nutritious—than that provided by Macaria's army, but it was sufficient in quantity to keep them from hunger.

It appeared that few accidents of fate could touch them in the world of eternal darkness. The only large animal which they saw during the first four days was a squat, humpbacked creature with a long nose and a sticky tongue which ambled around like a pale gray ghost, blindly snapping up insects. It fled from their light, but could not move quickly enough to avoid the glare entirely. No predators descended this far to chase such creatures, whose only enemies were parasites too specialized by long-standing habit to transfer their attentions to men. One night they heard thunder rumbling in the sky, and presumed that rain was falling on the canopy, but no raindrops reached them. Trickles of water running down grooves in the tree trunks were a familiar phenomenon, and were more or less constant, but it was not until some hours after the thunder that there was any noticeable increase in this flow.

Cheron became fascinated by the eyeless insects which inhabited the forest floor, feeding upon the fungi which reprocessed the decay products of the forest's wastes. The most common kind were flat and oval in shape, dressed with hard plates of white armor. If he caught one and held it close to the lamp he could see the shadowy outlines of its internal organs. Structurally, it was hardly modified from the cockroaches that had evolved billions of years before, having simply lost the function of its now-vestigial eyes and virtually all of its pigmentation. Some of the other creatures that coexisted with them still produced dark chitin, sometimes with colored patterns, and reacted to light. All were negatively phototactic save for a few fluttering moths which descended to the underworld from the middle reaches of the canopy.

Once he was accustomed to it, it was easy enough to believe that the evolutionary future of life on Earth might lie
with the forest rather than the semi-desert of Dahra or the
pastureland of Macaria. Perhaps, he thought, the human race
which would come to dominate the Motherworld in the long
run might be the forest savages rather than those who echoed
the dominant species of the ancient world. The forest was
new—there had been nothing like it on Earth ever before.
Perhaps now that it was here the Earth could never be the
same again. He had little enough opportunity to observe the
apemen, who clearly did not love the underworld, but he was
struck by their hatred of fire. Though they permitted him to
build a small fire each time the group stopped to sleep, they
would not go near it, and were emphatic in forbidding him if
he tried to build one on the march in order to heat coffee or
cook food.

Human society as I know it, he thought, *has four foundation stones in biological and social evolution. Upright posture,
the opposable thumb, language, and the harnessing of the energy of fire. Here, for the first time in evolutionary history, is
a human culture which has disposed of two of the fundamentals.*

He tried to pursue this thought, to imagine how different
the history of humankind might have been—and might be—
if men had never set foot on the ground; if they had cultivated manipulative ability in their feet as well as their hands;
if they had never adopted fire as their instrument. What
techology was possible for *Homo faber* without fire? What
culture was possible for a species whose agricultural endeavors were confined to the treetops? What religion was possible for a species who could not only witness the alternation
of darkness and light in the cycle of day and night but who
knew also of the existence of a world of eternal darkness far
beneath them?

Such speculations, not unnaturally, bore little fruit. He had
neither the intellect nor the imagination to follow through as
Cyriac Salvador might have done. Nevertheless, he found the
questions more palatable than those which might otherwise
have come to dominate his consciousness—questions of more
immediate concern like *where are we going?* and *why?*

Though Midas and Qapel were a little better on the fourth
day, Cheron knew that there was little prospect of their re-

gaining their health. The dispiriting effect of the cold and the dark, and the unfamiliarity of the diet on which they were expected to subsist, together with the necessity to keep walking for what must have been fourteen or fifteen hours in the twenty-four, made recovery almost impossible. The forest people were omnivorous, but only just, and the only animal protein which they offered their prisoners were the occasional egg and insect larvae which none of the four could stomach. The abundance of fruit and seeds in the diet caused even Cheron and Talvar to suffer periodic stomach cramps due to overacidity. The bread and hard biscuits which the apemen had plundered from the garrison's stores ran out on the fourth day, though the coffee promised to last for a further ten or twelve. They tried to negotiate with their captors for meat, but had no success.

"I don't understand it," complained Vito Talvar. "What do they use those blowpipes and arrows for if not to kill for food? Surely they didn't invent them just to attack Macarians?"

"Perhaps they did," replied Cheron. "Perhaps they use them for defense against predators. Either way, we'll get no meat."

"I could catch one of those waddling beasts with my bare hands," said Talvar. "But I couldn't skin it without a knife. I daresay they wouldn't provide one of those, either."

"They don't appear to believe in elaborate culinary preparation," said Cheron.

"What I don't like is the way they won't talk to us," Talvar went on. "They jabber away at one another, but they haven't tried to teach us a single word of their language, and they make no response whatever when I try to teach them *our* words. It's not as if they can't make the sounds—they might never be able to sound convincing but they could make themselves understood. It implies that wherever they're taking us there won't be any need for an exchange of opinions."

"Perhaps they can't spare the time," said Cheron. "They might be leaving such work until later."

The only one of the four who was able to offer any hypotheses at all about possible destinations was—not surprisingly—Midas. His ideas were curiously optimistic considering the dismal nature of his surroundings.

"It is possible," he told them, "that there is a land we

know nothing about hidden away in the middle of the forest; a land inhabited by men like ourselves, whose servants are these four-handed ones. It would be a rich land, of course, bathed in tropical sunshine but not too hot, with beautiful women, and grain to make bread, and grapes to make wine."

"The Merkadian Golden Age, still preserved in a lost valley far from Merkad?" asked Talvar.

"Certainly," replied Midas. "The Golden Age was the age when all the world was Merkad. There are stories told of travelers—and sometimes of men who go to sleep in queer places—who find themselves in the Golden Age for a little while, where everything is perfect. They always return to the world of today, sadder and older men, but they have had their taste of something like paradise. Something, in its way, a little better than paradise."

"How can anything be better than paradise?" asked Qapel.

"You are half-savage yourself, and would not know," said Midas, "but the ghostworld that claims us after we are dead permits us to exist only as shadows. The Golden Age, however, permitted men to live as men. Paradise has no beautiful women, and no wine—it simply has no pain. There is all the difference you can think of."

"*Our* paradise has beautiful women," said Qapel. "But no wine, though I am not sure why. *Our* paradise has green pastures, and clear streams, and perpetual sunlight. I do not know whether dead men are shadows, but I know that paradise permits pleasure. It would not be paradise otherwise. In the place of punishment men do not live as shadows, that is certain. And they are certainly not beyond pain."

"Barbaric fantasies," said Midas.

"And this dream of a lost world beyond the forest?" answered Qapel. "That is not a fantasy?"

"It might be a fantasy," said Midas, "but it is a *civilized* fantasy. There is nothing vulgar about it."

"I can remember the time when your imagination found nothing but demons and horrors," observed Cheron, cutting off the developing argument. "They seemed vulgar enough —especially the tales of northerners eating the children of other men."

"It was not quite what I said," Midas replied. "But no matter. There is no need now to imagine demons. We are imprisoned by demons in a dark world where none but demons live. I am too desperate now to invent horrors. I suppose you are different. Being forest men yourselves, you will be at home here far more than you were in Dahra."

"As a matter of fact," said Talvar, with a sigh, "I have never before set foot in a forest. Nor has Cheron. We have never been a single step farther north than the place where you first set eyes on us. I am as desperate as I have ever been, and I see no need in maintaining the stupid sham that Sarid Jerome invented for us—for the best of Prag reasons, no doubt. I am Vito Talvar, and I am not from the northern forests. I am not a barbarian and I am not a demon. I was not born on this terrible world and I mourn the moment when I was taken from my infinite sleep to be tortured thus. I see no reason why you should not know—we are from a world that orbits another star, so far from here that it barely twinkles in the clearest of nights. Our ancestors left Earth thousands of years ago, before the ancient world was destroyed."

"You see," said Midas, looking first at Qapel and then at Cheron. "When we are lost in darkness, our spirits fly to the stars."

"They do," agreed Cheron. "And for what it's worth, I hope you find your fabulous lost valley, open to the sunlight and thronging with refugees from the Merkad of legend. Perhaps you will see that your friends there do not treat us too badly?"

"Of course," said Midas, spreading his arms wide. "You are my friends, you have saved my life. At least, I hope you have saved my life, for I fear that my grip upon it is not as strong as it was. I would smuggle you into any Heaven you wish to visit, if I could."

"And also for what it's worth," added Cheron, "what Vito says is true. Every word."

"I believe you," said Midas. "I would be a poor friend if I could not. Qapel believes you too, don't you, my friend?"

Qapel responded with a weak shrug.

Talvar was not satisfied. "What the Marcarians say is true," he insisted. "The ancient civilizations whose cities they are digging out of the soil possessed machines far in advance of anything Macaria has. There were machines which could fly to the stars. Our ancestors left Earth in a starship, searching for a new home for man, because they knew that the old

world would be devastated, and they feared that no men
would survive there. I was born on another world, and my
size reflects the fact that my forefathers—and every generation since—had to be made specially strong in order to survive there. I swear that what I say is true. These are not
fantasies."

Midas studied Talvar's face for some time, then looked at
Cheron, who stared frankly back at him. "I don't doubt you,"
said the Merkadian eventually. "But I think you undervalue
fantasies. You need not insist so fiercely. It does not really
matter what is true and what is not. What matters is what we
do next. Always, that is what matters most. Can you fly back
to the stars?"

"No," said Talvar.

"In that case," answered Midas, "let us try to believe in my
lost land beyond the forest, where a life of pleasure awaits
us all."

"I cannot," said Vito Talvar.

"Nor I," said Qapel.,

Cheron, however, said nothing.

11

Sarid was presented with a new uniform: he was promoted
from private soldier to captain in one step. The new uniform
made little enough difference to his appearance, but all the
difference in the world to the way he was treated. On the
steamship which carried him back to Asdar he had his own
cabin and his own servant.

His servant—not by coincidence—was Baya-undi. Sarid
had offered him the job as soon as he learned of his enti-
tlement, and Baya-undi had accepted readily enough, well
aware of the fact that the alternative was another trip up the
Bela. If he did not seem properly grateful that was probably
because he considered the position to be somewhat demean-

ing. Toran Zeyer did not altogether approve of the decision,
largely because he had come to the conclusion that Baya-undi
was a Khepran spy and that Sarid's existence was something
he would rather keep secret. Sarid, however, pointed out that
Baya-undi already knew the truth, and that it would be much
easier to keep a check on his activities if he were close at
hand. The argument was not altogether competent, in that the
black man was far more likely to find opportunities to pass
on the information in Dahra than several hundred kilometers
up the Bela, but Zeyer was ready enough to give way to
Sarid's whim.

Sarid was slightly surprised to find that he was not kept
under intensive interrogation once he had told his story.
Zeyer appeared to be thinking over what he had been told,
and probably wanted to confer with his superiors before proceeding with any delicate negotiations with the Tanagarian.
He seemed to understand well enough that the kind of help
Sarid could offer was limited—chiefly, it would be a matter of
filling in gaps in Macarian understanding. His value lay primarily in his ability to help in the interpretation of the
material that the Macarian archaeologists were exhuming
from the ruins of the lost cities. Many things which puzzled
them would be perfectly clear to him; where there was difficulty in reconstructing written materials he could help—his
language was very much closer to the language of the ancient
documents than their own in terms of concepts which it contained and the representation of the world which it embodied.
Though Tanagarian was not identical to any of the languages
used in the documentation, it had words in common with
several of them and was solidly based in one particular
tongue. Sarid would have to learn a good deal himself before
he could become a full fledged archaeologist, but once he had
learned it, he would be in a uniquely privileged position as
far as understanding went: a genius of the Renaissance, who
could indeed lend an accelerative boost to Macarian intellectual history.

Sarid was a little apprehensive lest Zeyer and his colleagues
should expect more of him than this, and he took some pains
to explain that his actual technological expertise was slight,
but in fact Zeyer showed more interest in other aspects of his
story.

One day on the boat, while they ate a very good meal below decks, Zeyer offered his first tentative response to what Sarid had told him.

"Some of what you have told me about the ancient world, and how our world stands in relation to it, we already know, of course. We have been aware even as we have started our industrial revolution that it would be limited. Metals are a problem—too much of the iron that is easily available is in the form of oxides—but not an insuperable one. The real limiting factor is fuel. We have some coal, but it is expensive to extract it. We have no oil at all. If our ambition was to recapitulate the technological munificence of the old world, we would be very disappointed by these limitations. In fact, though, we are not as disappointed as you seem to expect us to be. You see, we have no real interest in recovering the circumstances of the old world in their entirety."

"I can understand that," said Sarid. "After all, the ancient world did destroy itself—and much of what went on in it must seem to you to be rather bizarre. I cannot imagine what archaeologists might make of some of its cultural artifacts."

Zeyer hesitated a little, and then said: "I suppose that is true, but really it misses the point. You do not seem to be thinking along the same lines as we do. You see, we are rather more interested in social history than you seem to be. You seem to be preoccupied by a notion of progress which is not altogether in accordance with ours. We pay much more attention than you do to the ways in which technological developments in the old world precipitated political changes. Your own comments on matters which are of vital importance to us seem both superficial and simpleminded. I appreciate that the analogy which referred to men sitting on donkeys was a mere illustration, but it seemed to me to be a misrepresentation at every level. It exaggerated the unimportant at the expense of the vital. We are not much concerned with *how* a particular social system obtains cooperation from its disadvantaged members. It seems to me that the distinction between promises and threats is a false one."

"It was a deliberately crude reduction of our own mythology," said Sarid. "I did not endorse it. Perhaps I was being too dismissive. One always tends to represent the ideas of others in a way that makes them look slightly ridiculous."

"It hardly matters," replied Zeyer. "The point is that what matters to us is the protection of the Macarian ruling elite—

ourselves, that is to say. You see, when we began to learn
about the science and technology of the old world, it was not
simply a matter of discovering new scientific principles and
ways to build new machines. Actually, that was for a long
time the least part of what interested us. It was not our first
purpose, as archaeologists, to become the fathers of a new
technology. The College has changed its nature and its ambitions over the generations, but there is some essential core of
commitment that has not changed. Do you follow?"

Sarid nodded.

"The early archaeologists were, first and foremost, historians. In a sense, that has never changed. We are still historians, and we are interested much more in the history of
technology than in technology *per se*. That may seem strange
to you, but I think you will be able to appreciate the importance of this perspective when I tell you that what *you* see as
the advance of knowledge and mechanical dominion over the
environment *we* see as a series of political changes made possible, or even directly caused, by the growth of knowledge.

"What you have to appreciate is that most of the scholars
of Macaria, two hundred years ago, were men of the Church,
and all of the ones who had the money to finance significant
researches were members of the nobility. This latter group
quickly became dominant, in that the aristocracy controlled
the finances of the Church, but there is still a strong Church
involvement in the College. Forget, for a moment, the science
and technology of the ancient civilizations, and try to imagine
what we saw in their *history*. We saw the history of a world
in which the kind of people that we were—and are—and the
social system which sustained them slowly fell apart. We read
the story of a civilization in which power was at one time
completely vested in an élite consisting of a landowning aristocracy and a Church hierarchy, but where power later
passed into other hands. There were different recipients, but
almost everywhere there was the same kind of redistribution.
As historians we saw technological development and industri-
alization as the chief causes of this transfer of power. Clearly,
it was not the sole cause or agent, but it was a vitally important one. It was easy enough to see that ownership of the
land was no longer the sole key to political and economic
power once factories had grown up to produce much of what
each society needed. Perhaps you will understand that to us,

the most interesting feature of the story revealed to us by archaeology, two centuries ago, was the rise of capitalism. *That*, and not what you call the Upheaval, was the end of the world from our point of view, for it was the end of the kind of world we had.

"At first, the College felt that the knowledge which was being recovered must be kept secret. The first response of those early archaeologists was that in order to preserve their own world, and their own power, they must protect it from the kinds of forces that had wiped out its equivalent in former times. The influence of the Church was powerful here—the priests were ready enough to condemn all technology as evil, and to regard the idea of material progress with as much horror as you do. The Church changed in its attitude to the study of archaeology itself: at first, it had approved of it as a fit activity for gentlemen, largely because of its impracticality. It had seemed to have an essential unworldliness about it. Now, it began to regret what the archaeologists had discovered, but dare not try to pretend that it had not ever been discovered. The Church read a story in the history of the old world, too—a story about the hopelessness of trying to condemn knowledge or overrule its implications. Really, there was only one lesson which could be drawn, and that was to continue the work, *but never to lose control of its products*. Instead of condemning the knowledge of the ancient world as heresy, the Church set out to reserve it as a kind of private property, so that any benefits accruing from it would remain with it, and could not weaken it. This of course, was the view that the aristocracy came to on their own account: the best course was not to suppress science utterly, and prohibit the development of technology, but rather to make sure that all its benefits were reserved for those already holding power.

"As far as the College could ascertain, the feudal aristocracy of the old world, and the Church that helped it sustain its moral authority, had declined because of the rise of a new class of individuals who achieved economic power—and hence political power—through their ownership of the apparatus of machine production. Some part of *their* power was then further usurped by the men who actually operated the machines. The College decided that the Macarian aristocracy should *not* be threatened in this way by virtue of making cer-

tain that it controlled both the land *and* industry. In brief, we
embarked upon a policy of maintaining our knowledge esoterically. A large proportion of our domestic population is
literate, but only in our own language. We deliberately refrain from translating documents from the ancient world into
the vernacular, and censor everything which is produced in
the vernacular. Only recruits to the College are given the
education necessary to acquaint themselves with even the
smallest part of the knowledge of the ancient world. All industrial endeavors have to be licensed by the College, and are
kept under careful control. We have no intention of recovering all—or even most—of the technology of the ancient
world, and would not even if we had the resources. We permit only that which we can control. In a sense, I suppose that
we have absorbed into our post-feudal aristocracy many of
the functions of your class of Intellectuals. Our aim is similar—the establishment of a stable society in which our own
class will never lose power."

"I must admit," said Sarid, "that none of this had occurred
to me."

"Of course not," replied Zeyer. "How could it?"

"It surprises me a little to find you so sophisticated in your
attitude to social philosophy."

"Why?" asked Zeyer. "Did you assume that we had recovered *only* technical information from our researches? Intellectual sophistication is not implicitly tied up with the extent of
electrical gadgetry."

"I see that," agreed Sarid. "It was stupid of me. I took a
man like Spektros as a representative of your entire race. I
should have realized that there is more to rediscovery than
... electrical gadgets."

"So you see that we are not so different from you as you
may have thought. Indeed, there are some surprising parallels. Save, of course, that we seem to be a little more pragmatic. What *we* are doing has one goal very clearly in mind:
we wish to retain and extend our power. In fact, we intend to
rule the world . . . and by we I mean the hereditary aristocracy of Macaria, not the whole nation. Indeed, I do not mean
all of the hereditary aristocracy. I mean the College, first and
foremost. Some of the old guard, as you will understand,
were too set in their ways to realize the kind of challenge and

opportunity presented by the discoveries of the last two centuries."

"Naturally," said Sarid, nodding.

"Curiously," mused Zeyer, "I did not hear much mention of power in your own story, except insofar as it concerned yourself. I can appreciate *your* motives, but I find your Intellectuals rather alien."

"They *are* rather alien," said Sarid. "They have the power all right, and they preserve it efficiently enough, but that's really a side effect of their endeavors. They do not like to speak of goals, but rather of duties and functions. They would not like to be thought to be Pragmatists, because they consider Pragmatism vulgar. They *are* pragmatists, of course, in a wider sense of the word, but they deemphasize the pragmatic aspects of their behavior, except sometimes when they are deliberately mocking. If ever an Intel gives a pragmatic account of his own behavior, he is talking to a Prag and enjoying a curiously subtle joke. It is a habit I have never liked, partly because it is insulting and partly because it is a double-bluff. An Intel invariably *is* pragmatic—he simply chooses to be hypocritical about it." Sarid paused, and then added, "I suppose that your telling me all this means that I'm to be coopted into your Collegiate aristocracy?"

"We could hardly do otherwise," replied Zeyer. "It would be terribly wasteful to kill you, and we could hardly let such a dangerous revolutionary run loose."

Sarid was silent for a few moments, sipping wine from his glass. Eventually, he smiled as if at some private joke.

"What is it?" asked Zeyer.

"I was just wondering how much of this Salvador could have anticipated," said Sarid. "Very little, I suppose. It takes a long time for a starship to travel to Tanagar and back—longer in Earth-time than in ship-time. Salvador must have decided to act on the basis on information three hundred years old. No doubt he continually updated that—but any more recent information must have come in while we were actually en route from Tanagar. He couldn't have learned *enough*. No matter how brilliant he is, he can't have known exactly how things lie. I wonder whether he'd approve of the situation as it now is. I'd like to think that he wouldn't, but that he'd somehow convince himself that he did. Intels are good at that."

Zeyer made no reply to all this, which did not interest him in the least.

Sarid let a few moments of silence go by, and then added, "It's a shame, in a way, that he's dead."

12

"Tell me," said Salvador, "how do you see the future of Macaria?"

Alaric da Lancha wiped his mouth with a napkin which he folded carefully before returning it to a pocket of his traveling bag. He had already discarded his paper plate and the cardboard cup from which he had drunk his coffee. He took advantage of the tidying-up process to gather his thoughts.

"It seems to me," he said, "that Armata's power will continue to increase. It can hardly do otherwise. But those who talk of a thousand-year rule will be sorely disappointed if they expect what they say to be literally true. Nothing can endure for that kind of period. The new nobility considers itself to be a whole organism, believing and acting as one. Even today, that is largely an illusion. There is already a degree of dissent; there are factions forming, internal power struggles developing. In time, as it grows through natural fecundity, there will be feuds between different bloodlines, jealousy regarding the distribution of privileges, and a war of ideas between those most committed to the Church and those who care nothing about it. At present, the harmony of the situation is preserved simply because everything else is changing so quickly. When matters in the world beyond Macaria's borders are stabilized, the internal breakup will begin. How could it be otherwise?"

"You take it for granted that no power group can achieve internal stability?" asked Salvador.

Da Lancha gestured with his right hand. "Power is always in short supply. Power is, by definition, power over others.

There are always far more people who want it than have it, and those who have it always want more."

"You do not admit the possibility of disinterested control? Rulers who do not desire power for its own sake?"

"I do not. It is a dream, no more. From the beginning of time men must have spent their time crying: 'If only our rulers were benevolent! If only we could be ruled by men who had the interests of *all* men at heart, and not simply their own!' If only snails had wings. . . ."

"Suppose that power were only important in circumstances where resources were short. In a situation where everyone could be fed and sheltered, where abundance could make life in general easy . . . perhaps then there might be a better balance. Political power would simply be less valuable, because there would be less advantage to secure."

Teresa, watching the faces of the two men, knew already how the conversation would go. Neither party would retreat, and neither would yield. Each man considered himself possessed of a superior wisdom, facing a naïve opponent. Nothing could come of it all; it was a game without an ending, whose only reward was that time would pass, and that both men might bring themselves to believe that it had passed more easily.

Her own impatience was not to be cured so simply. She found—somewhat to her annoyance—that the long train journey was more tedious than she had anticipated. The carriage was comfortable enough, compared to the hardships she had previously endured, but there was nothing to occupy her body or her mind. Each hour that passed was a mere repetition of another hour. Either the train moved, or it halted. Sometimes the engine was changed; sometimes coaches were added or subtracted; sometimes the passengers could stretch their legs, buy supplies, or even bathe at stations where they would wait for an hour or more. By now, though, Teresa was as sick of Macaria as she had been of Merkad. She was completely out of place in this world, like a fish out of water. All her habits, her trivial strategies of life, were useless to her now, and she could not make do as Salvador did by taking an obsessive interest in the details of their environment. Her place was among machines; ideally, in deep space. She could deal with information expertly, but only the information that was processed through machines. She was accustomed to mechanical complexity, mechanical delicacy and mechanical ubiquity. The rawness of this almost pre-mechanical world exerted a special friction upon her nerves.

She was still sick. She knew that the responsibility for this was entirely her own, and she dared not let Salvador know of her weakness. Her leg had not completely healed, and it never would. She lacked control, and she could not find extra reserves to draw upon. Her physical failure was a direct consequence—and, indeed, a reflection—of her psychological difficulties. It was a basic failure of adaptation, of self-confidence and self-awareness. She remembered that when the ship had crashed, and she had found Salvador dangling from a tree in his rotting parachute harness, she had imagined herself to be in complete control. She had seen herself as the dominant partner, and Salvador as the helpless one. It had not turned out that way. From the moment the snake had bitten her, she had been hardly a shadow trailing in Salvador's wake. *He*, not she, was equipped for survival here, because he was primed for understanding, while she was primed for action.

The most terrible irony of all, she realized, was that it would have been very different if she had been an experimental subject instead of an experimental administrator. The greater part of her troubles sprang from the fact that she had no object but to reach the Tanagarian base in the far north. If she had been dumped here, as Sarid Jerome had been dumped, and forced to formulate her own plans for an uncertain future, she would have had far more to occupy her mind. Alas, even this may not have been enough. Unlike Sarid Jerome, she was very much a citizen of Tanagar, shaped as Tanagar would wish. She was the kind of descendant the children of the *Marco Polo* had wanted. She fit in perfectly to her allotted place in Tanagarian society.

Unfortunately, she was no longer *in* Tanagarian society; and out of it she was losing the most precious gift that Tanagar bestowed upon its offspring.

She was losing *control*.

I'm dying, she thought, as she allowed the pain from her leg to bestir her consciousness. *I'm actually dying.*

She was less than two hundred years old, in terms of experienced time. Time in suspended animation, and the time dilation consequent of her travels in space, meant that much more time than that had passed since the actual moment of her birth. She had never before thought of death, which had seemed so remote. Never—until the moment when the malfunction light appeared on Salvador's console aboard the *Sabreur*. Now, she thought about it frequently, and knew that it was close at hand. It had been close at hand ever since that moment, and nothing she could do would make it go away . . . at least until they reached the base.

Salvador, she knew, was different. He had not thought about the possibility of death even when the malfunction was signaled. He had calculated the odds, and dismissed it from his mind, as any true Intel would. *She* had had the advantage then. But now, he had the same self-confidence perennially about him. He was still calculating the odds, and he still thought that they were comfortably in his favor.

He was probably right, but sometimes she could not help wishing that he might be wrong, and that some day he would find himself on the wrong end of a calculated risk that would slice him in half.

She returned her attention to the conversation in time to hear da Lancha ask: "Do you find Macaria so very inspiring, then? Seeing her through the eyes of a foreigner, I suppose, might make her seem infinitely more awe-inspiring than she really is."

"I don't think that's particularly important," Salvador replied. "Whether you see it through a foreigner's eyes or through your own, you can hardly avoid the conclusion that somewhere and somehow there must be a better way for people to conduct their affairs. The only question worth asking is whether Macaria—or any other nation on Earth—is capable of finding it."

13

On the sixth day, the darkness lightened, and they followed steep uphill paths which led them into a part of the forest where the trees were not nearly so tall and the canopy did not form a barrier impenetrable to light. It was dense forest still, and all the harder to penetrate because of the combination of precipitous ground and lush undergrowth, but the sight of the sky and the sun lifted their spirits in a marvelous manner. At noon they found a lake shaped like a fish without a head, three hundred meters long and a hundred meters across at its widest. It was flecked with small islets, and when they first saw it from the top of a high cliff they were tempted to make a dash down the slope.

When they reached the shore, in midafternoon, the forest man who had been leading them disappeared into the trees, leaving them alone. They bathed, and Cheron swam out to the nearest of the tiny islands. He estimated that the valley as a whole must be a thousand meters long and three hundred wide, and that it was surrounded by slopes bearing what he considered "normal forest" for a further two or three thousand meters in each direction. The lake was shallow, and there was not enough soil caught in the rock basin for the giant trees of the greater forest to take root, but it seemed as near to Midas's story of a hidden paradise as chance might provide. There were, of course, no beautiful women, no grain to make bread, and no grapes to make wine, but it represented a deliverance from the eternal darkness.

There were animals here—herbivorous mammals different from anything they had seen in the greater forest as well as monkeys and a profusion of birds. The lake had a colony of waders as prolific as the lower reaches of the Bela, and there were small ground squirrels so unafraid of men that they would approach to within arm's reach of the visitors from an

alien world. They could have seized some with ease, but
Cheron was reluctant to do so as he had not the means of
skinning them. He thought perhaps that he ought to provide
meat of some kind, for the sake of Qapel and Midas, but in
the end he settled for an attempt to catch some fish with
the aid of an improvised net. It took him much longer to do
so than he would have wished, but in the end he succeeded.

There was no sign of the savages during the remainder of
the evening, and Cheron began to wonder if perhaps they had
reached their destination. If so, then their journey made no
sense at all, but he was almost past the stage of expecting it
to make sense.

"Here," said Talvar, "I could stay. I would live the life of
a noble savage, trapping and fishing. I would build a hut by
the lakeside, and a small boat, and gather food plants to
make myself a garden. In all of Earth I have found nothing
so desirable. The world could not interfere with me, nor I
with the world. I would be content to ignore the forest savages if they would ignore me. This is where I would make
my home."

Midas and Qapel assumed that he was no more than half
serious in this assertion, and that his enthusiasm was inspired
by the contrast between this nightfall and previous ones, but
Cheron knew better. This little enclave could never qualify as
a lost paradise in Midas's view of things, nor Qapel's, for it
had too little of things they considered all-important—notably
the beautiful women of the Merkadian's dream. Vito Talvar,
however, was serious. Of all the places he had seen on the
surface of the Motherworld, this was the one that would have
suited him best. He had self-control enough to limit his needs
and desires—especially as he was safe in the knowledge that
the world beyond the forest had little else to offer. This might
be a poor second-best compared with Tanagar, but it had its
attractions even for someone familiar with what Tanagar had
to offer. There could be no noble savages on Tanagar, because life depended on the support of technology—the wil-
dernesses of their home world were far too hostile to be
endured—but the mythology of Tanagar had never quite
purged itself of the notion of Arcadia that the shipborne generations had nurtured through more than a hundred generations.

"I think I might be content to stay," said Cheron, "at least for a little while. It would be pleasant to be allowed the time which Midas and Qapel need in order to recuperate."

"What would happen," asked Qapel, "if we refused to go back into the darkness?"

"Who knows?" asked Cheron. "But I see no sign that this is anything but a way station. The most we can hope is that our real destination is a place like this, and not some remote spot in the dark forest. That would make a kind of sense. I cannot see that there might be a destination in the underworld, for us or for our captors. Eventually, we must come out . . . or go up."

"I have no head for heights," said Midas. "I cannot climb. Is there any way of making this clear to the demons?"

Cheron laughed. "I don't suppose that the concept of vertigo has any meaning for such creatures," he said. "And it would be unthinkable that any of their own people would be unable to climb. Whether they can make allowances for such as us, I don't know."

"We are no nearer guessing their purpose than we ever were," sighed Qapel. "Nothing has changed."

"At least we know that there are parts of the forest where the sun can be seen," Cheron told him. "We know now that we are not necessarily condemned to spend the rest of our lives in the underworld."

"How far have we come, do you suppose?" asked Talvar.

"I have no idea," replied Cheron. "I think we have come some way east and a long way south of our point of capture, but I had already guessed that before I tried to judge from the position of the sun whether I might be right. The impression may be false. In any case, we are too far from any vestige of civilization to contemplate reaching it under our own power. Our dependence on the forest men is absolute while so much of the underworld lies behind us."

The next morning, the forest men came in force to lead them back into the darkness. It was the first time in several days that they had seen more than two of the apemen together. Cheron and Talvar signaled their reluctance to leave, demanding in mime that they be left alone. Cheron attempted to impress upon them the fact that both Midas and Qapel were ill, and that their return to health was dependent on their being allowed to remain, but he could not tell whether he was getting the message across. In any case, the savages were implacable. Before the dialogue had lasted twenty minutes they were gesturing with their blowguns.

Talvar threw up his hands in despair. "Let them kill us," he said. "I no longer care. I stop here."

Cheron, however, had followed the gestures more attentively.

"I don't think they're threatening to kill us," he said. "They're saying that they can knock us out again and carry us back into the forest."

The black-polled leader of the group jabbered away at Cheron, pointing at the ground, and at the lake, and then stabbing with his finger urgently.

"I think he's trying to tell us that there's another place like this," said Cheron.

"Why should we believe him?" demanded Talvar.

"What choice have we got?" countered Cheron. He studied the pantomime a little longer, then said: "I think he's trying to tell us that there's a lot more high ground, and that the forest isn't so deep. Maybe the underworld is patchy in this region, and the journey won't be so bad."

In the end, they had, as Cheron had observed, no real choice. They shouldered their packs and set off. All four were walking now, though the effort was probably taking more out of Midas and Qapel than either was willing to admit. There was no way that both could be carried, though.

As Cheron had deduced from the furious signaling, the regions of Stygian darkness through which they had now to pass proved to be of no great dimension. They were continually interrupted by regions where at least *some* light filtered through the canopy. They found no more lakes, but there were several rocky regions where the giant trees could find no purchase, and where they labored in the full glare of the sun. The main effect of this was tragically ironic: by the time they paused for the next night, Midas was suffering from sunstroke and Qapel was running a fever. A few short hours of the glare of noonday had been too much for them. Even Cheron found that his skin was burning.

That night, Cheron's dreams ran away from him, and he spent much of the time he should have been sleeping turning and twisting in a waking delirium. It was not the first time that he had been tortured by nightmares, but the images that beset him were unusual in their clamor, and cut through his exhaustion.

The obsession that carried him away was the notion that they were being taken to some place that was sacred to the forest people; a place which all the scattered tribes and races revered, and where they sometimes gathered. What such a place might be like his dreams could not tell him, but he seized upon the image of a tree greater than anything he could imagine on the basis of anything he had seen in the underworld: a tree whose roots burrowed into the hot core of the earth, and whose topmost leaves extended beyond the stratosphere. This would be the tree of life and the tree of knowledge of good and evil combined into a single being, the spiritual heart of the empire of the forest demons.

We, his mind ran on, *are the first upright men ever to penetrate the forest to this sacred shrine. We are the emissaries of civilization, brought to stand trial for the crimes of all mankind. Pray that we are acquitted, lest we be destroyed.*

He rose in the morning, sick-headed, to find that he was not the only one to have suffered. Midas was no worse, but Qapel's fever was running high. This time, when the savage who came to rouse them demanded that they move, they refused and were adamant in their refusal. The black-crowned savage was called to arbitrate, and in the end accepted Cheron's judgment. He stayed to watch while Cheron and Talvar did what they could to control the fever.

They were not in darkness, but they were sufficiently sheltered from the heat of the midday sun to be comfortable. They were able to light a fire, and to replenish the liquid that Qapel sweated away while providing a little nourishment in the form of warm broth. In the afternoon, though, the Dahran began vomiting, and could no longer keep anything in his stomach. Whatever Cheron and Talvar did thereafter was bound to come to nothing.

In the middle of the next night, Qapel died.

Midas seemed considerably weakened, as much by watching Qapel die as by his own touch of the sun. He seemed to see in the Dahran's fate a prophecy of his own. When Cheron and Vito Talvar set off again, in a new gray dawn, they carried him as they had before, strapped to a makeshift stretcher.

In some strange way that his reason could not define, Cheron felt that the trial of mankind had already begun.

14

On the road to Ophidion the armored car carrying Sarid Jerome and Toran Zeyer was stoned by children. The missiles bounced harmlessly from the body of the vehicle, and the soldiers within ignored them. The windows of the car were covered with thin wire mesh rather than glass, and Sarid began to understand why. Previously, he had assumed that it was to ensure adequate ventilation.

"Is this usual?" he asked of Zeyer.

"Not unusual," replied the Macarian guardedly. "It is a kind of game. A way of venting frustration. They are harmless."

"You don't feel that they might grow up with the habit ingrained?"

"If we could find a way to stop Merkadians from hating Macarians, we would do it. There is no way. To shoot the children who throw stones at our vehicles would not solve anything. They do grow up with a burning sense of resentment against us. If it were not directed against us, it would be directed against other scapegoats within their society. They are a people much given to resentment. The only way to overcome this kind of display is to change their entire way of life—to bring the nation a new prosperity. It will happen, in time—it is already happening—but while things are changing they resist tooth and claw. It is mostly display, you understand—not real hostility. They rarely take to murder, except for a few ungovernable rogues who would be living as predators whatever the circumstances were. Resentment seems to be running high just now because we hung a man named Daran a few days ago. He went under the name of Machado when he was looting the region around Naryn, and pretended to be a hero of the nonexistent revolution. In fact, those he killed and stole from were his own people, and he always ran from any kind of confrontation with Macarian forces, but this has not stopped him becoming a kind of martyr. The fuss will die down in three days more."

"We appear to be passing through at exactly the wrong time," said Sarid.

Zeyer shrugged. "There are few right times. It always seems to be the case, if you listen to Merkadian gossip, that we have just destroyed another hero, or that another petty prophet has completed a meteoric career, trailing clouds of false hope. In Armata we say that Dahra is primitive in the hand and the heart, but Merkad is primitive in the head. A lack of civilized values is built into the way these people think, and they even boast of their irrationality by celebrating the loss of faith that started their long fall from some imaginary golden age."

The group of stone-throwing children was far behind them now, and Sarid was content to let the subject drop. The vehicle in which they were being transported was cramped, and had been built with people of lesser dimensions in mind. He was developing an awkward crick in his neck. The car was also crowded. As well as himself and Zeyer it contained four armed troopers and Baya-undi. This number did not include the driver and the machine gunner, who were in a separate compartment. Ever since they had set out from Asdar they had traveled with this kind of retinue—though mercifully not always in this kind of vehicle, which was a measure of additional protection deemed necessary only in Merkad.

They passed a convoy of oxcarts carrying produce from the surrounding farmlands toward the city, and Sarid stared through the wire mesh at the untidy train of people accompanying the carts. Most of them were on foot, because the carts were too heavily laden to permit them to ride without overtaxing the beasts of burden. The smaller carts were being pulled by donkeys; there were no horses or mules.

Only the children looked up at the armored car, one or two of them managing to meet his eye for a bare second. The adults were determinedly uninterested. The dust thrown up by the wheels of the car must have stung their eyes long after the vehicle itself had passed out of sight.

"Of course," said Zeyer, observing his momentary interest in the road's other users, "the fact that the harvest is in doesn't help matters. There are all kinds of traffic on every road into the cities and the ports. Ophidion will be crowded with transients, and a great deal of money will be changing hands in every direction. There'll be chaos outside the walls and queues at every gate. The walls should have been torn down long ago—they're like an iron collar strangling the city —but every move to accomplish that is greeted with total opposition. Even the city fathers have got it fixed in their minds that Macaria wants the wall down in order to render the city defenseless, and that to capitulate would be to put the last nail in Merkad's coffin. Absurd! The Macarians are inside the walls, it's their own rabble that bring the city under siege every year. In *that* sense, our timing is wrong. It will be almost impossible to move through the streets of the city."

In this, Zeyer was eventually proved right. Long before the city walls were in view the road became far more congested, and the car was reduced to the same pace as the oxcarts. By the time the tallest towers of Ophidion were peeping over the ridge of the horizon they were down to walking pace. By this time, there was no way that the vehicle could attempt to jump the queue, for the sides of the road were lined by a straggling shantytown thronged with people. This suburb did not cover a vast area, but it extended for several kilometers along the road, the huts and houses a dozen deep on either side. Such side roads as there were had become unavailable for use in time-saving maneuvers by virtue of being blocked by carts. A vast market had already been set up, and traders of all kinds were doing business. Many buyers had come out of the city to inspect the produce that was brought in, and many of the early sellers found themselves beset with a thousand enticements that would make sure some of their money stayed in Ophidion.

"Most of this is illegal, of course," said Zeyer, waving a hand at the crowds. "The crops on the ground belong to the landowners, and *their* convoys come into the city in a reasonably well-ordered fashion, with their destination already decided. The peasant-farmers are supposed to retain little more than enough to subsist, but as you can see, it doesn't quite work out like that. Fully half these carts are full of goods that have no official existence; they don't appear on anyone's tally. Yet no matter what the landowners do they can't control it. Their attempts are a little half-hearted, partly because this kind of theft is sanctified by tradition, and partly because it would be too expensive to hire the men required to make sure that everything happens as it should. As feudal barons the Merkadians are ludicrously inefficient."

"No doubt things work efficiently in Macaria?" said Sarid, and was not surprised to be assured that they did.

"What I object to," said Zeyer, "is the fact that it all causes so much *inconvenience.* If a black market has to exist on such a scale, why can't it be kept out of the way? Why do they have to block up *our* road?"

Sarid glanced at Baya-undi, and said: "I suppose it doesn't happen in Khepra, either?"

"Of course not," said the black man. For a moment, he was on the point of offering a homily on the superiority of the way that Khepra managed its affairs—with the usual lack of descriptive detail—but a venomous look from Zeyer reminded him that it would not be a welcome contribution to the conversation.

By now, the car had almost come to a halt. Eventually, the brake was applied, with a grinding groan of defeating finality. The driver came round to the rear of the vehicle to address Zeyer through one of the wire screens. He reported that the road ahead was temporarily blocked by a collapsed cart. Space was being cleared for the traffic to get around it while it was dragged from the road, but it was almost certainly not the only blockage between their present position and the south gate of the city. The driver, who obviously had experience in such matters, advised that if they wanted to reach their destination before dusk they probably stood a better chance of doing so on foot.

This information was far from welcome as far as Zeyer was concerned, but Sarid was a good deal more enthusiastic.

"It's not just a matter of saving time," said Zeyer. "There's the safety factor to be considered."

"We have an armed escort," Sarid pointed out. "There's no reason to suppose that anyone bears us any particular animosity. Neither Baya-undi nor myself is a ready-made victim for thieves or troublemakers. I think we can be sure that nothing will happen to us."

Zeyer—albeit reluctantly—agreed. The interior of the armored car was almost as uncomfortable for him as for Sarid.

Once outside, the prospect of a pleasant walk seemed a little less inviting. Indeed, there was little about it that was pleasant. The crowd had attracted a far greater swarm of flies, which had been excluded from the car by the mesh protecting the windows. The mesh had not altogether excluded the myriad smells that competed for the attention of their olfactory sense, but once outside these seemed to grow more clamorous and more offensive. It was a hot day and there was almost no wind. The one consolation was that by maintaining as determined a tread as the conditions allowed they soon left the armored car a long way behind. Their escort did not assure that they were spared the attentions of traders and beggars, but kept those attentions within reasonable limits. Nor were they spared a certain amount of abuse, but no one was stupid enough to raise a hand in anger to interfere with their progress. The four troopers had fixed bayonets, and held their weapons in such a way that they could easily use the butts to discourage any minor nuisance.

"All this should be cleared," said Zeyer, waving an arm to include the multitude of small huts and houses. "It's a fever-pit, with no properly planned water supply and hardly any worthwhile sanitation. These satellite towns which grow up around the roads should be properly designed to contain the population which they absorb. We would do this, if only we could obtain cooperation, either from the people themselves or from the authorities in Ophidion."

"No doubt the time will come," said Sarid, with no more than the faintest pretense of interest. Deliberately, he dropped back a little so that he was walking with Baya-undi rather than with Zeyer.

"Are you really his friend?" asked the black man, in a low voice. "Or are you his prisoner? Sometimes I cannot tell."

"He seems to have no love for Merkad," replied Sarid in a neutral voice.

"In Ophidion," said Baya-undi, "there are a million places to hide. There are men of every race and color, especially at this time of year. It is not too late, you know, to go to Khepra."

"Isn't it a little unwise to reveal such facts to me?" asked Sarid. "I am a Macarian now—I might consider it my duty to have you placed under restraint. Zeyer would not like it if you were to disappear. They would hunt you now—make no mistake about that. In knowing what you know about me, you know too much—though I am not sure that you believe it."

"I believe it," said Baya-undi. "I have known all along that you are not what you seemed to be. I have no trouble imagining that you are a man from another world. I know that all you have said is true."

"In Zeyer's eyes," Sarid pointed out, "that makes you more dangerous, not less."

Baya-undi did not seem disturbed by this. "I doubt that the rulers of Khepra would be interested," he said. "If there were a million men from the star worlds, it would not disturb their midday rest by the flicker of an eyelid. There is no need to fear the spies of masters such as those."

Sarid, slightly puzzled by the tone of the remark, said: "Try explaining that to Zeyer. Or to the army."

He had no opportunity to continue the conversation, because Zeyer had deliberately slowed his pace in order to fall back level with them.

"It will not be long now," said the Macarian. "One night in Ophidion—which has its civilized aspect, though you would not think so to judge by all this—and then we set sail for Solis. Within forty-eight hours you will be on Macarian soil, and your journey will be almost over. A new life will begin—for you, and perhaps for Macaria."

"Let us hope so," said Sarid, and realized as he spoke how tired he was of traveling. It would, indeed, be good to find a new point of departure, and a career more suited to his ambitions. For the duration of the tedious march he forsook the arts of conversation and was possessed instead by dreams which assured him that he was destined to become a powerful man in the affairs of Macaria—more powerful, perhaps, than a man like Toran Zeyer could yet imagine.

15

The moment the train ground to a halt at the little station Teresa knew something was wrong. There were a dozen men on the platform, all in police uniforms. No one was waiting to board the train. This was the last stop before Galehalt, and they were already high up in the mountains. The town at which they were stopping was a small one, but the railway was virtually its only link with the outside world. There should have been passengers lining up to get onto the train.

She turned to Salvador, ready to alert him to the danger, but he had already seen the policemen. She opened her mouth to speak, but he shook his head. His eyes commanded her to stay still, to remain calm. She did not know whether he was hoping that the trap was for someone else, or whether he still hoped to bluff his way through. She knew well enough what a faint hope the second alternative was. If these police were looking for two murderers who had fled from an insignificant port on the Bitter Sea, then they would be armed with descriptions that could fit no one else on the train. It would not take too much effort to penetrate the most crucial part of her own imposture.

Alaric da Lancha favored them with a curious glance as he noted their careful lack of reaction to the situation on the station.

"Police," he said, stating the obvious. "They've cleared the platform. They must be all set to arrest someone on the train."

"So it seems," said Salvador calmly.

Damn him, thought Teresa. *He'll face them with nothing but his deadly self-control. To him, it's a kind of challenge. He won't act until he's forced to. Damn his pride!*

She stood up, and was not surprised when he gripped her arm.

"Wait!" he said.

She looked him in the eyes, and said, "I'm sick of waiting. You can make a fetish out of keeping calm until they lay you out in a coffin. I'm getting out. You're coming too."

Salvador's lips were bloodless, and she could not help congratulating herself on the petty victory.

"Sit down!" he ordered, his voice deadly in its neutrality.

She reached inside her shirt to draw something out that had long been wedged in her belt, uncomfortable but comforting. He watched her as if fascinated, unable to act.

She pointed the gun at his face, and for a moment she said nothing. From the corner of her eye she could see da Lancha staring at her, aghast, and beyond him other passengers. Everyone in the coach had turned to watch her when she stood up; even that had been a signal that she might be the guilty one.

"We're getting off," she said rapidly. "This is the last coach, and we can get down on the blind side. My leg hurts, but in circumstances like these I can run like the wind. Once I've gone, you don't have a hope in hell. Are you coming?"

Salvador's fingers bit into the flesh of her arm, but then relaxed.

"You're crazy," he said. "Step outside with that, and they start shooting. They *know* what you did before."

She wrenched free, and ran to the back of the coach, not waiting to see whether he would follow. She was certain in her mind that he would, but his decision no longer seemed to matter. Her mind, at least, was made up.

Salvador watched her open the door at the rear end of the coach. Only the guard's van was behind it to provide shelter as she leapt down onto the track. She was seen immediately, and there was an immediate outcry. She ignored the demand that she should stop, and the moment the van was no longer between herself and the running policemen she released a shot. Immediately, the policemen began dragging their own pistols from their holsters.

Two men, with guns ready, launched themselves through the door of the carriage and commanded everyone to be seated. One or two of the people at the rear of the coach had risen to their feet, but now they subsided. Salvador had not moved from his seat. The policemen looked round, the muzzles of their guns moving slowly to keep pace with their gaze. Their eyes settled on Salvador, and there was no more need to wonder whether they had an accurate description of their quarry.

Salvador showed his open palms. "I'm unarmed," he said levelly.

When he stood up, da Lancha stood up too, motivated by an instinctive politeness which he found acutely embarrassing once he realized what he had done.

Salvador nodded to him, briefly but courteously.

"May I collect my baggage?" he inquired of the foremost policeman.

"No."

Salvador made the slightest of bows, and allowed the two men to guide him from the carriage onto the platform. There was still one man on the platform, though two or three others were on the train. The rest had set off in pursuit of the fleeing Teresa.

"I hope no one is hurt," said Salvador. "The gun had only three bullets. I doubt that my companion will do much damage with it."

"You're under arrest," he was told—rather needlessly. The speaker was a sergeant, but he was soon joined by an officer, who barely glanced at him before subjecting Salvador to a complete and scrupulous inspection. Without speaking, he directed the second policeman to make certain that Salvador was unarmed. The man removed the papers from Salvador's pocket and passed them over to the officer.

"They're not very good forgeries," he commented.

"They passed inspection four times," remarked Salvador. "They must be superficially convincing."

He received in return for this observation a stony and hostile stare.

"Get him into the car," said the officer after a pause. Then, to the second man, he said, "Get their baggage from the coach."

The sergeant, his gun still drawn, indicated which way Salvador should go, and the Intellectual led the way through the station turnstile to the pavement beyond, where a car was waiting. The man sitting behind the wheel jumped out, and began to unlock the rear door. Salvador got inside, meekly.

The sergeant followed him, and the driver returned to his place. A few minutes later, the second policeman brought Salvador's traveling bag from the train and opened the door on the sergeant's side.

As the sergeant turned away, Salvador plucked the gun neatly from his hand and turned it on him. With his left hand he jerked the man's body forward, and with his foot he propelled it from the car with considerable velocity. The sergeant and the other man went down heavily in an untidy heap.

Salvador reached across to slam the door and jabbed the muzzle of the gun into the back of the driver's head.

"Move!" he commanded. "Quickly!"

The driver fumbled with the starter, and Salvador drew back the hammer of the gun with an audible click. The officer appeared in the doorway of the station, drawing a gun.

Salvador watched him level the gun and fire, and ducked as a shower of glass sprayed the interior of the vehicle. The moment the gun went off the driver threw the car into gear, and it began to move forward. The engine screamed under the forced acceleration, and Salvador stayed down as a second bullet shattered the rear windscreen.

"Go north!" he commanded, as the car swung out into the road, heading for a junction.

Another shot sounded behind them, but it must have gone wild.

"You can't escape now!" said the driver. "There'll be men out looking for you on every road and in every town. You can't survive long in the mountains, even at this time of year. Believe me, you'd be better giving yourself up."

"If I were the man you take me for," said Salvador calmly, "your arguments would be quite appropriate. On the other hand, if I were the man you take me for, I would take no more notice of them than I propose to do anyhow. Keep driving . . . I won't take you far and I have no intention of hurting you. No matter what you may have heard, I have killed no one, and I don't intend to start. The shooting at the station was none of my doing, and the killing in the south was the result of the overenthusiasm of my companion, who has now gone her own way."

Privately, however, the tone of his thoughts was very different, and had he voiced the words that were in his head he would have spoken in a way that would have disgraced him forever.

Oh, Teresa! he was thinking. *This time your folly may get us killed!*

16

When they stopped to sleep on the twelfth day of their epic journey, Cheron, Talvar, and Midas received an unexpected gift from their captors and protectors: a large gourd filled with a sweet-tasting liquid. Cheron tasted it suspiciously, but found it extremely pleasant. Vito Talvar was delighted with it, and expressed some annoyance that it had not been provided before. That it was a drug delivering them into a state of euphoric intoxication became very quickly apparent, but they did not realize that it might have another purpose altogether until they were overcome by an insistent drowsiness.

Midas, still too sick to walk, succumbed immediately to the attractions of deep sleep, but Cheron and Talvar—accustomed to retaining control over their physiological states—tried to resist it. They were both aware of what was happening to them, and both were quick to realize that they were impotent to stop it.

"I only pray that it isn't poison," said Talvar, as he yielded to inevitability.

Cheron could not even find the energy to echo him, though he tried hard to thrust a subvocal question forward for the attention of his own consciousness.

Why? he asked himself.

Even his imagination could provide no answers.

He went to sleep inside the tent, in pitch darkness. They were once again in a deep part of the forest, but were climbing again, and during the daylight hours a certain amount of sunlight had filtered down to them. Though they had not dared to talk about it, they had hoped that they might soon emerge into the daylight—and even that their journey might be almost over.

When Cheron woke, things had changed so dramatically that it took him several seconds to remember what the situation had been before he slept.

He found himself in a bed, with a soft sheet and a single blanket—not his army blanket. The mattress was soft, and there was a ceiling above him, plastered and painted white. He sat up, in surprise, and then felt the back of his head, where there was a dull ache. It was not a generalized headache, but a much more concentrated pain, and the skin he touched, beneath his hair, was sensitive to pressure. The skin covering the ports in his skull was still intact, and there was no sensation to suggest that the artificial neural highways in his brain had been touched, but the pain was certainly in that area. For the moment, he could not estimate the significance of that fact.

Instead, he looked around him at the four walls. There was a window set in one—a glazed window with a small ventilation panel masked by a grille. There was a table beneath the window, but it was quite bare. There was no furniture in the room except for the table—not even a chair—but there was a neat stack of clothes on the blanket at the foot of the ample bed. He was naked, and he quickly moved to recover his undershirt.

All his clothes had been washed, but now they were quite dry. He put on a shirt and his uniform trousers, but ignored his jacket. The room had two doors. One of them opened onto a corridor, and he glanced out briefly before closing it and moving to the other. This one gave access to a room identical to the one in which he had found himself. In the bed, still asleep, was Vito Talvar.

This room also had a door opening onto the corridor, but he ignored it and went to the counterpart of the one he had just opened. Beyond it, as he expected, he found Midas. The Merkadian was awake, and his face creased with delight as he saw Cheron.

"Did I not tell you?" he whispered. "Did I not promise you that it would be so? It is the valley, every detail as I prophesied."

Cheron judged that he was whispering because he was so

weak rather than from any sense of tremendous reverence.
He went to the bedside to look down at the little man.

"Have you seen the beautiful women yet?" he asked.

"I have seen them," Midas told him. "One of them, at
least. She is black as Baya-undi, but she is beautiful. I will
not care if this place is full of Kheprans—I will not care if
this *is* Khepra—so long as it is the end. I feel it in my body;
peace is come. It is the valley."

"So it seems," said Cheron slowly. His last comment had
been half a jest, but now he realized how slow he had been.
Wherever they were, this building had not been erected by
forest savages. It had been built by men like himself—and
civilized men, at that.

He went to the window and looked out. There were trees
beyond a narrow corridor of cleared ground, cutting off his
view. They were ordinary trees, only fifteen or twenty meters
in height, and comfortably spaced. Their leaves were rustling
in a strong breeze, and he could feel the coolness of it
through the ventilator grille. All he could see beyond the
trees was the peak of a mountain, capped with snow even at
this latitude.

"Is it beautiful?" asked Midas, from his bed.

"I can't tell from here," answered Cheron. He turned as
the other door opened and someone entered the room. It was
not one of Midas's beautiful women, but a man. He was tall,
though not as tall as Cheron, and his skin was ebony black.
He was wearing a white tunic and white trousers, neatly cut,
and light brown sandals. He seemed surprised to find Cheron
in the room.

"Your powers of recuperation are surprising," he said, favoring Cheron with a small bow. The language he used was
Merkadian.

"Why?" asked Cheron, feeling that the situation was
slightly surreal. "Am I supposed to be dead?"

"Of course not," replied the other. "It would be a terrible
waste to have brought you so far only to have you die."

"One of us died," said Cheron flatly. "He would have lived
if we had been able to come a little more slowly."

"I am sorry about that," said the black man. "It was a miscalculation, I assure you. The Lu'el who escorted you here
were instructed to be most careful for your well-being."

"You had us brought here?"

"We did," said the black man. "Excuse me, please, for my impoliteness. My name is M'lise."

"You're a Khepran?"

M'lise shook his head. "The physical resemblance is strong," he said, "but I am neither Khepran nor Kyadian."

"You seem to speak Merkadian very well," observed Cheron.

"His accent is barbarous," contributed Midas. To M'lise he said, "Where are we?"

"On the slopes of a mountain, above the forest." He saw Cheron's eyes go to the window, and added: "Not *that* mountain. We are in the range where the Bela rises. From the peak, you can see its headwaters. Here, we are on ground that is almost level. There is a sheer cliff to the north, from which you can actually look back across the forest in the direction from which you have come. Instead of seeing its roots, though, you see its roof. It looks very different. A tribe of the Lu'el lives close to the cliff. Later, we will visit their dwellings, and you will see them as they really are. It is something that no white man has ever seen. I think that you will find it most interesting."

"How many men died at the river post so that you could take four prisoners?" asked Cheron.

The black man frowned. "We did not instigate the raid," he said. "We merely sought to take advantage of it. The Lu'el see the Macarians as invaders who threaten the forest. They burn and cut, and try to clear land. They shoot game. It is the burning that the Lu'el are afraid of, more than anything else. It is a threat to their homes. Already, this year, two forest fires have been started by the Macarians along the Bela. Both were deliberate, intended to prepare the way for the building of fortresses. The Lu'el of the region reacted violently, but they are not by nature a violent people. They neither use fire, nor do they kill animals for food, but they protect themselves and their homes against predators—the Macarians, to them, are simply a new and more dangerous species of predator. As they hunt down panthers, so they hunt down Macarians. We sent a party from here to save some men from death, not to kill in order to capture a few."

"You live here?" asked Cheron. "In these mountains?"

"Yes," said M'lise.

"The Macarians know nothing of your existence," said

Cheron. What he really wanted to say was that Cyriac Salvador—apparently—had known nothing of their existence, but he was still cautious about that.

"Why should they?" countered the black man. It was a reasonable answer, though it must be far easier to be hidden from the knowledge of Macaria than from the satellite-borne observers of Tanagar. Cheron looked again at the plastered walls and at the black man's clothes, trying to estimate what degree of civilization they implied.

"This is a hospital," he said warily.

"Of sorts," M'lise confirmed. "It is small, but it serves our purpose." To Midas he said, "You will recover, now. A few days' rest is all you need."

"And what then?" asked Cheron. "What *now*, in fact? Why have you brought us here?"

"To learn the truth," said M'lise easily. Cheron began to suspect that his uncommunicativeness was deliberate.

"Which is?"

M'lise laughed. "If the truth could be told and learned so easily, there would be no point in going to these extremes. I assure you, though, that we mean you no harm, and that you will be allowed to return to the outer world as soon as it becomes convenient. If it is any consolation to you, you have already seen some of what we intended that you should see."

"The forest—a worm's-eye view?"

"The forest."

"And what happens when we know the truth?" asked Cheron quietly. "What do we do with it? What message are we supposed to carry back to Macaria?"

"That depends on you," answered the black man.

"This is stupid," said Cheron. "You know what I want to know. What's the point of all this evasion? You say that you brought us here so that we can learn the truth—so why avoid every shadow of a question? Who are you, and why are we here?"

M'lise acknowledged the criticism with a slight bow.

"Very well," he said. "I will try to explain. One of you"—here his gaze alighted briefly on Midas—"is here as a result of a miscalculation. The Lu'el were asked to bring four men, but something went wrong. When the net closed not all the fish were there. We had *you* brought here because we are curious, and because we assumed that you, too, might be curious. We would like to know just what it is you plan to do here on Earth—and we would not like you to make any such plans on the basis of what you already know, because, as we see it, you do not know enough."

There was a moment's silence before Cheron answered. Then he said, "You know who we are?"

It was only half a question—the answer was already obvious. Nevertheless, M'lise confirmed the answer.

"Yes," he said. "We know who you are and where you have come from. What we don't know is why."

17

After they had washed and changed, Toran Zeyer took Sarid down to a private dining room in the basement of the hotel. The hotel was rather more impressive in size and in the comfort which it provided for its guests than the old palace, which they had passed in the course of their journey through the city. Though it was a hotel and not an embassy, open to anyone with the necessary finances, it was essentially Macarian territory, built to attend to the needs of Macarians whose business took them to the Merkadian capital. The contrast between its ostentatious luxury and the squalid back streets that could be seen from its higher windows was a deliberate political statement, aimed at the people of both nations. The building had electric lighting throughout and blazed like a beacon in the city night. It had thermostatically controlled heating; hot and cold running water; and an abundance of personal servants. It also had a squadron of Macarian soldiers guarding the spiked iron gateway and the neatly planted gardens that comprised its grounds. There had been trouble in the streets for the past three days, and it was only a matter of time before the tension erupted into violence. Nothing serious would follow, of course, but the guests were entitled to their peace of mind.

Sarid had a personal guard—two armed men patrolled the corridor outside his room. He was not entirely certain what their orders were. They were protecting him, of course, but they were also making sure that he stayed where he was supposed to be. Zeyer did not altogether trust him, though he would never be impolite enough to say so.

He was slightly surprised to find that he and Zeyer were not to eat alone, though on reflection he realized that Ophidion, so close to civilization, would have its own population of Collegians.

"I hope you will not mind if they ask questions which you have already answered for me," said Zeyer as they descended the stairs. "I have sent messages ahead of us, by mail-rider and by radio, but they have covered only the elementary details."

"I don't mind at all," Sarid assured him. "It will be a small price to pay for the hospitality I'm being shown. After all, I'm only a captain in the army, and a foreigner at that. The hotel staff can't have seen many like me."

When they entered the dining room Sarid felt like a specimen under a microscope as all eyes in the room turned toward him. There were four other people at the table, and all rose to their feet as he entered. They did not take their seats again until he himself was seated. From the way they acknowledged Zeyer's presence he gathered that in some important respect they all outranked him, but that his prestige had been temporarily elevated by virtue of his association with Sarid. The four who were to eat with them were introduced as Gedeon Macabel, Immanuel Spiridion, Raban la Cabral, and Vianna Cascorial. They all seemed to be in their fifties, or even older, though they were fit and healthy enough. Macabel and Spiridion already had white hair, and the woman's hair looked as if it had been dyed in order to save it from the same fate.

With impeccable politeness and mannered patience the four maintained a scrupulously trivial conversation throughout the dinner, asking Sarid only the most superficial questions and exchanging comments between themselves on matters of little interest—primarily the difficult situation developing in the city. Macabel predicted that someone would be killed before much longer, and no one doubted this opinion, though no one seemed particularly apprehensive about it. Whoever was killed, they were certain it would not be one of them.

They all apologized to Sarid for the sad state of Merkad, and Sarid assured them that everything had been quite adequately explained by Zeyer.

Only when the food was cleared away and they moved away from the table to a circle of armchairs in order to take coffee did the conversation become slowly more serious, and Sarid found that in the same light and polite manner he was being subjected to a searching interrogation. He repeated much of what he had told Zeyer about Tanagar, but found these people rather less interested in background information and rather more interested in his personal history.

"You were brought to Earth largely because you proved something of an embarrassment to the people of your own world," observed Spiridion, at one point.

Sarid confirmed that this was so.

"You've given quite an elaborate account of the reasons for your being shipped here, but as I understand it, most of that is conjecture. Is it possible that you might have been brought here just to get you out of the way? Might we expect a whole fleet of exiles?"

"I don't think so," answered Sarid. "It's possible, I suppose, that the population of the vaults has become a political embarrassment to the Intellectuals. Perhaps the morality of the sentence of eternal life has been called in question. But I don't think there's much chance of the Intels building a ship big enough to carry the whole lot of us back to Earth. They wouldn't be interested in mounting an invasion, and it's not their way of doing things to cause disruption."

"In that case," said Spiridion. "You may be the last of your kind we will see here on Earth."

"Salvador did imply that the Intels from the satellite sometimes send one or two of their number down to the surface. They have a base here, I think, but I doubt that it's permanently staffed."

"You don't know where this base is?"

"No, I don't. Salvador said that it exists, but he would hardly want me to know where."

"How do you like your allotted role—as a catalyst?" This question came from Vianna Cascorial.

"It's life," said Sarid. "That's infinitely preferable to spending eternity in suspended animation. If I'd been given the choice of all the lives I might like to lead, it wouldn't have been high on the list—but it's as good as anything else Earth has to offer."

"Suppose that you had an opportunity to go . . . elsewhere?"

Sarid smiled. "I wouldn't want to go elsewhere on Earth," he assured them. "Not even to Khepra. To Tanagar? . . . If it were possible, that might be a different matter. I don't think it will ever be possible, though."

"How long do you expect to be around, here on Earth?" asked Macabel, with the air of one who is asking a loaded question.

Sarid met his gaze, and said, "No one can predict how long he will live. If nothing goes wrong, I might have two hundred years in me, or perhaps three."

"You're older by far than any of us?"

"Not counting years spent in cold storage—yes."

"How, exactly, is that accomplished?"

"Mostly by self-control," Sarid told him. "But we do have help—treatment in early infancy, some prenatal adjustment. Preventive care is important too. If there is any cellular malfunction of the kind that would cause cancerous growth or trigger lysosome breakdown, it can be treated. It happens sometimes, even to Intels. If it were to happen to me here, it might kill me, though I'd be able to slow it down. I can't tell you how to extend your own life-spans, though I might do something for your unborn grandchildren. There's no elixir of life, and my knowledge of the drug treatments is very sketchy."

"How do you manage the prenatal adjustment?" asked the woman curiously.

"It's not difficult," said Sarid. "I was born ectogenetically, of course. We all are. The . . . natural process is considered unsafe and unhealthy."

Vianna Cascorial was not the only one staring at him. It seemed that for the first time they had begun to measure the extent of his alienness.

"You developed—as an embryo—in some kind of machine?" said la Cabral.

"An artificial placenta and amniotic sac," confirmed Sarid. "Intel design is a good deal more efficient than the work of natural selection—and it does permit prenatal treatment of any threatened malformation. There's some manipulation of the induction process to prepare for the development of efficient self-control, but it's nothing so very complicated."

"In spite of the fact that we lack such sophistications," said Spiridion slowly, "you could teach us to live a little longer— our grandchildren, at any rate. And there might be hope for potential further improvement?"

"I think so," answered Sarid. "But you have to understand that it's partly a matter of life-style. It's commonly said that in order to live forever you have to live in such a way that it's not worth it. An Intel has to maintain a moderately rigorous asceticism. You might have to ask your grandchildren to give up some of the things that you enjoy. It won't be as easy for them as it was for the children of the *Marco Polo*."

"The building of a true élite," said Spiridion, "was never likely to be easy. I think you will find that we are capable of doing what is necessary. You know, of course, what our intentions are? We have no intention of using anything which you can tell us for anyone's benefit but our own—by which I mean the members of the College and our protectors."

"I realize that," said Sarid dryly.

"And you have no objection?"

"Objections would be rather impractical. I have to work within the situation as I find it. I have no fanatical commitment to egalitarianism, if that's what you mean."

"But you are not the only one who needs to be considered, are you?" said Macabel.

For a second or two, Sarid thought that the Macarian was referring to Cheron Felix and Vito Talvar, both of whom were presumed dead. Then he remembered that the experiment was still in progress, despite what had happened to the *Sabreur*. The device planted in his skull was relaying all these questions and answers to the Tanagarian satellite. He had not told Zeyer about the implant, and had no intention of doing so. Zeyer might want it removed, and he was not about to submit himself to the risk of that kind of surgery in this kind of society.

"The Intels won't interfere," he said. "They want to see what will happen. If they thought they were under any moral compulsion to take action with respect to anything happening here, they'd have done it a thousand years ago, when Macaria hardly existed as a nation. They could have had total control of the whole planet before your antiquaries first started digging in the ruins of the lost cities. They won't stop you—you fascinate them far too much."

"Is there any way that we could dispose of the observers?" asked Macabel.

"No way at all," replied Sarid. "You might eliminate the ground base, if you could find it, but not the satellite. Even if we could build a ground-to-orbit missile, they'd have the means to take care of it. You'll just have to get used to the idea of being watched."

"Even the presence of watchers implies that we are not quite in control of our own destiny," said Macabel quietly. "You say that they will not interfere, but they have already done so. You claim that you are simply a catalyst, in their way of thinking. If we believe you—and if your conclusion is to be trusted—that still leaves the possibility that there might be other catalytic exercises. *You* have come to Macaria, but suppose others of your kind were in Khepra—or in the world beyond the western ocean—or in the lands to the south of the great equatorial forest? You do see my meaning?"

"I can't make any guarantees," said Sarid, after a pause. "The inferences I've drawn might be mistaken. Salvador may have lied to me about the *Sabreur,* and it's certain that he didn't tell me the *whole* truth. All of your plans might, at some future time, be frustrated if the whim takes Salvador's successor. Like me, though, you have to live with the situation as it is. There's nothing you can do about the satellite. It won't go away, and you can't pretend that it doesn't exist. It may not make you any happier to know that it's there, but you're still better off than you were when you didn't know. Ignorance may be blissful, but it doesn't help you to make decisions."

"It might conceivably help us if we had Tanagarian hostages," said Spiridion. "We *must* find the surface base, and when observers next come down to the surface they must be detected. If there are any on surface now, *they* must be detected."

Sarid permitted himself a wry smile.

Is all this coming in loud and clear? he thought, almost wishing that the mocking comment might be overheard by those high above. Even the voices, though, would simply be recording into a machine. It might be hours or days before any human ear heard them.

To Spiridion he said, "It won't be easy. Physically, we're distinctive, but men of our stature aren't really all *that* rare. I presume that the men of the northern forests really *do* have skins as fair as mine?"

No one answered the question. Instead, Macabel said, in a speculative tone, "The surface base could hardly be on the far side of the world. It would be useless there. On the other hand, it would have to be in a region so remote that transportation of personnel could be achieved without arousing undue comment. If we could follow up all reports of strange things seen in the sky. . . ."

"We'd be occupied full time on fool's errands," said Spiridion. "People always see strange things in the sky. If we were to take an interest in such reports they'd triple in number overnight."

"That's how I found Sarid," interposed Zeyer quietly. "I agree with Gedeon—the base must be somewhere in this hemisphere. It might be found, if there ever has been any extensive traffic between surface and satellite."

"*If* you found it," said Sarid, "there'd be very little chance of your finding it occupied. I wouldn't think there would be any chance at all of seizing an Intel hostage. The contents of the base, however, would be *very* interesting."

There followed a brief lull in the conversation. The pause was broken by Raban la Cabral, who leaned forward and said, "I'm curious about the extent of this bodily control that you have. It seems to me that something very like it is occasionally practiced here on Earth, by ascetics and petty miracle workers. Much of what they're reputed to do is undoubtedly cheap prestidigitation, but there are some stories which make more extravagant claims. I've recently come from Naryn, where they hanged the bandit Machado, and there were stories flying around the city about some holy man who'd been associated with him. Tell me, could your system of self-control allow a man to push a dagger right through the flesh of his forearm, and make cuts in his flesh that healed instantly?"

Sarid frowned. "I can make cuts heal, though not quite instantly. An Intel could do it. Parting the flesh to put a dagger through the arm is something I'd never try. Only an Intel could possibly bring off a trick like that."

He caught la Cabral's eye, and the locked gaze led their thoughts in the same direction.

"The holy man was said to be extremely tall," said the Macarian. "He came out of the Kezula and disappeared into the wilderness between Naryn and the Bitter Sea."

Sarid resisted an impulse to jump to his feet. Instead, he simply lifted his arm so that it stood up vertically from the elbow, and clenched his fist.

"It's Salvador!" he said. "He got out before the crash, and he's alive!"

18

Teresa looked up at the vertiginous heights of the mountains that lay before her. From where she stood, above the tree line, she could see a dozen snow-capped peaks whose glittering slopes seemed to jostle one another in the sunlight. Their shoulders were cloaked with dark coniferous forests, whose dull color and thick texture seemed to signal warmth, though the woods through which she had fled had been as cold as death itself. The icy wind that whistled through the pines bit deep into her flesh.

She seemed to hear Salvador's voice: a dry, cool voice dredged up from her memory, delivering one of his little lectures while they were safe and secure aboard the *Sabreur*.

"The soil of the region was redistributed after the Upheaval. The area wasn't bombed, but it suffered heavy fallout which killed ninety percent of the existing biomass. The rootless soil was blown and washed from the higher slopes, accumulating in the valleys. That the valleys became fertile again is no wonder, but the recovery of the mountain ecology is little short of miraculous."

Miracle or not, she thought, *it's dead, dead, dead. The trees are ghosts and so am I.*

She stepped back into the shade of a tree, leaning her back

against its ridged trunk, breathing deeply. The pain in her leg was far worse. If the break had ever healed, it was now undone. Every step that she took threatened to part the two sections and tear the flesh apart. Her body was on fire, and control was impossible.

The pursuers were not far behind. There were no more than a dozen, but she knew now that she could not escape them. Here in the forest the trail she left was all too clear. Out on the bare rock, climbing the ice slopes, she would be clearly visible for miles. If she could keep going until nightfall, she would surely lose her pursuers, but the night would kill her. She could not survive in conditions like these.

She no longer knew which way she was pointed. She had begun to run west, but which way her flight had turned her she could not guess. It did not matter in the least. The direction of the base was an irrelevance now. If it were less than a thousand meters away it would still be unreachable. It might as well be on the moon.

She lifted her arm, and stared at the gun in her hand. It was useless now, of course. She had fired all three shots. It was possible that she had killed one man, but she did not know for sure. It hardly seemed to matter.

Salvador, you bastard, where are you?

The silent words seemed to echo in her head. Anger, a crime of passion. A thought-crime, if not a deed . . . and if they were to pass judgment on her deeds, would they find them free of the signs of temptation?

I hate you!

She almost said it out loud. It might have echoed from some distant slope, and ricocheted around the crowding peaks: a cannonade of gossip. Malice, like anger, was listed in the table of temptations. It mattered little now. She had collected a full set long ago, as everyone did. She had tried to bury them all, as everyone did. She had never succeeded.

Perhaps no one ever did.

If anger and malice had been her only recurrent sins, it would not have been too bad, but she knew there was a third which she was guilty of—one far worse, as things had turned out.

Recklessness.

The table of temptations, she reminded herself, in a mock authoritarian tone, *is not a list of sins. Temptation will leave no stain on your soul. Nothing needs to be forgiven in the experience of temptation. It is necessary that we be tempted, in order that we should recognize temptation for the snare it is. Let us feel temptation, and learn to master it. Let us learn control.*

To recklessness, that most irresistible of temptations, she had yielded once too often.

It is not a sin to experience temptation.

It is only a sin to yield.

And yet, she thought, *it was recklessness that saved our lives. It was haste and panic that brought us from the Sabreur, instead of smashing us into bloody pulp. Salvador, with his table of virtues so neatly composed—his reason, his authority, his optimism, and his calm of mind—would surely have died. Sometimes, we need to act before we have paused for thought. Sometimes, to pause is to die.*

At other times, of course, to act is also fatal.

Put like that, it seemed so unfair. No strategy was good enough, it seemed.

And yet, she was dying alone.

Now she could hear the sound of her pursuers. They were close, but still hurrying. They could not see her—nor would they, until they had actually run past her, to the point where her snow tracks ended and looped around, signaling the last few desperate steps.

She knew that it was time to surrender.

She stepped away from the bole of the tree, holding her arms out. She was still holding the gun, but carried it in such a way as to make it obvious that she had no intention of firing. All they had to do was stop. It was all over.

It was all so obvious to her that she was quite astonished when she faced them, to see them raising their guns. She opened her mouth to cry out, but the breath was torn from her lungs. She did not hear the crack of the rifle until after the impact. As she was thrown backwards, her body burning now with a new fervor, she had time for one last thought.

You stupid, reckless bastards, she screamed inside her head. *If only you knew. . . .*

19

M'lise led Cheron and Vito Talvar across a narrow rope bridge that extended from the lip of the cliff toward the burgeoning foliage of the nearest of the forest giants. The cliff was not quite sheer, and eventually it was blotted out by the branches of smaller trees that somehow managed to make a living out of the single hour each day that sunlight poured down into the crevice. As far as they could see, the chasm was eight hundred meters deep. Cheron did not ask how much deeper it *really* was.

He felt safer once the causeway had run into the canopy and they were making their way through a world of leaves and branches. When he looked up, he could see patches of blue sky, and the leaves seemed to be translucent. It was easy enough to see the way they had to go. They passed the point where the far end of the bridge was anchored, and went on; the bridge had now become a road of rope. From time to time he would see Lu'el in the branches, going unconcernedly about their business. He was surprised to observe that they, too, made use of ropes, though not quite so carefully organized as the structure that he was following. The ropes were green, plaited from thin creepers. Some were toughened by secondary thickening, but none seemed to be dead. Apparently, the creepers could be induced to grow infinitely, and had no objection to structural reorganization. The sunlight still reached their curved leaves, and where their stems looped around branches they sent adventitious tendrils deep into the wood of the tree, holding as tightly of their own accord as they were made to do by the knots which secured them by design.

His first sight of the "village" where the forest men lived nearly took his breath away with astonishment. He had expected to find something like oversized birds' nests, or perhaps hollows cut into the junctions between the larger boughs and the trunk. What he actually saw was a vast three-dimensional web of creepers, arranged in semi-transparent nets and tunnels and curtains, in catenoidal and parabolic curves, and sometimes even hemispheres. The houses of the Lu'el *were* "nests" of a sort, but they hung pendulously from the boughs, or were knitted into the junctions of the web, like great wicker baskets twelve meters deep and five or six in diameter at the waist. The entrance holes were near the top, but always set slightly to one side, so that they could be covered by big broad leaves in the event of rain.

The most remarkable thing about these nests was their state of decoration, for every one was colored outside, with patterns in four or five different pigments. The woven strands were plastered with some kind of clay, and the colors were laid onto it with minute care. There was, so far as Cheron could tell, no representative art of any kind, but the abstract patterns were by no means careless in their design. Often, they had been planned with considerable subtlety. In the blue-green light of the dappled sky they looked magnificent. No two were identical, though a certain conformity was apparent in the color preferences (much use was made of red and orange) and in the predominance of stripes over spots.

As they began to move through the web—which was not an easy task, for it had not been engineered for the convenience of upright-walking men—Cheron began to appreciate the amount of time and effort that had gone into the construction of this place. The blend of natural substance and human ingenuity was marvelous in its subtlety, and he could not doubt that the intelligence behind it had been considerable. He had fallen into the habit of describing the Lu'el as *forest savages*, and thinking of them not merely as primitives but as subhumans, but the sight of the village shook this judgment considerably.

The Lu'el were plainly interested in the fact that they had visitors. There seemed to be a good many of them about—many of them young ones. They did not, however, gather in a crowd to stare and point, but simply took care that whatever path they chose took them closer to the strangers than convenience really warranted. They had seemed like spiders on the ground, but up here in their own element, they no longer gave that appearance despite the web that formed their streets and highways.

It was easy, as they passed among them, to imagine the nests as the bizarre fruits of the gargantuan tree—hundreds upon hundreds of them, and every one permanently ripe.

Cheron observed that M'lise was surefooted in negotiating the folds and curves of the web, and complimented him on the fact.

"I have spent a good deal of time here," answered the black man. "It is you who should be complimented on your sense of balance and your lack of fear. In fact, you cannot fall, but I think many men might be paralyzed with panic by the knowledge of where they were."

"Are we heading for some kind of meeting place?" asked Vito Talvar.

"The web has no real center," M'lise told him. "There is no vast arena—vertical or horizontal—where the whole village might gather together and form a crowd. The opportunities for collaborative democracy are not great, and a strict order of precedence exists to determine who will give way when two individuals meet in a narrow causeway. Despite their gregariousness the Lu'el have no egalitarian spirit. Hence, there are no meeting places, merely chains of instruction and invitation."

M'lise led them, eventually, to one of the nests placed higher than the rest. It was no larger, nor was there anything special—at least to Cheron's untutored eyes—about its decoration, but of all the houses of the village it stood closest to the sun. Cheron guessed that they were close to the main trunk of one of the trees, but there was no way he could be certain.

Obtaining access to the nest was the most difficult thing they had had to do in crossing the web, but they managed the maneuver successfully, albeit uncomfortably. The entrance hole let them down into a chamber some four meters deep. The woven floor was slightly elastic and gave way a little beneath Cheron's weight, which must have been three times that of one of the forest men. There was a hole in the floor which allowed access to the next chamber below, but this was displaced to one side. Waiting for them in the chamber were two of the Lu'el, each considerably older than those they had previously seen. They were squatting to one side, backs against the wall, and M'lise indicated that Cheron, Talvar, and himself should adopt a similar posture facing them. Cheron found it far from comfortable.

One of the Lu'el was crowned with black and red, the other with black and yellow. The former seemed to be the older; his frame was cadaverously thin and his hair was growing thin.

"The One Man," said M'lise, "is Gy'liu. The other is Or'u'um. Gy'liu will die within the next few days, and Or'u'um will take his place." Without pausing to permit a reply, M'lise began addressing the forest men in their own language, pointing first at Cheron, then at Talvar. The two Tanagarians looked at one another uneasily.

Gy'liu answered the stream of chatter with a long speech of his own, and then M'lise took up the thread again. Both of the Lu'el glanced occasionally at their white guests, but for the most part their attention was firmly fixed on M'lise.

Cheron was surprised when both of the forest men, suddenly heaved themselves up onto their toes, reaching for handholds in the wall of the nest, and swarmed up the wall to disappear through the entrance port into the forest.

M'lise turned back to Cheron and said, "He has granted permission for you to see what it is needful that you should see. It is a privilege, in their view. It represents a considerable . . . how shall I put it? . . . invasion of privacy. You will be allowed to look into a facet of their lives which is really theirs alone, to which no other race of man here on Earth can be admitted. You will catch no more than a glimpse, but they will be a great deal more conscious of your presence than you of theirs. Do not underestimate the value of this gift. I have explained to them why it is necessary for you to know. They know nothing of other planets circling other suns, but they understand the notion of other worlds."

Cheron made as if to rise, and said, "Where now, then?" The last syllable died on his lips when he realized that M'lise was not moving.

"Here," said M'lise. "They will return. Or'u'um will bring that which is necessary. Gy'liu will share with one of you— the other will watch. You should choose now which of you is to undertake the journey. No harm will come to you—that I can promise. You will travel in your dreams, and you will wake up in due course, wiser but unchanged."

"Wait a minute," said Talvar. "That isn't enough. I want to

know what's going on. I want to know who *you* are, and how it is that you know who *we* are, and I want to know a lot more about whatever kind of game you're playing. I've had my fill of dreaming, and if your friends are bringing back some other drug to take me out of my head they can keep it to themselves. I've had *enough*."

M'lise looked at Cheron. "It is necessary," he said. "In time, I will tell you everything. But if it is to make sense, you must catch a glimpse of possibilities that you know nothing of as yet. No harm can come to you."

Cheron turned many questions over in his mind. There were far too many for him to be comfortable. It was difficult for him to select just one. In the end, he said, "How do you know who we are?"

"We know," replied the black man, infuriatingly uncommunicative.

"I suppose you also know that everything that happens here will be known to the men who had us brought here? You know that the satellite is picking up transmissions from devices hidden somewhere in our bodies?"

"The transmitters were embedded in your skulls," said M'lise, with equanimity. "We put them out of action. That's why you had to be put to sleep before being brought up the mountain."

Cheron remembered the pain in the back of his head which he had felt on awakening, and which he still felt if he turned his head suddenly.

"Suppose we both refuse to participate in this educative experience?" he asked.

"Why should you?" asked M'lise. "I have assured you that it is the only way to reach the understanding which you desire so devoutly."

Talvar shook his head and said, "Not me."

A typical Hedonist's response, thought Cheron. *He's prepared to ask the questions, but in the end he wants the answers only to protect himself. Who can blame him?*

M'lise had not looked at Talvar to acknowledge the denial. His dark eyes were still fixed on Cheron. Cheron nodded, almost imperceptibly.

They all looked up at the sound of the forest men returning. The older one came first, then the black-and-yellow, carrying a bowl in which there was a viscous liquid.

"The One Man and you will drink from the same bowl," said M'lise in a low voice. "Then you will descend into the sleeping quarters. There is nothing to fear. What you see may be disturbing, but nothing can hurt you."

No, indeed, thought Cheron. *There is nothing to fear in drugs or dreams. Nothing at all. How can dreams be poisoned? And what can they really do to a man's inner self?*

20

Sarid sat down on his bed and began to take off his boots. A slight sound made him pause and look up, and he saw Baya-undi emerge from the bathroom.

"I thought you'd gone to bed," he said.

"*I* thought you might need me," said Baya-undi. He made no move to help Sarid with his boots, but added, "After all, I am your valet."

Sarid frowned slightly, but his voice was quite even when he said, "I don't need you. You'd better get some sleep while we have the opportunity of using such beautiful beds."

"I'm sure that your accommodation in Solis will be just as comfortable," replied the black man. He paused for a moment, and then said, "When I saw you first—before you saw me—you seemed troubled. It's the first time I've ever seen you wear your feelings in your face."

Sarid stared at his companion, wondering what had changed. It was not the kind of statement that he associated with Baya-undi.

"I discovered something that surprised me," he said. "I don't know whether I like it or not."

Baya-undi refrained from asking the obvious supplementary question, which Sarid would not have answered. Instead, the black man crossed the room and drew the curtains over the window, pausing only for a moment to look down into the street far below. He turned back to Sarid, but the Tanagarian had turned his attention once more to his boots, which he now managed to remove.

"I came to say good-bye," said Baya-undi calmly.

Sarid turned then, to look his companion in the face. After a few moments he said, "They won't let you go. Not now."

"They won't catch me," the black man assured him.

"I trust that you're not going to insult me with yet another invitation to accompany you?" asked Sarid.

"Of course not."

"Then why tell me? Suppose I were to warn Zeyer?"

"Is that what you intend to do?"

"No," answered Sarid.

"I once told you that I think of you as a friend," said Baya-undi. "I do not think that you believed me. It *is* true. I am not deserting you. It is simply that the time has come for me to go. Do you think that you will be happy in Macaria?"

Sarid shrugged. "Why not?" he countered. "It is the one place on Earth where a man can get things done."

"You cannot be sure of that."

Sarid permitted himself a small laugh. "You are a spy, aren't you?" he said.

"Yes," answered the black man. "I think that in your terms I am most certainly a spy."

"And what will your masters think when you tell them about me? Will they believe you? Will they care?"

"I have already communicated with my . . . masters. They know all about you, and they believe everything that I have told them. Your presence in Macaria might make a considerable difference to the fortunes of the nation. Their slow and unsteady progress in recovering the knowledge of the ancient world is certain to be accelerated. Their conquests will be accelerated also."

"Do you fear for the security of Khepra?"

Baya-undi smiled broadly, and said, "No."

"I thought you didn't believe in the knowledge of the ancient world. Not in its utility, at any rate. Or was that just for show?"

"Just for show," confirmed the black man.

Sarid studied his manservant carefully, Baya-undi moved aside from the curtains and leaned on the door frame, pausing before going into the sitting room—and then, presumably, out of the suite, out of the hotel, and out of Sarid's life.

"You've been acting the part of a fool," said Sarid. "But you're not a fool, are you?"

"There's a little of the fool in all of us," replied the black man. "The man who cannot play the fool is not a man but a carrot. So they say in Khepra, the one civilized nation on Earth, where they know how to value fools properly. Barbarians—especially Macarians—have lost the art through their relentless pursuit of knowledge and power. The same may happen to you, I fear, though not to your companions. Vito Talvar had a rare gift for foolishness, and I liked him for it. Cheron Felix was perhaps a little earnest, but there was something he saw in much of what went on around him which allowed him to retain that sense of wonder that is so essential in the man who is—occasionally, of course—disposed to be a fool."

"You sound like Midas," said Sarid, a little too tired to be wholeheartedly amused.

"A *real* barbarian," said Baya-undi. "But likeable, in his way. Perhaps we will meet again some day. Perhaps we will *all* meet again."

"I think the likelihood is small," answered Sarid dryly. "I cannot really believe that there is a life beyond the grave—and if there is, it must be far more populous than this tiny world where men live now. I doubt if we shall ever see Midas or Cheron Felix, even if we have eternity in which to search for them. For that matter, I doubt if we shall see one another, if you really do intend to desert. Wouldn't it have been easier in Asdar? Or even in Sau?"

"It might have been easier," said Baya-undi. "But it would have been less interesting." He made a small bow, and turned to go through the open door.

"Baya-undi!" called Sarid softly.

The black man turned, still smiling.

"Good luck," said Sarid.

Baya-undi bowed again, and then was gone, without returning the compliment.

Sarid began unbuttoning his shirt.

21

––––––

Salvador stood on the ridge far above the railway line and watched the train disgorge its human cargo: three hundred men in the uniform of Macaria's army. He watched them gather and parade, saw them split up into platoons, and watched them disperse again as a dozen search parties.

He frowned, more thoughtfully than angrily. He had seen army vehicles moving along the road earlier in the day. He had seen three small monoplanes moving between the mountain peaks. There had even been a dirigible balloon. He knew very little about the present strength of Macaria's air power—the last information transmitted by the satellite had not afforded such intelligence a high priority—but it seemed unlikely that a search by air could be mounted unless the situation was very special indeed.

It was possible, he knew, that Teresa had killed one or two of the policemen who had tried to arrest them. Even adding two policemen to a handful of Merkadian petty criminals, however, did not add up to a justification for this kind of operation. There seemed to be two probable conclusions. Either the search was for someone else and not for him or they had somehow discovered who and what he was. If the latter was the case, then they must have discovered it *after* the police had stopped the train, otherwise the opportunity would not have been left for him to get away.

If they had apprehended Teresa, and she had told them everything. . . .

Would they have taken her story as seriously as *this?*

Salvador had traveled far enough by now to know how difficult was the task facing the soldiers who had just left the train. Whether there were three hundred or three thousand, the odds were against them. There was plenty of forest to give him all the cover he needed, and the region was vast.

The weather was poor, and the Macarians, for all that this was their country, were less adaptable to these conditions than he. Neither cold nor hunger could threaten him in the short term. He could travel farther and faster than they, and if necessary could live on snow for twenty days. The worse conditions became, the greater would be his advantage. No longer encumbered by Teresa, he would be a difficult man to catch.

He was quite unafraid, but he was a little worried, because he could not be entirely sure what was going on. If they knew about *him*, they might know about the base. They could not know its position—but even he knew it only in terms of its positional coordinates. The degree of accuracy with which he could deliver himself to it would leave him a good deal of searching to do. It was bound to be well camouflaged, and would not be easy to locate. Once there, it was not certain that he would be able to walk in. Entering the base might still prove to be a problem, especially if there was no one actually inside it. It was quite likely that all personnel would be on the satellite.

Given these difficulties, his situation was not good. The Macarians could not catch him, but they might find the base before he did, if they knew what they were looking for. If it so transpired, then his ability to evade capture would become far less significant.

If only there were some way to tell the satellite personnel that he was still alive. . . .

He stood quite still for a few moments more, breathing deeply of the thin mountain air. He felt the pressure of the gun tucked into his belt against his abdominal muscles, and the momentary irritation caused him to snatch it out. It was, of course, the weapon that he had used to threaten the driver of the police car. He had retained it when abandoning the car, almost unthinkingly. Now he stared at it, and after a moment's contemplation, threw it away. It had served its purpose. He did not intend to go hunting, and if by some improbable mischance the searchers did catch up with him he certainly did not intend to start a battle.

He wiped the palm of his hand on the cloth covering his thigh, and then he set off along the ridge, still heading north.

22

Gy'liu drank first from the wooden bowl and then handed it to Cheron. He had taken only a few sips. Cheron tipped the bowl and watched the slow flow of the dark liquid with some apprehension. Then he put his lips to the rim and took some of the liquid onto his tongue. It was very sweet. It stuck to his tongue and teeth and he had difficulty swallowing it.

He handed the bowl back to the second forest man and looked at Gy'liu, trying to read some sign of approval in the inscrutable face. The ancient swung himself gracefully into the hole that gave access to the lower room, and M'lise signaled to Cheron that he should follow.

There was no light down below. The walls were woven more tightly here and there was no "skylight." Instead of a "floor" there was a cushion of soft, downy material.

"Lie down," said M'lise. "Allow Gy'liu to take your hands in his. In a few moments, you will find that you are unable to move your limbs. Do not worry. Try not to flinch from Gy'liu's touch. For the Lu'el, the experience which you are about to undergo is a kind of sacrament. It is an essential aspect of their being-in-the-world. You must respect that."

Cheron felt the thin fingers of the apeman groping for his wrists, and he accepted the double handclasp. Gy'liu said something in his own language, in a low voice. Cheron could not tell whether it was reassurance or some private ritual.

He felt a prickling sensation in his legs, followed by a sensation of heaviness. He tried to move his foot, and found that he could not. It was as though he had "lost" his limbs altogether. His brain felt light, as though it floated free within his skull. He seemed to be aware, in some special sense, of its convolutions and of the extending rod of his spinal cord.

He tried to blink, but found the greatest difficulty in opening his eyes once they had closed. In the end, he relaxed and let them close. He "saw" the random flashes of light which usually attend the closing of the eyes, but these faded. Then there grew what seemed to be a different kind of visual sensation: an even field of "light," colored blue. It was as though he were awake and alert, looking up into a cloudless evening sky, with nothing visible except the even, limitless blueness. He was not losing consciousness, and the continuity of his thoughts was uninterrupted.

There was something strange in this vision of blue, but it took him a little time to determine what it was. His vision did not seem to be unidirectional any longer—it was as though he had equal awareness of a whole three-dimensional manifold. He was enclosed by the blueness. He tried to imagine himself for a moment as a sphere completely covered by a retinal surface, but the image would not hold. He was not, in fact, aware of having any solid presence at all, nor any shape. His consciousness did not seem confined by the enclosing color, like a bubble in a blue ocean, but rather distributed *through* it, as one gas might be diffused in another.

He felt himself relaxing—psychologically, not physically— and slowly became aware of different kinds of sensation, which his mind construed as auditory and tactile stimuli.

It was as though there were a rustling sound, something like the sound of wind in dry grass, except that it ebbed and flowed with a steady pulse. It was similar to the occasional experience of "hearing" the flow of blood in his veins that happened when his idle mind reconstructed the feel of the pulsebeat in his temple as if it were a noise. What he *felt*, though, was a sensation which he could not liken to anything familiar. It was a feeling of *presence*, but it was not the feel of his own body, which he was used to—or, indeed, the feel of any body at all, human or otherwise. He was aware of *himself*, of *being*, but his imagination could produce no model to tell him what mode of being he had. He was real, but not solid. What kind of order and organization there might have been in him—what kind of structure and connection—he could not tell.

Is this the substance of mind, he thought, *detached from the mechanism of body?*

He rejected the Cartesian illusion, knowing that it was not the truth, except in some crude analogical way. He groped for an idea to express this uneasy sense of self.

I am not material, he thought, *but rather of the stuff of which matter is made—not substance itself, but the substance of substance. I belong to the world of the subatomic particles, which are the constituents of matter and hence cannot themselves be material.*

Whether it was true or not, he could not tell, but it satisfied him for the moment. He was no shape at all, but it was difficult to cope with his seeing all ways except with the aid of some fiction of shape. He imagined starfish, spider webs, wheels of fire, but none of it made sense. He thought of *Volvox*, of windblown clusters of fluffy plant seeds, but they did not help. He knew that his mind was throwing up hopeless barriers to understanding, trying desperately to locate him back in a matrix of being which could contain him, but he could not halt the imagistic experimentation until it had run its course.

The uneasiness and the consequent anguished writhing of his thoughts could not be healed, but changes in his new "environment" began to distract him. The blueness faded into twilight purple, and he was aware of an emergent mist of "stars." They never formed as distinct points of light against an empty background, but imparted to the "sky" a kind of granular brightness. It was as if there were stars and more distant stars, filling the sky and unobscured by clouds of dust, so that all this firmament, everywhere, was filled with light.

There were other kinds of awareness, which his imagination could not translate into the familiarity of his ordinary sensory apparatus. He could not say what he was aware of, or what he felt, but the immanence of *something* was indubitable. He found within himself a kind of resonance—a response to something not merely near but coexistent (as, indeed, all of this space seemed to be coexistent).

I am not within an atom, he thought, *but within a geometrical point. I am infinitesimal, and yet within myself infinite. This is the point within which all other points in the framework of space are included: this is the single moment in which everything happens. All of spacetime is no more than the unfolding of this single infinitesimal point in time and space, which in its unfolding may extend forever and forever. I am here, as is everything else, but I am aware of being here.*

As the thoughts ran through his mind, flowing like quicksilver, he considered himself intoxicated. There was a moment of great loneliness, sweeping in its wake a mixture of sadness and terror, but it was instantaneously overwhelmed by the impression of unloneliness, of response and reconciliation. There was a flux and reflux of identity, in which he was both self and other, interior and exterior, here and there, as if the surface of his soul had been contorted into a topological eccentricity such as a Möbius strip or a Klein bottle.

He was reassured.

He was content.

He was joyous.

He was also confused, afraid, uncertain . . . but all that seemed to be under control.

Somewhere within him grew the knowledge that the interchange might extend, that he was merely peeping through a pinhole in an iron womb, out into the world of daylight, and that he had not yet learned to see or speak in the terms that this new universe permitted. At present, he was aware of *it*, and of his presence *in* it, and of the presence of everything else in it, and of the fact that presence in it could be rendered meaningful, but there was no further step he could take, for the moment.

Once more he tried to get the thoughts straight, so that he could carry them back to his head in a way that still made a kind of sense. Only a *kind* of sense, for his head belonged to an order of things very different from this one. It was important that he see *some* kind of sense in it all, and desperately important, though he was not sure why.

There is, he told himself (trying to distort the truth as little as the ill-shaped words would permit), *a kind of touching point which unites all places and times in the universe. It is where everything that is begins and ends. It is the beginning and the end, the synthesis of Alpha and Omega. It is accessible to consciousness, though not through the sensory apparatus. It is real, and it can, in some strange way, be* used.

The words made it sound hollow. Not trivial, perhaps, but somehow minimized by its translocation into a vocabulary of concepts which could not meaningfully contain it.

I have seen! he cried in anguish. *But how can I know?*

There seemed to be shadows among the filmy stars; the echo of faint voices in the ebb and flow of the subliminal cascade of sound.

He tried to interfere with this reality which contained him, to cause change in order to be secure in his knowledge of being. He felt that movement of some kind must be possible, even though there was nowhere to move *to*. He felt that he could be a protagonist in this experience rather than an inert point of observation, if only he knew how.

He did *not* know how.

He was impotent, though he was sure he need not be.

I am dreaming, he thought. *It is only a drug-induced dream, chemical hypnopaedia. It is not real. It counts for nothing.*

He could not put his faith in that rejection. He knew too well that however unreal a dream might be it can change a man as completely as a man can change. Dream experience, he knew, was a genuine constituent of a man's personality, whether the dreams came from a clever machine or sprang spontaneously into being.

The "I" which tries to reassure me that "I" am dreaming, he told himself, *is not different from the "I" who is dreaming. The circle is closed, and I cannot alienate myself from my experience by pretending that there is another it could be happening to. Reality and illusion may differ, but we are the substance of our illusions just as we are the substance of our realities.*

Again, he experienced loneliness, sadness, and fear.

Again, *a response.*

Again, *reassurance.*

I cannot live here yet, he thought, *but I might, in time.*

He felt himself in the midst of change again, and for one dreadful moment he thought that this infinitesimal cosmos was breaking up, and he with it, but it was only a tremor in his sense of self.

Control, he advised himself.

Control.

23

As they got into the car, Zeyer said, "The Khepran seems to have disappeared. I suppose you know nothing about it?"

Sarid settled himself into the corner, and said, "I don't think army life suited him very well. He still felt that his induction was a rank injustice. It doesn't really surprise me that he decided to leave."

Zeyer closed the door behind him, and said, "We can't wait, of course, but I assure you that a thorough search will be made. He can't get out of Merkad. He knows too much to be forgotten. Wherever he finds himself, in the long run, I think he'll wish that he had stayed with you."

The Macarian looked round to check the strength of the escort as the car pulled away from the doorway of the hotel, heading for the high gates. Sarid, Zeyer, and their driver were in an ordinary limousine, but they were headed by an armored car and there was another car behind them, carrying four armed men in plain clothes.

"It's only a short drive to the docks," said Zeyer. "Then we'll be out of this accursed country for good. I'll be glad to get back to Solis."

"What did you do about Salvador?" asked Sarid.

"Sent a radio message to the north, top priority. They'll mobilize every man within a thousand miles of Galehalt. They've connected him with two men who killed a number of Merkadians in one of the Bitter Sea ports. With luck, they'll have been apprehended by the police already, but if not the search will have begun at first light. It's rough country, and one man might evade an army for years if he knew how, but if your Intellectual is trying to reach some kind of base then our men have a fair chance of finding it before he does."

Sarid nodded uneasily. He kept to himself the thought that neither Salvador nor Zeyer could know how the odds *really* stacked up. Since last night—though probably not before—the Intels on the satellite had known that Salvador was alive, courtesy of the transmitter buried in his skull. What they would do about it, he could not guess. Seemingly, they had as good a chance of finding Salvador as the army had, but it was presumably no better. Possibly, their first thought might be to protect the base. They might well figure that they could always pick Salvador up at a later date.

For himself, Sarid was uncertain of which outcome he would prefer. There was no way of knowing how Salvador would react if he became a prisoner of Macaria. He might render Sarid impotent by making him redundant, if he cared to—but he might not care to. Sarid was sure that his next meeting with the Intel would be an interesting one, but he was a little apprehensive about its result.

The armored car came to a halt ahead of them, and someone waved the limousine to a stop. A trooper ran back to inform Zeyer that there was trouble ahead. Some kind of dispute had broken out in the dock area and was building up into a small-scale battle.

"How close to our ship is the trouble?" asked Zeyer.

His informant shrugged and said that it was some way along the shore.

"Keep going," said Zeyer.

The convoy began moving again.

"It's a bad time of year," said Zeyer, half in annoyance and half in apology.

"The burden of empire," replied Sarid dryly.

The armored car turned left, and Zeyer nodded approvingly. "It's a little longer," he said, "but we'll be able to approach the ship from the other direction. It will only take a few minutes to embark. Then *nothing* can stop us."

"Unless we sink," suggested Sarid.

Zeyer was definitely not amused.

They sat in silence until they reached the waterfront, at which point the armored car turned right again to head east toward the quay where their ship awaited them. Sarid tried to see around the armored car for signs of trouble ahead. For a moment or two his view was blocked, and then—as the drivers of all three vehicles began to apply their brakes—he saw a crowd of people swarming along the shore, heading straight for the convoy.

"I think there's trouble," he said. "At a guess, the mob caught sight of the armored car and figured that it was headed for *them*. They don't seem to be disposed to discretion."

Zeyer opened his door and stepped out in order to look past the armored car at the approaching horde. They were still a hundred and fifty meters away, but they were running fast. The Macarian swore and got back into the car quickly, after making signs to the following car instructing its driver to back up. The armored car stayed where it was.

The driver of the limousine began to reverse, checking his distance from the other vehicle. The entry road was still fifty meters away. Sarid continued to watch the armored car, which began to move forward to meet the running Merkadians. He heard a quick burst of machine-gun fire, and hoped that it was directed above the heads of the onrushing crowd.

Just as the armored car met the mob, which divided and surrounded it, the car carrying the armed men reached the entry road. The driver tried to steer around in order to change direction and lead the way off the wharf, but he never got the chance. A large Macarian truck came hurtling out of the road and rammed the car. The impact was explosive, but the truck was not halted by it. It continued on its way, engine roaring as it shoved the smashed car clean over the edge of the quay and into the murky water a dozen meters below.

From the back of the truck a dozen armed men jumped down. They were Merkadians, but they were carrying Macarian army rifles.

Zeyer swore volubly, and howled at the driver, who changed gear and roared forward again. With the crowd ahead and the armed men behind there was only one obvious opening before them—the yawning doors of a large warehouse which sat opposite the only occupied berth between the car and their own ship. There were men at the rail of this vessel, shouting and gesticulating wildly, and others outside the warehouse who would be absorbed into the mob in a matter of seconds.

The limousine's tires squealed as it turned into the warehouse and jetted down the main aisle between the cages where various kinds of produce were piled high. The warehouse did have a rear door, but it was closed, at least to vehicles. There was a smaller portal cut in it that would allow individual people to pass through.

For a few seconds, Sarid thought that the driver was going to take a chance on the flimsiness of the big door, but in fact he thought better of it and put his foot down hard on the brake. The car came to a stop a mere meter and a half from the barrier. Zeyer was already leaping out, calling to Sarid to follow him. He never got to the inviting half-open doorway, because someone stepped out from hiding behind one of the well-stocked cages and felled him with a blow from what looked like a pickaxe handle.

The driver was already out of his seat, and he turned to run the other way, but already there were men waiting for him. He tried to dodge but had no chance. They laid him out within a matter of seconds.

Sarid leaped clear, and slipped immediately into a crouch, ready to grapple with anyone who came to tackle him. No one did. They seemed, in fact, singularly reluctant to approach him, as though aware that he would be a very different proposition from his two companions. They hung back, relaxing as they did so. The relaxation should have warned him, but in fact he was a little slow to judge its meaning. By the time he swung around to look for the gun it was already aimed at his broad chest.

He froze in astonishment. Every man he had so far seen had been a Merkadian, but the man who had stepped through the inviting doorway with a gun in his hand was black.

"You!" he said.

"I've come to invite you to desert again," said Baya-undi. "But this time, I'm afraid that you have no choice."

And so saying, he fired.

Part Four

MANIFOLD HORIZONS

1

Cheron took the cup that M'lise offered, and drank. His hand was shaking slightly. The cup contained cool, pure water. They were in the upper section of the nest, Gy'liu remained below, still sleeping.

"How long?" asked Cheron.

"About three hours," answered Vito Talvar. "Were they wonderful dreams?"

Cheron looked at M'lise warily. "You're going to tell me that it was more than a hallucination," he said.

The black man gestured briefly with his right hand. "A name," he said. "Why worry about what you may call it? Your body was here, and your mind with it. Your soul did not float free into the ghostworld. And yet, in some special sense, you were elsewhere. Perhaps you are always elsewhere as well as here, when you wake and when you dream—except that in wakefulness or dreaming you cannot quite discover the other ways there are to be."

Cheron gave him back the cup. "*Now* do we get an explanation?" he asked.

M'lise bowed his head slightly and then changed his position, so that he was squatting rather than kneeling beside Cheron. Cheron sat up. Talvar was already squatting and did not move.

"Can you walk?" M'lise asked of Cheron.

The Tanagarian nodded in reply.

"I do not think that this is the place for explanations," said the black man. "In a few minutes we will return to the mountain. For now—I do not have to ask you what you experienced. For everyone it is a little different, just as each man's experience of the world that surrounds us now is a little different; but in some essential sense it is the same for everyone, just as *this* world is the same. That is what makes it real. It is *all* that is needed to make it real. Do you understand that? Every man can experience it, and there are features of its innate order that can be perceived by all who can."

Cheron stared at him.

"I could see almost nothing," he said.

"Can you imagine what a newborn child can see when he first opens his eyes?" asked M'lise. "You have to learn to see, though I think you have seen enough to know that what I say is true."

"Perhaps," said Cheron.

"For the Lu'el, the world you have visited is no less important than the one you and I inhabit all the time. They live half their lives there. They believe that in some vital sense they are essential to its being—they did not create it, but they sustain it. Equally, it is essential to *their* being. It is their soul, if a soul can be a place. It is the identity of their race, where they are all *one,* in a literal sense of the word. The drug unites them. At any one time, some of the Lu'el are sleeping that special sleep. The world you have just seen is never empty. It could not *be* empty, though what might happen if all the Lu'el in this world were to be simultaneously awake they cannot say.

"From their point of view, what I am saying would be mistaken. I am speaking as if there were two worlds—ours and the one which you have just glimpsed. That is the way it must seem to us. To them, however, reality is seamless. When they take the drug, they do not go elsewhere. Rather, they regard the drug as a means of access to the true reality of *this* world. All that is happening, in their view, is that certain sensitivities are being replaced by others. Their awareness of matter, space, and time is being replaced by a different mode of awareness. Insofar as the world we live in is made up of the data provided by our senses, what happens is a translocation into a different world; but it is still the same universe— the *objective* reality has not changed. What changes is in the dreamer; in the way he perceives that which is external to his consciousness. Can you follow what I am saying?"

"*I* cannot," said Talvar.

Cheron hesitated before adding his own answer. "What you're saying," he said finally, "is that the drug's effect is physiological rather than psychotropic. Effectively, it blocks the usual channels of sensory experience—it destroys ordinary dreams, which consist of phantom sensory images, just as effectively as it destroys real sensations. It isolates some kind of pure consciousness, and allows perception of the universe through some unsuspected sixth sense—or perhaps not a sense at all, but some kind of fundamental process of intuition."

"That's right," confirmed M'lise.

"It doesn't make sense," advised Vito Talvar. "What's real is real, and what isn't is hallucination. I don't know what you saw, but. . . ."

"No," said Cheron, cutting him off. "You *don't* know." To M'lise, he said, "What you're talking about is something that's possible for us all, save for the fact that it's normally masked by the mind's dependence on the brain's sensory channels?"

M'lise nodded.

"The basis of religious experience," added Cheron. "The basis, in fact, of a good many occasional experiences . . . ones which can only happen when the mind's dependence on the senses is relaxed or distorted. The experiences that engender belief in telepathy and precognition, for instance. There's no actual transfer of sensory information, but there is some kind of empathy which transcends time, space, and identity. The drug won't permit the Lu'el to shoot imaginary thoughts from one head into another, but it will give them the knowledge that after all the evidence of the senses is suspended there's some kind of unity of mind and matter, in which all selves mingle and are part of one another. Is that it?"

"It is enough," confirmed M'lise.

"In that case," said Cheron. "I know what you want me to know. *Why?*"

"Sometimes," said the black man, "it is as well to remind ourselves that we can forget—that the advance of human intelligence is not simply a process of addition but a process of metamorphosis. Intelligence consists of the power to make effective use of the evidence of the senses; to sort out the information of the senses, to categorize and theorize, and hence to build a network of expectations which allows us to make better terms with the world than animals and infants. This can easily lead us into the error of thinking that animals and infants and savages are just like us—except that they have less intelligence. That is not so. They are actually *different*

from us, for our specialization in sensory information has
eclipsed something that they have—a different way of being.
There can be no doubt that *our* way of being works well, and
that it is valuable. I would not want to say that we have de-
prived ourselves in becoming as we are. But what I do want
to say is that it is not the only way to be."

"You don't want us to go back to Macaria to start a revolution in thought? To bring enlightenment to all mankind
through the agency of the Lu'el drug?"

M'lise stood up. "I am not talking to a soldier of Macaria,"
he said. "I am talking to a man of Tanagar."

"Oh yes," said Cheron softly. "For the moment, I had forgotten that you knew. You have not told me yet just *how* you
know."

"I think you can guess," said the black man, as Cheron
and Vito Talvar rose slowly to their feet.

"You're no more native to this planet than I am," said
Cheron. "You're the descendants of ship people, just as we
are. We aren't the only men to have rediscovered the Motherworld—and it seems that we aren't the first."

2

Later, they sat on the verandah of M'lise's bungalow, surrounded by fruit trees, enjoying the heat of the sun and the
slow mountain breeze.

Vito Talvar looked up at the wooden roof of the bungalow, and said, "Surely you could do better than this. You
don't have to live in wooden huts."

"Most of our equipment is inside the caves," said M'lise.
"Our machines, our communication systems, even our means
of transportation. They're out of sight there, and largely out
of mind. Who wants to live in caves, inside machines?
Wooden huts serve our needs very well out here on the
slopes."

"How long have you been here?" asked Cheron.

"Our ship made its landfall a little earlier than yours," said M'lise. "We did not wander quite so far in search of a new home. Once we had found it, we dispatched a small ship back to the Motherworld, to see how things stood. I suppose that our people were here some eight or nine thousand local years before the ship from Tanagar arrived."

"And you never announced your presence," said Cheron. "You lay in wait, and you watched. As long as the Tanagarians did nothing, you did nothing. Until now. You had us taken by your savage friends, eliminated the transmitters that would have told the Intels on the satellite what was happening to us, and now you have us prisoner. Why?"

"Why did we not make contact with the ship from Tanagar when it first came to Earth? Because, like you, we are cautious. We were not sure of our welcome. Our first instinct was to wait and watch. As you know, it is not difficult for a temporary hesitation to become permanent. There seemed no reason to reveal ourselves when we could devise ways of tapping the communications of the Tanagarians without allowing them to suspect that we existed. We needed to learn about the newcomers; at first, as you will appreciate, we did not even know that they were human. Once we were sure that they were men, we had also discovered that they were not as similar to us as we might have wished. There seemed to be a reasonable basis for caution and suspicion. The habit was easily formed, and there was never a need for us to act, until *you* came. Once Tanagar had decided on active intervention, we had to respond. If your people were landed here in any quantity, it would only be a matter of time before you found evidence of our presence—and evidence of *our* interference. Even if we could keep our presence here a secret for another thousand years, in the end it would be discovered. And in the meantime . . . your presence here would mean changes."

"You seem sufficiently similar to an Intel to me," said Talvar. "You talk like one, and you seem to share the same instincts. What's the big difference? Not the color of your skin, I take it."

M'lise shook his head. "The color of my skin is a mere convenience," he said. "As for the way I talk—I suppose that I am not so different from your own people. The dissimilarity is more fundamental. It relates to the experience of the ship that carried my ancestors away from Earth. You are children of the *Marco Polo*, culturally imprisoned by the social structures that grew up while your ancestors were wandering among the stars. *We* are children of the *Svante Arrhenius*, in much the same way. You have been further shaped by the world which you found and made into a new home for man. We have been further shaped by the world *we* found. I am as different from any man of your race as the ways our forefathers found for coping with the interstellar voyage, and as different as the worlds which our forefathers found when their voyages were over.

"The children of the *Svante Arrhenius* were faced with much the same problems as the men of the *Marco Polo*—they were part of an artificial ecology, strictly limited in absolute size. They sought stability, as your ancestors did, in social control and self-control, but they did not produce the same kind of society. They were extremely anxious about the possible effects of continued inbreeding in a limited population—about the loss of genetic variety and the steady depletion of the gene pool, and took steps to preserve the genetic heritage which they had. The children who could not be born were put into a kind of bank; every woman contributed half her ova, every man a sufficiency of sperm. There were many people on the ship who never had actual children, and the actual children who were born nevertheless duplicated only part of their parents' gene complement, but in spite of this fact very few genes were lost. The rest were simply deep-frozen, ready to make their contribution to the development of a new human race on a new world.

"Your own ancestors seem to have paid little attention to this matter, putting their main priority on medicine and education. Your strategy seems to have worked well enough—the loss of genetic variety does not seem to have impaired your efficiency as a race. Perhaps this means that my own ancestors were mistaken in their anxieties, though our experience as a race suggests that they were not. Perhaps your people were unusually fortunate; perhaps mine were unusually unfortunate; perhaps both were fortunate in their different ways. In any case, much of the scientific work that was conducted aboard the *Svante Arrhenius* while it searched for a new world was genetic research into the possibilities of cloning human cells, manipulating human tissue cultures, inducing mutations, and selecting the few useful genes thus created, tectogenesis, induced polyploidy, and so on. By the time we made our landfall, we knew a great deal more about genetic science and genetic technology than the men of the ancient Earth. As things turned out, we needed that knowledge.

"Tanagar, I believe, is not a particularly pleasant world. It is, I think, *physically* hostile. The environments which it provides for life do not permit organisms a great range of variety. Is that correct?"

"Yes," said Cheron.

"*Our* new world—which we named, on the basis of its first appearance, Emerald—was quite different. It was, in fact, a particularly bountiful environment, where living organisms found it easy to survive and thrive. The biomass of the indigenous ecological community was twelve times greater than the biomass of the ancient Earth. There was no intelligent life—it seems that intelligence may be the product of ecological meanness—but there was life in abundance and tremendous variety. There were plants everywhere, of magnificent size and multitudinous in form. The actual surface of the planet was open to the sun only in patches; for the most part the plant life formed its own stratum, limiting animal life over most of the world to an arboreal habitat. For this reason, the largest animals that existed there were about the size of human beings. Except, of course, for those in the sea depths."

"In short," said Cheron, "Emerald is rather like the forest which surrounds us."

M'lise shook his head. "This forest is a pale shadow of the ecosystem of Emerald. It compares to Emerald as the technology of Macaria compares to the technology of Tanagar."

Vito Talvar leaned forward suddenly. "You brought the forest here!" he said. "It didn't evolve after the Upheaval. You seeded the tropics with things you brought from your own world."

"That's true," said M'lise.

"And the Lu'el?" Talvar's voice was suddenly tense.

"We brought the Lu'el, also."

"They're not human!"

"Indeed they are," M'lise contradicted him. "They are the descendants of the children of the *Svante Arrhenius*, as am I. I am closer kin to Gy'liu than I am to you."

"You *created* them?" This time the question came from Cheron.

"They were formed for their world," answered the black man. "Just as the humans who descended to the surface of Emerald had to be formed for *theirs.* They had to be formed in a dozen different ways, and the process of gradual adaptation was a long one. Emerald's ecosystem was not easy to invade, and to every invasion it found a response. We adapted to Emerald, and in the end, Emerald adapted to us. Human life is secure now on Emerald, but you might have difficulty recognizing some of its forms."

"I don't call that human," said Talvar.

M'lise gestured as he had before and said, "A word. Meanings change with circumstance."

"But there are still people like us," said Cheron. "People like *you.*"

M'lise stared at him, his face quite expressionless. "Yes," he said. "I am like you, and my father, and his father too. But there is no way to say that *all* my fathers were as you are, in form or in thought. A creature like me may be created—or recreated, if you will—as easily as a creature like Gy'liu. There have always been men aboard the *Svante Arrhenius* and half a hundred other ships and space habitats, and there has not been the same need for *them* to be adapted in the same way that the colonists had to be. That does not mean, however, that they have held the ancestral image of man sacred. I am like you because I am here on Earth, and because I must sometimes move among men who are not too different in form from you. It is that necessity which dictates my form, and that necessity alone. *Now* do you begin to see why the descendants of the men who left Earth on the *Svante Arrhenius* considered themselves so dissimilar to the men who returned to Earth from Tanagar?"

"Yes," answered Vito Talvar. "I see it very clearly. I also see why you resented the possibility of our interfering with the course of Earthly history. You have your own plans for Earth, it seems. You intend to make it over in the image of your Emerald."

"What was the purpose of *your* coming here?" countered M'lise. "Was it not—however you may try to disguise the ambition—so that in the fulness of time Earth might become

a world made in the image of Tanagar . . . the Tanagar that
might have been had nature been kinder in designing it?"

"Tanagar is a human world," said Talvar. "I do not think
the Lu'el are truly human. If this forest were to grow to
cover the whole surface of the Earth, I think that would be a
kind of destruction. I do not see how we could tolerate that."

M'lise looked at Cheron.

"*Is* that what you intend?" asked Cheron levelly. "Are you
trying to make Earth into a second Emerald?"

The black man shook his head slowly. "What the children
of the *Svante Arrhenius* did in adapting themselves to Emerald was a matter of necessity," he said. "It was not, perhaps,
the price of survival . . . they could have gone on to another
world. But they had been searching for many generations.
Like your own ancestors, they had come to doubt that they
would ever find a home. What they did was the price they
had to pay in order to make Emerald a viable home for the
children of men. They had no alternative. They did not do it
because they thought, according to some abstract process of
reasoning or evaluation, that it was *good*, or *right*, or the will
of God. It was because they had to do it—because it was
necessary—that they revised their notions of good and right
and purpose. They accepted a new notion of humanity, because they had to."

"And was it similarly necessary to import the ecosystem of
Emerald to the Motherworld?" asked Vito Talvar.

"Yes," answered M'lise. "It was. Earth's ecosystem never
recovered from the Upheaval. When my ancestors rediscovered Earth they found it locked in a cycle of slow decline.
Men were preserving what they could of their way of life in
many different places, but in all of them they faced the same
problems, including the gradual and inexorable decline of the
level of oxygen in the atmosphere. Too much of it had been
extracted by combustion, and the gradual diminution of the
ecosphere meant that it was slowly being replaced by carbon
dioxide as Earth's plants failed to cope. When we arrived, the
situation was becoming critical. A few centuries more would
have seen the institution of a proliferating greenhouse effect
which would have converted the slow decline into a catastrophe. Nothing on Earth could prevent that. But our resources
were not limited to the Earth. We seeded the tropics with this
forest in order to provide the Motherworld with a lung that

would let her breathe. We did it quickly, without being able to calculate what the long-term effects might be. There was no time to waste in contemplation, and no possibility of experimentation. It was a matter of the life or death of a world.

"We did not know whether the descendants of the men who had been left behind on Earth could survive. We hoped that they might, but we had to face the possibility that they would not. We did not know then—and after several thousand years of observation we *still* do not know—what the long-term future of the newly hybrid ecosystem might be. So far, the genetic material introduced from Emerald has not diversified very greatly, and the forest has not extended beyond the tropics. There is no way for us to know whether it will eventually spread all over the globe, or whether it will reach an equilibrium. We know very little about the adaptive capacities of Earth's own ecosystem. When we brought the Lu'el here, it seemed likely that they might be the only men left on Earth after a few thousand years. As things have turned out, we were unduly pessimistic. The forest saved Earth's ecosystem. It saved mankind. The forest has made the rebirth of civilization possible. Perhaps the rebirth will be transient, but I think not. Within another thousand years, the Macarians will be as able to take an active part in the ordering of their affairs as men of Tanagar or Emerald now could. Perhaps they will be able to determine what happens to the forest. They might take control of the evolutionary history of Earth—and of their own descendants. All it requires is knowledge."

"That's what you wanted us to know?" asked Cheron quietly.

"It isn't just that we want you to know," the black man answered. "If it had simply been a matter of letting you know, we could have contacted the Tanagarian satellite at any time. We want you to *understand*. That's the difficult part. That's why we've done things so carefully and so elaborately. You see, before we reveal ourselves to *your* people, we want to be sure of our welcome.

"I think that you will understand well enough why we are afraid."

3

As twilight waned, Cyriac Salvador looked up at the castellate rocks above him, and then back at the tiny antlike dots spread in a rough line across the lower slopes far below. He paused to rest, feeling confident of his safety. He had evaded capture for several days now, and he knew that he could go on doing so forever. The problem was that he had not found the base, and the balance of numbers made it increasingly likely that they would find it before he did. He had led them to the region, and he was sure by now that they knew what they were looking for.

He had little alternative but to keep searching, but he knew that he had to make contingency plans. Once the base was in Macarian hands the Intels would have to come out of hiding. There would be no point in their sitting on high, waiting and watching, once their presence was known for certain. They would have to begin communication. That offered him the possibility of a new role, one which he was ready to take up even now, if only he could be sure of his welcome. He was quite prepared to return to Armata, save for several imponderable factors. He was being hunted, and was deemed a murderer. He did not know what had happened to Teresa. More important, he did not know what had happened to Sarid Jerome.

Physically, he was well. It was summer, and he had not found it too difficult to find food in the forests and the valleys. On the mountain slopes it was cold enough to make him uncomfortable, and occasional spells of bad weather threatened to make his situation temporarily desperate, but he had no doubt of his ability to survive. Isolation, doubt, and confusion, however, were having an effect on his psychological state. He felt trapped into this long search for the base—a quest which became more futile as time went by. It was not the fact that he might fail that bothered him; what troubled him more was the thought that it had become gradually less significant whether he succeeded or not. The moment the presence of the soldiers had told him that Macaria knew more about him than it should have, and that it cared, the prospect of an escape had lost most of its meaning. His experiment had been aborted, and now a new beginning would be necessary. He felt that it was up to him to make that new beginning, but he did not know how. The consequent feeling of powerlessness was not a feeling he enjoyed.

He resumed climbing, toiling slowly up the rocky path. When he got to the top, he resolved, he would stop to think—to reappraise the situation fully and carefully.

Darkness fell swiftly, but there was a bright moon and the stars seemed close at hand as they shone through the clear, thin air. He continued to make his way upward, wanting to reach the plateau before halting. He was not afraid that the darkness might tempt him into a false step and cause him to fall.

When the path petered out he had to climb, but the slope was not precipitous, and he continued toward the rim, carefully making sure of his handholds, feeling his way. He knew that he might get stuck, but was sure that he could find his way back down to a ledge where he might safely perch and wait for dawn.

In fact, the supply of handholds proved plentiful enough, and eventually he was able to pull himself over a jutting rim onto a large flat area just below the plateau proper.

He saw the light almost immediately. It was a patch of white, not particularly bright, but precisely shaped: a rectangle with rounded corners. There was no mistaking its artificial nature. It was some kind of doorway, no more than three hundred meters away.

A wave of exultancy swept through him, but he suppressed it quickly. It need not be the base. It might be a cabin used by mountain climbers. It might be a Macarian light that signaled the presence of his enemies rather than his friends. He began to move toward it slowly, picking his way over the uneven surface, trying to move silently as well as safely. He had to get much closer before he was able to get some idea of the shadowed shape that surrounded the light.

He allowed himself a sigh of relief when he saw that it was

a helicopter. The Macarians had small aircraft and large dirigibles, but they had no helicopters. The conclusion was obvious: it must have come from the base, and it must be looking for him. Perhaps it was one of several, each one perched on some coign of vantage, hoping that he would discover it, ready to take to the air if sighted first by the Macarians. Clearly, the men at the base no longer feared the possibility that their presence would become known.

It all added up in his mind as he approached, no less cautious because of his newfound confidence.

When he was less than ten meters away, a figure appeared in the doorway, silhouetted by the white light. There was something odd about the figure, but he was already raising a hand in salute when he realized what it was.

The man in the doorway was black.

"We've been waiting for some time," said the man. "We worked out from the search pattern the Macarians are following that you'd probably come this way. Come aboard."

Salvador stopped dead in his tracks, and the salute remained incomplete.

"Who are you?" he demanded.

The black man never got a chance to answer. Another silhouette moved behind him, and the man who had spoken toppled suddenly forward, crashing down from the doorway onto the cold rock. The man who had struck him down now took his place, smiling.

"Hello, Salvador," he said. "I've been waiting for some time, too. I knew you'd make it in the end. And I knew that all the stuff you taught me in those lurid dreams would finally see me through."

Cyriac Salvador stood as if petrified. Suddenly, the unanswered questions had multiplied, and the multiplication was hardly offset by the fact that one of them was solved.

He now knew what had become of Sarid Jerome.

4

Salvador put the inert body of the black man in one of the passenger seats behind the pilot's position. He lifted one of the man's eyelids briefly, and tested the bloodstained wound on his forehead with his fingertips.

"He'll be all right," he said, turning to look at Sarid Jerome, who was idly toying with the gun which he had taken from the unconscious man.

"I didn't hit him hard," said Sarid.

"He fell very heavily onto some hard rock," Salvador pointed out. "But as I say, he'll be all right."

Sarid gestured toward the control panel with the barrel of the pistol. "There's a radio set there. Is there any way you can contact the satellite?"

"I doubt the transmitter's up to it," replied Salvador. "I might be able to put a signal through to the base, though."

Sarid shook his head. "The base is empty. Sealed up tight behind a wall of rock. I doubt if the Macarians will find it. I doubt that *you*'d have found it. We have to contact the satellite, somehow. We'll have to attract the attention of their monitoring devices in such a way as to make them take notice."

"Why?" asked Salvador. There was not the least trace of tension in his voice.

"Where's Teresa?" countered Sarid.

"I lost her. I think she's dead."

"It doesn't matter."

"It matters to me," said Salvador evenly. "I wanted to get her out. Are you going to tell me what's going on?"

Sarid laughed, without humor. "While your fellow Intels have sat quietly in orbit watching the affairs of Macaria and her neighbors, there've been other offworlders on Earth all along. I don't understand quite how you could be so stupid, but you were. Perhaps you aren't as clever as you think. *We* were supposed to be planted on the Macarians, weren't we? A subtle helping hand, a gift from the stars. Well, within two days of our having landed *he* was planted on *us*. We played the clown for the army, and he played right along with us. His name's Baya-undi. He didn't altogether approve of your helping-hand project. He had to put on a race riot in order to get me out of Macarian hands, but he did it. The bastard shot me with an anesthetic dart without taking the trouble to tell me that is wasn't my last moment on Earth. He has a sense of humor just like an Intel."

"Why do you want to contact satellite? Why do you *need* to?"

"Because while I was out, they scrambled the little device you planted in my skull. As far as satellite knows, I'm as dead as the others. *They* think your entire project is washed out, and they still have no suspicion that anything is wrong down here.

"When I woke up, Baya-undi explained—if you can call it an explanation. He's descended from ship-people, like you and me—but his people rediscovered Earth a long time before we did. While we've been watching Earth, they've been watching us. While we didn't interfere, *they* didn't interfere. But your experiment changed all that. He'd already learned all he needed to know about what we were doing here by the time he took me out of Macaria's hands. He wanted to take me down to the surface headquarters of his people, somewhere in the far south, but he'd also found out that you were still around. *His* people were tapping the thing in my skull as well as ours—both sides must have realized that you were alive at precisely the same moment that I did. The difference is that *they* acted. Where the hell are *your* friends, Salvador? Conducting themselves in impeccable Intel style, no doubt, cultivating *mens sana in corpore sano* up there in free fall. Anyhow, Baya-undi shipped me out along the coast of Volokon, where we were picked up by this thing. Baya-undi borrowed it, and we made as much speed as we could getting up here. We stopped to refuel twice. This whole continent is full of their bases, but *you* couldn't spot a single one of them.

"I honestly don't know why he brought me along. Perhaps he didn't like to leave me behind. I assume that he felt sure he could handle me. After all, he had the gun. I knew I could take it off him, when the time came."

There was a moment's silence before Salvador said: "Is that all?"

"No," said Sarid. "It isn't all. You don't know the half of it. As I said, he's been explaining. Among the things he explained was the fact that his version of the human race goes in for elaborate genetic engineering. The fact that *he* looks human says nothing about his cousins. He also mentioned that the equatorial forest is part of an alien life-system, transported here from another world. If we're to control what happens on Earth, Salvador, it won't be enough to unfreeze a few deviants and sprinkle them lightly over the indigenous cultures of the civilized world. If we want control, we're going to have to take it. *They* already have it, and I don't like what they're doing with it. I don't doubt that they have far greater strength here than we do—maybe they could destroy the satellite if they wanted to. But if satellite can get off a message telling Tanagar what's happening . . . it'll take a hundred years to get to Tanagar, but it *will* get through. There's no way they can call it back."

Salvador stared at the gun which Sarid Jerome held lightly in his hand, deliberating carefully.

"Aren't you being just a little melodramatic?" he asked finally.

"Melodramatic!" Sarid's voice was sharp and high. "What do you expect? Within the last twenty-four hours I've discovered that the Motherworld, instead of being under the control of my own people as I'd hitherto imagined, is actually under the control of others. The others have mostly forsaken their own humanity and have imported alien life-forms which may well render the Earth unfit for human habitation in the fulness of time. I've been played for a fool by Baya-undi, and so have you. Can't you see what kind of a threat these people pose to Tanagar? What's going to happen to your carefully preserved social stability now we've made contact with *another* spacefaring society whose people—despite having the same ancestors as we do—are now alien? They've known about Tanagar since the moment a Tanagarian ship entered this system. Do you think they haven't been watching us? They might be established in Tanagar's solar system by now. Suppose they want Tanagar as well as Earth? Suppose they have plans to remake *our* world as they're remaking this one? And you think I'm being melodramatic! For once, Salvador, forget that your natural inclination is to sit back and ponder for a hundred years. It's time to *act*. We have to get a message to Tanagar, one way or another."

"What would you like the message to say?" asked Salvador mildly.

"I don't want to start a war," said Sarid, with noticeably less patience. "At least, not yet. I just want to alert Tanagar to the danger."

"Your solicitous attitude would seem to represent something of a change of heart," observed the Intel.

"It's a matter of priorities," replied the Pragmatist. "I don't like the Intel rule on Tanagar. If I'm to make a new career on Earth, I'd rather I wasn't a pawn in some clever Intel game. Now, though, there seem to be alternatives that are even worse. I'd rather be a pawn in *your* game than a pawn in *his*."

Salvador shifted in his seat, and said nothing.

Sarid let a few minutes go by, and then lost patience entirely.

"Salvador," he said, "we have to *do* something!"

The Intel shook his head slowly. "The best reason for doing something," he said softly, "is that there's something that needs to be done. The reason *you're* so desperate to do something is that you're confused and uncertain. I'd like to know what *he* has to say."

Salvador pointed at Baya-undi, but paused before drawing back his hand as he saw the muzzle of the gun swing to point at his face. Sarid's finger was on the trigger.

"Salvador," said the Pragmatist softly, mimicking the Intellectual's careful tone, "there were a good many moments during the weeks that passed after you dropped me here when I told myself how good it would be to kill you."

"I don't think this is getting us anywhere," said Salvador amiably.

"It would be a crime of passion," said Sarid. "I've already set the pattern, remember?"

"You're not in the grip of any unconquerable flood of emotion," replied Salvador. "It would be a crime of sheer insanity. You know that as well as I do."

Sarid kept the gun perfectly steady. "With a little effort," he said, "I could summon up the emotion. Anger, resentment, hatred. I don't have any cause to like you."

"I brought you back from the dead," said the Intellectual evenly. "We call it eternal life, but in our less hypocritical moments even we Intellectuals know that it's a kind of death. I gave you a second chance to live—not in the world into which you were born, and to which you were so ill-adapted, but in another world. It's not a very pleasant world, but a life is a life. Had things gone smoothly, you might have made an acceptable niche for yourself. Even as things stand, you still might. I used you, of course. I had my own reasons for doing what I did—good pragmatic ones that you ought to appreciate. But I haven't harmed you, and what I've done has been to your advantage. You see, I really do take my responsibilities as seriously as I can: my responsibility to Tanagar, and to its citizens. Self-control isn't synonymous with callousness, and certainly not with cruelty. If this project had been a success, it might have opened the way for the liberation of all the living dead. It would have set a precedent—it would have established the principle that the men in the vaults could be released to function in the interests of Tanagar despite the fact that their presence within Tanagarian society itself might pose a threat. *Think*, Jerome. That's all it needs."

Sarid's fingers relaxed a little, but his voice was still taut as he asked, "What's *your* plan?"

"That depends on your friend," said Salvador. "He came up here to fetch me; I'd like to hear his reasons. If there have been men on Earth for more than a thousand years, I'd like to meet them."

"You're crazy," said Sarid. "That's playing right into their hands. Don't you see . . . ?"

"No," said Salvador. "I don't see. That's precisely why I want the chance to find out the answers."

"They're *hostile*," insisted Sarid. "They could have declared their presence to your friends on the satellite at any time. They could have contacted Tanagar itself. Nobody hides unless he has a *reason*. You'd know better than I do what chance we have of contacting the satellite before they capture us or eliminate us. Maybe it's slim. But we have to *try*. Can you honestly not *see* that?"

Baya-undi groaned, and Sarid immediately switched the gun around so that it was pointing at the black man's skull.

The groan, however, was not a sign of returning consciousness. Baya-undi moved, but then lapsed back into inertia.

"Put the gun away, Sarid," said Salvador gently.

Sarid did not reply, and silence fell.

At any rate, silence *ought* to have fallen.

The two men heard the sound simultaneously—a distant
throbbing sound. Sarid looked around, but it was Salvador
who caught the direction correctly, and looked *up*.

"Switch off the light!" he said tersely.

Sarid looked wildly around, not certain where the switch
was. While he was searching for it, Salvador went forward to
peer upward through the clear plastic windows of the cockpit.
He could see nothing until the lights went out, and even then
it took several seconds more for him to realize that something
huge and dark was occulting the bright stars.

Sarid joined him, and whispered, "What is it?"

The sound of the motor was much clearer now, and the
shadow on the night sky was growing slowly.

"It's a dirigible balloon," said Salvador. "And it's coming
down. The Macarians have found us. Our lights must have
been visible for a kilometer or more, up there."

Sarid cursed, and threw himself into the pilot's seat. The
controls were still glowing though the cabin lights were off.
He flicked a switch, and the helicopter's engine roared into
life.

Salvador opened his mouth to say "Wait!" but Sarid had
not paused before activating the rotor blades, and their
gathering roar drowned out his voice. He looked up again at
the widening shadow and suppressed a surge of panic that
rose inside him. He reached out to touch Sarid's arm, but the
Pragmatist was in no mood to be held back and knocked the
hand aside.

Salvador shouted: "No!" This time he let the alarm show
nakedly in his voice, but it had no effect. Like Teresa Janeat,
Sarid Jerome was a firm believer in fast, decisive action.

The helicopter lifted into the sky, rising vertically. Sparks
spun away from the axle supporting the blades. Sarid steered
sideways as soon as he was clear of the surrounding rocks,
but the descending dirigible was almost on them by then. One
of the rotor blades slashed through the seamless silk of the
great balloon, and the jet of hydrogen released from the rent
turned immediately into a tongue of flame, licking out like

the forked tongue of a poisonous snake in the split second before the gasbag exploded.

The shockwave tore the helicopter apart.

Sarid never had the chance to understand what he had done. Salvador did, but it made no difference.

5

Midas was sitting up in bed, eating from a wooden bowl, when Cheron came into the room.

"It's meat," he said. "After so many days without, it tastes like the food of the gods. Did I not say that we had come to the valley of the gods, the paradise on Earth? Have I not always said that despite appearances I am the most holy and most favored of men? I have suffered, but my suffering is over. Is it not so?"

The way he asked the final question suggested that he would welcome reassurance on the point. He was too wary to put too much trust in his momentary good fortune.

"We're not in a valley," Cheron informed him. "We're on the slopes of a high mountain. As for the gods—well, perhaps. When you have seen the world *inside* the mountain, in the caves, then you will be all the more firmly convinced that we are in the place of the gods, but they are not your gods, nor even mine."

Midas put the bowl aside, and lay back against the pillows.

"What is going to happen to us?" he asked.

"To you—I don't know. I think I can persuade M'lise to return you to Merkad, or to any other place you wish to go. Your presence here is an accident of fate—the gods, such as they are, have no interest in you. Under other circumstances, they might let the forest men kill you, but to please us . . . I think they will do as we ask them to."

Midas looked dubious. "You are prisoners," he said. "We are all prisoners. Why should they try to please you?"

Cheron laughed softly. "They want us to understand," he said. "They are eager to win our support. Once they are sure of our commitment, *then* we might cease to be prisoners. If they do not win us over . . . I don't know. We'll see you safe, though, while they're still trying."

There was a moment's silence, and then Midas said, "They come from another world. As you do."

"I thought you didn't believe such nonsensical stories," said Cheron.

"I believe anything and everything," replied Midas. "If God had not meant us to be skeptical, he would not have created so very many liars."

"How is it," asked Cheron, "that you speak in one moment as if there is one god, and in another as if there are many?"

Midas shrugged. "It is hardly for one such as I to determine the number of the gods."

"I'm sure you're a clever man," said Cheron, "but I really do wish that what you said occasionally made some kind of sense."

"Who am I," countered Midas in the same mock-martyred tone, "to say that the world must make sense, and that I must know the sense of it? *You* are the one who is asked to understand, not I. It is you that is superhuman. I am only a man, who must rely on his gods—or any other gods who might be kind enough to take an interest—to deliver him from evil and promise him a few moments of joy, on this side of the grave or the other. It is simpler thus—it is an easier life to lead."

Cheron shook his head to show his bewilderment, but the gesture was partly admiring.

"Would you like to be taken to Merkad?" he asked.

Midas smiled. "Merkad is dangerous," he answered. "What is more, it is poor. As a Merkadian, I would not be welcome in Macaria, and I have already seen far too much of Dahra. All in all, I do not want to return to any place that I have seen. If I cannot stay here, I think I would like to go somewhere new."

"Do you have anywhere in mind?" asked Cheron.

"When I think of all the places I have heard of," the little man replied, "this world seems a dreary place. But then, I am not such a brave man at heart as I probably seem to you, and I am wary of places I have never heard of at all. Considering all that I have heard people say about all the places in the known world, I think I would like to go to Khepra. It is said to be civilized, after a fashion, and it is a long, long way from Macaria."

Cheron contemplated this decision, unsure whether to take it seriously or not. It was as difficult as ever to measure the extent of Midas's sincerity.

"If you *could* stay with us," he said finally, "you would find yourself in a world beyond your understanding. It would be completely alien to anything you have known. It may be that we shall be taking a journey through the depths of space, our bodies put into an artificial sleep in order that we may survive. At the other end of the journey would be a world as strange to me as it would be to you—a world of men that are no longer men. Do you think that you could do that . . . remembering that you may not be quite as brave as I might think you are."

"If there would be food and drink," answered Midas. "And light and warmth. And no pain. I could live in such circumstances, I feel sure. Of course, it would be better by far if there were women too, but I am not a greedy man."

Cheron nodded slowly and said—more to himself than to the man in the bed—"It might be as well to have as many friends as possible. In any case, you might get to Khepra and find that you didn't like it at all."

It was only to himself that he added one further comment: *And in addition, if you can handle it—well, then, so can I.*

6

Vito Talvar was sitting on a grassy slope, looking out over the forest, his eyes fixed on some imaginary point far off in the distance where the treetops blurred into a formless ocean of green. He turned around as Cheron drew close. His stare was quite impassive, and Cheron had the impression that the blue eyes were still focused on some distant phantom image.

"The news just came through," said Cheron. "It's been confirmed. Baya-undi, Sarid, and Salvador were all involved in some kind of freak accident. The Macarians were trying to spot Salvador from the air, using dirigible airships. The balloons are filled with hydrogen. They found Salvador just after Sarid and Baya-undi caught up with him. There was an explosion."

"Did Salvador cause it?" asked Talvar.

"I doubt it," said Cheron. "He'd have no reason. It must have been an unhappy coincidence—there's no other explanation."

"So that leaves us," said the blond man.

"M'lise doesn't want us to make contact with the satellite. Not yet, anyhow. In time, maybe the contact will be made here, but M'lise and his people want to make certain that the time is right. He wants us to go to Emerald."

"To add to our understanding, no doubt. Personally, I think he simply wants to get all the information he can out of us. He and his kind would be content to sit back and watch our people from hiding until the sun blinks out. And why not? If the positions were reversed, what do you think the Intels would do?"

"They'd do the same," answered Cheron. "And their reasons would be just as good. From the outside, Tanagarian society must seem rigid and intolerant. It must cause M'lise and his kind as much anxiety as the thought of a mutable race which recreates its children in order to colonize alien environments would cause among the Intels. In addition, M'lise and his kind live in a way that promotes a patient philosophy, just as the Intels do. An Intel lives seven hundred years, and he can afford to have his projects mature slowly. M'lise and his kind may not live as long, but when all your projects have to be measured in human generations, you have to cultivate a similar attitude."

Talvar stared at him, not bothering to hide the bitterness in his thoughts.

"That's right," he said bleakly. "They play their own kind of games, on their own kind of board. You and I are just pieces to be moved here and there, captured or killed."

"Not any more," said Cheron. "Salvador's death changes that. We're players now, not pawns. Whether we like it or not, we're Tanagar's ambassadors—not to Macaria, but to

Emerald. It's no longer enough to be controlled. Now we have to *take* control. We're not Hedonists any longer, in the sense that we can live entirely for ourselves. We have to take on Intel responsibilities. We have no choice."

Talvar looked away again, to stare out over the ocean of treetops.

"I could stay here," he said, following the track of his own thoughts and apparently ignoring what Cheron had said. "I really could. Not in this particular place, but somewhere out there, under the sun, with the forest forming a great wall around my little empire. It's the best that Earth has to offer. There's nothing here like Tanagar—that's lost forever, and I can accept that—but the world has rewards of its own. At first, I thought the simple fact of being *outside* was a kind of hell. The thought that I'd never again be inside a machine terrified me. But this world isn't Tanagar, and you don't need protective clothing to walk about. The kind of life that is possible here *is* possible. What I couldn't abide, though, is having to live as *other people* do. I can live in a way that's very different from the life I was born for, but I can't live in a way that other people are born for. That's asking too much. I could live alone, inside myself. If you go to Emerald, you go alone."

"What makes you think you have a choice?" asked Cheron.

"The purpose of taking us to Emerald," he replied, "is so that we may understand them. I don't understand, and I never will. I'm no use to them."

"Vito . . ." Cheron began. He stopped as Talvar turned to face him again, when he saw the way the blond man's face was set.

"Cheron," said Talvar, "I don't have to be ashamed of what I am. I didn't make myself—I was invented by Intels. They made me a Hedonist, and I can't break out of that. I don't *want* to break out of it. Certainly, I'm selfish. While you're standing there talking about ambassadors to other worlds I'm sitting here thinking about *me*. I'm thinking about what *I* can do. I don't *care* what happens to Earth, or to Tanagar, or to *anything* except as it affects me. That's the way I'm made, the way I was designed to be. Maybe you're different, coming from a time so far in the past, but I'm a Hedonist—a poor sensual—through and through. You know that. I can't change."

"Anyone can change," said Cheron. "You didn't create yourself, but you recreate yourself, day by day and hour by hour. You're not a Hedonist any more, and this dream of retreating into a solitary hermitage is nothing but a crazy illusion. Can't you see that it's *finished?* You have a second life, now, but in order to *use* it you have to be a new person. If you insist on being a Tanagarian Hedonist then this *is* hell, and you can never be out of it. You have to let go, and be prepared to rebuild. It's not as if you were a successful Hedonist in the first place. If you'd been as well-designed as you suppose yourself to be you'd never have been in the vaults."

Talvar scowled, but his anger was directed more at himself than at Cheron. For several seconds, he said nothing. Then, he asked, "Do you *want* to go to Emerald?"

"Yes," answered Cheron. "I think I do."

"Why?"

"I'm not altogether sure. Because, in a way, I think I'm on trial. I think the situation we're in is a kind of challenge. Perhaps I have delusions of grandeur, but I don't think it's just a personal matter. I think, in some sense, we're all on trial. Not just individual people, but whole races of people. Tanagar, Emerald, men on Earth, Lu'el. It could so easily fall apart—not in the sense that Tanagar and Emerald might go to war with one another, but in the sense that they never *would* begin talking to one another. The real danger is simply that of disconnection; the possibility that the men of Emerald and the men of Tanagar might never be anything to one another but things to be observed, separated by a kind of invisible wall. I think that the measure of what we are, and what we *can* be, isn't to be found in Tanagarian self-control or Emerald's genetic ubiquity. I think it's to be found in what we can make of our mutual membership of the human race . . . of the tree of life."

"That's nonsense," said Talvar.

"Perhaps it is," answered Cheron. "But it's something I feel. And, as Midas once said: It does not really matter what is true and what is not. What matters is what we do next. I intend to go to Emerald. I think Midas will go with me. Don't make your own decision too quickly. I think M'lise would let you stay here, if you want to, but you must be certain that your reasons are good ones."

Talvar shook his head, and said, "This *is* hell."

He had said it many times before, but always in jest. Cheron had always known, though, that the mock foolishness had masked a deeper discontent.

"Perhaps it is," he answered. "If so, our task is to find a way to live in it."

7

The men watched the screen in silence as the series of still pictures flashed across it, each one remaining for some ten or twelve seconds. No one moved until the run was complete. In free-fall there was no need for any continual readjustment of their positions.

When the lights came on again, a lone man came to stand before the others. His face was quite impassive, and his voice was level as he said, "We arrived a few hours too late. We actually saw the explosion. We had to get out again, quickly; the Macarians were already on their way up the slope. We think the pictures provide adequate evidence of what happened. The debris was mangled, but the vehicle that crashed into the dirigible was certainly a helicopter, and it certainly was not of Macarian manufacture."

"There's no doubt of that," agreed a second voice.

"Which means . . ." began a third. He left the sentence dangling.

"It means that if we'd been a little quicker off the mark when Jerome's monitor brought us word that Salvador was still alive, we would not only have rescued *him*—we'd have had a chance to meet the owners of the helicopter as well." *This* voice was deliberately abrasive.

"We weren't to know that," said one of the men who had already spoken. "And, in any case, there's no use in regretting what's past. The point is that we have to deal with a whole new vista of possibilities. If the helicopter hadn't crashed, we might never have discovered the unfortunate truth that someone else besides ourselves is interested in the Motherworld. *Some* good, at least, has come of our being late."

"The point is," put in a new voice, mimicking the phraseology of his predecessor, "now that we know—what do we *do* about it?"

There was a murmur that might have been gentle laughter before someone provided the obvious answer:

"We wait and we watch, more carefully than before. What else?"

10th Year as the SF Leader!
Outstanding science fiction